I0760605

# Pioneers of the Pathway

THE PATHWAY RING #1

Stuart Jaffe

*Pioneers of the Pathway* is a work of fiction. Names, characters, places, and incidents either are the product of the author's imagination or are used fictitiously, and any resemblance to any persons, living or dead, business establishments, events, or locales is entirely coincidental.

PIONEERS OF THE PATHWAY


Cover art by Luis Peres

ISBN 13: 978-1-963517-18-7

First Edition: November, 2024
First Hardcover Edition: December, 2024

*For Glory and Gabe,*

*this book never would have happened*
*without you both.*

# Also by Stuart Jaffe

*Max Porter Paranormal Mysteries*

Southern Bound
Southern Charm
Southern Belle
Southern Gothic
Southern Haunts
Southern Curses
Southern Rites
Southern Craft
Southern Spirit
Southern Flames
Southern Fury
Southern Souls
Southern Blood
Southern Graves
Southern Dead
Southern Hexes
Southern Hart
Southern Kin

*Nathan K Thrillers*

Immortal Killers
Killing Machine
The Cardinal
Yukon Massacre
The First Battle
Immortal Darkness
A Spy for Eternity
Prisoner
Desert Takedown
Lone Star Standoff
The Puppeteer
Blowback
Prime

*The Pathway Ring*
Pioneers of the Pathway

*The Ridnight Mysteries*
The Water Blade
The Waters of Taladoro
Waterfire

*The Parallel Society*
The Infinity Caverns
Book on the Isle
Rift Angel
Lost Time
Pages of Glass
The Bold Warrior
City of Infinity

*The Malja Chronicles*
The Way of the Black Beast
The Way of the Sword and Gun
The Way of the Brother Gods
The Way of the Blade
The Way of the Power
The Way of the Soul

*Gillian Boone novels*
A Glimpse of Her Soul
Pathway to Spirit

*Stand Alone Novels*
After The Crash
Real Magic
Founders

*Short Story Collection*
10 Bits of My Brain
10 More Bits of My Brain
The Bluesman
The Marshall Drummond Case Files: Cabinet 1
The Marshall Drummond Case Files: Cabinet 2
The Marshall Drummond Case Files: Cabinet 3

*Non-Fiction*

How to Write Magical Words: A Writer's Companion

For more information, please visit ***www.stuartjaffe.com***

# Pioneers of the Pathway

# ZILL GRACE

ZILL'S MOUTH STUCK LIKE DRIED PASTE. She had to concentrate to open her jaw, and her eyes proved equally difficult. With her muscles sore and her bones complaining, she finally lifted her reclined body to find she sat in a palatial office.

A vaulted, stone ceiling echoed little sounds while thick, crimson carpet swallowed them up. Massive bookcases lined the walls with enormous portraits hanging between each case. Two long couches formed a V with a hand-carved coffee table running along the middle. She had woken stretched out on the left side of the V.

With a dull throb in her head, she swiped open her holo. Nothing happened. She swiped the air over her wrist again. Still nothing. Her fuzzy mind noticed a red-crystal water pitcher and an empty glass on the coffee table waiting for her.

Grabbing for the glass, she sagged to her knees. The soft carpet saved her from bruising, but the slow fall reminded her that she had been drugged, abducted, and no friendly gesture of water would be enough. Still, she had to drink.

"Don't worry. It's safe." The voice came from behind.

A shocked gasp and she tried to spin. She flopped onto her rear. With an ungracious grunt, she pushed to her feet — teetering but managing to stay upright.

"Please, drink. You'll need it."

Several feet away, a comely man sat at an ornate desk the size of a queen bed. He swiped his deskholo off before standing in a trim, dark suit that made him appear older than his face suggested. Gesturing to the water, he strolled closer. With simple hand motions, he had Zill sit while he poured the glass halfway.

After presenting it to her, he waited.

Flashes of a man grabbing her from behind. Not this man. A bigger one.

"You are safe here."

She wanted to mock him with laughter but only managed a short grunt. Trying to fight her muscles, she finally grabbed the glass and guzzled the cold water. It rushed down her throat like a magic elixir, her body instantly reviving some of its senses and craving more. She gulped hard, coughed, sputtered, and drank again.

"I'm sorry for the way you were treated. When I asked Bracken to bring you here, he intended to approach you politely and with discretion. Unfortunately, matters changed fast, and he had to make a hard decision. I regret the method he opted for, but he had no real choice."

Finishing a second glass of water, Zill felt her mind processing again. Her mouth tasted horrible, like mold, but at least her lips no longer clung together. She inspected this man closer, and her chest tightened.

"Are you ..." The words croaked out.

He nodded. "Chovar Monclova."

Zill marveled that she did not pass out. Chovar Monclova sat before her. Head of Monclova Industries and descendant of the originators of modern civilization. A bit of a recluse, not one to enjoy his iconic status, yet not so shy as to avoid important government events. Professor Kovaric had often said that Monclova performed the bare minimum he needed to keep the money flowing.

*Professor Kovaric.*

Her hand dropped to her pocket. She could feel the pendant drive with all her research still there. "I was on my way to see the Professor." The rising strength in her voice surprised her. "Why did you do this to me? Let me go. I need to see —"

"Professor Kovaric is dead."

The world stopped.

Only the sound of the glass in her hand clinking against the coffee table grounded her. Without that noise, her mind would have disappeared — into memories of Professor Kovaric and their time researching together, then into the questions flooding her about why and how this could have happened, then into anger wrapped around regret, and finally, into a somber nothingness where she could float forever. But that steady sound reminded her that she held a real glass, that she sat on a real couch, that she saw and heard the real Chovar Monclova, and that none of this would vanish like a bad dream.

After setting the glass down, she rubbed the tears on her cheeks. Her heart climbed toward her throat, but she still managed to speak one word. "Dead?"

"Murdered."

Everything moved slow and cold and numb like drifting through space. She heard Chovar's words but struggled to make sense of them.

"Murdered?"

"You would have joined him had Bracken not intervened. Taking you away from a murder scene and driving you here was the best choice."

As slow as the world spun around her, it still moved too fast. She needed to think. Put things in order. She could do that. She was good at it. That was why Professor Kovaric had hired her.

Okay, then — start by getting details in the proper order. She had been heading to the Professor's house to deliver her latest research. He had insisted. She walked across the University campus, and had bumped into —

"Where's Rudder?" She heard her voice as if she spoke from far off and deep down.

"Your boyfriend? We investigated him long ago. His job at Southern City Networks hardly covers his gambling debts, let alone his lifestyle."

Part of Zill wanted to argue the *boyfriend* detail, but in a monotone, she said, "Gambling debts?"

Chovar had the decency not to point out Zill's ignorance of the man she had been sleeping with. He went on, "Mostly sports betting — jagball and balance racing. Lost quite a lot. I'm sorry, but he's been selling anything he could to the Dahtien across the border."

"He could go to jail for that."

"Not for now. We dropped him several blocks away and paid him half his salary to walk away and never return. He took the money."

Of course, he did. "Shouldn't we call the police?"

"Not when you and I both received the same summons to Kovaric's house shortly before his death. I think that'll look bad for us."

"He called you over, too? Why you?"

Chovar chuckled. "Who do you think funds all your research?"

And that was it. Earlier, she had been on her way to drop off her latest work for Professor Kovaric before attending a jagball game with a young man she planned to dump, and in a quick moment, she had lost everything. Though she could think the words, none of them felt true. Part of her still fought to exist in real space. Part of her saw the world in vibrant clarity.

*Is this what shock feels like?*

Taking a moment to pour another glass of water — her hands steady this time — Zill tried to wrangle her thoughts from shooting off in all directions. After drinking halfway down, she sat back on the couch, crossed her legs, and stared at Chovar. She stayed quiet as she evaluated all she had heard.

Whenever faced with overwhelming amounts of data, Professor Kovaric always told her to break it down into smaller units, search for linking data, find the common factors, and most of all, watch for the truth. Easier to do with diaries, journals, articles, reports, and other sources of historical record. A whole different matter when dealing with a living icon.

But to find out why anybody wanted to kill the Professor and who that anybody was, she had to swallow her doubts and get on with it. Turning her head from side to side, feeling the soft crackles in her neck release, she tried to clear her mind.

"You've made some big claims," she said. "Why should I believe any of this?"

Chovar's mouth widened with relief. "You're thinking now.

Good. We can begin."

"We can't do anything until —"

He raised a hand and gently patted the air. "I know this has all been sudden and confusing. But with the Professor gone, I need your help. We all do."

"We?"

"All of Newarl. All of Oxwala. Everything on this planet."

"Don't be grandiose. Why would anyone kill the Professor?"

"His research, of course."

"What are you talking about? The only thing the Professor worked on that could remotely be considered controversial is about the Dahtien origins, and that's only going to upset other academics."

Chovar leaned forward, elbows on his knees. "Kovaric posited that the human-Dahtien relationship has existed far longer than previously thought — possibly before the failed Ring, and that the border between the human state of Newarl and the Dahtien state of Oxwala might be called into question — though the original treaties have yet to be found. But I'm interested in the research you've done together."

She shook her head. This didn't make sense. Tensions over the disputed border continued to mount, but she could not see how any of it had reached the point of murder. In fact, the constant political bickering continued to point fingers at Monclova Industries for not providing better records of their early dealings with the Dahtien. That tied in with their joint research on … her eyes widened.

"Monclova. Your personal history. The company history. You don't have it anymore. You hire the best scholar of history you can find. But it must be for a greater reason than merely getting the politicians off your back. You don't like the spotlight, but this is a bit far reaching … oh … you have investments in Oxwala, don't you?"

Chovar snapped his fingers. "It is amazing to watch your brain work. And no, I don't break the law for investments. But you are close to the truth."

"Then what is the truth?"

He stood in a smooth motion and strolled to his desk. "When I first hired Kovaric, this nonsense about the human-Dahtien border was nothing but whispers. I certainly had no idea it would be calling attention upon me or my company. No, I hired Kovaric because I had — still have — an enormous decision to make, and to do so wisely, I need to know the full history of my family. Too much of Monclova's past has been lost or perverted. If I am not to repeat the mistakes of my ancestors, I must know what those mistakes were. That's why you've spent the last few years digging into my family name, our lives, everything Kovaric could find."

"And since Monclova is connected to the history of the Dahtien —"

"You see now? Choosing Kovaric was no accident. Neither was his death. Either you or he has uncovered something crucial. I need to know what that is."

Gazing at her empty hands, she recalled the odd way the Professor had sounded when he called her that morning. He wanted her research right away. "There's nothing we've found that —"

"Then you'll have to share with me everything the two of you learned. I know a lot of my family stories, and you'll know more. Between us, we might be able to piece together the truth."

Zill's fingers rolled tight as she lodged them against her knees. "No. I have no reason to believe anything you've said. In fact, you're the one who abducted me. For all I know, you killed Kovaric, want to steal his research from me, and —"

Chovar lowered his head with such a disappointed sigh, she could not finish her thought. After a few seconds of silence, he tapped something on his desk. A moment later, a large man entered and took away the water glass and pitcher.

"I now have your DNA, though I could have taken it from you while you were unconscious." He said the words calm and easy, the real threat simmering beneath.

Zill shivered. She glanced at the closing office door and imagined anybody sitting opposite Chovar Monclova in a business deal would quake whenever he spoke.

Turning his dark gaze upon her, he continued, "I'm hoping you will help me both to save all of this world from a grave danger or simply to finish the work you and Kovaric have slaved over for years. But if those aren't reasons enough, then know that I'll take your DNA, plant it into police evidence, and frame you for Kovaric's murder. Once you're in jail, I'll gain access to all of your files, all of Kovaric's, and while it'll take much longer and cost more money, I will eventually get my answers."

He delivered the threat with such casual grace, Zill nearly missed it. But the tension in her chest and the twist in her gut promised some part of her understood.

Closing her eyes, she pictured the Professor. His wrinkled skin and bulbous nose. His long, gray hair. That kind grin and friendly way of talking that promised his full attention.

If he had truly worked for Chovar Monclova, he had done so with good reason — not simply to save his own skin. He would never compromise himself to avoid consequences. Never had.

When she opened her eyes, she met Chovar's challenging gaze with a stoic, analytical stare. You have referred to this big decision. One that could be of *grave danger* to our world —your words. If I'm going to help you, I need to know what that is." She could see his objection and raised her hand, mimicking his pat in the air. "This is non-negotiable. Either tell me what is at stake or frame me for murder, and I'll risk the judicial system."

Anger flashed across his brow only to be replaced with a deep snicker. Crossing his arms, he leaned back against the edge of his desk. "You win. But you must understand that you cannot repeat this to anybody. If you do, well, I suppose I don't need to make more threats."

He held a long breath and tightened as if about to rip off an old bandage. "Over the last twenty-five years, Monclova Industries has secretly been building another Pathway Ring."

Zill could not think of a stranger set of words. "What?" she managed.

"Nobody on this planet outside of a few high-ranking officers in the company know about it. Not a single politician and certainly none of the Dahtien. Everyone working on it is forbidden to return here until it's done. If anybody on this planet learns about the Ring, everything my family exists for will be destroyed and I'll be arrested."

"If you turn that thing on, we'll all know."

"Yes, but if it works, the money will flow so strong, it'll deluge any objections. At least, that is what my father always claimed. But a few years ago, after he died and I took control of the company, I questioned what the truth behind the Ring was. Father taught me that the failures of the past had nothing to do with the Ring itself. He promised that this one would be safe for all, that we would avoid the great tragedies of yesterday."

"So, you hired Professor Kovaric to find out if that was true."

"Before I set that thing in motion, I've got to know." He walked back to the couch and sat. With an earnest face, he turned toward her. "Will you help me?"

She paused, letting his plea hang between them. Then: "Thank you. I think this is the most honest you've been. Please allow me to be the same. I don't like any of this, but I will do what you want and share all I know about your family on one condition."

"Yes?"

"You will help me find out who killed Professor Kovaric — even if the research is not the reason."

"You have my word."

She nodded. "Then you may want your man to bring another pitcher of water. This is going to take a while." Pulling together her thoughts, she waited until Bracken returned with fresh water. She wanted to make sure she presented the story in the clearest, most logical way. "Where to begin?" she muttered to herself.

"I assume with Lynia Monclova. She's the one who came here and built the thing."

"Not exactly. But before I fix the inaccuracies of your statement, I think it's clear we should start further back with Miguel Monclova, her father."

Chovar's eyes widened. "I never heard much about him. Lynia left us little in the family record except that she didn't like him."

"Professor Kovaric and I did uncover some unofficial records she left, and we pieced together the rest from snippets of information tucked around here and there. He taught me so much. You'd be amazed at the data he could pull out of something as simple as a billing laden or a flight manifest."

"I don't need the step-by-step. That's why I paid you both to do the work. I only want the conclusions."

"Of course. Well, Miguel Monclova was a hardheaded man, determined, and a big risk-taker. While Lynia is the heroine of the beginnings of your family legacy, she would never have been anything if not for Miguel. In fact, none of us would be here without him."

"Then start with him."

"I suspect you won't like him, but try to look beyond the surface. He did love his children, and he believed to his core that all his actions would create the legacy he did create."

"You don't need to protect my feelings. You won't insult me. The Monclova name has existed for centuries. Not all of us have been wonderful examples of humanity. I need the truth — good and evil — in order to make my decision."

"Okay, then. Miguel Monclova. We know little about his upbringing, little about his parents, not even their names, and we know nothing of the Monclova family reaching further back than that, but here is what I can tell you — long before Newarl, before the Pathway Ring, before the Dahtien, a father dreamt of ruling Mars."

# PART I

# CHAPTER 1

MIGUEL MONCLOVA SHOULD HAVE BEEN HOME already. His daughter, Lynia, celebrated her eleventh birthday while he poured a cup of coffee in the company breakroom before heading down the dingy hallway to his cramped office. Not that he had much work to do. Mostly, he waited on a call — an important call.

He sipped the coffee. Bitter, sharp, awakening. Tephen Hilt, the man in charge of Monclova Industries day-to-day operations, had promised that Earth coffee far exceeded the Martian variety, but Miguel noticed no difference. It was certainly good, but nothing special. Perhaps Earth beans lost some of their unique flavor in the long journey to Mars.

When he returned to his scratched desk, outdated computer, and fake red-stone walls, he set down his cup and rubbed his face. How had it all come down to a single call? He didn't want to think about it or the past that brought him here, yet sitting back in his squeaky chair, he removed his necklace with the *M* pendant made from Martian stone and pondered the small object. He rubbed his thumb over the *M*.

Rapping his knuckles on the wall, Tephen entered the office. Dark-featured, tall, lanky, barely filling out his suit, he held a youthful confidence Miguel appreciated. Tephen had ambition and intelligence. He had a great shot at success, too.

"Hey, Boss. Your wife messaged to make sure you wouldn't be too late attending the birthday party."

"I'll be there." Miguel tried not to grouse about the nagging tone in Annalia's paraphrased words nor the implication that he would ever forget a birthday. Lynia was the youngest of their four children — that didn't make her any less important to him.

"Is that a present for her?" Tephen indicated the pendant.

Miguel raised an eyebrow before gesturing the man closer. "Have I never shown this to you?"

"I've seen you wear it, but we've never discussed it."

"My father traveled to Mars to escape the American territory wars. With nothing but a week's worth of cash and an adventurous spirit, the old man created a new life here. Started out working in the mines, then managed the workers, then ran the main office, then owned the fledgling business that he eventually turned into the Monclova Company. He made this pendant from stone he mined with his own hands. Made it the same day he bought this company. After he died, when I took over, I took the pendant, too. I've had it ever since."

The rust-red stone deepened its color depending on the angle of light, and Miguel shifted the *M* in his hand to capture the effect in motion.

"It's lovely," Tephen said.

A catch in his voice pulled Miguel's attention. He looked up and saw pale fear in the man's eyes. Miguel's stomach clenched. "You've heard from Dytat?"

"I got the message right before your wife's call. I'm sorry, but they've decided to go with another company."

"Shit." He kicked at the table. "What about the rail contract?"

"We put our bid in, but that's a government job. It could be another year or two before they make a final decision."

Holding back the urge to yell, Miguel tightened his grip on the pendant. "We're a construction company with nothing to build." Nothing in the bank, either, but he couldn't let anybody know that part — not until the end. "Did you ask Dytat why they changed their mind after months of negotiations?"

"Of course, I did."

"And?"

"They wanted a company with a more modern image."

"An *image*." He growled the word. "If that doesn't say everything wrong about the new generation." He glanced at the young man. "No offense, but too many of your peers value style over substance. What's worse, Dytat is going to find out that while Monclova Industries might have too traditional an image, we know how to actually construct things. I'm guessing they'll go with Olympus Construction. That company is nothing but image. Dytat's going to end up with a subpar building that might even leak into the Martian atmosphere, and they'll call on us to fix it."

Tephen grinned. "In that case, better for us. We can charge them double."

Forcing a matching grin, Miguel said, "Sure. We can wait until then." He pocketed the pendant. "I need to get home for the party."

"I'll close up and be right behind."

"No. You need to stay here and find us a new client. Something big. Something that'll last years. Call on your political contacts. Surely, the dome needs constant repairs. We can't sit around waiting for idiots like Dytat to figure out where they should have put their trust and money."

Tephen tried to hide his disappointment. Miguel suspected the young man had taken interest in Sydney, the Monclova's eldest. But she was only seventeen, and even if she felt ready to date beyond the boys in school, Miguel did not feel the same. Annalia would laugh at him when he said such things out loud —*you can't stop our daughter from growing up*. Well, he could delay it as long as possible.

Resting his head against the car window, Miguel watched the Martian landscape drift by backlit with a pale sunset. Foliage dotted the dome, adding a touch of green life and, more importantly, helping to filter the air. Occasionally, a full-grown tree planted at the side of the trackway whipped across his view.

He had once considered buying a private car, but even when times were flush, the expense would have been ridiculous — especially with the monthly upkeep. Nobody owned a car here. They simply used their link to summon a DV — a driverless vehicle — tapped in a destination, and sat back for the automated ride. The government ran the entire operation and subcontracted the maintenance. It seemed they never had trouble finding the money for that project.

The DV kept a safe distance from other traffic. Not too bad for the evening rush, but then, traffic never bogged down unless an error in a car's software caused an accident. Not even the usual mass of Oxlo trucks delivering packages ordered via link could clog the best routes. At least, never up on the surface. Most of Catadonna had been built underground. With a much thinner atmosphere than Earth, solar radiation always caused problems. Special tinting protected those inside, but the dome was a fixed size. It could not grow with the rapid population increase of the city, and it limited the height of all buildings. Digging underneath was the main solution. The wealthy could afford to live on the surface, but most of the population burrowed below.

The city's growth had been one of Miguel's great victories early on. Excavating deeper and wider under Mars fueled Monclova Industries for over a decade. After all, skilled crews were needed to dig the space for the city, and skilled crews were needed to mine the ore. Monclova Industries had supplied it all.

After inheriting the company, Miguel had set about expanding. Making money had been easy back then. He had his father's political connections, and the government contracts flowed like a raging river. In a few short years, the Monclova Company became Monclova Industries, and Miguel became the wonder boy worthy of interviews, profile pieces, and a lot of female attention. Pretty soon, he met his wife.

Annalia's beauty had won his eye, but her kindness and rugged determination claimed the rest of him. He didn't account for her expensive taste. Nor the hefty cost of raising four children. A few bad investments and misjudging the market hurt, too, but the real blow came when the old politicians retired. Miguel discovered he lacked the people skills to gain new contacts. That was a big reason for hiring Tephen.

Too little, too late, though. The losses forced the company to shrink, and it should have forced a tightening of the belt at home. But Miguel couldn't do that to his family. Not unless he had no other choice.

The DV zipped along a wide curve, and he spied his home in the distance. Rising above the large single level structures and the digital signs for Oxlo's latest sales, Miguel's house stood three stories tall, built into the side of a hill, with clear panes looking over Catadonna. It announced to all of Mars that the name Monclova meant success. Even from afar, he saw the warm lights of Lynia's birthday party.

But it now stood upon a shaky foundation.

"I'm sorry." The whispered words sunk like iron in his gut.

Perhaps the time had come to retire. Earlier than he expected, but he had been only seventeen when he took over from his father. Rowan was sixteen, and while Miguel questioned the boy's business acumen, he couldn't do worse than had already been done. Or, if not Rowan, there was Varo. Only fourteen and lacking focus, but Miguel's retirement did not include death. He would be there to advise, to help, to usher in one of his boys.

He could hear Annalia in the back of his head — *why not Sydney or Lynia?*

She would hate his answer. But whether the people wanted to admit it or not, he knew setting out firm roles for men and women had helped the early Martian settlers to endure, to build, to thrive. Everybody had a clear job to do. Each job contributed to the group's survival, the group's security, the group's growth. *Law* and *order* were not simply buzzwords for ambitious politicians. They mattered.

Miguel smiled as he threaded around the numerous guests filling up his large house. Lynia's party appeared to have more adults than children, but that always happened. Other kids had parties and parents dropped off their child with a present in hand and a time to return. But when the Monclova children had a party, every single parent found a reason to stick around.

Some merely wanted to stand in the massive home, taste the wealth, see the gold banister, the crystal chandelier, and the endless vegetation hanging from the rafters. Maybe sneak a photo on their link. Others clambered for Miguel's time, hoping to pitch a great business opportunity or gain employment under Miguel's wonder boy guidance. Still others paraded their eligible sons in front of Sydney or their of-age daughters in front of Rowan, praying that their entire family's future would be secured through marriage.

As a result, Miguel learned the art of smiling in a warm yet non-committal manner. Annalia had taught him that one. With a bright flash of teeth, she could receive anybody to their home, make them feel welcome, while simultaneously stopping their mouths from uttering any of the wrongheaded, foolish, or downright immoral things they had entered the house hoping to utter. Though hardly such a master as his wife, Miguel had worked at the smile for years and found that he could pull it off occasionally.

Pleasant Martian music played in the background — a quartet of half wind instruments and half strings, and the stunning view of the Martian landscape through the dome bathed the party with a gorgeous, deep rusty red. Those parents that lived below the surface gawked at the sight.

From one of three balconies overlooking the main floor, Miguel gazed across the crowd. Sydney laughed as she helped wrangle the screeching eleven-year-olds while her brother, Rowan, dutifully handed out cups of water to rehydrate the little terrors. He looked as if a chain had been welded around his ankle, but he managed to smile at two children. Though only a year apart, Sydney and Rowan often acted if they came from different families. Nearby, Lynia hurried to take her spot at the large oblong table. At each seat, a doll from the show *Princess Tora: Warrior* had been placed. It was Lynia's favorite show — indeed, the favorite of many eleven-year-olds — and followed Tora's quest to reclaim her throne after her world had been destroyed when a giant meteor crashed into the land. At Lynia's seat, she found a Princess Tora doll dressed in animal hides and carrying a warrior spear. Soon, there would be the traditional cake, song, and presents, but for the moment Lynia and her friends gushed about the different dolls, characters, and episodes of the show.

Miguel flushed with warmth at the joy upon their faces.

That warmth chilled when he could not locate his other son, Varo. His heart skipped as he scanned the crowd but relaxed a second later. The fourteen-year-old stood in the corner, left hand propped against the wall, as he flirted with one of Sydney's beautiful friends. Though Miguel wanted to, he refrained from strutting downstairs and embarrassing his son with a comment about manliness. He admired the boy's ambition and figured his son should learn all the lessons that came from trying to seduce an eighteen-year-old. A hard slap in the face would probably do the trick. But even if the girl let him down gently, Varo would learn plenty.

Besides, Miguel wanted to enjoy observing everyone for a little longer. If Tephen failed to lock down at least one contract soon, all the parties would be over. The impressive house, the attention, the comfort — all of it gone. His children would learn how quickly people changed when they could no longer smell the money. Yet for now, for a few months longer, he could let his family pretend without knowing they were pretending.

Annalia attended the birthday girl before surveying the crowded room. With a radar sense developed over years of marriage, she lifted her eyes straight to him. A tilt of her head — *come down here so we can cut the cake.* He blew her a kiss and turned toward the spiraling staircase that provided a beautiful view that matched the balcony.

But before he reached the second floor, the timbre of conversations changed, grew hushed, gained tension. The front door had opened, and four men wearing gray suits entered. Not businessmen, though. Government men. Agents of one bureau or another. Miguel could sniff them out with ease.

By the time Miguel met them on the first floor, the music had ceased. Annalia glowered, but he hardly needed her prodding. Dropping his practiced smile, he leveled a harsh glare at the lead agent.

"This is my home and my daughter's birthday. We have guests. Whatever you want, you should come to my office during normal work hours."

The agent wore the same buzzcut style lately in fashion amongst the uptight, by-the-book types. Arrogance bled through every gesture, every motion, every word, as he said to the crowd, "We're sorry to intrude. Nobody's in trouble." He offered his boney hand to Miguel. "I'm Agent Grend Falcry."

Miguel held still until Mr. Falcry withdrew the hand. "Leave now, and I won't call your boss."

Leaning in and lowering his voice, Falcry said, "You don't even know what department I'm from, and we both know that your days of influence are waning. Why don't we go somewhere more private and talk. That way your guests can enjoy the rest of the party."

For a moment, Miguel considered throwing the agents out, calling the few political contacts he still had, and rolling the dice on the outcome. But this disturbance had already dampened the party, and he didn't want Lynia's day ruined any further. Even more, seeing Falcry up close, seeing the scars that intersected the crags of his face, seeing the eyes of a man far more confident, far more dangerous than Miguel's original estimation, left any idea of resistance standing outside the dome. This man didn't care about decorum or status, and he certainly didn't care about an eleven-year-old girl.

"My dear guests," Miguel said, all smiles and expansive waves of the hand, "when it comes to government contracts, they don't like waiting. Try to get them to fix the school system or handle the influx of Earthlings — well, that kind of thing will grind on for years."

Uncomfortable laughter ruffled through the room.

"A toast to my dear wife and our lovely Lynia. I'll be a few minutes, but feel free to enjoy the cake and open the presents."

Lynia shot to her feet, her face wrinkled and red. "No, Daddy. You have to be here. We can wait."

Miguel looked to Annalia for help, but his wife set the cake knife on the table. She stroked Lynia's hair and said nothing.

With a gentle chuckle, Miguel said, "Well, then, I suppose I'll have to be as quick as possible. Please, everybody, enjoy the party, and I promise to return soon."

The quartet took this cue to start playing again. Tightening his lips, Miguel sharply waved Falcry and his men to follow. Ushering them to his office in the back, he dared a final glance at his wife. Annalia grinned and laughed as she talked to the other parents, but Miguel saw the fury on her brow — nearly imperceptible yet directed straight at him.

He wanted to apologize. Except he would be apologizing for so much more in the coming months. Starting now wouldn't help.

# CHAPTER 2

THOUGH SOME WOULD CALL HIS HOME OFFICE GAUDY, Miguel loved the space. Indeed, when the final blow would force him to sell this home, he knew deep in his bones that he would miss the office most. Sumptuous, thick carpeting lay the foundation for cabinets and bookshelves of careful craftsmanship. A framed family portrait hung on one wall, perfectly lit from two sides and highlighted from above. His desk, however, stole the show. Made of red glass sourced from Martian sands, the unique swirling patterns never failed to get noticed by visitors.

Except Mr. Falcry.

That little bastard sat stiff and proper without a single comment. His agents stood ramrod straight in the back, arms at the sides, trying to intimidate by appearing ready for action, and yet Miguel spied the surreptitious peeks at the special desk. At least, they had some taste.

As he walked behind this desk, trailing a finger on its smooth surface — he never left any work out to spoil its appearance — one of the standing agents closed the office door. Miguel spotted a few guests peeking in from the hallway, and he clenched his fingers. The moment the door clicked shut, he pounded a fist onto the desk.

"How dare you come to my home, unannounced, ruining my daughter's birthday, embarrassing my wife and my family and me. Whatever this is about could have and should have been handled at my office. You sit there, smug and relaxed. You think my influence is waning? I may not be able to have you strung up by the balls, but I can certainly make things uncomfortable for you. Very uncomfortable."

With his eyes flared and his chest bobbing for breath, he set both fists on the desk and leaned close. Mr. Falcry did not flinch. Didn't budge at all. He did let loose an impatient sigh as he laced his fingers over one knee. Holding Miguel's glare a moment longer, Falcry then straightened, letting each motion command the room.

From his jacket's inner-pocket, he produced a handheld link and flicked it on. After tapping the screen a few times and swiping through several pages, he stopped to read. All through this performance, he never once bothered to look up.

"I've got a houseful of guests," Miguel said. "If you —"

Mr. Falcry raised an index finger and continued reading. At length, he put the handheld back into his pocket. "Mr. Monclova, thank you for agreeing to see us. I do apologize for this unorthodox approach, but we have time constraints that made it necessary."

Miguel's muscles tightened. He considered leaping over the desk and pummeling that idiot. But he could see the agents in the back tense up. If he made any threatening moves, he had no doubt they would act.

Pushing back, he crossed his arms. He hadn't intended to give away so much ground — perhaps that was the real reason Falcry and his cronies had barged in. They wanted to throw Miguel off. Stop him from thinking clearly.

"My daughter is waiting," he said, the grumble in his tone slipping through. "Say what you came for and get out."

Setting his posture with unambiguous authority, Mr. Falcry said, "Monclova Industries, once the darling of Mars, is now failing. Don't bother with denials. We can check the financials of any corporation. Today, your government has smiled your way by deciding that it would look bad for all to have such a notable Martian company fail. So, we're here to bail you out. But if you'd rather that we leave …"

Miguel held still. Perhaps it was childish, but he refused to give this smarmy whisk of a man the satisfaction of seeing him beg. Instead, he did nothing. Eventually, Falcry would have to deliver his message. Miguel could wait.

After twenty long seconds, Falcry smirked. "Right, then. Let's begin. Are you familiar with Project Needle?"

When it came to business discussions, Miguel despised circuitous explanations. He wanted a direct statement that cut clear through all the nonsense. Unfortunately, he did not drive this conversation. Falcry would take whatever route he wanted, and Miguel had no choice but to sit back for the ride.

*Unless I throw them out of my house.* Miguel knew it was a wasted thought and an empty threat. At least, until he learned from Falcry how the government planned to save Monclova Industries.

"Never heard of it."

"It's a joint venture between Mars and Earth. Teams of astrophysicists from both planets have been investigating several anomalies that have occurred near our planet. There are some unique features to these anomalies that make them special and worthy of our attention. First, and possibly most importantly, the anomalies have appeared in the exact same location."

Though Miguel wanted to stay silent, he couldn't stop his mouth from opening. "Unless my science teachers lied to me, we are all soaring through space right now. Any location your anomaly occurred in is long gone, and we won't ever get back to it."

"Forgive me. I misspoke. You are correct. No, the anomaly is maintaining an orbital relationship to the Sun and is close enough to our own that it appears to maintain a steady pace with Mars."

Miguel sat in his plush office chair. While all space-related projects had become significantly cheaper than in the early days of escaping Earth, he could smell the money. "I'm listening."

"Glad to finally have your attention. The anomaly occurs approximately two months standard travel from here, and so far, it has been recorded twice every standard year."

"I take it you want to have an observation post built out there. We can do that."

Falcry chuckled. "We already have a station set up. We've had it for quite a while. Long enough, in fact, that we've finally understood why we were getting such odd emissions readings from this location. Most theories surround black holes on one end and possibly white holes on the other, but obviously we don't have a black hole forming near Mars. That would be catastrophic. No, in this case, we've been seeing magnetic disturbances akin to a solar flare, for example. But that's not a good analogy."

"You can spare the details of this thing. Unless I need to know it to build whatever you're after."

"Of course. You're right. You certainly wouldn't understand it anyway. Let's simply say that we firmly believe this is the mouth of a, well, a wormhole."

In the distance, off key voices sang *Happy Birthday*. Others clapped, no doubt applauding as Lynia blew out eleven candles. Miguel did not raise a glance at the closed office door. All his focus narrowed onto Falcry. "You found a wormhole? Where does it go?"

"No idea. This is where Monclova Industries comes into play. Our teams have developed a device they call the Pathway Ring. It acts like a lightning rod for our wormhole. Once it attracts the wormhole, it locks into the object's frequency, if you will, stabilizes it, holds it together. With a Pathway Ring built at this location, we will create the mouth of a tunnel. Phase One is to build this device, and for that we need a company that can mine the raw materials, process them, ship them out to the location, and provide the knowledge to construct the Ring according to our engineers' specifications. Monclova Industries is the perfect company for our needs."

"That's a big project," Miguel said, leaning back as if under the weight of the job.

"That's only Phase One. There are countless challenges we're going to have to overcome to make this work. Above all else, though, you must understand that the Pathway Ring we build here is merely the entrance to the wormhole. The wormhole itself will spit out any traveler at some other anomaly point. It could be in another galaxy or another solar system or even right next to Jupiter. We have no way of knowing until we travel.

Then, we have the problem that, according to our mathematical models, the wormhole will not necessarily drop off subsequent travelers at the same location. Think of it more like a worm wiggling on a hook. The Pathway Ring is the hook keeping the worm locked in place here, but the other end is flipping around wildly. Thus, we have Phase Two."

Miguel's heart raced at the opportunity, but his mind had already calmed enough to jump a few moves ahead of his opponent. He didn't want to give away where those thoughts led him, however — that was a key negotiation tactic. Besides, something gnawed at him.

He could not put words to it, yet, but his instincts told him a crucial fact had been withheld. Perhaps the most crucial fact in this whole meeting. Keeping a close watch over every facial tell, every physical shift, and every odd breath from Falcry and his men in the back, Miguel observed like a poker player seeking out his opportunity to make a key play.

Though he suspected the answer, he asked, "So what is Phase Two?"

Falcry rolled one shoulder as if uncomfortable in the chair. With a thoughtful grin, he said, "We expect Phase One to require approximately ten years to complete. I will have a team preparing to journey through the wormhole starting around Year Five. Monclova Industries will have to provide all the materials for building a second Pathway Ring as well as detailed instructions on how you accomplished the first one. All of that will be towed by our ship through the wormhole. Those brave souls that make this journey will then build another Pathway Ring with which to capture the other end of the wormhole. If all goes as our models predict, we will have our galaxy's first stable wormhole with which we can travel back and forth as much as we want."

"Ten years? How large is this Ring supposed to be?"

"Quite large. It will have a radius of approximately three thousand kilometers."

"Three thousand? Are you insane?"

"Plenty of countries back on Earth are bigger. America is still slightly wider than that. I suppose only knowing Mars shrinks your perspective. Of course, you'll have to mine twice the material, so we've added in a few extra years. That will also provide our research team plenty of time to test the Ring's safety."

Miguel pretended to run some calculations in his head, but stalling did not help him figure out that missing piece. When he cleared his throat, Falcry raised one hand.

"I know. You're going to point out that such a massive radius works out to over a circumference of eighteen thousand kilometers. Well, nobody said cracking space to reach a wormhole would be easy. The more important question, the one you really want to ask, is also the most obvious question. As of now, I'm authorized to offer you four trillion in whatever currency you wish. That should be more than enough to complete the contract and give yourself a hefty profit."

*Four trillion.* That kind of money would do more than save the company. It would save his family. It would save him.

"That certainly is generous," he said in a neutral tone.

"A project this large is going to face setbacks. We don't want money to be among them."

Falcry removed his handheld link again, flicked through, and set it on the desk. "This is a basic agreement of commitment. We can let the lawyers work out the lawyering parts later. For now, we sign this, and you'll receive the first trillion in a few days. Enough to get things started. The rest will come once the formal contract is completed and signed. If that sounds okay, then let's sign this and you can go back to celebrating your daughter's birthday."

Miguel froze as Falcry's mistake hit — mentioning Lynia's birthday. That was a push too far and entirely unnecessary. It felt desperate. Why would the government be desperate? Monclova Industries was the one in bad shape. Miguel was the desperate one. Yet they pushed for him to sign the agreement when …

*Why did they come to Monclova in the first place?*

Miguel had learned long ago that he should never agree to anything if it had to be done that moment. Any deal worth making could endure a few days of scrutiny, and anybody pushing for an immediate signature either had a scam in place or had something to hide. Miguel thought over the deal from several angles. Nothing hinted at a scam. Which meant the government hid something.

Reaching for the link, Miguel noted the raise in Falcry's eyebrows — expectation. That solidified his opinion. Instead of picking up the device, he tented his fingers on the desk and made a show of careful consideration.

"Is there a problem?" Falcry asked.

*Absolutely.* "Not at all. I'm merely thinking over the deal. Something of this magnitude might be too grand for my little company."

"Please, no need for modesty. You have a reputation and a history that guarantees our success."

"I'll have to hire a lot more staff. Build infrastructure to get the tonnage into space. The local ports can handle things at first, but they'll get overwhelmed once all our mines are running at full."

"I see. You want more money. I'm afraid I cannot raise my offer on the front end. However, once we start getting income from usage of the Ring, there will be plenty of money flowing. I'm sure we can arrange a royalty of sorts for a set term. Probably net you another trillion."

Miguel rose to his feet and turned away. Gazing out his window at the double-moonlit sky over the vast Martian landscape, he focused on holding still. He had figured it out. The answer had been revealed as clear as the land after a sandstorm, but Miguel had to act ignorant. Falcry couldn't catch on that Miguel knew. Not yet. Because the real money, the real power in this, rested in building and controlling the other end of the tunnel. Since Falcry kept that piece of information quiet, the government clearly had no intention of sharing the wealth. The limited royalty offer only proved the point. The money made from controlling the wormhole had to be so immense that even a royalty meant nothing. Easily tossed to the peasants to keep them in line.

The question now — how best to use this revelation?

Miguel's first instinct leaned into his strengths. He could negotiate Falcry into a corner and swipe the wormhole rights out from under the government. Probably end up getting Falcry fired. That would cause several problems, though. The government would replace Falcry. Considering the value of the wormhole and the Pathway Ring, they would make sure the next agent had the right priorities — a by-the-book kind of person who would always be looking out for Miguel's maneuvering. That would be another major problem. Having outsmarted the government once, they would be cautious from that point on, and since the contract would last ten years on this end, and presumably another ten years on the other end, he would have to deal with them for a long time. Better to keep Falcry in place, exploit the man, and appear to have a good relationship with the government for the next twenty years.

"Mr. Monclova?" A slight quiver in Falcry's voice.

Turning back, Miguel beamed. He picked up the link and used his finger to sign the agreement. "This is such a wonderful opportunity. Overwhelming, in fact. I can't thank you enough."

Once Falcry had his link back and secure in his pocket, he offered his hand. "Welcome to the Pathway Ring project. We've got some exciting years ahead."

Miguel shook that hand with a tight grip. They smiled at each other with all the enthusiasm of two chess masters about to face off. In his mind, Miguel ground Falcry's bones into a fine dust, and he wondered if Falcry imagined the same of him.

# CHAPTER 3

WORKING OUT ENOUGH BASIC DETAILS to get underway took several hours more. When Miguel finally closed the front door on the government agents, the sound echoed through the house. Any other birthday, he would have felt hollow at letting down his family. He knew Annalia waited for him in their bedroom, pacing a gully into the deep carpeting that no force from above or below could assuage. But once she heard about the meeting, once they all did, Miguel had four trillion reasons to make them happy.

First, however, he wanted to see his children before they all went to sleep. Stalling to avoid the fight? Perhaps, a little. But he also knew that tonight had shifted the ground beneath them. Tonight marked the start of what would be a historic, monumental achievement for all humanity. His children needed to know, to prepare, because they would now inherit more than money. They would inherit a legacy.

He made a quick detour to his office to pull out one final gift for Lynia — a very special book. His body electrified as he climbed to the third floor and knocked on Sydney's door. He was going to change more than one world, possibly more than one galaxy. The name Miguel Monclova would be spoken with the same reverence as Madame Curie or Albert Einstein. Names that refused to die because of their universal importance.

Sydney sat in bed reading on her link. Dark hair, rich smooth skin, and brown eyes that dazzled even when she cried. She bore all the beauty of her mother.

Shining those eyes in his direction, she said, "You know Mom's cross with you."

"I know." He sat on the edge of the bed and kissed his

daughter's forehead. "I'm sorry I couldn't be at the party like I should've been, but your father has made a successful deal tonight, one that will keep you and your brothers comfortable for the rest of your lives. One that will make this family important. Famous, even."

"Famous? What kind of deal?"

"I'm not sure how much I can to say yet, but I'm going to need to hire a lot of people, and it'll involve going out into space."

Awe spiked her voice. "Space."

"That's right. And with you turning eighteen soon, there's going to be a lot of eligible bachelors who want to get a good position in our company. But I'm not worried. You're smart. You won't let anybody trick you into a false marriage."

"Daddy, come on. I don't even know if I want to get married."

"Of course, you do. How else are you going to have children?"

Rolling her eyes, she said, "I don't need to be married to get pregnant."

"You do in the Monclova family. Shendo is the foundation of our civilization. It's what has kept Mars alive and successful. We will follow it."

"I know, I know. All I mean is that I'm not even eighteen yet. Boys are fine, and I do want to have children eventually, but I've got other things to accomplish first."

"Like what?"

The way Sydney took a breath, swallowed a little, and shifted her eyes to the side, Miguel saw that she had been building up to this moment. Maybe for weeks. Or longer. Whatever she planned to say, she had guided their conversation to this point, and he had not recognized it until it was too late. He wanted to be proud of her — he was — but he could not stop himself from being on guard, too.

"Well," she said, as she set her link on the bedside table, "I know I'm not one of the boys, but I am the eldest, and you said you need more people, so I don't see why it would be a problem."

"You're giving me a preamble without actually telling me what you want. Be direct."

Another hard swallow. Then: "I want to work for you. For Monclova Industries. I want to learn how the business runs. I know you won't ever put me in charge, but if you want Monclova Industries to last, you'll need somebody in the family who understands things — and let's face facts, Rowan and Varo are not ready."

"Rowan is sixteen. He'll be ready."

"Rowan is sixteen going on twelve."

"He'll grow up fast when the responsibility falls upon him. And if he doesn't, then I have another son. Varo will be fifteen soon, and he shows a lot of my spirit and your mother's stubbornness. Those traits will make him a fine leader."

"But —"

"I know it's tough to hear, but Shendo teaches that we all have our places in society, our duties to fulfill. Yours does not include taking over the family business."

"Right. I'm just for pumping out babies."

"You think that's all your mother has done? She keeps the family together, keeps the whole operation running smoothly while I'm out running the business. It's a joint venture that cannot succeed without each other."

"But on Earth —"

"Mars is not Earth. Women have different roles here. This is a harder, more rugged, more dangerous planet to scratch out a living. Without our strict adherence to tradition, none of us would have survived to this point."

Lowering her head, Sydney said, "I guess it was a silly idea."

Miguel's heart clutched. He believed every word he had said, and yet, he wondered if the world might be changing. He knew every generation pushed the boundaries a little. Change was inevitable and only a fool pushed back. This Pathway Ring could potentially change more than a few traditional family roles. It could bring a seismic shift to all humankind.

He put a strong hand on his daughter's shoulder. "Perhaps

you're a little right. Not about Rowan and Varo — one of them will make a fine leader. But if you learn the business, I could see you being a great asset to them. An advisor, perhaps. You'd still be expected to marry and give me grandchildren. I want lots of grandchildren. But with the deal I made, this project will stretch out for the next twenty years or so. It might be good to have you in on things from the very beginning."

She hesitated a smile. "So, I can do it? I can work for the company?"

"You'll start a few afternoons each week until school is over. We'll see how that goes. If you haven't changed your mind after that, then we'll talk about you working full time."

Sydney wrapped her arms around him, squeezing tight, mumbling *thank you* into his shoulder. When he finally left, as he walked to Rowan's room, he decided that if he had made a mistake, at least it was a mistake that brought his daughter great joy. Besides, young men are often given a year or two after school to travel, to experience a larger life, before settling down to the business of living. Why not for his daughter, as well?

Rowan's door stood open a crack, and in the dark, Miguel spied his son asleep. But after a short time of watching, he could hear the uneven breaths and caught the tentative movements. The boy was faking.

Part of Miguel wanted to snap the light on and confront Rowan. Part of him knew he still had an argument with his wife ahead, and there seemed no upside to instigating more strife into the evening. He loved Rowan, but he consistently failed to get through to the boy. Sixteen going on twelve, indeed.

On the second floor, Miguel paid a visit to Varo's room. Just the room, though, because Varo was not there. Miguel thought of the pretty eighteen-year-old his son had been flirting with. Could the boy have actually succeeded?

Miguel had been putting off a discussion of birth control and consequences, but it appeared that talk had to happen fast. Otherwise, Mars might overflow with Monclova bastards.

He strolled down the hall and stopped at Lynia's door. The light was on — she probably waited to see him before going to sleep. The first of two ladies he owed an apology. He raised his knuckle to the door and swallowed the tinge of fear fluttering his chest. Armed with his present and his love, he knocked.

Lynia sat upright in her bed, her face twisted tight, overacting her anger as she glowered at her father. Miguel put up his hands, the wrapped present in one, and looked away in mock shame.

"I know, and I am sorry. I'm sure you think that I was a terrible father today."

"You were."

"I didn't plan on that meeting. But it was very important, and it has secured your future. That's what a good father does."

"I don't care about any stupid meeting. You weren't at my party."

Approaching his daughter, he bowed his head. "Perhaps I can make it up to you."

"I doubt it." Plenty of doubt resided in her voice. In fact, Miguel detected a hint of curiosity about the wrapped gift.

"You know I love you."

"I suppose."

Miguel barked out a laugh, and in seconds, Lynia laughed, too. Sitting next to her, he handed over the gift.

She ripped it open but frowned at the book. "The Bible?"

"Not any bible. That one has been mine since I was a child. Before I owned it, your grandfather owned it. It was among the first ever to be printed on Mars. One of the first to contain all three testaments — the Old Testament of the Jews, the New Testament of the Christians, and the New World Testament of the Shendo."

"That's you?"

"Us. Practically everybody on Mars."

"Because it was some kind of pioneer thing?"

Miguel's head pulled back. "You don't know your religion? I thought you went to classes at the temple."

"They were boring. And I got into trouble."

"Trouble?"

"I ask too many questions. What's wrong with asking questions?"

"Nothing. An inquisitive mind is good to have. But it's important to know how the universe works. That's in this book. When mankind first came to Mars to stay, it was a completely new experience. The ways of the pioneer had long been forgotten. Nobody on Earth had to forge new lands for centuries. Here we were on this inhospitable environment, struggling to build a workable society, but we had all these different types of people — Jews, Muslims, Christians, Buddhists, Hindus, Pagans, you name it."

"Shendo?"

"They didn't exist back then. Now with all these different types, these different religions, there was bound to be conflict. The success of these new settlements was threatened from within. It didn't look like we would survive. Until one night, God visited Hiroshi Shendo. Hiroshi stayed up all night with God writing the Book of Shendo. It is this book that gives us our traditions, our structure, everything we need to be a society that gets along despite our differences. It is the foundation of what makes Mars successful. It tells us how to best contribute to our civilization." He thought of Sydney's disappointed face. Well, he could make sure at least one of his daughters followed the Shendo way. "I'm giving this gift to you, so that you may read it and learn and wonder and marvel and experience all the most incredible thoughts and emotions that come through its words. Even if you don't understand it today, I hope one day you'll understand how much this means to me and how much I love you."

Lynia leafed through the book. "Wrote all this in one night? Seems a bit silly, but I'll try it."

Miguel laughed. "I love how open-minded you are." He kissed the top of her head. "Sleep well tonight, my dear. And don't worry if you hear a lot of yelling — I've got to face your mother."

Lynia's eyes widened. "I wasn't really mad with you. But I think she is."

"Don't I know it."

# CHAPTER 4

THREE DAYS. Miguel could not recall any three days lasting so long. Not a word from Falcry. Not a word from Annalia. Silence on both fronts.

With Falcry, the silence did not mean much. Government moved slow with each level of bureaucracy mucking up the simplest tasks. Even with authorization to make the deal, and with success in attaining Miguel's signature, there would be mounds of red tape for Falcry to cut through before the initial funding arrived.

Annalia's silence, however, meant far worse.

Morning breakfast and evening dinner hit the table on time and cooked to perfection, but she only spoke to the children. If he asked a question, tried to force a conversation, she acted as if she didn't hear. Or worse, one time, she simply stared straight at him, her eyes blasting through him, incinerating any chance to speak. At night, of course, she refused to share a bed. With no words spoken, she made up the living room couch with sheets, a comforter, and his pillow. He didn't argue.

His children were aware. Sydney's excitement to start working for Monclova Industries kept her from saying anything. She probably feared he would change his mind. He didn't bother asking Rowan — the boy would take his mother's side. As for Varo, he would figure it wasn't any of his business. Especially since his parents fighting meant they didn't come down hard on him for the birthday party. That first morning, Miguel saw right away that the young man had not attracted Sydney's lovely friend, but rather, he had filched a bottle of cerio — Martian rum — and drank his head into a horrible hangover. Which left Lynia. For her part, she gave Miguel a hug and kiss goodbye each morning, as well as a secret report on the situation. *Don't worry, Daddy. She's calming down.* or *Be patient* or *She laughed today. I think you're almost there.*

At least, Miguel had a massive workload to distract him. Though he would have preferred to boast in front of his wife as each thrilling day ended. Even at that moment, standing at the edge of the city dome, staring out at the endless kilometers of Mars, knowing he would purchase most of what he could see — well, he felt bigger than the dome itself, taller than the large-leaf trees towering above. Yet he could not stop wishing Annalia stood at his side.

Instead, he had Senator Bashir.

The man had deep-set eyes that pinched his nose, graying hair shaved close to the skull, and a long face that stretched caverns along his dark skin. A strange combination that created shadows in every crease. He wore a fine suit, one meant to instill authority and envy. It failed on both accounts.

"Did you know we went to school together?" Bashir said.

Miguel tried to picture the massive complex he would build. "I'm sorry, I don't remember you."

"Oh, you wouldn't. I was two classes below you. Everybody knew you, of course. The heir to the Monclova fortune. Every girl wanted you. Even the ones already spoken for."

"Didn't seem that way to me." In fact, Miguel recalled plenty of lonely nights in which he wondered if anybody would ever fall in love with him.

"It's always different when you're the one sitting on the perch. I know all about it. When I first became Senator, I had no idea how isolating it would feel. A gilded cage, right? Isn't that the old Earth phrase? And now, look at us. Two wealthy, powerful men, standing on Mars and gazing at its empty, barren land, visualizing the greatness we could create."

Bashir snapped his fingers, and one of three assistants standing a respectful distance away hustled over. She handed him a link already displaying the pages he required and rushed back to the others. Miguel swore she bowed her head a tiny bit.

"I have here my authorization from the Martian Coalition

Government. This makes me your point of contact for the duration of the project."

"What happened to Falcry?"

"Oh, he's still involved as your main business partner. Nothing has changed. But he's from Earth." Bashir held the link out to the side, and the same assistant returned to take it away. "Think of me as the facilitator for things that need to actually get done through our government."

"Like getting paid? Falcry hasn't delivered the first installment yet. It's going to be difficult to hire all the workers I need, if I can't pay them."

Clasping his hands, Bashir lined his pointer fingers together and shook the whole blob at Miguel as if making a poignant gesture. "That's exactly the kind of thing I can help with. I promise you'll have that first payment before the end of tomorrow."

Miguel noticed that two of his people started tapping on their links.

"You can start hiring right away." Bashir inclined his head. "We can really use the employment."

"What about this land? I'd like to build a few launch pads on it. Further out, of course — I wouldn't want to put the dome in danger. We'd have to make sure there isn't anything important underneath. I'd hate to destroy property values because homes are shaking every time we send a rocket into space."

Bashir frowned. "We have a fully-functional port already."

"Which will require me to load trucks with all the materials, haul it to the other side of the dome, go through the red tape at the port, load it onto a ship, and wait for a launch window that doesn't conflict with other traffic. If I had my own port, I could have the finished materials go straight aboard a waiting ship and launch at my convenience. The Ring will get what it needs far faster, far more efficiently. That means the job might get done earlier than estimated. The sooner its done, the sooner we can all profit."

"But —"

"I'm sure you have some way to get cash out of the deal."

Miguel paused as it clicked in his head. "You were planning to skim off the port fees."

"There's no need to cast aspersions."

"Doesn't bother me. A job this big invites all kinds of interesting accounting. A little misplacing of funds here and there is expected. But I need this land, and I need my port." He stepped away with a thoughtful bounce of his head. All theater — he had factored in Bashir's greed from the start. "I have an idea."

Bashir moved in so fast, he stumbled. "Oh? I'm always open to creative solutions."

"This land is government owned, and I have no doubt that your superiors gave you a final price you can't bargain lower than. What is it? Thirty-percent discount? Forty?"

"Well, actually, I can go as low as fifty percent. But I shouldn't tell you that."

"Not if we were planning a straight-forward sale. You already know that's not what I'm proposing. Now, I have a reputation of being a hard negotiator. So, let's tell the government you managed to stop me at a forty-two percent discount. I think they'll believe that — especially when they were expecting to go all the way down to fifty. In reality, though, I'm agreeing to only forty percent. I'll give you the full amount in cash, once the government pays me, and you can pocket the two percent difference."

Bashir's mouth stood agape. "You're going to buy this land from the government and bribe me, a government official, all with the government's own money." He laughed. "Mr. Monclova, I think I'm going to really enjoy working with you."

Miguel decided to walk back to the office. He inhaled the fresh air and watched people strolling the numerous suspended pathways. Automated cars zipped along the trackway. The rumble of the larger city beneath his feet vibrated up his legs. In the distance, parents brought their children to the park to enjoy as much nature as could be provided on Mars. Maybe one day, a statue of Miguel would stand in that park, and all those children would learn about how he had changed their lives.

His link vibrated a double-pattern in his pocket — a message. When he checked it, he could not hide the wide smile on his face. Annalia had asked him to lunch. *It's time we talked,* the message read.

# CHAPTER 5

MNW, THE LITTLE DINER two blocks from his office, had been a favorite for years. The owner, Giji, once told him the letters stood for *Mars Needs Women*, a relic of Earth's movie past, and that made sense considering Giji had decorated the walls full of authentic movie posters, stills (he was pretty sure that's what she called the framed photos), bits of actual film, and any other Hollywood paraphernalia she could get her hands on. "Also," Giji once whispered to Miguel, "I prefer women."

"So do I," he had said. She laughed about it for weeks.

Annalia sat in the front corner to the left of the entrance. A large window cut dramatic light across her face like something from one of Giji's old movies. Miguel took a seat across the table, waited for his link to connect with the diner, tapped in their order — Annalia always ate the same fried veggie plate here — and sat back with his legs straddling the chair. He intended to strike a relaxed, open posture but something about it made him think he looked aggressive. He came forward and placed his hands down on the table. He trembled a smile.

"Only you can make me so nervous," he said.

Her lips curled for a second before returning to a straight line.

"I'm sorry." He blurted the words harsher than he had wanted. Calmer, less aggressive, he went on, "I really am. I never asked for, I never expected anybody to interrupt our party. But you must understand, I couldn't afford to turn those men away. I've done all I could to let you and the children remain in comfort, but the truth is that our situation was not good. The company was failing. The meeting that night — it's changed everything. We're going to have more money than you ever thought possible. We're going to be famous. The name

Monclova will live on forever."

She let out a breath as if releasing smoke. Flicking her hair aside, she lifted her gaze to look directly into his eyes. "You really don't understand."

"I'm trying. I truly am sorry. I've apologized, and I made sure to apologize to Lynia. She's okay. She told me she was fine, a little disappointed, but no harm done. I could tell she told the truth."

"She adores you. She'll put up with anything. I should know."

"What's that mean?"

Miguel had come prepared for anger. Anger he understood. It was the main method of communication in his line of work when things went wrong. But this — he had never seen her react this way. Besides, it was just a birthday party.

Angling her head, catching the light even more, Annalia said, "Do you remember our fourth date?"

"Our fourth? I don't think so. Did I do something stupid?"

She snickered. "Dear, that was our first date."

"That one I remember. I was charming on our first date. And a gentleman. I don't know what I could've done that I was stupid."

"On our first date you were both charming and a gentleman, but you were also arrogant and set on making me know how important you planned to be in the world. I didn't mind. All that bragging sounded ambitious and exciting and even a little sexy. But that was all I got of you that night. On our second date, it became clear that you were more than a gentleman. You were a traditionalist. Not a prude, but extremely careful. On our third date, I realized your ambitions had a quality of dream to them. Not that you couldn't attain them, but that your goals involved something larger than what anybody could accomplish in a lifetime. You dreamed then, you still dream, of a dynasty. All of that was intoxicating and nearly had me falling in love with you."

"Nearly?"

"It was the fourth date that I fell in love with you."

"What did I do?"

"Nothing. We went to my apartment, I made you dinner, and

we sat at my little table eating and talking. Really talking. Mostly about our families. You liked that I came from a large family. You liked hearing about all my brothers and sisters. You told me about the values you were raised under, and I could see how your whole life shaped you into the man you are. But even then, I had not fallen in love. I was certainly attracted to you, I certainly was interested, but if I was going to fall in love with somebody —"

"You wanted to make sure it would last."

She reached out and clasped his hand. "Near the end of that evening, all the posturing, all the attempts to make ourselves look our best, all the facades faded away. I saw the real you. Do you remember what you said?"

Miguel thought back. He did remember the evening — just not that it had been the fourth date specifically — and he knew what came after. But his exact words? "I'm sorry, I don't."

"You told me that if we ended up together, I should be prepared for reality. You knew you had big dreams and that they might not happen. In that moment, I saw your fears — healthy fears. You were going to take big risks, and you wanted a woman who willingly took those risks, too. Because if you failed, it would all come crashing down. All these promises of fame, fortune, importance — we could have every bit as easily ended up in the gutter. I fell in love with you because I saw a man willing to show me his sheer will, his ability to fight and risk and push, even knowing he might lose it all. That's why I pulled you into a kiss that night. That's why I pulled you into my bedroom that night."

Miguel winked. "You thought I was pretty good-looking, too."

"You're passable."

"Passable?"

Annalia giggled. A delightful sound. A forgiving sound. "That was more than a birthday party you missed. That was a moment in Lynia's life that cannot be replaced. All the money, all the fame, all of it cannot fill the hole you left that night. Don't do it again."

Miguel squeezed her hand. He had apologized. She had accepted. He raised his head toward the sky as if the sun could shine through the ceiling and warm his relief. "I want to reassure you that we don't have to worry. The risks we took are a thing of the past. The deal I've made will bring in more money than the Monclova family has ever seen."

Dropping her shoulders, Annalia let go of his hand. "I don't care about the money. I swear, sometimes I wish we'd never had any success."

"Easy to say when we're living extremely comfortable. You and I might be okay going back to the days of struggle, but we never had it too bad. Not like our parents. And our children? They wouldn't survive one day without their links, without their super-padded bedspreads, without their high-end foods and —"

"I've worked hard raising them to not be spoiled by our good fortune. They could live without all of that. What they need is their father."

"I'm right here."

"You weren't there for Lynia's birthday. You weren't there when Varo broke his arm last year. Rowan knows so little of you that he doesn't even understand the purpose of a father. And Sydney — why that girl still idolizes you is beyond me."

"That's not fair. I've had to work hard every day to provide for them."

"You had to work hard every day to build your empire. And once built, you didn't have to keep working. You've chosen to."

Giji served their lunch, glanced from Miguel to Annalia, and quickly escaped. Miguel looked at his plate — a pulled pork sandwich made from pigs dome-born and dome-raised, some of the finest, most succulent meat on the planet. He pushed the plate aside.

"I know I haven't been there for every key moment in our children's lives, but I've been there in spirit, and I've made sure they understood why I was away. I made sure that they saw what hard work and determination can accomplish. Sydney and Lynia are growing into beautiful young women, and when they seek out a man, they will seek out a man who will work just as hard to provide for them. That's a good thing."

"What if they want more than to make babies?"

Miguel scowled as a deep fire burned up his chest. "Lynia said she hasn't been going to temple classes. I figured we would discuss it once we had made up, but I can talk now, too. You've been undermining me for a long time. Sydney wants to work at the office, Rowan shows no initiative, Lynia's already questioning her role in society. Varo's the only one acting his age. I wanted our children brought up in the Shendo traditions because those are the beliefs and values that have brought us such incredible fortune."

"And I have shared those with you. But the pioneer days are long gone. Do you really think our children want to follow those antiquated rules when they can get on their link and see people all over this world, all over Earth, who are free to do what they want with their lives, to be who they want to be? Our traditions were good and necessary to get us to this point, to provide our children with the freedom to pursue anything, but if we're not careful, those same traditions can build walls around us. They invite a prejudice which I do not want our children to have."

"That was not your decision to make alone."

Annalia stared at her plate untouched. "I love you, but you're wrong."

They sat in silence for several minutes, neither one moving a muscle. Miguel replayed the argument, trying to figure out how he went from the success of his apology to this ravine of doubt.

He checked the time. "I've got to go back to work."

"I'm sure."

"We've had disagreements before, and I'm sure we'll have them again. We both know what needs to be done. Take some time, cool off, and talk through this carefully. Maybe tonight when I get home?"

Her only response — an unenthusiastic shrug. He stood, hoping he believed the words he had said, hoping she would be ready to talk that night.

As he moved to leave, however, she clutched his arm. "Promise me. No matter what happens with this new deal, with our future, promise me that you will always protect our children."

"Why would you even ask that? Nothing is more important that our children."

"Promise me. Even if they don't turn out to be what you want, always protect them."

He knew he had missed a step in this argument — really more of an intense discussion — and that he would go over it again and again throughout the day, sifting through each word to understand what had transpired, but for the moment, he had no trouble answering her. "I promise."

She released him. As he walked back to the office, dark thoughts clouded his mind. He had the distinct impression that he had changed something which he could not go back on. And while he had always followed the teachings of the New World Testament, he found a new desire growing within him. He decided that after work, before he went home that night, he would do something he had not done in many, many years. He would go to the temple and pray.

# CHAPTER 6

ONLY ONE YEAR INTO THE PROJECT and Miguel already felt the pressures mounting. The logistics were a nightmare, but finding and training enough workers proved an even greater challenge. There were a limited number of people available on Mars, and not all wanted to work for a huge construction-mining operation like Monclova. However, the most pressure came from recruiting the extra people Miguel required — the people beyond those he told Falcry about or reported to the Martian government. They were his insurance policy, and he needed to get them in place before anybody noticed.

He wished he could tell Annalia about his plan. Maybe she would have understood why he had to be away for the entire month, making appearances at the office or via link-calls while skulking around the lower-levels, forging deals to acquire all he required. Not only choosing the right personnel, but he had to acquire special equipment, special people to operate it, and above all, to keep it secret.

"I was home for Lynia's twelfth birthday party," he had said before leaving.

Annalia raised an eyebrow. "I'll throw a parade."

He wanted to say that she damn-well should. Did she have any clue how difficult his job had become? Did she understand even a little of the sacrifices he made so that his family would be secure and immortalized? Sure, he hadn't been around much. He knew that. Rowan and Varo still needed Shendo instruction, and he had failed to push Annalia on that. Lynia needed it, too. But it was hard to influence their upbringing when he spent most of his time away. He should have been able to trust his wife to handle that duty. As a result of their mutual neglect, they often argued whenever he was home. In fact, if Sydney had not started working for him and sharing the occasional lunch, he probably wouldn't know anything that went on at home.

But even she was tight-lipped when he returned from his sojourn into the belly of Mars. He entered the house to find the family sitting at the dinner table waiting for his arrival. When he had called to say he would be home that night, Annalia promised to have a meal ready, but she never mentioned presenting the children this way — all dressed up as if for a holiday meal.

Nobody shouted a joyous greeting. Nobody burst from their chairs to rush into his arms. They looked at him with a darkness that churned his stomach. This shadow hung over Lynia, in particular.

"Everything okay?" he asked.

A few nods. A grunt. Nothing more.

After the near-silent meal, the children rushed to their rooms. Lynia moved the slowest, as if held down by the weight of guilt. Miguel looked to his wife with an expectant gaze.

"What?" she said. "Life continues while you're gone."

"That's no reason to shut me out of whatever happened."

"It doesn't matter. It's been handled, and if you didn't hear about anything in public, then I've done my job."

"What could've happened that threatened to go public?"

Annalia gritted her teeth. "You don't understand anything."

"Then tell me." He made a fist but refrained from pounding the table.

With an exasperated huff, she said, "Every single moment of their lives is under a microscope now. We are the Monclovas, after all. If one of them farts in class, news of it will reach Earth."

"Okay. I understand that's difficult, but —"

"Stop. Don't pretend you have a clue what's going on here, and don't ask to know. We have our roles to play, after all. I make sure the family runs smooth, and since you made that deal for the Ring, smooth now includes protecting our name from public smear. So, accept that if you don't hear anything, then I'm doing my job."

Later that night, he kissed her. It was an apology kiss, one they both knew too well, and she accepted. Yet as their kisses grew stronger and their clothes came off, Miguel noticed an absence in her eyes. She went through the usual motions, made the right sounds, smiled when she thought he looked at her, but he could feel part of her missing from the experience.

Hours afterward, while Annalia slept, Miguel sat in bed with his link bathing the room in digital blue. He intended to catch up on mail, but his mind kept racing through the evening, the odd glances between his children and the odder conversation with his wife. He didn't know how to feel, but he agreed that she had done a good job. Except for one thing — the children's religious training.

Usually, that fell upon the father's shoulders, and now he wondered if he had asked too much by expecting Annalia to provide that as well. No wonder she had been mad at him. Sure, it was partly his absences, but they had succeeded in life by following their roles. She had said as much after dinner. Except he had failed to do his part with the children — making sure they knew Shendo. He had left that on Annalia's shoulders.

"Tomorrow, that changes," he whispered.

When morning came, he had his schedule reorganized so that after school, he could be home. He had thought through the matter and decided that he would focus on Rowan and Lynia first. Varo would resist too much, but Miguel figured that if his son saw a successful experience by his siblings, he might be convinced to try. Sydney was old enough to decide for herself, and Miguel had to hope that she would follow the right path. But Rowan and Lynia were ripe for a proper Shendo education.

Annalia laughed when Miguel explained his plan. "Good luck with Lynia."

"She still adores me."

That brought a dark scowl. "More than you know."

He wanted to ask again about what had happened but so no upside to broaching that conversation. Instead, he said, "She needs to learn these things. Otherwise, she won't be prepared for her role in society."

Another laugh. A bitter one. "Lynia is too strong-willed to be married off for making babies. And even if you persuade her to visit the Shendo monk, I guarantee he'll throw her out after her third question. She doesn't take non-answers."

Though Miguel wanted to argue further, he had to admit that Annalia knew their daughter better. If she thought Lynia was not ready for a Shendo education yet, then perhaps he needed to wait. He would have to find time at home to teach Lynia proper manners when receiving the wisdom of a monk. Or perhaps Annalia could do that.

He ordered Rowan to a DV and headed to the Shendo temple.

From the outside, the temple did not have much impact. A squat cube painted gray, it had only two adornments that set it apart from neighboring buildings — a red pillar on each corner and a green plant on either side of the entranceway. As Miguel led them in, the front doors slid open and cool air wafted across to chill their skin. The temple had dim lighting, shrouding much of the place in darkness. Along a wide hallway, the walls displayed several of the founding principles in the Book of Shendo in colorful script that shined in the dimness before disappearing like smoke, only to reappear in a continuous loop:

> *Each person has a place. The Lord wants them to find theirs.*
>
> *We have been led to our freedom by the will of the Lord.*
> *Shendo will show us His path.*
> *Shendo is the will.*
>
> *To lead or follow, to rule or be ruled, each finds their path when they find Shendo.*

Miguel noticed Rowan reading the inscriptions with interest. He smiled inwardly for his son. They should have done this long ago.

Monk Crozet approached with a wide smile. Portly and pale, he wore the traditional red-swirl robes that dragged on the tiled floor, always connecting him to the planet. In one hand, he pressed the Book of Shendo to his chest. The other hand led the way to his guests.

"Mr. Monclova, it is an honor to have you and your boy in our humble temple."

Ignoring the pleasantries, Miguel turned to face his son. "This is Monk Crozet. He'll teach you all about Shendo. You listen to him, and you learn it. Understand?"

"Yes, sir." Rowan stood stiff — nearly saluted.

An instant later, Monk Crozet walked deeper into the temple with Rowan at his side. Their murmured chatting sounded friendly, and Miguel swore he caught a fond gaze rise between the men. It caused a strange, sharp reaction in his chest. He had never seen that look on Rowan's face before — not only respectful but enthusiastic.

*Am I jealous?*

Walking back to the waiting DV, Miguel considered the possibility before dismissing it with a shake of the head. Part of Monk Crozet's job was to build respect and enthusiasm for Shendo in his pupils. Of course, the monk would be good at it. He had been doing the job for most of his life.

With his one son's education now set on the proper track, Miguel allowed a moment of relief. His plans for the company, for the family, had him juggling so many risks. To accomplish this one thing, to see it blossom in an instant, at least he could hold onto that. As he headed to the office of Monclova Industries, he refocused his mind toward the remaining few hours of the day and what he could accomplish for the Ring.

# CHAPTER 7

SINCE THE DAY THAT MIGUEL FIRST UNDERSTOOD he would grow up to take over the family business, he imagined the success he would bring to it. He dreamed how all of Mars would know the name Monclova, how his mining operation would add a construction operation and maybe even a space transport operation, how Earth might even come to know the name Monclova, and everywhere he stepped foot, people would stop, point, and marvel that they had glimpsed one of the wealthiest, most powerful men alive. He strived for it. Worked hard for it. Gave up so much. And when he thought it had all come crashing down, this one government contract rescued him. Five years in, and he had learned that his big dreams had been foolishly simple.

He nestled back in his private DV's luxury seat as it drove him to the office after a lovely and expensive lunch. The exquisite Martian landscape whisked by. Four fading vapor trails like smoking pillars marked where the latest Monclova transports had blasted away. Every twelve hours, those rockets rumbled the ground as they headed into space full of iron, steel, aluminum, and other basics. Some contained methane or nitrogen. Mars had plenty to offer. More than Earth in some cases — especially iron — and Mars had plenty of unused land to dig up. Best of all, Mars was significantly closer to the wormhole. Much cheaper to send a rocket on a journey of weeks instead of years.

"Are you still there? Did I lose the connection?" Senator Bashir's static-filled voice pulled Miguel back.

"You have nothing to worry about. Monclova Industries is in an excellent position."

"For now. But if the government were to stop funding the

project —"

"Do you know something I don't?" Miguel didn't truly believe the threat, but a tiny piece of him always worried the same.

"No, no. Everything's fine. After all, the money's already spent. No point in stopping the project now. In another five years, we'll start making our return. No need to be concerned."

Bashir babbled on, repeatedly taking both sides of the discussion, and Miguel barely listened. Politicians tended to be this way — always searching for a new crisis to become the central figure of fixing. Still, from the start of the Pathway Ring project, Miguel had made sure to keep Tephen seeking out new contracts. Once Monclova Industries started spending the project money, people noticed, and Tephen had little trouble strengthening the foundation of the business. Several interviews and articles and annual reports helped matters, too. After all, a project this big, with the money of two planets behind it, could not be kept secret. Nor did anybody want to keep it secret. Lots of money flowed from just the potential of the Pathway Ring.

"It's not the money, anyway," Bashir rattled on. "I've asked you before, and I completely understand why you don't want to discuss the matter, but you need to have a clear successor, a clear plan should something happen to you or should you choose to retire. This is very important — not only to the government but to outside investors."

Ah. Bashir had been making side deals. Miguel wasn't surprised.

"Plus, once you name a successor, I can build a relationship with that person now. That way, when the day comes, there will be a seamless transition, and no harm will come to the project or to Monclova Industries."

A good point. However, Miguel suspected Bashir cared less about the company or the project and more about buttering up whoever Miguel named, making sure that person kept Bashir's interests in mind.

"I fully understand," Miguel said. "It's a big decision, a crucial one, and I appreciate how my decision will ripple through the company, the project, and even the government. Which is why I'm taking my time to weigh all the details instead of jumping to one name or another."

"But you still plan to use one of your sons, yes?"

"The company is named Monclova."

A few minutes later, Miguel extracted from the call, but his DV had already slid into the underground structure. He had missed his favorite part of the drive — seeing the large swath of barren land he had purchased five years back now teeming with the life of his company. Launch pads in the distance with control towers, support buildings, fuel dumps, office buildings, and endless rows of warehouses. Spidering away from this central hub, long rail tubes reached out to the various mines and factories all over the planet. It should have taken decades to construct — some of it still had a few years to go — but with a huge amount of money and a massive number of employees, entire cities could be built in a fraction of the time.

Shortly after, the DV slowed at the building entrance and two assistants stood waiting for his arrival. The first, a young man from the notable Armstant University, rushed to open his door. The other, a young woman from the equally worthy Kensdale University, had her link syncing with his to download the afternoon agenda. Both had started their internships a few days ago and Miguel had yet to learn their names.

Marching into his building as his private car slid away to park itself, he flicked through the agenda now appearing on his link. The lobby's immaculately-detailed architecture — two-story vertical windows, receptionist counter an extra four inches higher than the average person stood, colossal sculpture of a rocket hanging overhead — reminded visitors of the imposing power and wealth Monclova Industries wielded. Miguel hardly noticed it anymore.

They took the elevator to the third floor — reports and data collation. He could feel his assistants tightening as he made an unplanned stop. With a firm stride, he crossed the busy room. Several employees straightened as they caught sight of him. Others never glanced over their desks. He stopped eight rows in.

The young woman sitting behind four screens glanced up and pouted. "Daddy, you shouldn't be here."

"It's my company. I'll go where I want."

Sydney grinned despite blushing glances to her fellow employees on either side. They stared back in shock. As she stiffened in her chair, Miguel thought she hadn't told them her last name. With a formalness he had never heard before, she said, "I'm sorry, Mr. Monclova. How may I help you?"

"Your performance reports continue to be excellent. Keep it up."

"Thank you, sir."

"I'd like you to find and send me the leadership reports on Varo and Rowan. They should be done with finals tomorrow. Don't read them. Your brothers would be twisted up."

"Please don't try to talk like our generation. Besides, *twisted up* is a few years out-of-date."

"Well, they'll be angry. Just get the reports to me, please."

"Yes, sir."

Miguel wanted to give his daughter a big hug and kiss, but he figured he had embarrassed her enough for one day. Heading back to the elevators, he used his link to check on Lynia. She continued to dominate her academic classes, charming her teachers and showing great intelligence and creative thinking. Her return to Shendo studies, however, had not gone well.

He guessed that a lot of her resistance stemmed from the problems at home. He tried to explain that separating with Annalia did not mean getting a divorce. They needed space to learn how to appreciate each other again. At least, that was how Annalia framed it when she left. But Lynia saw through it all, and somehow, the Shendo verses about marriage offered her little comfort.

He tried to make the transition easy on all the children. Annalia and Miguel agreed to let Sydney, Varo, and Lynia live with him. But Rowan had a closer bond with his mother, and frankly, Miguel knew that he had no connection with the boy. He once thought Shendo would bring them together, but that only moved Rowan closer to Monk Crozet. So, other than leadership classes at the company offices and weekly dinners, Rowan stayed with his mother. The other children must have thought the whole thing crazy, yet they never once questioned the arrangement.

Miguel questioned plenty enough for all. He prayed about it nightly.

"Oh," the young assistant to his right said.

"What is it?"

The elevator doors opened to his outer-office where all his assistants and secretaries had their desks. Glancing up at Miguel like a terrified mouse, she said, "Um, apparently, sir, um, Mr. Falcry is making a surprise visit."

Annoying, but certainly not worth all this fear. Miguel peered around the desks. He didn't see Falcry, and nobody would have dared let the government man into his office. "Where is he?"

"That's the thing, sir, because, well, he's not here. He's out there. Warehouse 11, sir."

Punching the elevator for parking, Miguel tried to hold his composure in check. Still, he couldn't stop from muttering one word. "Shit."

# CHAPTER 8

ONCE MORE, MIGUEL SAT IN THE BACK of his private DV. He wasted too much of his life in these things. This time, he wanted to override the system and force it to race along the trackway. If he caused a few accidents, so be it. But he had to wait impatiently as the car brought him to the first internal trackway of Monclova Industries. He could have cut through the offices and picked up the trackway without leaving the property, but he guessed Falcry would have agents standing around, scouting. Miguel wouldn't surprise Falcry. He could, however, arrive with as little notice as possible.

A tiny monitor on the door read — *Time Remaining: 00:02:38.* For a first, Miguel found himself wishing he had not made the Monclova Industries property so damn big.

Tapping his link awake, he connected to his company's internal network. A quick sign-in via voice verification — *Pelicans Don't Live On Mars* — and he pulled up a listing of all his warehouses and their current contents. Warehouse 11 — iron.

Miguel eased a notch. Iron. The most basic item they mined. Something Mars had far more of than Earth — or anywhere else nearby — and one of several major reasons for Martian involvement in the project. The sheer volume of iron pulled from the ground, loaded onto rockets, and sent to the Ring in a never-ending flood made it difficult to keep exact numbers. Discrepancies in all sorts of counts were common, allotting for plenty of wiggle room. If Falcry thought he'd find a problem in the iron warehouse, Miguel had nothing to fear.

The trackway lowered underground — far easier to keep the buildings cool and free of significant radiation. Warehouse 11 sat on the western end of the warehouse block, and Miguel considered that Falcry had chosen this location not because of a problem with the iron counts but simply because it put a lot of distance between them and the offices. Maybe Falcry had learned of Bashir's games which, over the years, had extended well beyond the money made off the land deal. In fact, Bashir had managed to get a piece of nearly every transaction on the books and several off the books, too. Miguel had always assumed that if Falcry figured out Bashir's skimming and corruption, he would either have Bashir removed from the project or accept the loss as the price of doing business.

Perhaps Miguel was wrong. If so, then he merely had to explain how the system actually worked and leave Falcry to huff and whine. Nothing to worry about, there.

Miguel's pulse relaxed a bit more. He had one concern left, but even if Falcry suspected some level of misconduct, Miguel didn't think the man bright enough to guess the truth. Then again, Falcry had chosen the iron warehouse to inspect.

When he finally arrived, Miguel strode through the enormous facility like a king. Workers paused to nod his way before getting back to work. Heavy duty vehicles beeped and growled as they maneuvered tons of iron to different staging areas. In the back, an enormous conveyor system sent the product either to be used for steel, shaped into other products, or simply to the next rocket launching for the Ring. Miguel's eyes locked on the office high above, overlooking the entire operation. The lights were on, and he spotted Falcry standing over Ms. Geysler, head of the western warehouse block, as they studied several information screens.

He quickened his pace. When he entered the office, the two inside raised their heads. Ms. Geysler looked terrified; Falcry looked calm, in control, as if a trap had already been sprung.

Rushing around the desk, Ms. Geysler stammered as she repeatedly bowed her head. "Mr. Monclova, I'm sorry, but this man has government credentials. The government agreement for the Pathway Ring Project says I must let him into our systems to check our inventory. But I've been watching to make sure he does not go outside of what is legally allowed."

"Oh, yes," Falcry said. "She has been quite the good

employee. You should give her a raise."

Miguel thanked Ms. Geysler, assured her no harm had been done, and that she should go elsewhere in the building to do other work. Once alone, Miguel rolled a chair over. The bitter scent of burnt coffee reminded him of the days before the Pathway Ring had begun. The corner of his mouth lifted.

Lacing his fingers around one knee, Falcry said, "I can assure you that my visit here is not a pleasant one."

"Don't be like that. We haven't seen each other in years. The least we could do is be hospitable."

"Hospitable? We'll see."

Falcry stood and tugged on his jacket before tapping away on his link. "I'm sending you the latest images of the Ring. Everything on our end is being performed according to schedule. I've even chosen my Phase 2 transit team that will go through the Ring to set up the other end. They've begun physical training and will soon start their education regimen on all the systems and construction techniques required to build their copy of the Ring."

Miguel flicked the image onto his link screen. A sense of awe flushed through his body. Floating in space, surrounded by emptiness, an immense tube had been constructed into an enormous circle. Some sections looked complete — solid with a gorgeous rusty red Martian coloring. Other sections were composed of nothing more than a skeletal framework. With such an enormous diameter, the Ring could have sat atop Mars like a crown. And none of it would have existed without Monclova Industries. Without Miguel.

As he understood it, the Ring would require an overwhelming tonnage of material to pass through and be *consumed* into energy, generating enough to jumpstart its main functioning. Once it connected with the wormhole and stability was achieved, it would be able to pull power from within the wormhole itself. But that initial outlay of material — any kind of matter, really — would be far more than Mars could handle on its own. Earth, too. While both planets would make significant contributions to the required mass, several joint venture teams had been sent to the asteroid belt to capture the remaining matter.

Miguel had known about this, but the difference between reading the proposal and seeing the half-finished project floating in space struck him deep in the chest. No wonder Falcry had so easily offered up a transit royalty during their negotiation five years ago. This was much greater than money.

"If we're not careful," Miguel said, closing his link, "there will be wars over this thing."

"Absolutely. The fact that you understand this makes me even more curious — why are you stealing from me?"

Falcry's calm demeanor kept Miguel in check. Admit nothing. Deny nothing. Let the man speak his piece. Miguel needed information, needed to understand if Falcry knew anything concrete or if he fished for some type of edge.

Perhaps thinking he had shocked Miguel, and there had been some degree of surprise, Falcry bounced as he paced around the room. He clearly wanted to command the space, to intimidate Miguel, and to let Miguel know who had the real power. Miguel listened.

"I've been going over your numbers regarding the iron mines — I picked those because they were the most plentiful — and I see nothing to indicate a reason for any shortfall. In fact, Monclova Industries has been doing exemplary work. You have not missed any launch windows apart from weather-related delays — mostly sandstorms." He paused, making a performance of being confused by the calculations in his head. "The problem is that there is not an equal amount of iron being sent into storage near the Ring for Phase 2, for my transit team. Naturally, I assumed you were stockpiling it here and simply sparing the fuel cost of sending it into space until it would be necessary — which, admittedly, is five years away." Another pause. Another dramatic squeeze of his face as if he could not quite reach the answer. Then: "There are plenty of reasonable explanations, and I thought I might be satisfied with filling in the blanks myself. However, it is part of my fiduciary responsibilities to keep an eye on all aspects of this operation — our governments are putting a tremendous amount of funds into this

— and so I came to make sure things were going according to plan."

Miguel matched Falcry's agreeable tone, putting on a subtler performance of his own. He doubted that he fooled Falcry any more than Falcry had fooled him. Both men seethed, wishing the other was not necessary to accomplish their goals. But Miguel had dealt with such men before. Too often, they thought themselves smarter or more capable than others. Too often, they proved to be weak and cowardly. Falcry might have the business smarts — Miguel would have to be more careful — but he doubted the man had anything else to offer.

With an expansive gesture toward the bank of link screens, Miguel said, "You've clearly had a chance to inspect our work. Are you satisfied?"

"Everything is in order. But then, I would expect as much."

"Are you accusing me of skimming? You already said I was stealing, and yet my books show you that I've not stolen anything. Every last ounce is accounted for."

Falcry halted, his focus snapping onto Miguel. His tongue flicked the top of his lip. "Your bookkeeping is fine. My problem is all the storage of iron you have in these warehouses yet none of it is earmarked for Phase 2. Plenty is set to launch into space and reach the Ring to complete the project, and I've even found where you have held back iron for the required mass of turning the machine on, yet I find not a single entry about Phase 2."

Miguel forced a pleasant chuckle. "Is that why you came all the way out to Mars?"

"We're talking about hundreds of billions worth of iron. No small matter."

"A simple logistical choice. It makes more sense for us to keep the iron flowing into space at this point. After all, Phase 2 cannot happen until Phase 1 is complete. On the advice of my engineers, I decided to focus all our operations on Phase 1. Once we've reached the eighty-percent mark, we'll then begin launches for Phase 2. According to our forecast schedule as well as our actual performance data, all the contract requirements will have been met on time."

"That's not what was agreed to."

"If you read the contract, you'll see there is no mention as to how Monclova Industries decides to fulfill the contract, merely that it is fulfilled. A little trust would go a long way."

Falcry's features pinched together. "My transit team —"

"That brings up an interesting issue." Miguel smelled the weakness and guessed he would never have a better opportunity to strike. "The one area where we are concerned that matters will fall short is in the training of your team. Even with my people's considerable expertise, we had to learn a lot over the last five years in order to accomplish Phase 1's goals. Quite frankly, I don't think your team can be brought up to speed fast enough to actually build anything worthwhile on the other side of that wormhole."

"That's not for you to decide."

"Don't mistake me. I'm not saying they're stupid. I'm sure they can read instructions and learn from my experts. Operating some of this equipment is not difficult. Some of it, however, requires precision, skill, and experience."

"Which is why they need training now."

"But when something goes wrong, and something always goes wrong, five years training won't be enough. It will happen out there, in some remote part of the universe, inaccessible and probably inhospitable. Without my team to fix it, this entire venture is pointless. You won't even know if anything went wrong until ten years later when nobody has connected with the wormhole. Maybe you try again with a new team, but I think volunteers will be slimmer. And I guarantee that by then my experts will be more expensive. Not that I'm going to gouge you, but fifteen years from now — they'll either be running this place or have moved on to other, more lucrative opportunities. Price in the laws of supply and demand and that these experts know what they're worth …" With a placating shrug, Miguel put out his hand as if serving tea. "No need to worry about all that, though. I propose that you add five of my people, my best experts, onto your transit team. I already have the volunteers, and they understand that they will be under your team's authority."

"Absolutely not."

Speaking as he would to Lynia when she didn't get her way, Miguel said, "I can see you're angry, but from one businessman to another, I think we can handle this in a professional manner. After all, you really have no choice. Without my people, your team will never learn what they need to learn. My men will happily teach them, once they have reached the other side. It will be hands-on training."

Falcry dropped his chin to his chest, and Miguel enjoyed a moment of triumph. But then, with a regretful sigh, Falcry tapped his link before walking to the observation window like a man expecting to be imprisoned. With an iciness slicking each word, he said, "People always push without thinking. Please, take a look."

This sudden change gripped Miguel's chest with a chilling hand. Moving with a confident stride he did not feel, he approached the window. "I see my warehouse. So?"

Falcry pointed to one corner. Near the side wall, out of view of the workers but within a clear shot of the observation window, one of Falcry's agents stood behind Ms. Geysler, brandishing his sidearm. She had no idea of the threat, but the message was clear. Miguel's heart jumped.

"You should be smarter than this." Falcry shifted to the side so that he faced Miguel head-on. He looked nothing like the Falcry of the past. The weasel had transformed into a hyena, teeth bared, ready to pounce. "With a signal, your warehouse manager will be removed from the premises and executed. That should make you compliant. For now. Unfortunately, I don't believe I'll be able to trust you for the next five years."

Miguel's fingers curled in. He wanted to punch Falcry. Dig his fingers into that monster's throat until he broke the skin and ripped out whatever he could grasp. Instead, his features pinched tight as he remained pinned in position. Barely opening his mouth, he said, "Did you bring an army with you? Are you going to oversee everything I do?"

"Don't be ridiculous. That would be highly inefficient."

"Then why threaten me? I'm not the man from five years ago with no political connections worth anything. I provide jobs for half the city. You really think the Martian government is going to condone this? One call and you'll be fired."

"Probably. But only if they ever know. Let me be blunt. Five years may have changed you, but I'm the same man. You've never had to know me, though. Now, you do. You will start shipping material for Phase 2. You will send your experts to teach my team now. If you fail to do this, there won't be any warnings, no second chances, I won't even ask you why there was a delay. Miscommunication, sandstorms, sunspots — I don't care. I will simply murder your children."

Miguel flinched. He couldn't have heard that right.

Falcry went on, "I'll make it quick for them. But I will then go to wherever your wife is living, and I will have her head separated from her body. Slowly. I will also burn your lovely home to the ground." Falcry stepped closer, his eyes as dead as his words. "I won't waste a second thought about any of it."

In the silence that followed, Falcry tugged on his jacket, tapped on his link to release Ms. Geysler, and exited the office. Miguel did not move. He only heard his heart pounding. He only thought — *who the hell am I involved with?*

# CHAPTER 9

THE REMAINING HOURS OF THE WORKDAY DRIFTED. He made sure that Ms. Geysler received a bonus, three weeks off for recovery, and as much therapy as she required. Not only did he want to make sure his employee was well-cared for, but her expertise and attention to detail made her ideal for managing several warehouses. He did not relish having to train somebody new. Beyond Ms. Geysler, though, he could not think straight. Even arranging for her care kept the threats against his family alight in his head.

Tephen visited the office several times, but Miguel could not summon the energy to focus on the young man's words. How could he when his mind swirled with vile images of Falcry standing over his children, soaking in their blood, baring his teeth like a rabid animal? And whenever Miguel managed to banish those thoughts, the vacuum filled with pictures of the fires Falcry would start — fires that burned his family into screaming cinders.

Miguel tried to tell himself that these were empty threats. He had become too important, too connected, too visible. But he knew better. After Falcry razed him and his family to the ground, any half-formed story would be swallowed with glee — as long as the work continued, as long as the rivers of money flowed. Monclova Industries would fall apart, but someone else waited for their moment on the stage — someone easier for Falcry to control.

When the workday finally ended, the horrors continued to play in Miguel's mind, nauseating him, scalding his nerves. All through the drive home, he heard Falcry's threats and visualized the gruesome results. He had suffered threats against his business and against his life numerous times over the years, but nobody had ever gone after his family. Nobody had ever looked so thirsty to follow through on those threats. He had misjudged this man. Falcry bore a sadistic streak that promised every appalling word he had said.

Folding his hands in his lap, Miguel slowed his breathing. He had been shaken, but no good would come from racing around in a panic. He needed to regain his self-control and then think through this problem. He always knew a clash with Falcry would arise, but he had intended for one of his making. He never expected his opponent's viciousness. But he had dealt with violent men before — mining and construction have always been filled with such men. He could handle Falcry.

As his confidence mutated fear into determination, his DV descended into a small private garage. When he entered his house, all set into its right place. Sydney and Lynia bustled in the kitchen, filling the air with delicious aromas and the enticing sounds of sizzling. Varo hastened over to take his father's coat while rushing through a story about meeting a beautiful girl at school.

Miguel glanced around, but Rowan had not arrived. Normally, Miguel would have picked up the boy himself, but after meeting with Falcry, he needed time alone. He also wanted to avoid arguing with Annalia.

Seeing her would only remind him of the great failure in his life. He still hoped to reconcile with her, reunite their family, and somehow bring Monclova Industries and the Monclova household into harmony. With every petty disagreement and outright argument, that hope diminished. It hurt his heart almost as much as thinking about Falcry's vicious tactics. But it also centered him on his children. Annalia mattered, but they mattered more. So, he had ordered a DV to gather Rowan from his mother's house, and soon, the new family dinner would be complete.

When Rowan finally arrived, he slumped into a chair at the dining room table. He had sprouted during his final teen years, and now in his early-twenties, he often hunched over to diminish his size. Miguel tried to prod the boy into standing with pride and confidence, but he failed to find the right words. Much like he failed to find the right words for anything regarding Rowan.

As Sydney brought out a piping hot dish filled with Martian beans, cheeses, spices, and pasta, baked until bubbling and filling the house with its tempting aroma, Lynia cleared a spot. Varo plunked down into the chair opposite his brother while Miguel took the head of the table. When the girls sat, Miguel nodded to each before picking up the serving spoon.

But as he scooped out the first helping, Rowan's meek voice said, "Aren't we going to say grace?"

Varo snorted a laugh. "When have we ever done that?"

"Never." Though he remained quiet in volume, Rowan did not back down. "But Shendo tells us that —"

"Isn't that all about men building things and women tending the home?"

"Shendo's book fixes many of the errors of the previous testaments and codifies many traditions that were not specified in the older versions of the Bible. The first one Monk Crozet taught me was that saying grace —"

Varo turned to Miguel. "Make him stop."

Miguel swallowed dry as he nodded. "Rowan is correct. We should give a moment to be grateful for the food we are about to eat."

Miguel stumbled through an awkward, impromptu prayer — one Monk Crozet could have improved with ease — and then quickly served the food. The sooner mouths were chewing, the less chance anybody would question the matter. Enough plagued his mind. In fact, hearing his children playfully bickering brought him out of his thoughts. It appeared half the food had already been eaten.

"Everybody knows," Varo said.

Sydney blushed. "Stop it."

"Knows what?" Miguel asked, and all grew silent. Sydney looked down while Varo grinned wide and expectant. "Varo? What does everybody know?"

Sitting straighter, the young man said, "Well, I was saying that, um —"

"Lynia, help your brother."

Wiping her mouth, Lynia sighed. "We're not little children. Except maybe Varo. You can see from Syndey's face that she doesn't want to talk about this."

Miguel turned to Sydney. "Your sister's right. You are an adult now. Far too old to be hiding things from me. What is going on?"

Still not looking at him, Sydney said, "Apparently, my interest in a young man has become the subject of office gossip."

"Ah. That's the *everyone*. Well, is this true? Are you interested in somebody?"

"Daddy!"

"I'm your father. I have a right to know. Who is this man?"

Reddening deeper, she finally said, "Tephen."

Miguel chuckled. "Oh, well, that's a good choice. I think he might like you, too."

"Can we please talk about something else?" Though she looked relieved as Lynia directed the conversation elsewhere, Miguel thought he caught a glint in her eye.

A flash of Falcry as a jagged-toothed serpent slithering toward his eldest filled his mind, but he shoved it away. Sydney, however, watched him every bit as carefully as he watched them.

"What's wrong?" she asked.

The others, once again, turned their attention to him. Grabbing his wine, he drank down a bit.

"Nothing." As he set his wineglass on the table, he thought of a diversion. "This morning, I spoke with Senator Bashir, and he posed an interesting question. He asked which one of you would be taking over when I retire."

"Are you retiring?" Varo asked.

"No, no. Not yet, anyway. But he wanted an answer. Which one of you —"

Rowan said, "Which son, you mean."

"Hey," Lynia said. "I could do the job better than you, and Sydney's already working there."

"I'm sorry, Sis, but Shendo is clear on what a man is and a

woman, and it doesn't leave room for you to run a company. Isn't that right, Father? Isn't that what you believe?"

"I'm surprised your mother lets you still study with Monk Crozet. Do you follow Shendo closely?" Miguel thought it was a good question, but the perturbed glower on Rowan's brow suggested otherwise.

"Monk Crozet was a nice man, and he helped me start my journey. But I have read the entire Bible as well as the Quran, the Bhagavad Gita, the Tao Te Ching, and some Talmudic discussions. I'm studying all the religions."

Varo smacked the side of his own head. "Why would you want to do that?"

"Because Shendo was supposed to unify them all."

"We got enough reading to do in leadership training."

"If you read the actual books, then you'd know that it doesn't say what people think it says."

Miguel stiffened. "Careful. You don't want insult a man's religion."

"Have you even read the Bible? The Book of Shendo does not say that a woman's job is to make babies and tend the home or that a man's job is to make profit and provide that home."

"Shendo says men and women have their roles in life —"

"Yes, and that each person should find their role. *Useful to the group*. That's the line. Back when Mars was being settled that sometimes meant women had to have babies and raise them. But if a woman was more useful engineering air filters or digging ditches that's what she did."

Lynia said, "Then maybe I'm more suited than you to run the company."

"You're not."

"Hey!"

"I remember what you did when you were twelve. You're not suited. You don't have the temperament. What does it matter, anyway? You don't believe in Shendo."

Miguel eyed Lynia. He still recalled those odd looks at that tense dinner when she was twelve and had returned from a month belowground. He wanted to ask her, but the last drops of what Rowan had said took precedence. "Is that true? You don't believe?"

"Why should she?" Rowan raised his voice in excitement. "Did you know that the Book of Shendo has nothing to do with rest of the Bible?"

Varo laughed. "That's crazy."

"It's true. Hiroshi Shendo wanted to unify the split religious views of the settlers. And since the Bible is based on Judaism and Christianity but also is the backbone for Mormonism and Islam, he figured tacking onto it would cover more religions than starting his own."

Miguel slammed his fork flat on the table. "Hiroshi Shendo did not make up a religion and stick it onto another. The Lord spoke to him. He wrote that book because the Divine told him to do so, and he made it the third testament because that was what the Lord wanted."

As if he expected nothing more, Rowan returned to eating, holding back whatever comments filled his head. Miguel couldn't stop the image of Falcry severing that head from its body, and he wanted to forgive his son's impertinence and beg his son's forgiveness for scolding him. But he held back. Thankfully, Lynia saved the awkward silence by asking if anybody wanted more food. Miguel drank the rest of his wine.

Sensing the fouling mood, Sydney attempted some levity. She told a joke that fell flat — Varo groaned while others merely grinned — but Miguel only saw those grins split wider and wider, blood gushing down their chests, while he heard Falcry cackling in the distance.

"Maybe I've been wrong." He thought he had muttered the words to himself, but all activity around the table ceased. Clearing his throat, he decided in that instant to find an answer. He glanced up and saw Rowan's eagerness. "Not about Shendo." The young man's face dropped. Miguel pressed on. "I'm curious what everyone here thinks of the Pathway Ring. What value is it to us?"

"Are you kidding?" Varo said. "It's value? The project pays for everything. Right?"

Sydney said, "I think Daddy means what value does the Ring bring besides money. Is it even worth building? Of course, the answer is yes. Think about all the great achievements of humans. They didn't always begin with a practical purpose. Even the first colonies on Mars had no idea if living here could create any value. It's not like they looked at the landscape and thought that it was wonderful, fertile land."

"Who cares? The Ring made us rich."

Lynia said, "It really depends on what we each value."

"What about you, then?" Miguel asked.

"I think it will depend on what we find on the other side."

Miguel perked up. "That will certainly be a big part of it, but is that all?"

Taking a moment to consider, Lynia finally said, "There is value in the effort. In the things we will learn or invent regardless of the success or failure. Sydney mentioned coming to Mars despite it being a dead land. She's right. Even if we had never settled the planet, just coming out here and trying created entire new industries."

Varo said, "And those industries made money for people. Why am I the only one trying to be honest? There's no noble cause behind the Pathway Ring. A bunch of governments from Mars and Earth are throwing tons of money at Monclova so that we can build this machine so that they can make a bunch of money, too. It's always about money."

"No." Miguel pictured his children at this table, heads flopped forward as thick, crimson streams flooded across the white cloth. "Money for the sake of money, for the sake of buying things, is the way poor people see it. The ones at the top — the ones that I answer to — they see it as more. It's power. It's always about power."

Later, after the house quieted into slumber, Miguel sat in bed wide awake. While he could not stop the tempest of horrors swirling through his mind, he could push it down long enough to think clearer. He had thought Falcry wanted money, wanted riches, wanted wealth all for the sake of buying things. But Falcry was no poor-minded man. That feral glower in his eyes, that evil grin, the way he casually threatened to annihilate Miguel's family — these actions came from a desire to control, a desire for power.

That made Falcry more dangerous. But it also gave Miguel an opening. Because now he knew what motivated his enemy, and knowing that, Miguel could prepare.

Thrusting his bedcovers aside, Miguel hurried down the hall to the narrow, closet-sized room near the laundry. In it, a low table waited under a square window. Two candles wrapped in plastic sat on the table with Miguel's Bible between them. The only other furniture in the room — a padded kneeling-bench.

Brushing dust off the table, Miguel winced at the guilt stinging him. Still, he always found comfort knowing the room existed. He believed in Shendo, believed God watched over him, believed that without Shendo there would be chaos, anarchy, and a descent into immoral animalism. At least, that was the teaching. Rowan was right — Miguel had never fully read the book. There never seemed enough time.

But he picked up the Bible now and pressed it against his chest. Praying had always given him comfort, and his success in life meant that he must be following the path his god wanted for him. That also meant that Falcry and his vile threats could only be seen as an obstacle to overcome, meant to challenge Miguel into being a more powerful, more faithful servant.

Kneeling on the bench, eyes closed, he whispered, "Please, Lord almighty, I pray for the strength to see this through."

# CHAPTER 10

TIME MOVED FAST. It always seemed to do the opposite of what Miguel needed yet also provided just enough to accomplish his goals. Or, at least, he could accomplish something that resembled what he had set out to do originally. His plans for the Pathway Ring fit this model with perfect imperfection.

The latest addition to his growing roster of conspirators was Mr. Slater. The man had done fine work at Monclova Industries focusing on IT and other computer related fields. Every report Miguel could find suggested Mr. Slater was highly-skilled and creative but off-putting and grumpy. Not a social man, but that suited Miguel. Anti-social meant less likely to reveal anything important.

Thankfully, the man had no ties to Mars or Earth — at least, none that Miguel's people could uncover — and offering Slater the opportunity to head up all the software programming for Phase 2 was more than enough to get his signature, thumbprint, and retinal scan on the contract. With Mr. Slater in place, Miguel thought he might be able to pull of his audacious move. He had one final position to fill before he could allow more than basic confidence into his heart.

Miguel's link flicked on from its connection to his office desk monitor His head secretary appeared on the screen. "Sydney Monclova is here to see you, sir."

He glanced at the time — too early for lunch. His heart skipped. The secretary was too composed to betray a serious problem. With a soft sigh, he put away his worries and said, "Send her in."

Those worries reignited when he saw his daughter's tight

brow. "What's wrong?" he said.

She shook her head with a stern gesture around the office. He didn't understand. He grew more confused when she plastered on a bright smile and said, "Daddy, I thought we might take a break together and go for a walk. You always said you'd show me the launch pads. Maybe we can catch one of the cargo ships going into space."

He was about to dismiss her with a growl, but the pleading in her eyes raised a warning in him. "Um … sure."

Neither said a word as they drove out to the launch pads. It would be several hours before the next launch, a fact he thought she already knew, but as they walked along the railing that overlooked the massive rockets through protective, transparent walling, he started to understand. They hissed and rumbled as fuel and cargo were loaded in. Large supply vehicles whined, beeped, and roared as pressure-suited workers maneuvered the vehicles through their daily actions. Even from the safety of the observation building, a symphony of noise surrounded the area.

"You think Falcry has my office bugged?" he said.

She nodded. "I don't trust him."

Miguel grimaced. "You shouldn't."

Pausing, Sydney made a final decision. She pulled out a thin wire, inserted it into her link and then attached it to Miguel's. With a direct connection, she could transfer information without it going through the airways — without anybody intercepting, interfering, or even copying the files. After a few swipes and taps, the transfer completed. She then removed the wire and waited.

He looked at the first file — the personnel information on Browit Cot, the man Miguel had tapped to head up the mining operation on the other side of the Ring. A major player in the Phase 2 plan. Miguel swiped to the second file — Runi Nire, one of the best factory architects on Mars and the one willing to go through the Ring. She risked everything for the riches she would gain helping Monclova Industries prosper. Plenty of other names flashed by as he swiped through the list — Critto Lig, expert in security; Ghee Tsung, expert in engineering; Marcel Fletcher, expert pilot.

"Don't worry," Sydney said. "I made sure to remove this stuff from the company servers."

"How did you —"

"I doubt anybody else noticed the little tags you put on these files, but considering how you want to keep this all secret, I think you should be more cautious. None of this — whatever it is — should be done anywhere near the office. You should work from home. Or maybe that's not safe. Maybe you should rent a place down below. Move again every few weeks."

He stared at his daughter, trying to comprehend how she could think this way.

She read his expression easily. "I'm not an idiot. I don't know what changed between you and Falcry, but about a year or so back, something clearly changed."

"That's an understatement."

"I want to help. What are you planning? What can I do to make it work?"

All the people involved in his efforts kept silent because of money. If Falcry caught any single member of his little conspiracy, that person did not know enough to matter. Miguel maintained secrecy over the entire plan. Each person only knew their part, and in a lot of cases, their part would not seem suspicious or wrong if revealed.

But the whole plan — nobody knew that except Miguel. He had intended to explain things to Varo or Rowan, but perhaps Sydney should know, too. After all, she was destined to be more than a mere assistant when the time came. While she would not hold an official title, Miguel thought of her as Vice CEO. She knew the company better than his other children, and that knowledge would be paramount to their success once he left. But beyond all, Miguel thought it might help to have another Monclova aware of his plans — as both a sounding board and a backup, should anything happen to him.

"Okay," he said, leaning closer to whisper despite the loud noise of the launch pad activities. "Here's how we're going to take control of the entire Pathway Ring. On both sides."

# CHAPTER 11

THE NEXT SEVERAL MONTHS proved Sydney's immense value in the office. Miguel found every decision of the plan easier to make and the execution of each facet easier to conduct. Above all else, though, she was honest and reliable — rare and admirable qualities. So, when she told Miguel that she worried about Lynia because his youngest had been sneaking out late at night, he took the matter seriously. Sydney did not tattle out of spite or vengeance. He saw true concern for her sister and a desire to help. His options for handling the matter were limited, though.

He could tell Annalia, but that would solve nothing and possibly exasperate the situation into something more than it was. He could pay a detective to follow Lynia, find out what she was up to, but that brought outside focus into his home life. Lynia did not need her personal problems becoming worldwide news. In fact, any outside involvement meant opening his daughter's life and his own to the scrutiny of the public — which also meant Falcry would learn of these things. None of that would be good. Miguel had a single option — follow her himself.

For three nights, he pretended to sleep while waiting for Lynia to sneak off. On the fourth night, she finally did. No slipping through a window or working her way through an airduct. She merely disabled the alarm and walked out the front door. From the security cameras, he saw that she dressed down in a plain, humble outfit. That worried him. If she had been a dazzling display of excess, he would have known she went to a party with her wealthy peers. That level of teenage rebellion made sense. Instead, she had dressed to avoid drawing notice by blending in with those living below the surface.

Miguel's clothing for underground hung in his office closet. He couldn't travel all the way out there, get dressed, and return without losing track of Lynia. But two simple ideas popped in his head.

First, he deployed a mini-AV — a drone smaller than his hand that he could control with his desklink. Nearly silent, the drone would lock onto the target — Lynia — and follow her with ease. It had limited range, but he hoped it would last long enough for his second idea to kick in. He called Mr. Slater and had the man hack into the police cameras that monitored most of the underground.

Mr. Slater did not ask any questions. Merely stated it would take a few minutes and that he would have the feeds sent to Miguel's home office. In the meantime, Miguel watched the fuzzy display from the mini-AV and offered a fast prayer that his daughter had not become involved in anything immoral or dangerous.

Lynia headed straight for the hoverlifts that lowered to the first level beneath the city. The smooth and quiet lifts only operated three levels deep. After that, she had to take a less-capable elevator that ran on thick cables. This brought her to the seventh level.

As the mini-AV dropped through the elevator shaft and caught up with her, Miguel wondered if perhaps she had learned his secret — the plan that only he and Sydney knew in full. If Lynia had found out a small part of it, she could have been trying to uncover more. Perhaps she had been coming down this way in search of the people he had recruited.

The mini-AV cut its transmission, and Miguel tapped the home button to bring it back. Now, he had to wait on Mr. Slater. Staring at a blank screen for several minutes, Miguel's breathing shallowed as his heart raced. His youngest child, his sweet Lynia — she should never have been down there alone. The people were good, mostly, but they had been raised under rougher circumstances. She didn't know them. Couldn't understand them. And he did not want her to learn hard lessons in hard ways.

When his desklink erupted with numerous camera feeds,

Miguel had to bother Mr. Slater again to help find Lynia. The man snarled as if the challenge was beneath him, but he agreed nonetheless. Miguel thought he caught a glint of pleasure on the man's face. He still didn't know Mr. Slater that well, but he had figured out this much — the man always liked to show off his skills.

Shortly after, they located her on the fourteenth floor. She did not stop to question anybody. She did not seek out specific addresses. Instead, she merely passed along the hardened roadways amongst the dark and lonely streets as if on a pleasant afternoon stroll.

As she walked by sketchy bars and even sketchier people, she watched them closely. Not out of caution, it seemed to Miguel, but rather with a scientific curiosity. Maybe he projected his thoughts upon her, but he swore she seemed to be on an adventure of interest rather than an escapade of defiance.

He reached over to turn off the desklink when she turned off the main road. The bright light displays for the various vices available disappeared. On this darker street, Miguel spotted a skeletal man, hunched over and approaching Lynia. He must have said something because she paused and moved a step towards the man. Thinking better of it, she turned to leave when another, more menacing oaf appeared behind her. Miguel's stomach dropped. If he called the police, they would never reach her in time. He could do nothing but watch.

A third man, a young man, yelled at the other two. When they turned their attention, Lynia kicked the small one between the legs and ran off. The young man jumped in the way to stop the oaf from giving chase. As the two men fought, Miguel could see the young man watching Lynia, making sure she got away safely.

Later that night, she returned home. She slipped into bed, and from the satisfied sigh Miguel heard in the hallway, she sounded pleased with her journey. He wanted to ask her about it, warn her to be more careful, but he suspected that any words he offered would be shooed away. No, if he wanted her to listen, the concerns would have to come from Sydney. Anyone else would be ignored.

Sitting in his office with the lights off, Miguel wondered how things had gotten to this point with his children. His plans relied on them. They were the Monclovas. He had no choice. Yet managing these four required skills undeveloped by running a massive corporation.

"There's still time." He muttered the words as he closed his eyes, and he hoped they were true.

# CHAPTER 12

IN THE MEDIA HALL, the crowd gathered. Miguel could hear their growing voices while in the auditorium the shuffling chairs, the technicians prepping, the final touches being placed — all for him. No, not really him, but rather they had come to hear what he would say. They knew that this could be a historic speech. They knew that they might witness a phrase or moment that would be remembered and repeated for centuries, and every person in that audience wanted to tell their children and grandchildren how they sat there and heard those words and in a small way, that they were part of it all. Miguel knew it, too.

His visi-link displayed the speech in the air before him to go over once again. In reality, the words splashed millimeters before his eyes like a personal HUD. Just one of many new technologies developed over the last few years for the Pathway Ring Project.

Other companies had invested in hands-free link displays, but the visi-link had the right combination of freedom and comfort. No special glasses. No cumbersome unit worn on the belt. Nothing more than a small device that fit over the ear and ran toward the temple.

Many on the tech side warned it was easily hackable, but it was still too expensive for the average person. Miguel figured that its vulnerabilities would be fixed by the time it went to market. For now, only large companies could afford the device. With workers in space who needed both hands, with workers deep underground who couldn't waste time fumbling with a small handheld link, with workers in any dangerous or precarious positions, the visi-link had changed lives — possibly saved them, too.

It also had made Miguel a lot of money.

His employees, too. Everyone had received a hefty bonus. The equivalent of four month's pay. Nearly a half-year of profit distributed to his entire workforce.

The media argued whether Miguel did this out of charity, duty, insanity, or as a publicity stunt. Miguel never answered the reporters. They wouldn't understand. Oh, they might comprehend the side point — that by sharing some wealth now, he insured most of his employees would remain, work hard, and thus, help the company make even greater profits in the years to come. But the real reason would only mystify them all.

Annalia.

Though the divorce had been finalized over a year ago, he still loved her. He thought she still loved him, too. She simply couldn't share his love. During the last three years, their arguments always centered on this. She wanted him to leave Monclova Industries — they had more than enough money to live off — and the two could travel the planets, enjoy each other, and be there for the children. He would say that it sounded nice. But he never left work. He loved work. And she refused to understand that he had built more than a company, more than a piece of history — he worked at an empire, a legacy, a name that would exist forever.

The media was right about one thing. He gave all that money for the publicity. But only so Annalia would find out. If she saw how little the money meant, maybe she would finally understand him. Maybe she would come back. With a frustrated grumble, he shut down the visi-link and flopped back onto a lumpy couch in the green room.

With a black door to the hallway and another leading to the auditorium stage, Miguel had no idea why they called it the green room — even the walls were tan. Two couches facing each other, a small refrigerator, and a table with a lit-up mirror for makeup completed the dingy room — none of it painted green. Right when he decided the question worthy of searching on his visi-link, Senator Bashir entered from the hallway.

Miguel glimpsed two bodyguards stationed outside. He also heard the excited crowd gathering further down. Shutting off his speech, he stood and shook Senator Bashir's hand.

"I don't know how you did it," Bashir said, pumping Miguel's arm while flashing his politician smile. "To come in two years ahead of schedule — it's amazing."

"I suppose Mr. Falcry could be thanked for that. He gave me a lot of motivation."

"You see? I always knew you could iron out your differences." Glancing around to make sure they were alone, Bashir stepped closer. "To be honest, I'm a little mad at you. We're leaving a lot of money on the table by not stretching this out the full length of the contract."

Miguel forced a friendly laugh and thumped Bashir on the shoulder — harder than necessary. "Think about how much money you'll make over the next ten years. We'll build a whole new infrastructure on Mars to prepare for when the transit team completes the second half of this wormhole tunnel. Think about that. You've got ten years of local profits, my friend, and when that wormhole opens, when all that trade starts going back and forth through it, you'll get a piece of that, too."

"I will?"

"You've managed to get a piece of every part of this job so far. I have full faith in your ability to figure something out over the next decade."

Bashir chortled as he strolled to the refrigerator. Glancing inside, clearly unimpressed with the options, he said, "There is a matter I'd like to discuss, but it can wait until you're done making your big speech."

Miguel glanced at the door to the auditorium. Nothing wrong with having the audience wait a little in anticipation. "What do you want to talk about?"

"Just trying to weed out truth from rumor. I understand that you have made your decision concerning who will take your place when you retire."

"I have."

"My sources have told me that you chose Varo."

"I have."

"Well, he's a fine young man, of course, but —"

"But?"

"Well, and this is not to disparage your youngest son in any way, but it seemed to me and everybody on my staff, everybody that I talked with about this, that, well, you should have picked Rowan. He's oldest, and he seems more — how should I say this? — serious minded."

Miguel had been expecting this conversation, just not today. His plans required a lot to happen in the coming weeks, and he had hoped to put off this type of discussion until then.

"I understand the concerns, but your sources have limited access to the reality going on in my buildings."

"This is why I wanted to talk with you. I need to know the truth."

"Varo has been heading teams on various projects important to the Pathway Ring. I've monitored him closely, even had problems thrown into his work to see how he handled the matters, and I can say with complete confidence that I have no hesitation in turning control over to him when that time comes."

He hoped he sounded more confident that he felt. Bashir said, "Have you considered —"

"Have you? Have you given any thought beyond your own petty little fears? I brought you into this when it was in its infancy. I could've left you to be nothing more than a go-between. But I saw in you strength, character, and most importantly, loyalty. I've cut you in on every deal and made you a rich man. A very rich man. Why are you questioning me now?"

Bashir locked his hands together in front of his waist. He nodded. But Miguel could not tell if the nod agreed with the statements or confirmed some suspicion. At length, the senator headed toward the hallway door.

"I'm sorry to have disturbed you. You're right. You have done great things for me and for Mars. I should never have doubted you."

He opened the door to find Sydney and Tephen about to knock. After a few awkward stumbles around each other, they switched places. Senator Bashir gave a short bow to Sydney before making his escape. Sydney, looking both amused and confused, closed the door and turned to her father.

"Are you okay?" she asked. "I know you have your speech, so if you'd rather we leave —"

"No, no." Miguel beckoned them with a wave of his hand. "Come. Sit. I could use the distraction."

Sydney's eight dangling earrings jingled as she fidgeted with the bottom of her shirt. Sitting next to her on the couch, Tephen appeared equally uncomfortable. With a hard swallow, she said, "We have something important to tell you."

A peek at her hand confirmed his suspicions when he spotted the small, respectable ring on her finger. He didn't bother waiting. He grabbed his daughter and spun her around.

"Congratulations. This is better news than anything." Setting her down, he reached over to shake Tephen's hand. "I couldn't ask for a better match. You'll make a fine husband."

"Thank you, sir." Tephen blushed.

Sydney said, "I'm so glad you're happy. I was worried to tell you, and I didn't mean to do this right before your speech, but Tephen asked me moments ago, and I'm so excited, and —"

"It's wonderful news," Miguel said, giving her another hug. "Why would you worry to tell me?"

"Because Tephen works for you. I thought you might think he was trying to advance in the company through me."

Baffled, Miguel said, "But you've been dating for a long time, and I would never think that of Tephen. He's been a great asset throughout the years." Turning to Tephen, he added, "Now that you'll be family, I may rest more responsibility on your shoulders."

Tephen puffed. "I'll do my best."

"As you always do."

"Daddy, with Tephen now being my fiancé — oh, that feels weird to say — anyway, shouldn't he know about the plan?"

Miguel chuckled. "He already knows. How could I possibly pull this off without him?"

She turned to Tephen. "You never said —"

He said, "I didn't know you knew."

They talked for several minutes, all three beaming while also scheming, until Miguel's male assistant entered to say they had five minutes until the speech. Tephen and Sydney wished him luck and hurried out. Miguel stood in the empty green room. Alone. His mind a jumble, confused by the ricochet caused by the speech, Bashir's visit, and the jubilant news from Sydney.

He pulled out his necklace with the *M* pendant made from Martian stone. One last moment. That's all he gave himself. Time to concentrate, focus, and find stillness. Because soon — but he didn't want to think about all of that. The plans were in place. The moments would arrive. For this one solitary, silent moment, he put it all aside and allowed the happiness he saw in Sydney to shower him with joy.

A red light above the door to the auditorium flashed twice. A quick prayer. Time to go.

He re-opened his speech on his visi-link and selected the prompter mode — an application he had added recently. In seconds, the entire speech had been fed into the program and would flow before his eyes as he recited the words. The link would listen to his voice and move at his pace. If only the rest of the world would do the same.

Rolling his shoulders back, Miguel opened the door and stepped onto the stage as the crowd roared applause. Lights flashed. Music thrummed. As he waved and made his way to the podium, he wondered how many of them would still throw their support when they discovered why he had finished the Pathway Ring Project so early.

# CHAPTER 13

THOUGH THE ROOM HAD BEEN CALLED AN AUDITORIUM, it only sat about a hundred people in a sloped rectangular space. From the stage, Miguel guessed two hundred had crammed in. Media recorders hovered near the ceiling between the lights, streaming every moment across the planets. He had never spoken in front of such a large crowd before — plenty of interviews and board meetings and business negotiations but nothing like this — and he suddenly felt gases brewing in his gut, threatening to humiliate him with a crude noise.

Standing at the podium, he tried to focus on the words of his speech hovering in the air. It began with a string of acknowledgments to those involved at the top of the project — Senator Bashir, Mr. Falcry, the various Earth and Martian governments — and then he hit the main body of the speech. Gripping the sides of the podium, he coughed and forced a pleasant grin.

"Eight years ago, we set out to build an incredible machine, the largest manmade object in space."

The words sounded hollow. Worse, they sounded boring. The best AI had pulled upon the greatest speeches throughout history, yet these words fell dead to his ears. That would have been bad enough, but Miguel noticed two figures standing by the back corner exits — dressed in gray suits, eyes roving, mouths grim. They would have blended in most crowds, but to Miguel, they flashed like dying neon. He had seen them only twice in his life, but he knew them well — Falcry's agents.

Damn. He had not expected Falcry to move so quickly. He had been naïve. Of all days to strike, this was a prime choice — celebrating, distracted people, large crowds, and all the usual security measures under strain. All would change now. Very well. He had made his career like any successful businessman — pivoting on a moment's notice to take advantage of opportunities, no matter how slim.

He heard the uncomfortable rustling from the audience and gazed across the swath of faces waiting on him. Shutting down his visi-link, he said, "My apologies. One moment."

To startled murmuring, he walked toward the stage wings. Tephen hurried to meet him. "What's the matter?"

"Listen carefully and do exactly what I say. No questions."

"Yes, sir." Tephen did not hesitate. Did not question. Perfect.

"As discreetly as possible, I want you to get Sydney and Varo, put them in a public DV, and send them to my new home."

"Sir?"

"That's right. My new home. You understand?"

Tephen's eyes roved beyond Miguel. If the man noticed the agents, Miguel couldn't tell, but Tephen managed a steady nod.

"Once they're on their way, I need you to send another DV to get Lynia and have her also taken to my new home. Nobody can know what you're doing. When you're finished, return to your office and work as if nothing has happened. This is the last you'll see of me for a while. Sydney, too. But don't worry. I'll bring her back to you."

"But the plan was to —"

"Falcry is already seizing the company. We have to adjust."

Tephen's face riddled with questions, but the man simply swallowed hard and left the auditorium. Returning to the podium, Miguel offered a humble laugh.

He scanned the crowd but didn't see Falcry. No other agents, either. They would be maneuvering through the facility.

Miguel poured a glass of water and took a step. He would have to buy time for his children, but he refused to ramble. If he had to make this speech, if it was the last speech he ever made, he would make it a good one.

"I owe you an apology. I began with gratitude and praise for the politicians who funded this amazing project, but I forgot to thank all of you. Those of you sitting here and those of you watching on your links elsewhere — the great people of Monclova Industries and the great people of Mars. My people. Without your labor and creativity, of problem solving and discipline, none of this would have been possible.

"As you might imagine, this is a momentous day. Events are planned throughout the afternoon, including a parade, as I understand it, and for my part, I was asked to stand here and say a few words. That's what our president messaged me — *a few words.* Of course, the implication is that these words would be suitably weighty as the event itself. Words that might make history.

"Well, I don't know if I'm that powerful a speaker. I know how to dig holes in the ground and build things in the sky. I am no politician. Thankfully." That got a laugh. It eased him a little. "What I can tell you, if you'll indulge me, is how I know this is not merely an important and historic day, it is not simply a celebration of great human achievement, but rather it is a turning point for us all. Once the Pathway Ring is used, Time itself will forever be delineated as *before the ring* and *after the ring.* We sit on the cusp of that moment. We celebrate its birth. In less than a week, a ship will fly through that machine to be thrown to some other part of the universe, and the gears of history will turn forward. But there will always be those who seek to deny the masses of the wonders we should all share."

Miguel leaned his elbows on the podium and softened his voice as if speaking to only a few people. "When I was young, I remember asking my father why the family ever came to Mars. I had never been to Earth, but I had read about it. I had seen pictures and video. Even back then, I knew Earth had air I could breathe without filters, sunlight I could feel on my face without fear of radiation, food and animals that existed in the wild. Water flowed in such plenty that it literally cries from the clouds. Why would we ever leave that?

"He said to me that it was all true. Earth had many riches and could be a wonderful place. But only if you had the money to claim it. For the rest, the air was polluted, the waters undrinkable, the plants and animals going extinct. All the good land, the good water, the good food — all of it was reserved for those who could afford it.

"So I asked him, is that why we left? But he said no. Despite all its problems, a man could still start from the bottom and work his way up, gain wealth, gain position and prosperity, and achieve great success. The problem, he told me, was the government. All of them. The moment you start to succeed, he told me the government would come in and take what you had created. Sometimes just pieces of it; sometimes the whole thing. It depended on the government. But none would simply allow you to continue unmolested.

"And here? Well, here on Mars, especially back then, the government existed simply to keep us all alive. Keep the dome intact and the air filters running. They had too much to worry about to be bothered with whether you or I found our way to success. Besides, we all began with nothing on this planet. The rich didn't show up until the dome existed, until everything was settled. Unfortunately, it appears that we have learned nothing as we shifted from one planet to another. The Pathway Ring has been a phenomenal project and will continue to impact our lives forever. It should not come as a shock that the governments of Earth, and even those of Mars, all want to exact a price." Concerned looks and quiet words shifted throughout the crowd. "As I stand here, I don't know if Monclova Industries will be allowed to continue. Oh, the name will, but don't be surprised if they try to break us up into smaller units, easier to control units. What I do know is that the spirit which my father had, the desire to build a future for himself and his family, that ambition was a seed planted in the red soil of Mars that grew into a great tree. Those days have been gone, and I have been told they would never return. But once we send someone through that Ring — the pioneer will live again. On the other side, somewhere, there will be planets. Maybe they will be dead like Mars was or perhaps they will be thriving like Earth. It doesn't matter — as long as we have free spirits willing to risk and push and discover.

"So, as we embark on this new adventure, as we step into the world of *after the Ring*, I stand before you not to receive praise for what we have created but rather to offer my praise to those brave souls who will truly change the course of humankind. And hopefully, get rich along the way. Thank you."

Laughter and applause and cheering erupted. Miguel could not stop the swagger in his step as he exited the stage. But it did not last. One of Falcry's agents blocked the green room door. She made sure to have her jacket pulled back enough to display a holstered weapon.

He turned around. She would move fast, so he shifted straight to the small ramp off the stage and into the audience. He nodded and shook hands with those who gathered around. Ahead, the two guarding the exits tapped on their old wrist-links. Apparently, Falcry didn't spend enough to keep his people up-to-date.

One agent sidestepped between the two exits while the other attempted to push through the crowd. Miguel thanked those around him, never ceasing to move forward, weaving in one direction, then another. Searching, searching … until he found an opportunity.

Two lengthy men and a rotund woman made a human hedge near the left door. He guided the surrounding throngs in that direction. A peek over his shoulder — the female agent lacked the height to see above all the people and headed toward the wrong door. The other agent, the one that abandoned his post to enter the audience had vanished from sight. Miguel would have to hope the man was also lost.

Gazing ahead, he eased further left which forced the entire crowd to ease left as well. As if it had been planned all along, the three people he had picked out also moved left — enough to obscure the agent's view. Miguel increased his stride, his pace, and hurried right out of the room.

He moved faster now. The agents would eventually report their failure, alerting other agents in the building to look for him. There were plenty of other agents around. Miguel spotted them as he navigated through the building.

But it had been his building, not theirs. He knew the back routes, the seldom used corridors, the service elevators. Though sweating at every turn, he made his way to the garage without trouble.

Tephen had Miguel's private DV waiting. After tapping in the address, after the car slid onto the trackway, Miguel hunched over and let out a long, shaking breath. Monclova Industries receded behind him, and he wondered if he would ever see it again.

# CHAPTER 14

POURING A STIFF DRINK FROM THE CAR'S SMALL BAR, Miguel focused on calming his jangling nerves and adjusting his plans. He could still make this work. The timetable had been altered, but he refused to accept defeat. Not ever.

His visi-link chimed — Falcry. With a swig from his glass, he rolled his shoulders back and answered.

"Quite a rousing speech," Falcry said from Miguel's office chair, feet propped on the desk. Over the years, Miguel had decorated the office with items celebrating Mars and Martian culture. Covered in rusty red hues, sculptures by local artisans as well as furniture from the finest craftsman, the place stood as a monument to his love of the planet that had given him so much. No doubt, Falcry would remove it all.

"Sorry I couldn't stay after, but business calls. You understand."

Falcry jumped to his feet. Stabbing the desk with his index finger, he said, "You're being childish. Give me your passwords and full access to the company, and we can avoid any unpleasantness."

"Why would I do that?"

"Don't act like a fool. You know what's going on. If you don't give me the passwords, I'll have my programmers brute force their way into your systems."

"I don't think my employees will appreciate that, and you certainly need them to keep things running. Eventually, you'll replace them, I have no illusions about that — I doubt they do, either — but for now, you better play nice."

"Have you forgotten what I'm capable of?"

Hoping his face did not betray the terrible nightmares he had suffered for three years, Miguel said, "Oh, I know what you can do, but you can't do it today. All the cameras, all the reporters — you move against my family today and you're done."

Falcry's face clenched. "You think you're so clever." He bit back on his anger, still trying to salvage the situation. "Why didn't you just do your job? Nobody asked you to accelerate the production timeline."

"You did. You insisted that your transit team's supply needs be brought up to the same levels as the Pathway Ring Phase 1. I took your motivational words seriously. I had to."

The DV changed lanes and at the next exit ramp, slid underground. The travel clock estimated another four minutes until arrival. Two levels further down and one district over — far, but not too far.

Spitting out his words, Falcry said, "I didn't tell you to finish two years early. My transit team isn't close to ready."

"Then we wait two years. It's not a problem."

"It would be an embarrassment, and you know it. In your little speech, you said that we're only a week away from the future." With a rueful grin, he wagged a finger at the screen. "Oh, you think this will force me into using your people, your experts, put them onto my team."

"No." Miguel pushed all venom from his voice. "You made it clear that my people were not welcome. When they finished their jobs on this project, I had them assigned elsewhere. They are scattered around the world, helping build a better Mars. Although, I suppose since you're stealing my company, you could call them back in. They are your people now. I can't speak to their loyalty to you, but perhaps you could trust them."

Falcry pounded the desk with both hands. "Turn around, right now. You understand me? This is a direct order. You will give me those passwords, and you will turn yourself in. If you don't, if I have to send agents to apprehend you, then you'll be tried for treason and executed."

*"Arriving,"* Miguel's DV said as it parked.

"You can't hide from me," Falcry said. "I can track you with ease."

Miguel snickered. "Please, do me a favor — send me video of you trying to get a court order to arrest me — the man who just gave a speech which will be remembered for centuries."

"If you make me go after you, I'll get your kids, too. I swear I'll —"

Miguel cut the connection. Exiting the car, he commanded it to return home. As it drove off, he glimpsed the estimated time to arrival — twenty minutes — and started a timer on his visilink. Tightening his coat, he walked at a brisk pace.

The narrow streets of belowground, the lack of sunlight, and the constant noise closed firmer around him. People shouted at each other — some with friendly waves; others with menacing gestures. The scents of various meals competed as did the different music styles playing out of numerous windows.

There was a life to the area. A beat. A pulse. The streets breathed the people, and in turn, the people made each street unique, special.

No wonder Annalia had chosen to live down here after the divorce. She could have stayed topside. He had offered to purchase an enormous home for her. She declined.

"There is far more to the world than the small knit of wealthy friends we know." She had said those words when she walked out the door for the last time. He thought about Lynia's secret jaunts down here a few years back. Had she sought the same as her mother? A wide sense of the world?

He checked his timer — two minutes, so far. He picked up his pace.

Turning the corner, Miguel bumped into an elderly lady wearing old, dented Herif supports. Another invention created from the Pathway Ring Project's needs, the user wore metal strips along the outside of the legs and, when turned on, the Herif supports replaced the need for a cane or walker. They firmed up the leg muscles — or something like that, Miguel wasn't too sure.

At three minutes twenty-four seconds, he reached a door painted blue with the number 72 in white. He knocked. When Annalia answered, his heart clenched. He adored her. Seeing her lovely eyes and heart-warming lips only reminded him that the divorce had been her decision.

"What do you want?" she asked as if addressing a troublesome stranger.

Miguel had hoped there might be a glimmer of happiness, but her eyes narrowed to slits as her mouth tightened into a small dot. "Please let me in," he said.

"You're not allowed to be here without both our lawyers present. You also need to have scheduled the visit."

With a quick glance in either direction, he said, "Which is how you know this is extremely important." He tried to see over her shoulder. "Is he here?"

"Rowan doesn't want to talk to you."

Checking up and down the street again, he said, "Would you please let me in? It's not safe out here."

That word — *safe* — cut straight through to her. "What's going on? Are you bringing trouble to my door?"

"Please."

Her jaw pushed out. She looked ready to throw a punch, but she stepped aside, allowing Miguel to enter. She closed the door, leaned back against it, and crossed her arms. Annalia lived in a modest two-bedroom apartment and seemed comfortable in the space.

Metal walls, lighting that ran along the perimeter, Martian stone floor — quite a step down from their home together. Miguel knew not to say that. A short hallway led off the main room to a small kitchen. Rowan sat on a metal folding chair and glowered back.

Miguel checked his timer — nine minutes fourteen seconds.

Glancing back at Annalia, then forward at Rowan, the words escaped, leaving Miguel fumbling to convince them what he needed. Annalia cocked her head and raised an eyebrow. "Well?"

Closing his eyes, Miguel muttered a fast prayer. Then: "I'm sorry for what I must do. It's not fair, and it's not what you want to hear, but I need you both to pack three- or four-days' worth of clothes and necessities. Right now. We have to leave."

Rowan popped to his feet as Annalia spewed out rapid-fire

insults.

Miguel put up his hand. "Please, please, listen. We don't have time. In about ten minutes my DV will arrive back at our house."

"Your house," Annalia said. "I don't live there anymore."

"When it gets there, agents that work for Mr. Falcry and the Pathway Ring Project will discover that I'm not in the DV. It won't take them long to break into the vehicle service computer and pinpoint where the car last stopped. From there it'll be easy to figure out where I've gone, and they'll be knocking on the door."

"Then why did you lead them right here?"

"I have a plan. The first part is to leave now. Even if I hadn't come here, Falcry would have sent his people. My divorced wife is an obvious move." Snapping his finger at Rowan, he said, "Start packing. Falcry is not thinking clearly at the moment, and he's a bit insane to begin with. He's threatening all of you."

Annalia slapped Miguel across the face. Hard. "You promised me. You were to protect the children."

"That's what I'm trying to do."

"By pushing and pushing further into this madness of a business? We were fine before. We had everything. We didn't need trillions and trillions. But you want the fame. You want to be immortalized. Isn't that right? You only care about the children that will keep your name going. Sydney, Lynia — they don't matter. Only the boys. The ones that carry the Monclova name."

"Fine, fine. I'm a terrible monster. Now, take your scorn and your ass and go pack. Or would you rather stay here and watch Rowan have his head cut off?"

Miguel thought she might slap him again. She appeared to weigh the option. At length, she motioned toward Rowan, and the young man hurried off to pack.

"Thank you," Miguel said.

"I hate you." Annalia stormed toward her room.

# CHAPTER 15

DURING THE NEXT SEVEN MINUTES, Miguel called a public DV on his visi-link and chose a pickup location one block away. He would have preferred dropping down a level and several blocks over, but they couldn't wait that long. Also, he doubted his family would go that far willingly. He'd rather not give them time for a change of heart.

Rowan exited his room with a stuffed backpack over one arm. For a man of twenty-four, he looked meek and unsteady. "What?" he said.

A torrent of thoughts raced through Miguel's mind, but he settled on a simple one. "I'm sorry."

Rowan met those words with a hard stare.

When Annalia joined them, she carried nothing. Her eyes were red, swollen, and her arms crossed tight once more. Rowan's brow knitted as he tried to parse out his mother's actions. Miguel, however, understood. *Brave woman.*

She sniffled, then jutted her chin toward him. "You will keep your promise?"

"Always."

"How?"

"Not now. I'll explain once we're on the way." He knew it wouldn't work but held on for hope.

She shook her head slow and with pity. "I'm not going."

Rowan whipped towards her. "Then I'm not going, either."

"Yes, you are. You heard your father. Dangerous people are coming here, and they want to kill you."

"Why me? I'm not part of this."

"You will be," Miguel said. "We have to leave for a while, and when you return, I'll have stepped down. You will take my place running Monclova Industries."

"I don't care about your stupid company."

"I know that's not true. Your leadership training scores prove that much."

"Well, I'm staying with Mom."

"No." Both Miguel and Annalia spoke at the same time.

Cupping her son's face, she said, "I know this isn't what we want, but that's part of life. You must go. It's too dangerous to stay."

"Then come with us."

"If I go, your father's enemies will figure things out faster. But if I stay, they'll be stalled up talking with me, trying to get information from me. Since I don't know anything other than your father came here and took you away, I can't say anything."

Miguel wondered if Rowan would decipher the true meaning of her words. The sudden shaking as tears ripped down Rowan's cheeks gave the answer.

"No, no, no. I won't go."

"You have to."

"They'll torture you. Maybe even —"

Annalia wrapped her arms around her son as tears filled her eyes. Those same eyes glared at Miguel. With a sharp jerk of her head, she made it clear that he should leave for a moment.

He gave a slight bow and stepped outside. Mother and son needed time to say goodbye. He checked the timer — twenty-seven minutes. Every second made their situation worse and his timeline tighter, but he would give her whatever she wanted.

Miguel paced in front of the blue door and watched the empty street. If anybody suspicious appeared, he would run. He'd make a show of running. Do his best to lure away the agents. But for the moment, all was quiet.

He thought about what he had said in that apartment. Until the words had left his mouth, he had not truly considered Rowan for the job of running the company. Miguel hardly knew his eldest son. As a boy, and even as a young man, Rowan had clung to his mother. His interests never aligned with Miguel's — even his brief time with Monk Crozet only pushed him beyond Shendo into other religions. Or maybe all of them. Something like that. Miguel didn't know because Rowan had kept a wall up between them.

Still, Rowan was strong, though he always looked weak, thin, ineffectual. But as Miguel paced, he recalled an incident years ago. At ten, Rowan got into a fight at school. While unclear in the principal's office, Rowan later explained that his closest friend had been singled out by the school bully. Rowan thought it his duty to intervene. That sounded good enough for Miguel, but the part that remained with him all these years later reminded him that his son had integrity, grit, and courage. Rowan had knocked out four of the bully's teeth and broken two of the kid's ribs.

When asked about his excessive response, Rowan shrugged. "I guess I was overcome."

For several minutes longer, Miguel waited. He tried not to think about his other children. Tephen would get them to safety. Sydney would listen because she knew the plan, and Lynia would go along because it would be a big adventure. Varo, however — he balked at every rule, every norm. He rebelled when nothing existed to rebel against, and when he couldn't do that, he drank.

Miguel hated to admit it, but now was not the time for fancy denials. He youngest son lived at the bottom of a bottle. Leadership training had worked, at first. Varo had performed well, earned high marks, and showed a real aptitude for organizing a team and seeing them through a project. But once he started full-time employment for Monclova, he fought against the job's constrictions.

"All jobs have rules," Miguel had told him one night. "All jobs have things you can and can't do, can and can't say. Rules are how we keep order and civility in society."

"It's not about being polite," Varo said. "Monclova Industries needs a lot of work done. What's the problem if I have my team push an extra hour? I was right there with them. I was putting in the time, too."

"Yes, but afterward, you go to a spacious home, eat expensive food, and sleep in a beautifully comfortable bed. They live well — I pay a good wage — but they don't live as well as us. Some of them, those that can't manage their money, they don't live well at all. Stealing an hour from them —"

"They got paid."

"It was an hour of their lives which did not belong to you."

There were other such conversations, and the more Miguel tried to align Varo's views with reality, the more the young man shrunk. Until one day, Varo failed to show up for work. Tephen eventually located him at a bar, four-levels belowground, drunk and getting drunker.

Miguel cringed. Annalia blamed him for their son's downfall. Maybe she was right. Maybe he had pushed too hard. Then again, with Rowan, maybe he hadn't pushed hard enough. It was so difficult discerning the right pressure to put on a boy to make him a man.

The blue door opened. Rowan shouldered his backpack, looking grim but determined. Drying tears stained his cheeks. Behind him, Miguel saw Annalia crumpled on the floor, heaving long sobs. Rowan closed the door.

"Let's go," he said.

# CHAPTER 16

As Miguel and Rowan stomped up the block, neither spoke. In a nearby apartment, somebody blasted Miguel's recent speech at full volume. Half-a-block over, another apartment chose the latest pop song — *I'm Yours for Now* — and Miguel offered a quick word of thanks. He didn't want to hear his own voice, and he certainly didn't want others to have that in mind when they saw him hastening along the sidewalk. People rarely recognized him, yet they might remember a stern but nervous man who resembled the guy that made that big speech earlier, the one that was on every media outlet around Mars.

Turning the corner, Miguel halted. Their DV waited for them, but so did two of Falcry's agents. Back around the corner, Miguel led his son.

"How could they know that DV was for me?" he said.

Rowan lifted an eyebrow — too much like his mother. "It's not that hard to hack into a visi-link. The stupid things have serious security issues."

Gazing at his visi-link like it was the enemy, Miguel shut the device off. "We've got to get a DV without using a link. Is that even possible?"

Rowan readjusted his backpack and huffed. "Welcome to the rest of the world. Come on. I'll save us."

Without breaking stride, Rowan headed straight to the nearest downway, a spiraling ramp giving access to lower levels. They dropped two before Rowan brought Miguel through a narrow alley. Vendors selling trinkets, snacks, and used electronics lined either side. At one point, Rowan waved to an elderly woman sitting on a brick step.

"Mrs. Huang, how are you?"

The tiny lady squinted as she lifted her double-chin. "Oh, it's you. Checking up on me, eh? Such a good boy. Is this your father? You should be proud. He's a good boy."

"Do you mind if I use your link to call a DV? My battery is dead."

"Sure, sure. We've got to help each other out when we can." She turned her face toward Miguel. "Want to buy a charm? Very cheap. Very good."

Miguel started to decline when he saw Rowan's expression. Clearly, the use of Mrs. Huang's link had a price. "That's very kind of you. I'd love one."

"Just one? Your son told me once that he has two sisters and a brother. Surely, your whole family could use the luck."

"Surely. Okay. Five charms, then."

Mrs. Huang handed her link to Rowan while she bagged the charms and handled the money. Twelve minutes later, a DV pulled to the curb. Caked in red dirt with flickering lights and a burnt smell, the car fit in perfectly with the area. Miguel took the rear-facing seat — might as well make it harder to be spotted — and tapped in the destination on the door console. As the DV drove off, he gave Rowan a firm slap on the knee.

"Good job. Quick thinking. I like it."

Rowan stared out the window.

The city drifted by — hundreds of faces, hundreds of activities — but Miguel ignored it all. He sought signs of the enemy. Any hint that Falcry's men had figured out his location, and he'd have to shift tactics again. At the same time, he had to focus on Rowan. His son's sullen eyes and slouched posture suggested the young man would need more convincing. Protecting his mother would only motivate for so long.

"You're quiet," Miguel said. "Aren't you curious where we're going?"

"I'll find out soon enough."

"True. But I would think —"

"I don't care." Rowan refused to look away from the window.

Miguel gripped his chair's armrest, trying to stay pleasant. "I told the truth back there. You are going to head up the company.

It'll all be yours."

"I don't want it."

No words could have stung worse. "Of course, you want it. You'll practically be the king of Mars. Who wouldn't want that?"

"I'm not interested. I never have been. If you'd taken the slightest bit of time to learn anything about me, you'd know that. You'd know what I want from my life. And you wouldn't have to struggle to figure out which of us kids should run the company. In fact, if you hand me the company, I'll turn it over to one of them, pursue my own goals."

"Your brother has a lot of good qualities, but he's drinking is a problem, and he's a bit erratic."

"You stupid —" But Rowan cut himself off. He angled his head toward Miguel — looking too much like his mother — before he finally spoke. "All you hear is about the company. You just had an opening to talk to your eldest son about his life, his dreams, anything, and you latched onto the last part. Why can't you do the one thing you're supposed to do? Is it really so hard?"

The DV climbed several levels, working toward the surface. By now, Falcry's agents would be knocking on Annalia's door. Miguel hoped Tephen had done his job right or all of this would crumble into pieces.

Miguel said. "Soon, we're going to be with your siblings, and I'll explain everything that's happening. It's not that I don't care about what you want from your life, but you must understand that without Monclova Industries, none of your dreams can happen. Right now, the decision about who will run the company is the most pressing."

"Then do the smart thing, the obvious thing. Give it to Sydney."

"Sydney?"

"She's the brightest, she loves working at the company, and now she's engaged to Tephen — the guy who knows the most about the company with the exception of you."

"Sydney is very intelligent. But she is getting married, and then will come children. She'll not be able to —"

"Utter shit. You had me study Shendo when you've never

even read the book. You don't know what it actually says."

"I know what I've been taught at the temple."

"Here we go again. Trying to talk with you about your own religion is useless. You refuse to think about it honestly."

"That's not —"

Covering his face, Rowan let out a long moan. "Stop. I don't care. You're going to do whatever you want anyway. Listening to me or any of us has never been possible for you. You'll smile that stupid, fake smile and nod like we're important in your life, but we're only important as a trophy. Part of your accomplishments. Why do you think Mom left you?"

Miguel clenched a fist and brought it down hard on the armrest. "Disrespectful and ungrateful. You're right about one thing. I didn't pay close enough attention to my children, to their education, to making sure they thought right. I trusted your mother, and then I trusted Monk Crozet. Both let me down. Well, it's never too late to fix a mistake." He leaned his elbows onto his knees. "You will run Monclova Industries. If you don't, you'll be sentencing your brother and your sisters and even your mother to a life of poverty and humiliation." Before Rowan could respond, Miguel sat back and glared out the window. "It's best we don't talk until we reach the launch pad."

"Launch pad?"

"We're leaving Mars."

# CHAPTER 17

THEY DROVE BY THE ENTRANCE to Monclova Industries. Miguel counted four agents guarding the wide bank of doors leading to the main lobby. No longer hiding in gray suits, these people wore body armor, carried pulse rifles, and looked ready to charge against a fortified position. Miguel had hoped Falcry's takeover would have progressed slower, but no matter — all good plans had contingencies.

After tapping in a new destination, the DV continued onward, took the next exit, and headed underground. Five blocks away, the DV dropped them off.

"Up there," he said, pointing to a private Monclova Industries DV parked ahead.

Seeing that vehicle spread warmth throughout Miguel. It meant that the rest of his children were safe. Tephen would only have left the DV as the last part of his assigned tasks — at least, those that kept him out of the office. He had plenty more to do before this day ended.

One more drive, a rather short trip, brought Miguel and Rowan to an underground launchpad. A massive rocket loomed within the deep cavernous site. The ship's crew and Miguel's family would already be aboard. Another twenty-five volunteers filled out the passenger list — experts in construction, engineering, mining, and electrics. Those handling the final prep outside of the ship had no idea they serviced a clandestine enterprise. Tephen had given the orders, and he would handle the launch from his office.

While normal rocket launches involved a room full of people, their presence was a matter of safety and insurance. If those were not concerns, then blasting a chemical reaction to propel a hunk of metal into space required little. Tephen could probably do the whole thing off his visi-link.

Stepping out of the DV, Miguel gazed up at the towering rocket. Steam hissed out of vents as workers drove vehicles to and from side panels for fuel and coolant. It was an older ship — the kind only available through a month-long negotiation with unsavory types belowground. But purchasing a newer ship required more of a digital trail, and this one would do the trick. At nearly three-hundred billion, it better.

Lights surrounded them, all with different meaning and purpose, but to Miguel, it was a kaleidoscope of wonder. He had accomplished many victories over the years, but nothing struck him with such weight as this moment.

Rowan gazed up. "If that isn't phallic overcompensation, I don't know what it is."

A woman in yellow overalls and a white hardhat rushed towards Miguel. "Sir, an urgent message."

She handed him an old comm device. It had been Tephen's idea to use the aging technology — not as easy to be hacked, not as easy to be overheard.

"Yes?" Miguel said.

Though scratchy with static, the voice of Captain Fletcher came through. "Please, sir, you need to board now. We have to push the launch up."

"We can't. The point is to leave during the regular launch window with the cargo ships. If we leave early, they'll know right away what's happening."

"If we wait to launch, we'll be caught. Somebody has figured out we're here."

*Damn.* "We're boarding. Start the launch process now."

Dashing ahead, sure that his son followed, Miguel led the way to the elevator that would whisk them to the main door of the ship. When he entered, he saw Sydney, Varo, and Lynia all strapped tight in their wall harnesses. The other passengers spiraled down the long tube, each getting strapped in as well. Varo looked upset and busy processing what Sydney must have explained. Lynia appeared trapped between concern and excitement.

At the back, a porthole door led to storage for supplies and then the engines. Above him, another porthole door opened onto a corridor with several small rooms to be used for privacy, conversation, meals, and anything else not requiring a gaggle of people. There was also the head, the galley, and an observation room. The final porthole door gave way to the bridge.

"Daddy, you're here," Sydney said, relief rushing with her words.

As Miguel pointed Rowan to a harness, he smiled at his children. "This is the fruit of our hard work. The birth of the Monclova legacy."

Over a speaker, Captain Fletcher's voice said, "Everybody check your straps, and make sure you are secure. Agents are at the entrance to this facility and closing in. We'll be launching the moment we are clear."

Sydney said, "I wish Tephen could be here."

"He needs to stay," Miguel said.

"I know, but we just got engaged."

"He'll be the first to hug you when you return."

While Miguel strapped in, he flicked on his visi-link. No point in hiding now. A flood of missed calls accompanied long messages — all from Falcry.

Warning klaxons wailed. Tapping into various surveillance cameras, Miguel watched as the workers servicing the ship hurried to reach protective bunkers. Once the klaxons ceased, five enormous metal clanks reverberated from the outside. The enormous metal doors covering the top began to open. The cavernous launchpad depressurized with howling winds and a Martian soil range from above. Sunlight flooded the area.

With many safety precautions pushed aside, Captain Fletcher did not bother with a countdown. He punched the engines into life. Chemicals and flames delivered beneath, shoving the rocket upward. If any of Falcry's agents had dared to enter, they were incinerated.

Miguel sunk into his seat, the pressure building on his chest. His body vibrated with the ship. He wished he had a window to see the Martian surface disappear underneath him. Instead, he closed his eyes and prayed — for success, for the Pathway Ring, for his family.

No stopping now. Miguel and his children, twenty-five loyal volunteers, and the crew of the Martian ship *Veteran* left the grasp of Mars and entered space.

# CHAPTER 18

OVER THE NEXT SEVENTEEN HOURS, Miguel barely had a chance to speak with his children. New experiences filled the first few hours for the whole family. None of them had ever been in space before, and when they weren't stuck vomiting the last contents of their stomachs as they discovered zero gravity, they crowded around any viewport to see the awe of Mars receding into the inky void.

Any questions they had — and they had plenty — went to Sydney. Miguel was impressed with how well they adjusted to this sudden life disruption. He wanted to consider it more, but much of his time had been filled with calls to his various conspirators to make sure everything continued as expected. He also needed to speak with Senator Bashir.

"Have you gone insane?" Senator Bashir looked less angry than angling to find his advantage.

Miguel provided. "It should be clear to everyone by now that I intend to go through the Pathway Ring. In ten years' time, if successful, we'll have completed the other end of the Ring and opened the wormhole for trade. Our deal still holds. You will get plenty of money from this."

"That won't help me for the next ten years."

"Which is why you're going to make sure the Martian government does not allow Mr. Falcry to retain control of Monclova Industries. In a few days, one of my children will return to Mars provided you do your part. Work with Tephen Hilt. He is soon to be my son-in-law and after me, he knows the most about how everything operates. Together, you'll get rid of Falcry so that it is safe for my children to return. Then you'll make sure the company continues. Do that, and you'll find that we can and will work on several of the government's most desired construction projects at cost. No profit to us. Just pay for the materials and we'll eat the rest."

Bashir nearly choked from salivating so much.

With that set in motion, Miguel completed several other important steps, contacting influential people, sending messages to others, and thanking many ahead of time. Two hours of sleep followed, and he finally gathered his children in one of the small privacy rooms.

A round table bolted into the floor provided a sturdy surface to hold onto. Lacking experience with zero gravity, the Monclova family all floated and bounced as if caught in unseen currents. Holding onto the door latch, Miguel looked at his children and wished he could cast back to when they were little, when they adored everything he did, when it seemed simpler.

But they were adults now. He presented every detail to them.

It began when he had agreed to take the Pathway Ring contract. He recognized back then the importance in controlling the far end of the Pathway Ring, but it wasn't until Falcry threatened his children's lives that Miguel planned in earnest. Right from the start, there were several steps that needed to happen almost simultaneously.

He increased production — no secret there — with the intention of completing the order at least two years in advance. He sent extra workers to the Ring to speed up construction, as well. The original timetable had been based on maximizing profits while minimizing risk. But with extra hands, Miguel knew the job could be finished sooner. He guessed correctly that Falcry would not question the sudden influx of deliveries. After all, the man had asked for them. That these deliveries far exceeded the transit team's needs would go overlooked.

The crucial parts, however, had been kept secret from Falcry, from Senator Bashir, from everybody not directly involved. A team of one hundred workers, technicians, and experts began training to be the real transit team — Miguel Monclova's transit team. Some of them were sent ahead to educate Falcry's team as Falcry expected, but when their service finished, they did not return to Mars. Instead, their ships were diverted to another ship where they could hole up until the day of action arrived. Little by little, other volunteers joined them. It gave them time to practice agriculture in space, dealing with zero gravity for long terms, and the myriad other challenges they would face when they traveled through the wormhole.

While this process continued, Miguel set his escape plans in motion — which included the ship they all were aboard now. This ship would carry the last of the crew and had been outfitted with two X-25 booster rockets capable of quadrupling the average speed of a typical transit ship.

"We will have no trouble catching up to our team and joining them. At this very moment, they are headed for the Ring. In addition, the huge block of ore and metals should be on its way toward the Ring as well. When my experts taught Falcry's team how to do things properly, they reconfigured the thrusters on the ore block so that they could control it from afar."

Sydney laughed. To the confused looks of her siblings, she said, "The Ring needs a massive amount of raw material to jumpstart. All that material is what we've been amassing under the guise of it being there for Falcry's team. There are going to be people running the Pathway Ring who won't want to start it for us. They work for Falcry or Earth. But when they see that mass coming through, they'll have to make a hard choice."

"Exactly. Either they will do what I want and start the Ring, in which case they will use up all that mass and when finished, our transit team can fly right through to wherever the wormhole takes us. Or they do nothing, and that ore block passes straight through untouched and maybe smashed into Jupiter or just keeps going forever. If they choice that, they'll have work another five to ten years to accumulate the necessary amount of ore once again. And Mars might not be willing to give up another city's worth of its precious resources after this whole debacle."

"The Ring operators have no real choice. They will start the Pathway Ring or lose every chance of seeing their dreams come to fruition in their lifetimes."

Raising a lazy hand, Varo said, "Doesn't that mean when our

guys go through, they won't have any materials to work with?"

"I never intended them to have anything," Miguel said. "The men and women who volunteered know that they'll have to find the nearest planet or asteroid field to mine for material. But our people are excellent at that very job. Falcry's team needs the material because they wouldn't know how to get it otherwise. All we need is the people to run the equipment. They've got the know-how. What they require is a leader."

Rowan bristled. "I already told you I don't want —"

"No, son. You're to stay here. I promised your mother you would return, and I meant it. When this is all done, you'll go back to Mars and run Monclova Industries."

Snickering, Varo said, "Don't look at me. I'm not going to hurl myself through that crazy machine and hope it spits me out somewhere with a decent bar and decent women."

Miguel's disappointment soured the air. Hearing his son speak so crudely gave form to the thoughts Miguel had tried to suppress in the past. Varo would never rise to the challenge. Rowan fought against the idea of running the company, but in the end, Miguel knew the young man would do so. He'd succeed at it, too. If not for any other reason, Rowan would do the work for his mother. But Varo …

"I will be the one going," Miguel said. "Rowan stays here to run things. Sydney is getting married to Tephen, so she'll stay, too. Varo will join me —"

"I won't go."

"— then you'll end up in prison or executed. After all, the leadership work you've been doing for me was part of this." While true that Varo's assignments involved Miguel's secret plans, Miguel doubted anybody would harm his son — especially once Rowan took control.

"That's not fair," Varo said, straightening too fast, the momentum sending him into the ceiling.

"All of you should dispense with the idea of *fair*. Nothing is ever fair or not-fair. It just is. This is the situation, and nothing will change it."

Lynia waited. But not patiently. Miguel noticed the way her

mouth set and her eyes continuously surveyed the room. Though tense, she showed calm acceptance.

But as she motioned to speak, the ship's comms presented Captain Fletcher's static voice once again. "Mr. Monclova, please come to the bridge. Urgent."

# CHAPTER 19

As Miguel floated toward the bridge — really a glorified cockpit — he feared he had made a grave miscalculation. None of his children had looked pleased. He had pulled off an incredible feat that had taken years to accomplish, a feat that would benefit them for their entire lives and the lives of their children, yet they acted as if he had ruined the family name. He could admit that he had not been the perfect father. He had relied too heavily on Annalia to give Rowan and Varo a man's proper upbringing. But why should that stand in their way? Surely, his sons were smart enough to seize the opportunity before them. Any idiot could see it.

As much as he wanted to solve this problem, he knew the captain would not call him on an idle matter. Family would have to wait. After all, if this gamble failed, none of his children's foolishness would matter.

He sighed.

Four kids and not one of them could make his life easier.

Pushing his concerns aside, trying to focus on the present issues, Miguel reached the circular, red-metal door and entered the bridge. Captain Fletcher drifted over, moving with the ease of a seasoned veteran to space travel. All the more impressive considering the narrow area he had to maneuver. Old control panels, wide flat monitors, and dented bulky links had been crammed into every available space. A crew of three worked their stations with Fletcher overseeing the entire operation.

Newer ships — heck, ships from the last few decades — had a sleek, open design with everything handled at a central row of screens. But this ship had been scrapped together from parts purchased without drawing notice. Had they bought a modern control screen, Falcry would have uncovered Miguel's plan years ago and stopped it. Probably would have executed Miguel, too. For fun.

Despite the ship's antiquated technology, Captain Fletcher looked pleased. His young physique and thick, blond hair suggested more of a heroic figure than a well-paid lawbreaker, but he clearly enjoyed the thrill and challenge of making this ship succeed. However, as he reached Miguel, his expression turned dour.

"We've been monitoring Mars since we left. The usual cargo launches occurred on time, however, we noticed another ship hidden within the group."

Miguel nodded. "That'd be Falcry's agents using the same idea we had planned to use. I expected them to follow us. Falcry would never simply sit back and wait."

"The problem is that they're using a military ship — the *Horizon.* Not what we had counted on. It's armed and significantly faster than us."

"We've got a huge lead."

"It won't matter. I've had the AI simulations go through all likely possibilities. We can't outrun them."

Gazing across the array of twinkling lights and flashing displays, Miguel asked, "How long until they overtake us?"

"If I push the *Veteran,* maybe three to four days."

"Then do it. We need every second that you can gain."

Fletcher's heroic image swiped away, leaving behind his true visage — cold-eyed, snarling, ready to fight. "Let me be clear — I don't care about your goals or your reputation or anything like that. I agreed to ferry you on this old ship for one reason — the payday. You never said we'd be pursued by a military-grade arsenal. I'm not abandoning the job, but I want you to understand that I won't risk my life or the lives of my crew for an overblown science project."

If he thought the sudden attitude shift would scare Miguel, he was wrong. Miguel preferred it this way. More honest. "You only have to keep us ahead of him for four days. Long enough to reach our transit team. Do that, and it'll be too late for Falcry.

There will be no point in attacking. You'll be in the clear."

"And the second-half of my money?"

"In the bank. Waiting. Mr. Tephen Hilt is back on Mars, and he's monitoring all that's going on. Once he sees the transit ship go through the Ring, once my daughter contacts him to confirm, the money will be posted to your account."

Captain Fletcher held his gaze as if trying to wring out where the double-cross awaited. At length, he uttered a dismissive grunt and floated back toward his chair. A few rapid commands, and Miguel heard the increase in engine power.

*Four days. At best.* That would have to be enough.

After exiting the bridge, Miguel paused. His heart pounded as if he had sprinted across a field. His chest tightened like he swallowed too large a bite without proper chewing. He rested his head against the cold metal wall and closed his eyes.

Sleep. He wanted nothing more than to drift off into a dream. The last time he had felt this exhausted, his father had died and he fought to keep the company afloat. But this would be different. He had the money and the knowledge to make this work. In four days. Maybe less.

"You're doing this wrong," Varo said.

Miguel opened his eyes to see his son approaching from beneath his feet. His body had coasted away from the wall. He struggled to realign with Varo — which also flipped the ship's corridor upside down — and breathed slowly to settle the churning in his gut.

"Are you even sober enough to start this conversation?"

With a smirk, Varo said, "Thrust into space on a rocket that might fall apart any second does wonders for clearing the mind. And straight down, you're not making the best decisions right now."

"*Straight down?*"

"It means —"

"I know what it means. I didn't know you had taken up street slang."

Varo's head bumped the ship, snagging the bravado out of his words. "You don't know much about me at all."

"Maybe so. But now is not the time to deal with family wounds."

"Only proves me right. You're not doing —"

"I'm doing all I can to save our company."

"You're running away."

Miguel's eyes flared. "Watch yourself."

"I'm sure it seems like a manly step into adventure, but even I can see that you belong back on Mars. The idea that you want to go through the Pathway Ring, well, that's straight down vanity. Nothing more. Forcing me to come along? That's a control move mixed with some punishment. Neither are good reasons."

"Wrong on all counts. If your brain wasn't so fogged up, you might be able to recognize that fact. And stop with the slang. You're better than that."

"No, I'm not. I don't belong on this ship, and —"

"One more complaint and —"

"What? You've already thrown me into space and threatened to send me through a damn wormhole. You really think there's anything more you can threaten me with?"

Miguel's hand twitched at his side. He wanted to grab his son by the shirt and shake the boy into understanding. Instead, he gripped one of the many handholds lining the walls, his fingers squeezing as he spoke.

"I took you off Mars so that you stayed alive. Falcry would have hunted you down and murdered you in the most painful way he could dream up."

"Nah. He told you that, sure, but what good would killing me do? You would've blasted into space without me, and any doff-fool could see I wasn't going to try taking over the company. I mean, yeah, I worked for you, but be honest, straight down, I'm not good at any of it. I don't want to be. I'm much happier with a mug in one hand and a woman in the other."

With a rising growl, Miguel said, "Do you think that makes you more of a man? Drinking and whoring?"

"You want me to believe you never?"

"Drink? Of course, I have. But you take it too far. As for women — no. I never played around with loose types. I dated a few respectable women, and then I was introduced to your mother." Cautioning against the heat lifting in his chest, he tried to let go of the handhold, but his fingers would not unlatch. "I want to help you break free of that life, to make something of yourself."

Varo mocked him with a laugh. "When have you ever shown any real interest in me? In any of us? Your life has always been about you and your company. Mom, Syd, Rew, Lyn, and me — we're nothing but accessories."

"That's not true."

"I'm not hurt or upset. None of us are. We understand how we fit into your image of a perfect life, and since you never bothered to intervene too much in our lives, it worked fine. We've accepted you for who you are. Why can't you do the same for us?"

"I should accept that you're a drunkard? Never. My job is to make sure you live a good life, find a wife, have children of your own."

"I might already —"

"Legitimate children."

"There it is. I was wondering how long before you'd start in on that Shendo crap."

Barely above a whisper, Miguel said, "How dare you." Only a few words, but enough to pry off the lid he had clamped tight. He had spent years orchestrating every detail to protect his family and guarantee their prosperity. Years fending off attacks from other businesses, from greedy politicians, from the media. Years toiling late into the night while his family slept warm and safe. Yet not one of them showed a speck of gratitude. Annalia took it even further by divorcing him.

Miguel placed his free hand flat on Varo's chest and pressed hard, locking the young man against the wall. "I have given you opportunity after opportunity to do right, to act like a man, to accept the situation and adapt. But you are spoiled. You think you can talk with me, debate with me about how to run this family? You don't have enough brain cells left. You've partied them all away. And while you were out fathering an army of bastards, I protected you."

"You think you deserve the Greatest Father on Mars Award? Because I don't remember you being around much, and when you were, you'd have work to do or simply ignored us."

"Then consider yourself lucky now because you're about to get years of my undivided attention."

"I'm not going, but even if I did, even if I stood right by your side, you would hardly notice. You have another big project to build, another Pathway Ring, so I don't think you're going to be around for that good father-son bonding. Besides, if I go and you bother to take notice out there, you'd probably find that I spent my time fathering an entire company of workers for you."

Miguel raised his open hand but stopped when he saw his son flinch. He had never hit his children, and he refused to start now. Instead, he grabbed his son's jaw. "You will go with me, and you will do what I say. Your wild days are over. Time to be a man. Stop being a disappointment."

As he coasted away, Miguel heard gasping — but he could not tell if it was shock, fear, or tears.

# CHAPTER 20

THROUGHOUT HIS CAREER, Miguel rarely experienced uncertainty. There were times — plenty of them — in which he did not know the outcome of his actions, but once he chose a course, he continued with confidence. When he made mistakes, he tried to own them. When it came to making the actual decisions, though, regardless of right or wrong, he acted with certainty.

He had none of that with his children.

The morning after his argument with Varo — at least, he thought it was morning, time had become rather fluid in space — Miguel could not feel certain what the correct path forward should be. He had spent hours going over every detail, trying to ascertain where things had fallen apart, how he had lost control of his emotions, but could not reach a satisfactory answer. If this had been a business negotiation, he would have treated Varo as an opponent, an enemy, and could have ruthlessly dissected the disagreement until he had reached clarity. But this was his son. This was family. The rules of business did not apply.

After using the bathroom — a unique experience in zero-g — Miguel drifted up through the center of the sleeping area. His volunteers hovered around in quiet conversation, all glancing his way, some waving, some nodding, each making sure to give him the respect of being their boss as well as the distance of pretending not to have heard yesterday's outburst. The ship's crew remained on the bridge. He suspected they slept there, as well. And his children — he did not see them. They must have commandeered one of the private rooms.

Closer to the bridge, Miguel ducked into what he considered the observation deck — a small room with an entire wall panel viewport. He kept the lights off, centered himself before the wide window, and took in the vastness of space.

He wanted refuge in that void. Maybe absolution, too.

He thought about his own father. A hard man. A cold man. A man who had no concept of how to deal with children, so he simply chose not to. Miguel's mother handled family matters while his father worked in the mines, and eventually, built the company.

From an early age, Miguel knew the expectations laid out for him, and his parents instilled in him a desire to fulfill those expectations. Why had his own children failed the same? What was different that made him want to achieve the goals of his father where his children shunned those things? Perhaps he had shown them too much affection. Perhaps his children did not crave his approval enough. Or perhaps the fall rested in Annalia. Her lax attitude towards less traditional ideas may have harbored the root of this dysfunction.

But Miguel shook off those thoughts. Blaming Annalia or his children was too easy. The fall had to be his. Deep down, he had to know it, even if he could not admit it at the time. After all, that failure, that certainty of his failure, would explain his shameful outburst at Varo. He needed his children to behave a certain way, to step up and face the challenges before them, and he had assumed they were ready. But perhaps he had been lying to himself — about them and about the job he had done in preparing them.

Rubbing his face, he stared into the dark.

He spent hours in the observation room. Easier than dealing with his children. Not that he condoned the idea of hiding from anybody, but he needed a workable plan forward with them. He had to convince Varo to want to go through the Pathway Ring while also convincing Rowan the value in staying behind to run Monclova Industries. The biggest obstacle that Miguel could see — he really didn't know these young men well. He didn't understand their wants and desires nor their weaknesses and vulnerabilities. Essential information in any negotiation.

Part of him balked, knocking his mind out of seeing his children as another business deal. His boys, in particular. They were an essential part of his plan, and he had not prepared them properly.

He shook off the thought. Regret over mistakes would not change anything. He had the boys that he had, and those were the tools at his disposal. He would make it work.

At some point, he fell asleep. When he woke later, he had drifted toward the top corner of the observation window. From that angle, he spotted the edge of the Ring. His chest swelled at the very idea — he had built something so massive that a person could see it in space from this distance. A true marvel.

The door clanked as somebody turned the lock and slid it open. Lynia entered.

"Come here," he said, excitement charging his voice.

Perhaps bouncing off his energy, she sped over with curiosity. Craning her head, she let out a gasp — a small sound that puffed his chest more.

"It's incredible." The way she whispered her words, Miguel knew she meant it for herself. That fact broadened his broad smile.

They stayed there for several minutes, both hovering against the window, snatching peeks of the Pathway Ring as it slipped in and out of view. Miguel thought that he should take Lynia to the bridge. They would be able to observe the Ring in full as the *Veteran* headed straight towards it. But before he could speak, she pushed back with the look of a child about to broach a difficult topic with a parent — which, a breath later, he realized was exactly the situation.

"Have you come here to tell me that I'm doing everything wrong, too?" He didn't intend to sound so rough, but once the words blurted out, he couldn't stop them.

She glared at the doorway. "Varo? He's never happy when anybody tries to get him to do anything — even if wants to do it. Once, I saw him rambling on about wanting new experiences in life and then getting angry because some girl he was dating suggested they go to a different bar than the usual one. Ignore him."

"I wish I could. But he's my son. When I go through the Ring, I'm going to need someone I can trust at my side. That's supposed to be him."

"You have another option."

"Rowan must stay behind to manage the company. I had hoped Varo would be ready for that, instead. I had been training him to fill that role, but it's clear I was wrong."

"Not Varo, not Rowan. Me."

Instinctively Miguel dismissed the idea, yet part of him held back from saying anything. He looked at his daughter, really observed her, and he saw the woman she had become — strong, athletic build; stronger, more determined stance; possibly the strongest, most confident eyes. She had always been the one that loved adventure, loved taking a big risk. At least, that was how he had perceived her. But the last thirty-some hours had made it quite clear that he did not know his children. Still, he could not embrace the idea of taking her on such a treacherous journey.

"My dear —"

"I don't want to hear *my dear* unless it's followed by *of course you can come*. The boys are not prepared for the physical hardships you're about to face, and Sydney should never go. She's about to get married, and she's the smartest of the three of them. You need her to keep your company alive, not Rowan."

Miguel appreciated the fire he saw in her but not enough to change his mind. "You might be right about them, but the people who go through the Ring will become the new pioneers. They will face more than hardship. History has taught that to function, to grow, to become a healthy group in such a difficult situation, they will have to rely on a unifying code. That means Shendo. I'm learning that I don't know you children well enough, but unless I've missed everything about you, the idea of Shendo is not one you agree with. In fact, I'm guessing you're an atheist. So, you deny God altogether."

"I am an atheist," she said without hesitation. "But you don't understand what that really means. I don't deny the existence of a god. I simply admit that I don't know, that I have not seen any credible evidence to prove to me there is a god. If you could show me that evidence, I would believe in a heartbeat. I'd be happy to believe. What a miracle it would be, and how much easier life would be, if there truly was more to it than the short time we are given."

"There's evidence all around you. But it doesn't matter. I'm heading this mission through the Ring, and that means we will be following the Shendo code. If you want to go through, you would have to accept that."

He figured that would end this foolish debate. Lynia surprised him when she maneuvered closer so that they hovered on an even plain. "Prove it to me."

"What?"

"You say there's evidence everywhere, show it to me. Give me real evidence of a god that comports with reality, evidence that can be objectively, repeatedly verified, and I'll finally, happily believe."

Though he did not see how this would change his decision, he admired her gumption. For the first time since launching into space, he saw before him a challenge with his children that he could handle with certainty.

"It says in the Bible —"

"That's not evidence. It's just a book." She lifted her chin as if to say she had scored a point.

"It's Scripture. It's the word of God."

"Just saying something doesn't make it true. We have no way to prove who wrote those books or what they said before they were translated and re-translated and re-translated through centuries — often shoddy translations. Even if we could know, it wouldn't prove anything. What is written in the Bible has no bearing on what's true. I could write a book and get people to follow it and it could be no more or less true than the words of the Bible."

"But look at any of the books — Old Testament, New Testament, New World testament — it doesn't matter, they all point to the same truth."

"There have been thousands of gods throughout history. Most of the religions of those gods have sacred books. The people who believe in those gods believe in those books and would say the exact same words you're saying about your god and your books. Even if there is a real god, how are we to know that your god is the correct god? What if one of the other religions has it right? You're going to say it was in the Bible, but they're going to say it was in their book. You see the problem?"

Scratching his brow, Miguel said, "Well, if you don't like the Bible, then how do you explain wormholes or dark matter or any of the other mysteries of the universe? Science doesn't know the answers."

"And neither do I. That's okay. I accept that there may be limits to what we could ever know. That's what science is all about. Pushing our understanding, finding the truth." Lynia's initial apprehension disappeared the more they debated. Miguel saw power flare in her eyes. She went on, "The fact is that every time religion has drawn a line in the sand and says that this is where science ends and a god begins, science figures out the mystery and religion has to move further down to draw another line."

"What about morality?"

"Who is more moral? Me or Varo? That should be proof enough right there that you don't need a god to be moral."

Miguel chuckled. "But religion does put down a moral code for all to follow. Even though you are an atheist now, you were brought up with some Shendo teachings. You probably learned your morals through that."

"I hated those classes. If anything, I should be the most amoral person ever, simply because I reject Shendo. But I'm not. You go through history, though, you'll find many of the horrific atrocities mankind has inflicted upon itself were done in the name of one god or another. If your god wants us to follow some moral code, he's doing a lousy job of getting the point across."

"I'm not sure that's true. Plenty of secular atrocities have occurred."

"We can look it up, but even if you're right on the debate of morality versus atrocity, it doesn't prove truth to the claim that a god exists."

While he enjoyed the debate, Miguel had to admit that he was unprepared. Clearly, Lynia had given the subject plenty of thought whereas Miguel had no reason to consider these points until now. He believed in Shendo from an early age, and that settled the matter. He did not live a life of religious doubt. Smoothing down his hair, he gazed out the window again.

"I suppose it all comes down to faith."

Lynia clasped her hands behind her back. "A poor substitute for the truth. I want to know what's true — good or bad. That's what your team will need, too."

He wanted to reach out and hug her. Kiss the top of her head as if she were a little girl still. But she wanted the truth, and he would give that to her.

"I'm sorry, but you're wrong. I can't let you go thinking the way you do."

"That's all right. I never thought you'd give me real consideration anyway."

She turned to leave, but he caught the change on her face — the tears she hoped to hide.

"If we were only going for a matter of weeks or a few months, then I would bring you along without reservation. But this is going to take years. Not the simple eight years we worked on the Pathway Ring here. Out there, it might be years until we find enough raw material to mine. Years to set up all the equipment and factories necessary to make that raw material usable, and years more to actually build the darn thing. Why would you want to waste the prime of your life on this craziness? All that is assuming we don't wind up dying before we even find the first planet or asteroid to mine."

Lynia stopped at the doorway. When she looked back, he saw that he had been mistaken. Her eyes were dry, and the corner of her mouth raised. "It would be a lot more fulfilling than sitting around Mars going to parties, waiting to be married, and popping out some kids. But most of all, it's simply what I want."

# CHAPTER 21

HOURS PASSED. A DAY'S WORTH? Miguel couldn't tell by looking around, and part of him resisted finding the answer. The more hours gone, the closer Falcry's warship came.

Miguel had underestimated Falcry's ability to organize a launch so fast, and he never expected a military ship to be sent. He assumed Falcry would throw together a team onto the next cargo hauler. Those ships were slow. Slower than the *Veteran.* Every brain Miguel had running the numbers said he would be through the Ring long before a cargo ship came anywhere near. But Falcry had changed things.

That was part of business — of life, really — and Miguel had to adjust. Only problem — he was stuck in the belly of a rattling ship with no real possibilities to outmaneuver his enemy. Tephen would be working with the Martian government to regain control of Monclova Industries, and until that happened, he wouldn't be able to exert any significant pressure on Falcry to cease this pursuit. Of course, Tephen couldn't truly get the government's attention until Miguel's team went through the Ring to establish control.

Miguel needed a clear mind. Back home, he would have walked the company campus, gazed across his wealth of land and mines and factories, watched the cargo rockets lift into the sky. But on this ship, he only had the observation room, and that brought no solace.

Worse than thinking about Falcry and that military ship, Miguel could not stop going over his last conversation with Lynia. On the one hand, she had amazed him. Her strength, her confidence, her daring, her firm and considered arguments — all traits he wanted in his children. He wished Varo had learned some of what Lynia had. Which made him wonder why one child thrived and the other wasted away? Miguel wasn't fool enough to think he had influenced the outcome — at least, not in a positive way.

Before more maudlin thoughts could take over, he shifted away from Lynia's character and focused on the content of their discussion. He wouldn't reconsider his position — Shendo was the true path. It hurt that she didn't believe, that she had been pushed from it. But he had to admit there was a simple logic to what she said, and he could see how that steered her further away.

The idea that other people who believed other religions also thought their book spoke the truth — well, of course. Probably some Muslim father and daughter had the same conversation. Or a Hindu father and daughter, or a Cherokee father and daughter, or a Catholic father and daughter. But Shendo had proven itself to be true by the simple fact that Mars flourished under it.

That should be more than enough evidence of a god. It wasn't cold, analytical proof, but that's where faith came in. Yet she refused to accept faith as an argument.

He paused to peek at the Pathway Ring once more. He didn't have to strain to see it, now, and it thrilled him that soon he would be among the first humans to ever witness a new section of the universe. All his problems would disappear. He'd have new problems, but they would be those of survival, at first. A pioneer's problems. Not all this mess with the way his children thought and behaved.

Then again, if he brought Lynia with him — something she wanted — then he might influence her, bring her back to the Shendo fold. He hoped to do that with Varo, but now he wondered if Varo was too far gone. Perhaps the Lord had put Lynia in his path so that he might save one of his children.

A harsh beeping interrupted his thoughts. Flashing red lights near the door reflected off the observation window. An alarm.

Captain Fletcher's voice came through the ship. "Mr. Monclova to the bridge."

By the time Miguel reached the bridge, a short journey of only twenty seconds, his adrenaline had kicked in again. Based on the crew's flurry of activity, he wasn't the only one.

With a grave expression, Captain Fletcher spun over the heads of his crew, using handholds to stop near Miguel. "The military ship has fired upon us."

Miguel held back all expressions of shock, though his body jolted within. He kept underestimating Falcry. He never thought the man would fire so soon. "How long do we have?"

Glancing at a screen with a three-dimensional display of their location as well as the pursuing ship and the missiles, Fletcher's shoulders dropped. "Current projections say the missiles will arrive in seven hours. We can plot evasive maneuvers for that position in time, but there are no guarantees."

"Can we outrun them?"

"Captain," a woman said from the workstation tucked nearby. "Incoming message."

"Image?"

"Yes. You want it on screen?"

Fletcher hesitated with a glance at Miguel. "Might as well."

Several monitors flickered to life with grainy video of Falcry. From the surroundings, Miguel caught another surprise — Falcry was on board that military ship.

In his most authoritative tone, Falcry said, "Captain Fletcher, you are in violation of numerous Earth-Mars treaties as well as the binding agreement for the Pathway Ring Project. Each violation will not only cease your career, but they will come with prison time attached. Cut your engines and wait for my ship's arrival. If you cooperate, we can find a solution that helps you avoid such unpleasant outcomes. However, if you continue onward, I will order for the missiles we have launched to be armed. Mr. Miguel Monclova, I sympathize with your predicament, but I urge you to consider the safety of your crew and your family in this dangerous hour. I have no desire to destroy your ship and kill all of you. Don't make that necessary."

"End of message," the crewmember said.

Miguel scowled. "You said they were three to four days behind."

"No, I said we could outrun them for three to four days. That was the ship. Not its missiles."

The frozen image of Falcry remained on the monitors, but Miguel's eyes drifted beyond to the front viewport — to the Pathway Ring. Suspended in the darkness of space, it had all the splendor of an aerial photo of a city at night. Enormous in scope, dazzling with lights of activity, a lovely portrayal of potential, of dreams. To be so close now. His stomach cramped at the thought of backing down.

"Sir, I know you want to keep going," Fletcher said, "but I have to think about my crew."

"I'll double your fee."

"I can't spend money if I'm dead."

"He won't arm those missiles. He's a government man. If he blows up this ship, he'll spend the next five years answering for it, and the press will keep milking the story anytime he shows his face. It'll follow him forever. Given enough pressure, the government will have to convict him. Put him in jail for a few years. You really think Mr. Grend Falcry wants to risk that? He's a psychopath, but he's not crazy."

Fletcher's focus shifted to the side, and Miguel could feel somebody there. He whirled around, ready to yell at the person eavesdropping, but Sydney stood at the back. Her eyes had fixated upon Falcry's image on the monitors.

"How long have you been there?" he asked.

She stood firm, reminding Miguel of his recent talk with Lynia. "I heard most of it."

"Well, don't worry."

"I'm not."

Her normally girlish attitude had vanished, and her reply concerned him. Perhaps she was in shock.

He approached her, placing a hand on each shoulder, and he did his best to project calm assurance. "I promise that I'll do everything to make sure no harm comes to us. Trust me. Of all my children, you have always stood by my side, always believed in me. Keep doing that." He gestured to the bridge. "This is no different than business back on Mars."

Sydney watched her father with a softer gaze. The word *pitying* came to mind, but Miguel rejected the idea. Why would she look at him like that?

"I love you, Daddy. And you're right, I've always stood by your side. In fact, over the last several days as the boys, Lynia, and I have talked, I've been defending you and the plan. But I'm starting to see their side of things. I saw it just now. You seemed truly surprised that Mr. Falcry has launched his missiles, but Lynia, the boys, and I expected it sooner."

"Sooner?"

To Captain Fletcher, she said, "Cut the engines. Let them catch us. You've made it clear we can't evade them, and we don't want those missiles armed."

Captain Fletcher looked between father and daughter. His perfect hair and chiseled features lost all their strength and charm. His chin quivered.

Sydney's authoritative tone rang of a Monclova leader. "Would you rather have our bodies scattered across space?"

With a decisive nod that did not match his nerve-wracked body, Fletcher commanded his crew to slow the ship until they stopped. Miguel wanted to yell, threaten, retake control, but Sydney put her hands on his shoulders.

Though still holding a stern expression, she winked. "It's your turn to trust me. We have our own plan."

# CHAPTER 22

SYDNEY LED MIGUEL INTO ONE OF THE PRIVATE ROOMS where he confronted his other three children waiting. As he found a set of handholds to cling to, he noticed the hard stares in their eyes. Not towards him but rather wearing the look of those prepared for a great and difficult task. They had the eyes of explorers before climbing the tallest mountain, of performers standing in the wings of a great theater, of soldiers awaiting the attack order. These were not his children anymore. They were not children at all. Somehow, the little boys and girls that had thrilled when he managed to come home before they had fallen asleep now floated before him as full-grown adults.

Sydney pointed to Varo. "Get Mr. Slater."

To Miguel's amazement, Varo scurried off. No complaining, no sarcasm, nothing but the simple obedience.

"Daddy, I need you to listen with an open mind," Sydney said.

"I'm starting to think that *Daddy* might not be the right name for me anymore."

Sydney reached over and squeezed his hand. "No matter what, you'll always be Daddy. At least, for me." When she let go of his hand, her posture straightened like a leader. "First, from the moment we left Mars, I started planning. We all have. We're not idiots, and it's clear that we're in serious trouble. We refuse to simply sit back and hope you figure a way out. Not that you couldn't, but we have brains, too. And we've used them."

Rowan said, "I tried to tell you she's the smartest of us."

"We're not doing that," Sydney said, stern enough to quell Rowan. "This is not the time. Maybe someday in the future we can deal with family issues, but none of that will happen if we're dead."

The gentle rumble of the ship's engines cut out. Retrofired bursts shot to slow them down. Part of Miguel could not grasp how he had lost control so quickly. Another part of him wanted to be impressed. Still another part screamed in his head, told him that he acted in shock, and that they would all die soon if he didn't pull together and do something.

But with a new, unsettling hardness to her voice, Lynia said, "Pay attention to Sydney. She speaks for us all, she'll tell you the plan, and you need to hear it. We can fix this mess that you've made, but I'm certain you're not going to like it."

Sydney put up one hand. "Everybody stop. Daddy, I apologize for these outbursts. I'm sure you can understand that this is all new territory for us. But it won't be long before Falcry and his agents arrive, so if everybody's done interrupting, I'm going to have my say."

Disoriented from the sensation of being in a room filled with familiar strangers, Miguel said, "I'm doing my best to listen and pay attention. You have my word that I'll keep trying."

Sydney pushed forward, locking her feet into floor rings so that she could splay her fingers on the table and not lose her position. "We have identified three goals that need to occur in order to secure this family's future. First, we must make sure that our team goes through the Pathway Ring. Nobody else. Second, we must make sure that we end up controlling the Pathway Ring. And third we must make sure that we retain control of Monclova Industries both on Mars and at large. We can achieve all three goals, but Daddy, you will have to go along with what I say."

"I already have a plan for all of that. You know."

"But your plan relies on the wrong people."

"Rowan? Varo?"

Rowan said, "Exactly — the wrong people."

Continuing in her strong voice, Sydney said, "Over the last several weeks, the four of us have been making our own plan. With all that's happened, we've adjusted — used some of your old plan, too."

Miguel recalled how calmly his children had accepted these recent days. He should have seen it. They didn't panic, didn't fight hard. They were upset — so was he — but Sydney must have prepared them, kept them focused.

Because they had a plan.

With a laugh caught between incredulity and amusement, Miguel said, "This is insane."

"No, this is reality."

"I built this company from the feeble little mining operation my father started and turned it into a powerhouse industry that spans beyond one planet, that influences governments. I've made us ridiculously wealthy. I maneuvered us through difficult negotiations, complicated contracts, labor disputes, resource shortages, public backlash. I spent a lifetime learning how to be the best leader of this company, and you have the gall to think you can come in and, over a mere few days of conversation with your brothers and sister who have never shown any interest in this company, you think you can suddenly solve everything. It's disgusting."

She didn't even flinch. "You are a disgusting fool if you think you know anything about us. You've never been there for Rowan or Varo or Lynia. For me, you were around a bit, but not much. Because I showed interest in the company, you showed interest in me, but it only went so far — I'm a woman, after all."

"That's right. Even if I grant that you and your sister are the smartest of you four, it doesn't change Shendo law. Neither of you will continue the Monclova name."

"You're wrong," Rowan said.

Miguel flailed a hand towards his son. "Ah, yes, enlighten us all. I suppose since she's CEO that makes you the next prophet."

"Hardly. But I know what Shendo says about your name. You don't. You've based your whole life on this notion of our societal roles, yet you've clearly never bothered to read the New World Testament. It's sad."

Wrapping her knuckles on the table, Sydney said, "The two of you are not going to fight religion. The point here is Rowan found that we don't have to give up our names upon marriage. Now I've talked with Tephen, and he's agreed that when we marry, he'll change his name to Monclova. Our children will carry the Monclova name. Daddy, you've nothing to fear about that."

Squeezing the handholds, Miguel snatched a peek at the doorway. He needed space, freedom from this claustrophobic room. He needed to think about next steps. Captain Fletcher had cut the engines on Sydney's order — what did that mean?

Lynia snapped her fingers, locking his focus as she cleared her throat. "I know you want to run back to the observation room, lock the door, and stare into space. I know you believe that you can think of a way out of this. I see it in your eyes. But instead of fearing your children and the actions we're taking, look into your heart, into your bones, and find the pride. You've never been proud of us before."

"That's not true."

"None of us follow the path you wished for us. But we are following strong paths, and in the end, we're doing exactly what you want — just not how you envisioned it. We're taking charge of the company, protecting the family, and most importantly, we will take control of the Pathway Ring. We knew this would be hard on you. We're sorry about that. But our plan is the best option. You can either hear us out, perhaps even help us, or you can become another obstacle in the next evolution of Monclova Industries."

Miguel pressed two fingers against his forehead and rubbed a circle. The idea of a little uncertainty had blown apart like a volcano spewing out endless flows of the unknown. Surveying the room, he watched the eyes of his children, their expressions, their body language — they had hope. They saw a light at the end of this dark tunnel where all he saw was emptiness.

"Answer me one thing," he said, trying to organize this new reality. "Did you ever consider Varo?"

She glanced at the door. "Daddy, you have entirely too much faith in him. We all love him, but he was never going to lead any part of this family's business. He has too many distractions, too many indulgences. From the start, he would be vulnerable to outside pressures. Our enemies would attack all his vices. I promise you, Varo will never lead this family. Now, do you want to hear how we're going to save everyone?"

When Miguel first took over Monclova Industries, he learned a valuable lesson — always be ready to adapt as new information entered the picture. That simple concept, though often difficult to follow, had served him through decades of strife. With Falcry closing in, his missiles closing even faster, and Miguel's children the only ones with an apparent plan, he did the best thing he knew how to do. He adapted.

With a nod at Sydney, he folded his arms. "Let me hear it."

# CHAPTER 23

After explaining the details, after Miguel agreed to do his part, the entire ship became involved. Lynia and Rowan spoke to the team of volunteers. They explained what would be happening and the risks. Miguel hovered at their side not only to offer his support — which, admittedly, his children did not need — but also to offer his presence as a stamp of approval. The volunteers recognized that he had given over his power. He never said a word.

Lynia did the talking. She spoke for a few minutes, enough to present everything clearly and concisely. When she finished, every member of the team watched her closely. It hit Miguel — they awaited orders. He remembered the first day after his father had died, standing before a room full of hardened miners and trying to convince them that he would save the company, save their jobs. It took several hours, but he succeeded. Here, now, in mere minutes, Lynia had won the volunteers' support, their approval. Her leadership would not be questioned.

The team lined up as she handed out assignments. Their first step — convert a portion of the ship to look like one of the private rooms.

Off to the side, Varo appeared with the man he had been assigned to bring — Mr. Slater. Together, they hunched over a computer terminal.

"Oku Slater," Rowan said, following Miguel's gaze.

Miguel nodded. "All the way from Earth. South Africa."

"When you recruited him, Sydney made sure he would side with us, too."

Mentioning Sydney sent Miguel's focus behind him — to the bridge. At the end of their family meeting, she had gone to visit

Captain Fletcher. The captain never once came out to ask Miguel if Sydney should be followed.

"I've been usurped."

Rowan chuckled, and Miguel thought his son sounded exactly like him. "Nothing so drastic. You taught us well. That's all. Maybe you didn't realize we were paying attention — well, Varo and I might not have been, but Sydney and Lynia certainly were."

As the team continued to set up things, Sydney slipped alongside her family. "Daddy, you're only hearing parts of what we've been telling you." She turned to face her father straight on. "I love you. I still need you. On Mars. I need you to keep teaching me."

But he had been listening. That was what his children kept missing. He had heard every word, every detail of what they had to say. He had swallowed it, processed it, and recognized acceptance on the horizon. They were too young to understand that a complete paradigm shift in one's life could not occur in an instant. At least, not easily.

But he tried. He would get there.

"Besides, we need you now," Sydney went on. "Our plan won't work unless we can get Falcry to agree to our terms. That requires the best negotiation we could ever dream of, and you, Daddy, are the best negotiator. Nobody can do it like you."

As a volunteer placed a table for the makeshift room, as two lighting units had been ripped from the walls to be used behind the camera, as a visi-link was connected to Mr. Slater's computer terminal and adjusted to film the set, Miguel took one final, deep breath. His eyes narrowed, his chest lifted, and he ran through Sydney's plan — particularly, the specific steps he needed to negotiate for. To his children, he said, "I'm ready."

He floated down to the set and positioned behind the table. One of the volunteers crouched under and held Miguel's feet in place. Everyone else hovered and jostled on the other side of the camera.

Sydney said, "It's important that you keep him talking for several minutes. It will take Mr. Slater time to piggyback the connection."

"Don't worry. A negotiation like this is going to give you more than enough time. It's the rest of what we want to achieve that concerns me."

She dashed in closer and kissed her father's cheek. "I have full faith in you.""

From his spot low on the floor, Mr. Slater said, "Connection's good."

Sydney pushed back behind the camera. To the left, a small monitor had been set up and it now flickered to life. Mr. Falcry's tense face appeared, and behind him, the bridge of his ship.

"Miguel, how did we come to this?" Falcry spoke with a grandfather's pity toward a wayward child. "When I brought you this opportunity, so long ago, I thought you were smart. You were brave and intelligent and, quite frankly, you had the balls to reach for greatness. Where is that man now? I'd admonish you for being greedy, but I can't believe you would do this only for money. How much more could you possibly need? Greed cannot be motivating you." He waved off any reply. "Whatever your reasons, you have tried to take more than you should, more than you deserved, and you have failed. You've made a real mess. But don't worry, I'll clean it up."

As Falcry rambled on, Miguel settled into his role, feeling the familiar warmth of negotiations surrounding him. Sydney had been right. This was his element. In his world, negotiations were ruthless, bad faith exercises in screwing over an opponent worse than he screwed back. They were not equals in a zero-sum game. They were high-stakes poker players, and Miguel always won.

He had already begun to analyze Falcry's tone, Falcry's appearance, Falcry's little facial movements — all to help navigate the proper route for success. Based on Falcry's gloating, Miguel knew the first step would be contrition — make Falcry feel even bigger.

Lowering his head slightly, Miguel said, "I owe you my sincerest apology. I've always believed I could outthink anybody. I guess I was wrong."

Twisting his tight face into the approximation of a forgiving smile, Falcry said, "We all make mistakes. Unfortunately, with a project as big as the Pathway Ring, our mistakes tend to be equally big."

"It does seem that way. That's why I'm contacting you. I want to negotiate our surrender."

"It's a simple matter, really. You do exactly what I say, or we'll destroy you."

This next step had been easy to spot coming. Falcry's overconfidence and arrogance had always been the man's blind spot. He knew he had an advantage, so it never occurred to him to consider the downside of winning.

"I'm sorry," Miguel said as if he truly regretted things, "but that threat is no longer a good one."

"Don't try to smooth talk —"

"You misunderstand me. You see, there are a couple of reasons that you will not destroy us. First off, there are too many people watching. We're close enough to the Pathway Ring that all the workers there are paying attention. That will bring you a lot of bad media coverage. I'll be dead, it won't bother me, but you may find when you return to Mars that Monclova Industries is no longer yours. The government won't want to be seen as supporting a murderer, and while you are certainly smart enough to outmaneuver that, it's the tail end of my comment that's important. Because not only is the Martian government watching, but Earth's government is watching, too. I'm not sure you'll be welcome back on your homeworld after Mars forces you to leave. Even if you don't care about how any of this will look, even if you prove better at political maneuvering — which I grant you probably are — the third reason is the most important. On board this ship are all the final experts your transit team needs. Without them, your team will be unable to build anything useful. You might be smarter than me, but I'm not a fool. I made sure that the most crucial experts came last."

Falcry held still and silent for ten long seconds. All his cockiness drained, leaving behind the nasty man Miguel knew too well. With a sharp sniff, Falcry said, "I guess we have a little to negotiate then."

Sydney threw her hands up in a silent cheer. Miguel wanted

to warn her not to celebrate too early. This had been the preamble, the easy part. The actual negotiating for all the things Sydney's plan required would be much more difficult.

# CHAPTER 24

LIKE POKER, THE ART OF NEGOTIATION had less to do with the cards and more to do with playing the opponent's character. In this case, Falcry's personality centered around distrust and control. So, Miguel opted for his biggest ask first, knowing Falcry would assume the real big asks would be hidden later in the conversation.

"I will agree to surrender and board your ship peacefully along with my daughter, Sydney, and my son, Varo, but only if you allow my other children, Lynia and Rowan, to remain behind. None of them were aware of what I attempted. They only learned of it once we left Mars. Lynia and Rowan have nothing to return to now — only shame and humiliation. Between us, I think they want to join your transit team as a way to hurt me."

Falcry agreed. Clearly, his interest was in acquiring Miguel. "When you come aboard, captain and crew must also join you. They are to set your ship on an auto-course directly to meet my transit team. Any deviation and I will fire missiles — armed ones."

Miguel then launched into a series of demands he cared nothing about. They appeared like important points — indeed, they would be very important should he return to Mars a prisoner of Falcry — but Miguel trusted his daughter. If her plan failed, none of these little details would matter anyway.

"I do have one minor request," Miguel said, sprinkling his words with a nonchalant tone to arouse Falcry's suspicions.

"I'm listening."

"My daughter, Sydney, is returning to Mars because her fiancé is still there. My son, Varo, is returning because he has nothing anywhere else. My money has spoiled him, and I suspect he will continue to live as a playboy, if he can. They have done nothing wrong. They came with me against their will. Since it takes several days to return, I ask that you allow them freedom of movement on your ship. They should not be treated like prisoners because of me."

"No." The man did not bother thinking about it. He had decided that this was part of Miguel's tricks and congratulated himself for rooting it out with such ease. Miguel saw it all in the man's narrow eyes.

Adding a crestfallen sigh, Miguel nodded his weak acceptance. "I'd ask you to reconsider, but I don't suppose I've earned that right."

"Certainly not."

"Would you at least house us in the same room? I have failed as their father. You'll be sending me to prison for a long time, no doubt, and I'd like to spend my last few days trying to repair some of the damage."

This time, Falcry paused. Good. He probably went through the conversation, trying to determine if he had been maneuvered into accepting this request. Miguel tamped down the smile threatening to creep in. Poor Falcry never had a chance. The original request worked either way. Had he allowed them freedom of movement, everything would be easier, but his men certainly understood the denial. Turning down this request, however, Falcry would look heartless. Some of his men had to be fathers, after all. If that did not motivate Falcry, however, if he chose to keep all three prisoners separated, Miguel still had options once they were aboard. In her brilliance, Sydney had accounted for all eventualities.

Thankfully, Falcry had a moment of humanity. "I can agree to that. I believe we've covered everything. My ship will reach you for transport in thirty-seven minutes. Any deviation from our agreement will result in the use of our missiles. Be ready."

Falcry cut the call.

Miguel felt the volunteer beneath the table let go of his feet, and as he rose toward the ceiling, he looked at Sydney. She looked towards Mr. Slater. In fact, everybody in the room looked toward Mr. Slater. After a few moments, the man raised his hand, and keeping his eyes on his work, he gave them a thumbs up.

The entire team erupted into cheers. They had cleared the first hurdle. Thirty-seven minutes to prepare for the next.

# CHAPTER 25

THIRTY-SEVEN MINUTES EVAPORATED IN SECONDS. Amongst the hectic and nervous preparations in the ship, Miguel sought a quiet place to wait, but those thirty-seven minutes ripped away. Before he had a chance to still his racing pulse, Falcry's ship drew alongside the *Veteran*. It would not take long for a docking tube to be connected.

The only reprieve from this mounting tension came when the conglomerate of metals sent to jumpstart the Pathway Ring finally entered. Briefly, all activity on both ships ceased. Miguel pictured the equally hectic activity aboard the Ring as engineers, technicians, managers, and all manner of employee rushed to perform their individual duties, adding their small contribution to history. He could hear the held breaths around him and imagined the same occurred aboard the *Horizon* as well. Everybody watched that enormous hunk of ore and metal crawl into the Ring.

A flash of suns. The space within the Ring flooded with light. Miguel shielded his eyes, squinting as others turned away. Hushed gasps filled the ship.

When the dark of space returned, when the ghosting images in every eye dimmed, tensions returned. But Miguel sensed a growing excitement, too. The Ring had not been destroyed. Reports flew across space suggesting that the jumpstart had worked. Minutes later — precious minutes nobody could afford to wait upon — further reports arrived. The wormhole had been stabilized on this end. The next step toward an unfathomable future had succeeded. People smiled as they prepared for the dangers ahead.

What had started with a desperate conversation in Miguel's

home that interrupted — no, *ruined* — his daughter's birthday, now filled hundreds of people with a new reality. Soon, all people on Mars and Earth and the Moon would discover this shift. Everything would change. Eventually. For the moment, though, lives continued as before. Only those on the *Veteran* and the *Horizon* were truly changed. For some of them, an uncertain and deadly future awaited.

But none of that altered Miguel's future. Sitting in one of the private rooms — a real one without a visi-link camera, a computer hacker, and an audience — he worked out final strategies. Each step ahead required careful consideration — what he would say to Falcry given different situations, how he should handle the different scenarios that might arise, what limits he placed upon accepting certain reactions. Unlike the gambling of a negotiation, this work was more akin to chess. He thought over his opponent's possible moves and developed countermoves for each one.

Outside the room, he heard the voices of his children. His daughters commanded the ship, answering questions and ordering tasks like a seasoned professional. Varo's laughter resonated through the walls as he charmed the team, lightening their mood during this stressful moment. Even Rowan helped in his own way. His deep murmurs drifted by Miguel's closed door, and though Miguel could not make out the words, he suspected his son offered theological answers for those seeking reassurances about their survival.

Miguel should have been proud. He was. But rather than electrifying his blood with joy at the wonderous adults they had become, he soured at his failures. They had not become great children because of him but rather in spite of him. Annalia had done the real work. He could stand upon the old, foundational belief that while she raised and guided the children, he had provided the house, the food, the money that made her work possible — but that structure did not feel so sturdy anymore.

A knock on the door as it opened, and Lynia poked her head in. He marveled as she entered. So beautiful, so strong, not a hint of fear, only an eagerness, an eagerness for what was to come.

"It's not fair." His voice cracked. "I feel like I've only met you, the real you, and now you're here to say I have to go. We have to split apart."

"Only for about ten years. Twenty if things turn out harder than we expect."

A bitter smile graced his lips. Scratching his stubbled cheek, he said, "I know I haven't earned the right to give fatherly advice. I do want to give you a warning, though. Because I'm starting to see all of you for the first time, and in you, my sweet Lynia, I'm seeing too much of myself. That same adventuring spirit which makes you so powerful can isolate you, too."

"I'll be careful."

"You don't even know what I'm talking about. But that's okay. At your age, the realities of living a long life are impossible to know." A loud clank of metal on metal announced another step completed in hooking up the docking tube. "You never really knew your grandparents. My father died long before you were born, and my mother died when you were only two. Sydney would remember her. Maybe Rowan. But I wish you had a chance to talk with her. She was always better at this kind of thing."

Lynia's stoic expression suggested she tried to focus on what he said, but he knew he had muddled the whole thing.

"When I was young," he said, hoping to salvage the moment, "my mother worked to keep our home together and keep me healthy. Not easy on a struggling planet like Mars. Dust coated everything, the air couldn't be trusted, simple things on Earth like plumbing had to be built from scratch, and complex things like gravity had to be discovered from scraps of nothing. She hated it. She hated Mars. But more than the struggle, she hated how it changed my father. Later in my life, after he had died, she often said that the mining business consumed him. I thought she meant that he devoted everything to it, and that was true, but she once said it more explicitly. She said, *Those mines ate him up and didn't even leave behind the bones.*" He paused as he felt tears welling from his chest. A few breaths to regain his composure. Then: "These last days with you and your siblings — I see that Mars consumed me, too. I've lost you to the planet, to this Pathway Ring project, to my own ego. I even lost your mother."

"You haven't lost us. We're still here."

"When you're older, you might understand. For now, I can only warn you — don't do what I have done. Don't continue this family flaw. If you have people you care about, be there for them. You don't want to be like me, discovering too late that I never really knew my own children."

Lynia put out her hand. "Don't worry. I'll lead this team well, and I will return in ten years. With a little luck, maybe sooner."

She listened, and that was all Miguel could hope for. He prayed that someday she would understand, too. But her pitying gaze told him that she thought he panicked knowing that he only had minutes left. He didn't feel that way, but perhaps it was true.

He bit his lip and shook her hand. Her skin scraped against his palm, and her biceps flexed a bit as she gripped his hand tight. When she released and turned to leave, he said, "Wait. I have something for you."

She rotated to face him, and for a flash, he saw the little girl she had once been — except he now knew that he only saw her as that image. He didn't know who she had been. He paused, so many conflicting emotions filling his heart, his chest, his head.

Another clank of metal. Hovering at the door, she looked at him expectantly, and he realized he had told her that he had something to give her. But he had only said that to stop her. "Ten years is too long," he whispered.

"What?"

He couldn't bring himself to say it again. Instead, he reached around his neck and removed his necklace with the *M* pendant his father had made from Martian ore. As he handed it over, his throat swelled. "Remember your family." He strained out the words, managing to hold back his tears.

Pushing off the door, she soared across the tiny room and wrapped her arms around him. She held him tighter than she had shaken his hand, and he swore he heard her sniffling. His eyes blurred as he buried his face in her neck. Far too quickly, though, she kissed his cheek and pulled away, taking the necklace with her. A final smile and she left the room.

Before Miguel could recompose, Rowan entered. "We've got confirmation the docking tube is secure. They said to cross in five minutes."

Miguel tried to nod, tried to speak in a normal voice, tried anything to stop the eruption rising within. Rowan paused, clearly concerned. That look set Miguel's heart open. He coughed a short cry.

"I'm sorry, son. I'm sorry I never got to know you. I'm sorry I let all these years go by without seeing you, hearing you, without being a good father."

Shrinking back as if from a diseased man, Rowan said, "You were fine. No need to apologize."

"There's no more time. You've got to know that when I look at you now, I see a bright man, a thoughtful man, someone who is trying to be so much better than I ever was." Tears streamed down his face.

"Please, you've got to get ready to go."

"That's exactly what I must do. Listen to me. Understand that you are every bit as special and smart as a father could hope for. You have followed Shendo like I never could."

"That's not true."

"It is. It is. You called me out, and you were right. I never even read the book. Not all the way through. But you —"

"I'm not Shendo. I'm nothing. I've read the books, but I've read from all sorts of religions. I've studied them, yet I don't know what's right. I've been trying to hear what the Lord is saying, but no clear answer has come."

"It will. I know it will." Gasping, Miguel clutched the edge of the table and used it to drop to his knees. Though he bounced off the floor, he managed to stay low. Another wave of distraught tears ripped through him. "Watch over your sister. She's strong, but she needs more guidance than you. I've seen that much. And forgive me." Another wracking gasp. "Forgive me for all of it. You are the better man. Follow the path before you. Be strong. Be brave. Please, please forgive me."

With his head bowed before his son, Miguel shook as all the

great years of business and failed years of family caught up to him. He closed his eyes, knowing Rowan felt uncomfortable and unsure. He again begged for his son's forgiveness.

When the thought struck that Rowan would leave in silence, that Miguel had failed his son yet again, a tentative touch brushed his head. Miguel held his breath. The touch grew heavier until Rowan had placed his entire hand upon Miguel.

"I forgive you," Rowan whispered.

Another emotion blasted out from Miguel's chest — relief. Joy and happiness slipped in, too. He covered his face, embarrassed by this outburst but unable to stop from smiling. Straightening up, he said, "Thank you, son. I … I love you."

Rowan looked at his hand, then at his father. "Sure. Love you, too."

The door opened. Varo glanced in, paused, shook his head to dismiss it all, and said, "Time to go."

# CHAPTER 26

THE ACCORDION DOCKING TUBE stretching between the *Veteran* and the *Horizon* had been checked over several times before and after pressurization. Little more than oval rings sheathed in plastic, the slightest tear would cause a disaster. Miguel guessed Falcry wouldn't mind such a tragedy other than the headache of forms to fill out and the possibility that the death of Miguel Monclova might be blamed on him. Standing at the *Veteran* side of the tube, Miguel hoped that would be enough to prevent any "accidents".

With Sydney and Varo behind him, Miguel led the way across. Captain Fletcher and his crew had already boarded the *Horizon* after they assisted in securing the docking tube. Knowing they had used the tube with success earlier should have been reassuring, yet Miguel couldn't help imagining all the ways Falcry might double-cross him and his family.

Drifting through the tube, he peeked off to the side. Though warped by the plastic, he still had a good view of the Pathway Ring. He wanted to reach out, touch the tube, stop his momentum, and simply stare at the engineering marvel. He wanted to dream about what it would feel like to travel through a wormhole, to emerge in some unknown section of the universe, to discover everything anew. But that was not for him. This was as close as he would ever get.

He faced forward and concentrated on the airlock at the end. The Ring was no longer his. Monclova was no longer his. He had work to do. Work that would protect the lives of his children far better than all his company or his money ever had.

After entering the airlock and cycling through the pressurization process, the inner-door to the *Horizon* opened.

Falcry stood between several soldiers armed with stun-prods. He wore a business suit and a condescending smirk.

"Hold still, please," one soldier said as another approached with a handheld scanner. She ran the device over each arrival, checked the readouts, and gave an affirmative grunt to a third soldier.

That one — the name Yoon on his breast pocket — faced Falcry. "No weapons, sir. All clear."

As he spoke, another soldier collected their visi-links. No connecting with Mars allowed. With that task completed, the soldiers returned to a line and stood at attention.

"Well, well." Falcry took one step forward, keeping his hands at his sides. "I never thought this was how we'd end up, but life is always filled with surprise. I never thought I'd have worked with you in the first place. In fact, when your name came up, I laughed. Monclova Industries? The failing mining company? I thought the Secretary was joking. Yet years later and here we are. Looks like I was right to question working with you — just not for the right reasons." He turned to the soldier. "Major Yoon, have our guests taken to their room."

"Yes, sir." Yoon gestured for Miguel, Sydney, and Varo to follow him. Two more soldiers brought up the rear.

While Miguel and his children floated through the metal corridors, the soldiers had mag-boots that clicked as they latched onto the floor and clacked as they released with each step. Security cameras had been posted at either end of the corridor, and all the doors were unmarked. Apparently, the soldiers were expected to memorize the ship's layout. Sydney had warned that would be the case, and Miguel wished they had been given enough time to memorize the ship, too. But she also said not to worry, that she had it figured out.

They were deposited in a room designed for one person. A single bed with harness straps, a flat piece of metal attached to the wall for a desk, three containers stacked and locked down — cramped, but at least they were together. Varo swung an arm through one of the harness straps to claim the bed. Miguel bounced toward the desk, nestling one knee under to keep in place. Sydney, however, required movement. She pushed off one wall, reached for the next, pushed back, and in that way, achieved zero-g pacing.

Miguel wished he could ease her nerves, but he understood how futile any attempt would be. His daughter led this operation based on her own strategies. She had to rely on everybody doing their part as she had envisioned it, and the consequences of failure would devastate her. He had been in her shoes many times. The fate of the company, the fate of the family, the fate of the employees and their families — all rode upon her not only being right but also being able to get others to perform properly.

Worse — she had nothing to do now. They had to wait for the *Veteran* to be searched for any of Fletcher's crewmembers, wait for the docking tube to be released and retracted, wait for the autopilot to start the *Veteran* on its way, and wait for the *Horizon's* engines to kick in. Until all of that happened, Sydney was stuck.

She checked her watch.

Varo said, "Relax. It's going fine."

"Shh. We don't know if they have surveillance in here."

"I'm not giving anything away. I'm saying that Lynia is tough. She'll have no problem dealing with anybody."

Miguel said, "None of us will. You both have nothing fear. Falcry's suspicions won't ever include what we're going to do."

"Daddy, I expect Varo to be an idiot, but you know better than to talk about this out loud."

"The room is not under surveillance. It's clearly an officer's room, and Falcry had not planned on using it. He wanted to send all of us to the brig. I have no doubt."

Sydney scowled. "They've had plenty of time to install a microphone or something. Or maybe they're simply listening on inter-ship comms."

"Then they catch us. All that you have planned is now set in motion and, without some way to communicate with the *Veteran*, none of us can stop it. Don't drive yourself crazy finding problems where none exist."

"That's all fine, but still —"

"I'll speak quieter. Will that make you feel better?"

Sydney's stressed expression did not match her gentle nod.

Miguel went on, "I agree with Varo. We can trust Lynia. It won't be easy for her to take over Falcry's team, to convince them to join her, but she can do it."

"Join her? Was it ever your plan to have them join you?"

"No, but I thought —"

"It's not our plan, either. The only difference is that we've convinced Falcry otherwise."

Varo said, "It's why Lynia is the perfect one to be out there. She can always make the hard call." To Sydney: "You remember the suitcase incident?"

"What's that?" Miguel asked, a small voice in his head suggested he didn't want to know.

Jolting up — which sent his body spinning until he could stabilize off the ceiling — Varo said, "This happened long ago. I think Lynia was ten."

"Twelve," Sydney said, her lack of enthusiasm for the tale bothering Miguel even more.

"Twelve? Really? Well, whatever it was, this one day, she gets in a fight with Mom over something stupid."

"It wasn't stupid. She wanted to visit where Daddy worked."

"Quit correcting me."

"Then tell the story correctly."

Rolling his eyes as he pulled on the harness to return to bed, Varo huffed. "Twelve years old, wants to visit Daddy's office, Mom says no. But Lynia doesn't like being told what she can and can't do. So, she throws a fit and storms into her room. The rest of us go about our day. Dinnertime comes around, Mom calls us, and we all come. Except Lynia. This launches us into a four-day search for her involving the police."

Miguel said, "How could I not have heard about this?"

But he knew. He remembered coming home from a month-long trip belowground and the weird behavior at the dinner table. He remembered later that night when Annalia said she had done her job keeping it out of the media.

"The point isn't you in all this, it's Lynia. We eventually found out that she got it in her head to climb into a security container and have herself shipped to your office. Only problem was that she had no idea how to mail a package properly. The post service got the container but couldn't figure out where to send it. So, for four days, they shoved it in a warehouse corner. Lynia is sitting there and realizes something in her plan has gone wrong. She's not moving anywhere. She tries to get out, but there are containers stacked on top of hers, and she's not strong enough. She's stuck. She's also hungry and needs to go to the bathroom."

Sydney said, "Will you get to the end? Please."

"We've got time to kill. Might as well make it entertaining." To Miguel: "There were a few gaps in the container's corners. It wasn't much of a security container. She peed out one of them. On the second day, she notices rats have squeezed in. On the third day, she turned a hairpin into a weapon and killed one of the rats. Drank its blood and ate it raw. Killed another on the fourth day. The stink of urine finally got noticed and a worker discovered her."

"You understand now, Daddy? Lynia is brave, smart, and ruthless. But none of that will matter if she's dead before she reaches the transit ship."

As Miguel digested the story, he wanted to pace the room, too. Instead, he asked, "How much longer?"

Sydney checked her watch. "An hour, probably." She patted her necklace. The soldiers had been preoccupied with scanning for weapons, nobody bothered to look at her pendant — a datapod provided by Mr. Slater. "Get ready. We're going to save this family."

# CHAPTER 27

When the engines rumbled to life, Miguel wanted to mark the moment, even if only with a simple group huddle. He'd always run his business that way. Before every big meeting, every milestone earned, every promotion or valuable change to the company, he wrote a speech, proposed a toast, sent a gift, or slapped a back. Something to show appreciation. But this was not his company anymore. He had to defer to the new way of things and allow his daughter to develop traditions of her own.

He looked to Sydney and waited for her decision. She had slipped close to the door and listened intently. Once satisfied, she pushed off, snapping her fingers at Miguel. He shifted his weight, sending his body in a gentle coast until he reached the position Sydney had just abandoned.

With one ear on the door and an eye on his daughter, Miguel became a guard. He snickered. On the other side, a soldier stood guard as well. They both guarded against each other.

Groaning, Varo disentangled from the harness and gave way, allowing his sister to work. She moved fast, running her hand along the wall by the bed. Miguel noticed the slight tremor in her fingers. That was a good sign. She should be nervous. That energy would keep her focused and aware.

When her hand traced the outline of the wall panel she had sought, she snapped her fingers and reached back without looking.

"Not very polite," Varo said, sounding more like sibling ribbing then true complaining. From his pocket, he produced an expensive set of vintage earphones. Though digital, the headset used some ancient analog tech — more for show than function.

Removing the padded cushion, he slipped out a large cup from each side.

This all followed Mr. Slater's instructions. The cups were made of a soft material that originally vibrated to amplify sound. Decorative now, but still authentic, they could also be pressed against a flat surface to create suction. After Varo passed them over, Sydney placed one on the top left corner and one on the top right, pushed them down, and in seconds removed the wall panel with ease.

She glanced back at Miguel. He put his ear to the door. Hearing nothing, he motioned for her to continue.

She hunched over the open panel. With her datapod, her bare hands, and — apparently taking a page from Lynia's brutal experiences — a hairpin, she got to work. Miguel could not see her progress from his angle, but he knew what she was supposed to be doing. Mr. Slater had given his explicit instructions to all three of them — in case one did not make it this far. If all went as expected, she would be able to connect the datapod into the ship's main data line. Once achieved, the datapod would instantly upload several programs designed by Mr. Slater. The passwords he had hacked during Miguel's negotiation provided all the authentication the illegal program needed. The ship should never know.

Several of the team had suggested Slater create a virus, but he dismissed the idea. After all, if things played out as hoped, Miguel, Sydney, and Varo needed an operable craft to fly back to Mars. The downside to not using a virus — it took more time.

Sydney cursed twice as something metal clanged against the inside of the wall. The sound triggered Miguel to push his ear against the door harder. Holding his breath, trying to slow his heartbeat, he closed his eyes and listened.

Nothing.

After three more interminable minutes, Sydney backed away with her arms out as if the merest vibration might destroy her work. She waved for Varo to bring the wall panel. Using slow and gentle movements, she eased it back in place. Peeling the suction cups off, she ran her fingers around the edges, pushing in at certain points.

To Varo, she said, "It feels loose to me. Be careful."

Varo rolled into the harness, pressing his back against the wall panel. "It'll be fine. I'll be fine. All I've got to do is sleep. I can do that."

Sydney checked the time. They had to wait until the *Veteran* would have reached Falcry's transit team on auto-pilot. Soon after, Lynia would board the ship, and her people would begin their takeover — violently, if necessary. Sydney and Miguel had to achieve the next step ahead of news of that takeover. A narrow window, risky, but as long they started before Lynia boarded the transit ship, they thought it should work.

Miguel watched her, admired her. Every passing minute should have raised his fear. Instead, he grew more comfortable with the idea of her leading Monclova Industries. And with her getting married to his most-capable employee, she would be in a great position to take the Monclova family into the future.

"Get ready," she said.

Miguel shifted to face the door head on. "Whenever you say."

Silence filled the cabin. Even Varo had the sense to stay quiet. Then, Sydney floated next to Miguel and brushed his shoulder. "Okay."

She opened the door, and as the guard turned her head, Miguel braced his legs against the jamb throwing all his weight behind a punch to the nose. Bubbles of blood scattered into the air — some moving steady until they splattered on the walls; others spinning in place like red raindrops frozen in time. The shock of the attack gave Sydney seconds enough to get behind and lock the guard's head in the crook of her arm. Miguel wondered where she learned a sleeper hold but decided best not to interrupt.

The guard went limp. Together, father and daughter pulled the unconscious soldier into the room. They sat her in the only chair and locked her hands with her own handcuffs.

Varo's harness had a pillow sewn into it. With an impatient gesture, Sydney had her brother rip the casing off. She tore it in half — part of it tied as a blindfold; part of it as a gag.

Hissing as he spoke, Varo said, "Why are we doing this in here? I thought I was supposed to just sleep and block the wall."

"Safer this way," Sydney said. "If you get discovered or she wakes up and gets loose, they'll all assume you were left to guard her. Nobody will start poking at the walls. We leave you alone in here, it looks suspicious."

"No, it looks like I'm incompetent and you left me behind. I'm okay with that."

"Get okay with this."

Without another word, she pushed off, leaving the room and not glancing back. No problem, though. Miguel made sure to follow close behind.

They drifted through the middle of the corridor, silent as clouds, always keeping one hand trailing against a wall in case they needed to make an abrupt shift. At doorways, they paused to listen. The click-clack of magboots made it easy to know if a soldier approached. Though the large ship contained three levels and numerous twisting paths, Sydney had memorized the routes she required. Miguel was glad for that. As he got older, his ability to remember that many details in such short time under heavy pressure had dimmed.

She led them down a drop tube to the bottom level and toward the back. The ship design included a separate regulator line for the engines. If the main data line was damaged or corrupted, control of the ship could be maintained through this auxiliary. This bit of knowledge came via Mr. Slater's assistant, Ms. Rhukov — apparently a fan of ship design, holding a particular fascination with military ships.

As they neared the final turn, Miguel knew what to expect. He had not memorized the entire path, but he knew the endgame. A short corridor led to a thick door and into the engine room. On either side of the door, tiny spaces had been allotted — one as a limited office, mostly for engineers to file reports; one as a breakroom. Both rooms bore a single, clear wall looking onto the corridor.

According to Ms. Rhukov, they did not need to enter the engine room, but rather, their best access point for the auxiliary data line was in the ceiling of this corridor. The lines then cut toward the outer walls of the ship, running straight to the bridge. Sydney needed to remove a ceiling panel, crawl inside, attach a datapod, and slip back out before anybody noticed.

One final check behind and she pushed up to the ceiling. She counted the ceiling panels until she hit number five. Using the makeshift suction cups once more, she worked at removing the panel.

Miguel watched her until he remembered he needed to be the lookout. Moving toward the corner, he tried to listen to both the hall ahead and the ceiling behind. He glanced back over his shoulder.

One of the suction cups slipped, and the ceiling panel tumbled out of her arms. It floated and flipped at a sharp angle, hitting the clear wall of the breakroom, then cracking on the floor. Shards of panel blasted into different directions. A second later, clacking magboots grew louder along with mumbled voices speaking into comms.

"We have to go," Miguel said.

"I'm already up here. I can finish this, first."

"No time."

"I'm in charge."

He wanted to argue or grab her ankle and yank her down, but she was right. It was her call, and the longer he tried to change her mind, the more time they spent in the open. With a grunt, she lifted halfway into the ceiling.

But it was too late. Three soldiers rounded into the hallway.

One robust soldier thrust Miguel against the wall. Another did what Miguel had previously considered — grabbed Sydney's ankle and yanked her down. Much harder than Miguel would have done. The third soldier tried to cuff Sydney, but she put up a fight. The soldier backhanded her and pulled out a knife.

"Hey!" Miguel tried to move, but he couldn't break the hold on him.

The soldier that had brought her down from the ceiling now turned to Miguel. He blocked view of Sydney, but sounds of struggle filled the hall. The soldier had perfect teeth and a vicious grin. He punched Miguel in the side.

As Miguel doubled over, the soldier said, "I'll take care of the old man. There should be another prisoner around here. Go find him."

The first soldier saluted and click-clacked away. Miguel figured if he would ever get an opening, this was it. While Perfect Teeth thought he had all under control, Miguel kicked off the wall, burying his shoulder into the bastard's gut. He heard a satisfying groan, but the man didn't stumble back. Of course, not. He had mag-boots. A blow to the back slammed Miguel into the floor. He bounced off, heard the click of a single mag-boot release, and floated up to meet a vicious kicked into the wall.

"Daddy, don't resist." Sydney had been forced over her knees with her arms locked behind.

Miguel attempted to right himself, find air in his angry lungs, and haul off a hook to the face. He never finished the first step. Perfect Teeth rushed in — *click clack click clack* — and threw an elbow into his chin. Miguel's teeth jammed together. The inside of his mouth spewed bubbles of blood. A thick hand grabbed his shoulder, keeping him from rising to the ceiling. The hand pressed him to the floor.

That should have ended it. In a different circumstance, Miguel would have stopped. But Lynia counted on him. Sydney counted on him. They probably didn't know it, but he did. Even if their faith in him only lived deep in their marrow, he believed it was there. All he had to do was be the man he should have been throughout their lives. A man of honor to his children, of integrity. A man who would sacrifice a lucrative business deal in order to sing *Happy Birthday*. That man would do anything to buy as much time for his daughters as possible.

Miguel bellowed a raging cry and clasped the nearest part of Perfect Teeth he could find — the man's leg. He bashed his fist into the knee. Twice. Hoped to break the bone but only managed to break his own fingers.

"You old shit," Perfect Teeth said, unholstering a weapon hidden beneath his shirt.

"Wait," Sydney said. "You don't have to do that. We give up."

"You crazy?" the other soldier said. "You smuggled a gun onboard? Why? You can't shoot in here. Hit the wrong thing and we're all dead. Just stun them and —"

Perfect Teeth shot.

A flash of light. Sydney and the other soldier ducked. The bullet dug into Miguel's gut, tearing through intestines, sending bile into the hallway. Miguel screamed. He clutched his stomach, blood seeping through his fingers in little floating globs.

The other soldier jaw quivered. "Shit. You could've killed us. You could've … that's it. We're taking them to the bridge. These are Falcry's prisoners. You want to explain to him why they died? Why you shot a gun in this ship? Just stop, okay? Let Falcry decide what to do."

Perfect Teeth shrugged but holstered his weapon.

Miguel looked to Sydney and forced a smile. It'll be okay, he tried to say. But already, the soldiers had him moving through the corridors, a trail of blood balls forming behind.

# CHAPTER 28

MIGUEL WAITED FOR HIS BODY TO SLIP INTO SHOCK, for adrenaline to brace his muscles, for anything that would cut off the messages of pain to his head. That glorious relief only arrived in erratic bursts. During those brief moments, he saw the corridor float by, heard the grumpy groans of the soldiers, and Sydney's shaking hand guiding him by the elbow.

Miguel knew that his daughter's fears no longer revolved around the plan or their failure to secure the backup contingency at the engines. They had accomplished all they could. It was up to the others now. The agonizing jolts his gut produced promised he had no more to contribute.

But he had to admit that he experienced a slight pleasure in Sydney's fear. It was for him. She actually cared. Despite all his shortcomings, she still found space in her heart for him. If only dying had not been the cost for that moment of joy.

At some point, they had entered the bridge — a sleek, well-maintained, and well-designed control center. He heard Sydney's repeated begging, but his brain could not decipher her words, only the tone. Yet shortly after — or perhaps far later — he felt a sharp sting in his arm. The pain receded. Not entirely, but enough to become aware.

He and Sydney and Varo all had straps tied around their thighs that secured into the floor, forcing them to their knees. Two soldiers held stun weapons aimed at their heads. Perfect Teeth stood in front of Falcry, gesturing in broad forceful movements. Falcry did not appear pleased.

"What about Private Han?"

Not happy with the shift in focus, Perfect Teeth said, "She's been taken to the infirmary."

Sydney said, "So you do have an infirmary. Take my father there, now. He needs serious medical attention."

"Open your mouth once more, and you'll need —"

Falcry raised a couple fingers. "Now, now. No need for all these threats." He strolled away from Perfect Teeth, his magboots clicking softer than the soldiers. He crouched in front of Miguel. "I knew you would be mad when I took over your company, that was obvious, but you had to expect it was going to happen. Looking at your response, you evidently planned for it. Such an unnecessary route to go. We could both have prospered. Your family —"

"You know nothing about my family."

Falcry sauntered back to the control panel. Displays lit up with a clear view of the Pathway Ring and the transit ship *Pioneer* heading towards it. "Soon, my people will go through the Ring, and all this will be behind us."

Varo smirked. "Don't be so sure."

Miguel cringed and hoped Falcry would assume it came from pain. Varo's yabbering mouth might spoil their plans. But Miguel had nothing to fear. Falcry's arrogance blinded the man. He uttered a condescending laugh as he wagged his finger at Varo.

"My whole life, I didn't have enough money, didn't go to the right schools. Brats like you wasted their days with lust and drink, never did and never would amount to anything — you are corrupted. It happened to your father, too. He came from humble beginnings, yet the attitude of the snob poisoned him against his own. Only one generation and his children are the worst examples of this." He whipped his head towards Miguel. "You talk of family? Look at your son. You've allowed him to become nothing but a waste."

"Maybe I am nothing," Varo said. "That won't change the fact that you're going to spend the rest your days in jail."

Damn. Miguel observed the change on Falcry's face. The man had started thinking, started questioning Varo's boasts, Varo's confidence. Miguel wanted to glance at Sydney, gauge her expression, but he didn't dare. The fact that she said nothing told him enough — she would not betray any reaction.

Pivoting to the display screens, Falcry pushed his newly concerned face in close. "Private LaMotte, contact the *Pioneer* now."

A pause. "No reply, sir."

"Try again."

Another pause.

"Why aren't they answering?"

The angular face of a stark woman appeared on the screen — Lynia. She sat in the commander's chair of the *Pioneer's* bridge. "Mr. Falcry, your crew is dead. Only two were disloyal and offered to join us, but we didn't trust them. Our replacements have already boarded the *Pioneer,* so we have left your dead in the *Veteran.* Please see that they make it home to their families. I would see to it myself, but we'll be busy going through the Pathway Ring. We claim it on behalf of Monclova Industries and the Monclova family."

Falcry tried to speak in a constrained voice, but she cut the call.

Puckering his little face, he pounded his fist against the desk console. "You are all stupid. When will you realize that I am smarter than you. I am smarter, and I am steps ahead, and more than any of you, I am willing to do whatever it takes to win." Shaking a finger towards a soldier at the wall display, he said, "Mr. Foster, arm the missiles and fire."

"Yes, sir."

Miguel and his family kept quiet. They watched the display screen report the release of two armed missiles. The plan had been for Lynia to get through the Pathway Ring without trouble. Only after she had crossed over would Sydney reveal the truth to Falcry. But Varo had ruined that. Now, they had to rely on their contingency plan. With the second contingency of controlling the engines no longer an option, this had to work.

Twinges of pain punched out from Miguel's gut. His fingers felt sticky as if slipped in ooze and his belly felt filled up with sloshing liquid. It probably was. He suspected blood pooled within him, his heart unknowingly pumping him closer to death. Grinding his teeth, he watched the graphics display as the two missiles neared their targets.

"Intercept in thirty seconds," Mr. Foster said.

"You see?" Falcry's feet clicked as he walked back and forth in front of the Monclovas. "Your daughter and your employees have wasted their lives. They won't make it to the Pathway Ring."

Miguel's vision darkened. Time disappeared. But his head snapped up, and he saw on the display fifteen seconds left. Worry threatened his heart while the rest of him oscillated between pain and numbness.

At ten seconds, he heard Sydney choke down a cry. Miguel reached over and squeezed her hand. He leaned his head toward Varo, but his son showed no fear, no concern. Varo smiled.

"What?" Falcry said.

Miguel checked the displays. As if possessed, the missiles diverted course. They arched away in wide loops until meeting each other, colliding in a massive explosion both bright and silent. The flames died out fast in the vacuum leaving debris to float forever.

As Falcry uttered one curse after another, as Sydney eased back with the knowledge that Mr. Slater's plan had succeeded, Miguel watched while his youngest daughter guided her ship of two hundred souls through the Pathway Ring.

"What did you do?" Falcry's face turned bright red.

Sydney said, "Hacked your ship and took control of your missiles. I thought that was obvious. Now you need to get my father medical attention."

"You think you've accomplished anything? I'll put together another transit team. I'll send them through the Ring, and they'll end up somewhere else. It'll be a race between our two teams."

"Nobody's going to finance another team for you."

"Believe what you want, but I am much smarter than you and much more determined. I'm also a bastard. So, I'm going to let your father die. Because I can."

"Incoming communication, sir," someone called out.

"Not now."

"Um, sir, it's Senator Bashir."

Though Miguel winced with another stab from his gut, he

managed to warp it into a smile. With equal pleasure, Sydney said, "You better get that. You're about to find out how smart and determined we are. Also, that I can be a bitch, if I have to."

The sickened flush overcoming Falcry warmed Miguel's chilling skin.

"Mr. Falcry, it seems you failed to send your team through." Senator Bashir did not get many opportunities to gloat — too much compromise in government — but clearly, he wanted to savor this day.

"Yes, well, there were some unforeseen disruptions. But don't worry. We will still continue as planned."

"I don't think so. My people have been going through your reports, particularly taking notice of your financials. I'm told the numbers are not adding properly. It seems that you've been untruthful in your accounting practices."

Of course, Senator Bashir's own accountings were far from clean. In fact, record of Bashir's skimming now showed Falcry as the culprit — thank you, Mr. Slater. Falcry knew better than to say anything. Miguel wished the man would, though. He would have loved to see that.

Senator Bashir continued, "I've also been in contact with Mr. Tephen Hilt who has made it clear that the employees of Monclova Industries refuse to work for a man that has seized the company without any regard to their well-being. That may be fine on Earth, but it is not the Martian way. Now, according to my records, Lieutenant Camden is the highest-ranking officer aboard your ship. Is that correct?"

From deeper within the bridge, a voice said, "Yes, sir. I'm here."

"Excellent. Lieutenant Camden, please arrest Mr. Falcry as he will be facing trial when he returns to Mars. Both the Pathway Ring Project and Monclova Industries are now under the control of Sydney Monclova. Please obey her orders as you would have done so under Mr. Falcry. I trust she will be a more pleasant person to work with."

"Yes, sir. Right away."

With swift, practiced motions, Perfect Teeth had Mr. Falcry

down and cuffed in seconds. Other soldiers released Miguel and his children.

"Thank you," Sydney said. "Now get my father medical attention."

But Miguel shook his head. He lifted one hand to his daughter — slow and weak. He shivered, unable to rid himself of the cold digging deep into his marrow.

She dropped close to his face. She smelled like he remembered from her early days, those days when she brightened at the sight of him arriving home. "Daddy? Hang on. We'll get you help."

Too much he wanted to say. Too much he wanted to accomplish still. She needed to know that he did not fear his future or the future of the family. She had saved the company — he knew that. Lynia would lead her people to build the other end of the Pathway Ring, and one day, it would all work out. No, he didn't need to tell her any of that. What he needed to do, what he should have done so long ago, raced up his spine and into his brain, barely outpacing the deadly chill.

Touching her cheek, he said, "I'm proud of you."

He closed his eyes.

# ZILL GRACE

ZILL EMPTIED THE PITCHER OF WATER and finished her glass. Even when she planned to give a full lecture, she often experienced a lot of dry mouth. This lecture certainly had not been planned.

"That is an impressive tale," Chovar Monclova said, smoothing his pants as he digested all that he had heard. "But you must admit that it's hard to believe. I accept the notion of Mars and Earth, but that's only because I know the Pathway Ring as more than a story from long ago."

"True. For the average person, there's no real evidence that such places ever existed. As you've pointed out, though, you and I have access to other information. We know the Pathway Ring is more than legend. We know that Lynia Monclova and her people kept diaries and journals and recordings. No information pre-dates that. If we didn't come from Mars, if we didn't start by going through the Pathway Ring, there would be a fossil record or ruins or some other evidence of our existence on Miguel long before Lynia. But there's nothing."

"Except the Dahtien."

"Nothing human."

Chovar stroked his chin. "What happened to Sydney and Tephen and Varo?"

She shrugged. "No way to know. Our history doesn't really begin until Lynia flew through the Ring. We only know what she and the original settlers knew. They never had contact again with that other galaxy."

"But if I order the new Pathway Ring to be used, we would reconnect with that galaxy, with Mars and Earth — if they truly exist."

"Maybe. Doubtful, though."

"Oh?"

Zill sipped more water. "It's been generations upon generations since Lynia left there. Assuming Sydney succeeded with Monclova Industries, it's conceivable that she would keep the Pathway Ring open for a couple decades. Eventually, though, when nobody ever returned, they would have to assume that Lynia failed."

"She didn't, though. That is, we all didn't."

"They don't know that. And keeping that machine running would cost a lot. The best we can hope for is that they had organized another transit team and tried again. If that team succeeded faster than we did — and didn't suffer the unfortunate outcomes we did or worse — then perhaps there is a robust Ring system in place by now."

Chovar sat straighter. "Then we might be able to connect with that."

"That's a big *might*. There's also the tech issue. When Lynia came through with her people, they were chosen for their expertise in specific fields to build the Ring in this galaxy. We started our existence here with a tremendous amount of knowledge, but also a tremendous amount of gaps. Things important for the building of a society, a civilization, weren't always important for maintaining a camp of construction workers. We've had to rediscover a lot."

"Yes, but math is math. The answers don't change."

"But what we choose to do with them changes. If Lynia's recordings are factual, then back on Mars they had DVs to drive them around. We have the capability to do the same thing. But we don't. Why?"

"Because we've designed our cities to be close-knit systems."

"Exactly. We rely on other methods of transportation, and we've built our cities to benefit from those methods — including walking. Having a DV system is a waste for us. If you want or need a car, you'll drive one. Or, in your case, you'll pay for somebody to drive it. But that idea holds true for all our developments. We are a different type of human. We've made different choices because of our history — a history that deviated from our originators on Mars and Earth."

"That is a lot to consider."

Zill chuckled. "It might even be true."

"That's not amusing." Chovar's face darkened. "Why would you say that?"

"Oh, I don't mean that I lied. Only that we're relying entirely on the memories Lynia recorded in her final years and Rowan recorded at the height of his ... well ... more verbose rantings. Even with the scant accounts from others who were there, so much has been lost over the centuries. If you think I've painted a complete picture, then you're mistaken. I'm just good at filling in the gaps with educated guesses. There are, however, a lot of gaps."

Licking his lips, Chovar said, "I see. I trust the closer we get to our present day, the fewer of these *gaps* we will encounter."

"That's how history usually works."

"Then let's continue. I very much want to hear how we survived Lynia and Rowan."

Sitting back in Chovar's lovely couch, Zill jutted out her chin. "No."

"We've already made an agreement. Don't try to renegotiate. That's a bad faith maneuver, and one that will collapse unfavorably upon you."

"I'm not trying that at all. I agreed to tell you what I know of your family history, and you agreed to help me find out who killed the Professor and why. I've now told you about the foundations of your family. What have you done to fulfill your end?"

Tenting his fingers on his lap, Chovar said, "You'll have to be patient. We cannot do anything until the police have finished their investigation of the crime scene."

"So, they've started the investigation?"

"As of my last update, no. I'm not sure they even know Professor Kovaric is dead, yet."

Zill popped to her feet. "Then let's go now. We can search through the whole house before the police show up."

"And if we are caught while there?"

"You're Chovar Monclova. Isn't that enough to get you out of a minor infraction?"

"I wouldn't call disturbing a murder scene *minor*, but I suppose most people would look the other way. Not everyone, though. Plenty despise the Monclova name. We get stopped by an officer who feels that way, and you'll end up behind bars before the night is over."

"Your call. But I know that house top to bottom. We should be able to look through it very fast, and I'll have no trouble spotting anything out of place."

She had no idea if he would accept this — she worried she had pushed too far already — but Professor Kovaric deserved her best.

Rising, Chovar said, "I'll call a car."

"Don't you think that will be conspicuous? An actual car parked in front of his house?"

"You have a suggestion?"

"Drop us off. If it makes you feel better, have your man park a block over or drive around as many times as we need. But if we're trying to avoid the police, then the longer it takes anybody to notice something off, the better."

He thought over it for the briefest moment. Then: "Done."

Bracken — the same man that started this mess for Zill — drove them with quiet professionalism. He looked cramped and bored at the controls. So few people owned vehicles in the city, Zill thought he would have felt special, maybe even important. Then again, from the way Chovar spoke of Bracken, the man had probably spent his life serving the Monclovas. Driving an expensive car or meeting famous people or dining in the most unique locations would all become mundane when it occurred every day. Zill shuddered at the idea that Bracken also found abducting her and sneaking onto a murder scene mundane.

Sitting opposite her, Chovar tapped at his holo. He had the blur function on so she couldn't see his work beyond a swash of colors. Probably for the best. She had enough troubles piling on her shoulders. No need to add *accidentally learning corporate secrets.*

At length, he closed the holo and looked straight at her. "Professor Kovaric's murder has still gone unnoticed, and one of my police contacts is now scouting for when that information arrives. She'll try to slow it down until we're out, but I wouldn't expect that to go far. She doesn't have the clout she likes to portray, and a murder in such a peaceful neighborhood will draw tremendous attention."

*He would have hated that,* she thought. Even the small bit of celebrity the Professor had received bothered the man. He couldn't understand it. Why would anybody care to interview him or be curious about his life? Media, eager students, faculty — they were a nuisance.

She smiled, recalling how he taunted and pranked those he deemed unworthy of his time. Once, when forced by the University to be filmed for a poorly-researched documentary about the mysteries of Earth, he showed up speaking his best approximation of the Dahtien language. Zill had to translate everything, including an explanation that even the Dahtien could school these filmmakers about Earth, so he figured that language better suited the moment.

Nearing their destination, Bracken drove by Dushefs Dumplings, a small store consisting of a counter under an awning and a long line stretching down the block. Zill remembered when she noticed how often Professor Kovaric purchased dumplings from that store. She had only been working for him a few months and wanted to make a good impression, still fearful he might fire her if she failed at anything. As a gift, she purchased a loyalty card granting Professor Kovaric dumplings for a year.

When she presented the gift, he glanced up from his work. "Why?"

Trying not to squirm under the weight of his single word, she said, "You eat these dumplings a lot. I thought it would be a nice gesture."

"I don't like dumplings."

With a perplexed squint, she said, "You get them every day."

"And I don't eat them. I only bite enough to taste."

"I don't understand."

Professor Kovaric's face brightened. "That is a wonderfully honest and important thing to say. We must never be afraid to admit that we don't know or that we don't understand." He returned to his work.

"Are you going to explain?"

"Oh yes. Of course." He awakened his holo and searched through it for a moment. "When Dushefs Dumplings first opened, I heard word of how delicious they were. When I tried one, I was both disappointed and amazed. Disappointed because the taste did not live up to the praise. Amazed, however, because I tasted a strange combination of flavors I had only read about. In fact, I read about them right here."

He brought up a page from the diary of Kep Pradan — one of Lynia Monclova's engineers who liked to experiment in the kitchen as a hobby. In her diary, she left several recipes, including one for dumplings. Professor Kovaric had been tasting these dumplings for weeks attempting to figure out if the store was using this original recipe.

Zill asked why he didn't simply approach the owners of the store, but Professor Kovaric refused the suggestion. His research had to be carefully guarded. Private benefactors paid for this work, he had said. Sharing anything in interviews or in articles or other media had to be strictly and carefully handled. He did not think it appropriate to bother his benefactors with matters of a recipe for dumplings.

She had no idea that he referred to the Monclova family, but knowing the goal of this research now, she finally understood. Too many revelations released to the public might allow others to draw conclusions, to create suspicions, and either accidentally or on purpose, to figure out that Chovar Monclova and his family had developed a new Pathway Ring.

And if Professor Kovaric could go to such ridiculous lengths over an innocuous recipe, what might he do with truly dangerous information? A man like that might be willing to fake his own death.

The idea sparked within her, warming embers of hope — dangerous and terrible. Holding hope for something reasonably possible did not give her license to hold hope for something reasonably impossible. Like all children in Newarl, Zill had been taught the importance of truth. The search for truth, the acceptance of truth — good or bad — always outweighed the human desire to believe lies.

Professor Kovaric was dead. That was the reasonable, logical truth. The idea that Chovar had lied to her in some elaborate scheme or that Professor Kovaric had fooled everyone into thinking he was dead to protect those around him — these were highly unlikely possibilities. If she did not see his body when they entered Professor Kovaric's home, then she would have a kernel of evidence to consider the unlikely. But until that moment, until she received evidence to the contrary, she had to accept the most probable reality as being closest to the truth.

As planned, Bracken dropped them off several blocks over, and they approached on foot. With every step closer, her logical mind and hopeful heart fought, each claiming to be the holder of truth. The answer would arrive in moments, but she could not stop feeling a false elation, thinking that she might open that door and see her professor sitting in his reading chair with a bowl of soup and a bright smile. Chovar neither slowed his stride nor showed any hesitancy about entering the house. If this had been a hoax or an outright lie, the truth would be revealed in moments. Except Chovar would never allow her to enter this house if doing so ruined the lie. Which meant that only an unsettling reality awaited them.

As Zill crossed the threshold to the Professor's home, the war within her peaked. Her heart saw the narrow entranceway covered with stylized wall rugs popular over a century ago, smelled the musty aroma of a bachelor scholar who should pay for more frequent maid service, and bathed in the unique sounds she had grown familiar with over endless hours spent in this building.

She noted the lack of music playing — Professor Kovaric

always played music — and the off-putting stench of death. Several steps down the short hall, an opening on the right led to the main room which the Professor used as one of two studies. Chovar stood at that opening. The fact that he did not step forward in a commanding manner left Zill empty of doubt — the Professor was there, and she did not want to see him.

Still, she walked ahead.

When she peered into the main room, her eyes dashed about, trying to focus on anything but the human-sized lump in the middle. Yet wherever her gaze rested, she saw only horror. To the left, blood spatter dotted the Professor's favorite reading chair. To the right, a work table had been overturned, seemingly as a shield or blockade. Several wall rugs had been torn askew, and even gazing upward, she saw splotches of green — thikay leaf soup, his favorite. Probably thrown high in surprise.

Chovar remained quiet as she summoned the courage to lower her view onto the floor. Whether from shock or politeness, she didn't know, but she felt grateful for his silence. Then she clamped her mouth to hold back any shocked utterance, and she looked.

Professor Kovaric lay curled in a fetal position. If not for this unusual placement, Zill would have assumed he simply took a nap. His gray hair flowed over his collar, and part of her rebelled against looking any closer. But she noticed his body did not rise and fall with breath.

A surprising explosion of energy propelled her across the room, spun her around, and dropped her to her knees. Blood pooled in front of him, staining his white bushy beard where it fell on his chest. Both his mouth and eyes were locked open in shock.

When she reached out, Chovar said, "Don't touch him. We can't leave evidence that we were here." Chovar stepped behind, gripped her by the shoulders, and assisted her to her feet. "This is about answers, not mourning."

"You don't have to be heartless."

"I've known him longer than you. It hurts me terribly to see him. But our time is limited. Neither of us will get what we want if the police arrive and we're still rummaging around here. We can cry over his loss and gather our memories and cherish his life at his funeral. Later. Right now, we need to search this house."

He continued to hold her shoulders until she wriggled free. "I know. You're right. I'll be okay."

Swallowing her pain, Zill turned away from the corpse. She lifted her chin and cleared her thoughts with a strong inhale. "I'll start upstairs." It would be easier without the Professor's body in her way.

The upstairs consisted of a bedroom and another study. Both had sparse furnishings and plenty of old wall rugs. The man loved his wall rugs. The only major difference between the rooms — the study had a small table set up in the middle.

She started in his bedroom. Not much to look at. No bed, no furniture. Just another wall rug spread out on the floor to sleep upon. Professor Kovaric had said sleeping this way brought him closer with those he studied. After all, all the original settlers often rested on the hard, cold ground.

"This, at least, is cushioned." Professor Kovaric had snorted a laugh.

Assuming he had been murdered for some information he possessed, she could not imagine where he would have hidden a holo in here. Still, she pushed aside each wall rug and folded back his sleeping mat. Nothing.

Perhaps he had been murdered for something he had seen or written about or discussed as an idea — intangible things that would not be discovered in this house. If that were true, then why the urgent call to deliver her data? No. Either he had wanted to give her something for safekeeping or he had wanted to secure her research. Since nobody had attacked her, and nobody had demanded she turn over her work, she thought it a safe conclusion that Professor Kovaric held the offending material.

She checked his second study. Like the bedroom, the lack of furniture offered few hiding places for even a small holo. As she returned to the first floor, she had to admit that she never expected to find much up there. She simply needed some space to breathe and regain her composure without the head of Monclova Industries looming nearby. Ignoring the body on the floor, she crossed to the adjoining kitchen where she found Chovar sliding open each cabinet.

"Any luck?" he asked.

"Everything looks normal." She nudged her head toward the main room. "Almost everything."

"Then look again. Look harder. Something must be off in here."

Standing still, she scanned the kitchen while thinking about the upstairs. She even pictured the main room with its disorder and its blood and its corpse. When living such a sparse life, any changes should be easy to spot. Unless this was another case of dumplings.

Perhaps Professor Kovaric lived his meager style in order to hide his truth. Perhaps he knew or believed that somebody watched him. His enemies? How long could something like that have been happening and she never caught on? Was it possible that the Professor Kovaric she knew did not really exist? He may have been putting on an act to fool those who would do him harm.

Except no evidence supported those thoughts. Unless he had been some type of master spy, the kind she read about in fiction, the kind that lacked all proof for ever having truly existed, then he simply did not have the skills to hide such a big secret from her for two years. Which brought her back to the simple idea that whatever he called her for had to be within sight. Perhaps hidden a little, but he needed access to it for her visit.

Unless he carried it on himself.

Crap.

She peered back at the main room. "You're not going to like this," she said as she shivered at her own thoughts.

"What have you found?"

"Just come with me."

She re-entered the main room with Chovar. With a flick of her wrist, she pulled up her holo, swiped through to the Professor's contact info, and pressed the call button. Two seconds later, the arpeggio of a mon-mon bird chirped from his pants pocket.

With her heart hammering, she approached his body. The room warped around her in a surreal bubble. She moved, she made decisions, each breath came as the world continued to spin, yet it all tumbled away from feeling real. Even as her brain recognized the sensation as a defense mechanism, a protection of her sanity, she continued toward the corpse. Yes, a corpse. Professor Kovaric had been murdered, and rather than call the police or run or hide or cry or shout, she had played along with Chovar Monclova. All for one simple reason.

"I'm truly very sorry," she whispered. "But I've got to know the truth."

She shifted the Professor's right leg back which gave her a better angle on the pocket. Cringing as if forced to handle a highly unstable chemical, she slipped her hand in. Professor Kovaric always preferred an old, bulky holo, and her hand bumped it right away. As she pinched it between two fingers, and eased it free so as not to disturb the dead man's sleep, she wondered why the killer had not searched the Professor's body. That made no sense — unless the killer's only intent was to kill.

"Well?" Chovar said. "What's on it?"

She stood back from the body, happy to put any distance between, and flicked open the Professor's holo. She knew his passcode, but the holo did not ask for it. The home screen appeared. Turning the small device in her hand, she said, "This isn't his."

"No?"

Her stomach lurched. She called his holo again. The mon-mon bird chimed from his pants pocket. "If his holo is still in his pocket …"

"Then what's this?"

She didn't want to say the word, didn't want to think where it might lead, but the truth demanded evidence, and in her hand, she held evidence. "A second one. A secret one. A burner, maybe."

Wincing as if about to open a door that might be

boobytrapped, she brought up the main screen of the secret holo. Only one message existed. She tapped it open — *7291 Orstead.*

Chovar brought the address up on his own holo. "That's on the opposite end of the city. Almost an hour away. Let's go."

Once Bracken collected them and sped off, Zill had to brace her arm against the door and clench her fingers. Three deep breaths. Each one helped submerge the image of Professor Kovaric's body. Down, down, deep into her mind, into the parts that she could not summon with ease.

Chovar called the police telling them he and his secretary had paid a visit to Kovaric but found him dead. Of course, Chovar would be happy to appear at the station later for questioning, and he'll have his attorney with him. Yes, he did touch the body in his shock. Yes, he did leave right away. Well, if he remained at the house, the media would blow things out of proportion. The police would have a much easier time investigating without the trouble of a Monclova around. No, he could not go to the station immediately. Running Monclova Industries required a lot of time. He promised to have his schedule rearranged so that a sufficient block could be set aside for the police. His people would contact the police by the end of the day to set up that meeting.

After cutting the call, Chovar said, "I know it was upsetting to see Professor Kovaric, but I promised to take you there, and I have. It's time to continue our talk about my family history."

"Now?"

"We have a lengthy drive, and perhaps digging into the history will help relax you. We might even uncover something important regarding the Professor."

Zill bumped her forehead against the window. She knew Chovar tried to manipulate her into talking, but she also believed he deserved to hear it. He had done as he said he would. That alone earned some respect. There also might be some truth to the idea that she could uncover an important detail by delving into the Professor's work. Besides, it was her work, too.

Mistaking her thoughtful pause for an outright rejection,

Chovar said, "I do know a little about my history from when Lynia entered our galaxy. I know it took her and her people a long time before they found a planet to mine. I also know that she fought a rebellion consisting of Falcry's agents, and that she defeated them nearly single-handed."

"Not quite." Zill perked up. "A revolt did happen. But Falcry's people never went through the Ring. Not one of them. Rowan led the charge against Lynia."

"Rowan? Her brother?"

"That's right." Sparkling with the thrill of teaching truth to a powerful person, she leaned forward. "She also had a lot of help. Including that of the locals — the Dahtien. Listen close, and I'll tell you the whole story."

# PART II

# CHAPTER 29

LYNIA STROLLED THROUGH THE FACTORY FLOOR, it's black-red brick walls stretching high overhead, sunlight breaking through wide windows at the top, and for the first time, she thought she might live to see the completion of the Pathway Ring. The small crowd of engineers and workers eager for her approval followed several paces behind, their pattering steps as tense as their held breaths. They needed this success as much as she did.

Turning to face them, she said, "We have all endured so much in order to reach this moment."

The first challenge had been getting to the Ring — a success mostly due to her sister and Mr. Slater. She thought about Sydney often. Varo, not so much. Not to be cruel, but she figured Varo wouldn't last long in this world. He sure would have a good time hastening his end, though. Sydney, however, had the burden of continuing the Monclova name and making it flourish on Mars. Maybe Earth, too. Perhaps Lynia had become an aunt, already. She wondered if she would ever see her nephew or niece.

Once they had crossed through the Pathway Ring, they faced the challenge of the wormhole itself — the sensation of traveling through warped space stretching for eternity while simultaneously occurring within an instant. On several occasions, she had tried to put into words what she had experienced. It never seemed enough. Others wrote about it, too. She had heard a few poems and several songs had become popular. In fact, she suspected well over half of the team kept detailed journals and diaries which would include what they went through traveling the wormhole. Hopefully, some had better talent at such things. The poems were good to pass the night and the songs usually filled folks after the third round had been drunk, but none of it brought the full truth.

She remembered it like great pain. Searing, anguishing pain at that moment — but only a distant memory now. She could relive the memory but never truly the sensation. The best she ever described it — like being on fire while doused in ice.

When the wormhole spit them out into the darkness of space, everybody erupted in cheers. They had survived. They had taken the next great step in the destiny of mankind. People sang and hugged and kissed and clapped and cheered again. The Pathway Ring had worked. But it only took one person, out of habit, attempting to use their visi-link, and all the exuberance slid away into horror — the Pathway Ring had worked.

They flew in unknown space. Alone. Unlinked. A morose silence overtook them. The only route home — they had to build it.

Lynia's next challenge arrived immediately. Solidifying her command. She didn't know all the people on board. Her father had spent years selecting them, but she only had a short time to prepare. Thankfully, simply acting as if there was no question that she was in charge and expected everybody to follow worked wonders.

For several days, they prepped for the job ahead and astronomers searched for useable planets or moon-sized asteroids. But the search stretched on, and the longer they went without finding anything, the more restless people became. Lynia spent hours staring at the empty data, trying to wish a planet into reality. Wherever they pointed their scanners, however, they only found the endless void of space, small debris of failed planets, and a star.

They were in a solar system, thankfully, and traveled towards that star. All they needed was a large enough rock that could be mined for raw materials. At the same time, several of the team searched the stars and used computer modelers to determine where they might be. It became clear they had no answer. They couldn't even tell if they still traveled in the Milky Way. Space was simply too damn big.

Browit Cot, an expert in mining techniques within adverse environments, became Lynia's first personnel problem. He had been one of Miguel Monclova's prized recruits not only due to his knowledge but because he believed in the project and in Miguel. Maybe that should have been a warning — that the man so readily jumped in on an unproven idea — but Lynia juggled so many other troubles, she never noticed him until he started mouthing off. The growing dread that all members of the team harbored — the biggest being that they might never find a planet — stoked Browit into a fury. He let loose during mealtime.

The mess hall consisted of two metal tables bolted into the floor of an area the size of a high school classroom. Barely enough to hold thirty people. Lynia often ate alongside the team to build a rapport. But as the latest failure to find a planet filtered through the team, Browit Cot stood from one end of the table, his magboots clicking as his bulky body settled.

"This is ridiculous." His face puffed from behind a dark, thick beard. "I didn't sign up for spinning in circles, accomplishing nothing."

"None of us did," Lynia said, barely gazing up from her lunch pouch. "We all want to find a rock to mine and get this project going."

"Yeah, but you ain't found nothing. Promises were made, and right when your father was about launch his great plans into action, you and your sister screwed it all up. Now you're still screwing it up." He pointed at one of the engineers — Kep Pradan. "You were saying earlier that it don't seem right for her to be leader. We were supposed to get Miguel Monclova, not his reject daughter."

A few murmurs of agreement flitted around.

"And you —" Browit pointed to Palew Tonne, master electrician. "— you said all this busywork she's been giving us ain't helping get any closer to starting on the Ring."

"That's right," Palew said.

"And I say we've had it. We need some real leadership here, and she doesn't cut it."

"Enough." Lynia sealed off the pouch to avoid food floating

away, taking her time until she had the entire room's attention. Then she stood. "We all knew the Ring could toss us out anywhere, including nowhere. It was a risk we took. Complaining won't make us find a rock faster, but it will cause trouble."

Browit stomped up the aisle until he reached her. With a menacing stance, breathing hard, and spitting his words, he said, "That worries you, don't it? We get angry, and you'll have to face facts — you can't do this job. Maybe we should toss you into nowhere. Get ourselves a new leader. There's still another Monclova onboard, after all."

Lynia reached out and grabbed Browit between the legs. She squeezed hard, stepping forward, forcing him back. He gasped at the sudden pain. Before he could shove or punch or react in any useful manner, she jabbed twice at his throat. His size, his beard, and her attempt to control her strikes saved his life, but he fell over when his magboots failed to connect properly. Wheezing as tears bubbled from his eyes, he finally shrieked for mercy.

"Am I going to have a problem with you?" she asked.

He shook his head. But it wasn't enough. She growled and tightened her grip. He brought his hands together as if praying. "Please, stop. I swear I'm sorry."

When she let go, he curled into a fetal position, whimpering as he cupped his groin. Lynia returned to the table, reopened her lunch pouch, and finished eating.

After that, she had few discipline problems.

A good thing, too. The next day, they found the planet she would name *Miguel.* While that news brought out the celebrations once more, the reality hit soon afterward — they had to travel seven years to reach the planet. Maintaining order would become her daily battle. And she was determined to win.

However, seven years locked in a small metal box had another name — prison. Though her people had more freedom than a convict, they still had plenty of limitations. The obvious one — a limitation on movement. But they also had limited access to food since it had to be rationed until new food could be grown in abundance. They had limited space to call their own. Activities like gambling, drug use, and prostitution all crept into their world, and Lynia had to limit or outright stop those, too. She often felt more like a warden than the leader of mankind's brave future.

Chief Critto Lig, head of security, offered little help. "I can keep the law once you decide on some laws." Except they both knew that she had to be careful — too much law in a confined space could turn the whole populace into Browit Cots.

Her best solution to maintaining order — keep people working. Make sure everyone had a job. Some people were easy to place. Those brought along to work in hydroponics or coding or systems maintenance all found much to do. But those like Browit Cot would not be useful until they started mining. For them, Lynia had to find jobs to keep them busy, to keep them thinking they contributed, or at least, to keep them too exhausted to cause trouble.

In addition to work, she imposed mandatory exercise. Lost muscle in zero-g could become a serious problem over such a long period in space. Regular resistance and mag-weight exercises, as well as periodic time spent in a spinning gravity simulator she had ordered built along the way, would mitigate much of the damage. She hoped.

Relationships formed and severed — many romantic — but thankfully, few ended in violence. Those that did had to be handled with brutal methods. Lynia saw no way to keep this team together for so long if she allowed morals to fall apart. She had a storage room converted into a brig, she made the rules clear, and she had no qualms over a public beating. Chief Lig enforced her will, and it instilled respect, fear, and most important, compliance. Stealing, assaults, domestic violence — these were held to a minimum after only a couple public displays.

She wondered at times what such strictness would have done to the next generation, but that was not a problem she had to deal with. All employees on this project had been implanted with the latest birth control. The last thing Monclova Industries needed was to raise children in an unknown section of space while trying to build the other end of the Pathway Ring.

Not that any of it mattered for Lynia personally. She avoided all romantic and physical relations with the team. It would only undermine her authority, and she had enough mechanical options to keep her satisfied without the human complications.

As the years drifted by and they closed in on planet Miguel, when they finally started getting a good look at their worksite, the excitement grew. The planet had locked in its orbital axis so that the northern hemisphere always pointed toward the sun. As a result, that hemisphere flourished with blue waters and green plants. The southern hemisphere, however, looked to be a frozen wasteland. Always bitter winter. If anything lived out there, Lynia figured they didn't want to meet it.

Analysis of Miguel continued during the final years of approach. The planet had a thirty-one-hour cycle with only six to ten hours of night depending on latitude. Because the planet's orbit was further from its sun than Earth, the longer day helped Miguel reach comfortable temperatures for humans.

The air mixture resembled Earth. Not exactly, but enough that they would survive and adapt. That bit of news spread throughout the ship with thrills and whoops. None of them had ever breathed fresh air on Mars. To walk the surface of a planet without a pressurized suit, to inhale air that hadn't been filtered and processed — nothing could have seemed more alien. Or more enticing.

No signs of civilization were detected. While this disappointed the more romantic, Lynia thought it a good thing. They had come to rip apart the land and mine away its resources. If they only had to contend with the wildlife, so much the better.

Everyone measured the last year of travel by the size of Miguel in their viewers. They mused on what it would be like to live there, what challenges they might face, and how they could heroically overcome those problems. Then suddenly, feeling as if seven years had not crawled by, they were in orbit. They picked a landing site in a temperate area. They suffered through the physical adjustments — the weakness, the nausea, the headaches, the disorientations, all of it. And they settled in, ready to build their first camp. Then the real challenges began.

They lost several lives to animal attacks — large, razor-toothed creatures with dark green skin as if dappled by shadow which were quickly dubbed *shadowbacks*. Even with the attacks, it was difficult getting people to be cautious with all the wildlife. Most of them were Martians. They had only experienced animals in zoos. But after the fourth death, Lynia had the camp move a few miles away until they left the shadowback territory and imposed strict guidelines for encountering new species of anything.

They lost forty-three lives to illness. That had been expected. Every person had to build a new set of instructions for their immune systems. Short colds, stomach ailments, chills, rashes, fevers, dizziness — each day brought a new set of symptoms for a new set of sicknesses. But all the medical staff invited on this journey had also been trained in vaccine development — some receiving their education during the last seven years. Whenever possible, vaccines were created and issued. Those with botanical training used local flora to create other medicines.

They lost three lives, including Lynia's assistant, due to mishap. One was a construction accident. One was lost during a storm with hurricane wind speeds. And one was trapped in a cave-in while searching the surrounding area. She survived two days but couldn't be reached in time.

Still, gaining a little ground each day, the people of Monclova Industries grabbed hold of their small encampment. They discovered what was edible and what was poisonous. They learned what sounds cautioned danger and what promised peace. They uncovered the rules to living on Miguel, and they stayed.

Then they started upon the real work — the work they had come here to do. This factory marked that first great step.

"How soon before we can get this running?" Lynia asked.

Runi Nire, the woman that designed the factory, organized its construction, and would oversee its operation, folded her dark hands across her hefty belly. With a proud sway, she said, "We are ready now. We only need the raw materials."

A boney man, Marcus Winslow, stepped forward. "My survey team has identified three healthy sources for iron and coal. We can start blasting them open right away, provided you allow the miners to focus on their actual jobs instead of tending to camp."

Lynia let the jab pass. She knew many were discontent having to wait for the infrastructure to be built. Just as she had done on their long voyage across the stars, she tried to maintain order by keeping people busy. The results had been less than positive, but she hoped they could hold a little longer.

"Once those mines are completed enough to operate," Winslow continued, "we'll have plenty of steel coming out of here. We're searching for other useful things like silver and copper, too, and have some hopeful leads on bauxite. That plus the more specific metals we brought with us should be enough."

"This factory," Nire said, "is best suited for steel production since iron and coal are the most abundant so far. But if we locate the materials needed for aluminum or titanium or anything else, I'll be ready. I've had many years to plan the basics for each factory and only have to adjust to the physical space I'm given."

"Thank you." Lynia gave an approving nod — still catching a few less than enthusiastic looks. "You should celebrate tonight. This factory puts us on the road we've all been wanting for years. The road home."

The small group smattered applause before congratulating each other. One man caught Lynia's eye — Pel Garner. A handsome man, good physique, and the confidence that came with his position — one of the main engineers brought along to oversee the entire Pathway Ring project. Every step, every facet of construction would go through him and those like him at the Planners Office. They had spent little time together, so far — running Monclova Industries meant running the entire camp, not just the one big project, and there were more senior engineers that appeared at the update meetings — but she knew eventually they would have daily interactions.

That thought sent a trill across her cheeks. She hoped nobody had noticed. Foolish of her. Entering the Ring had been the end for such girlish ideas. Still, she couldn't stop from glancing at him once more. His eyes caught her. He gave a short nod, and as she felt heat rise in her face, thankfully Marcus Winslow stepped into view to ask him a question.

Others approached her to shake her hand or chat enthusiastically about their great hopes for all that awaited the team. Their delight ended too soon, however, diminishing as the rapid footsteps of Graham Torson approached. As one of the top welders on the project, he had spent much of his travel time learning to pilot spacerigs. Lynia thought him capable, bright, and enthusiastic. She looked forward to seeing him work on the Ring. Welding and piloting in space — two crucial skills one day, but useless for now. Until that changed, he was her main assistant, and she tried to hide her concerns at his frantic expression.

"It's your brother, ma'am," he said, through gasps.

"Is he hurt? What's happened?"

"No, ma'am, he's fine. But he's at it again. In the Square, this time."

Damn.

# CHAPTER 30

DEFYING ITS NAME, THE SQUARE was an off-shape octagon in the center of camp where several dirt roads converged. Lynia marched along the roadside while various vehicles rolled up the middle. Much of the camp had been built from prefab units held in storage aboard the *Pioneer*. Other units had been designed as part of the ship that could detach and be used both as dropships and then repurposed. Basic hauling vehicles, drillers, and other necessary equipment all came along, too. The rest would be manufactured as required.

Runi Nire's factory had been built on the eastern edge of camp, and the walk toward the center grew longer with each step. Graham hurried by Lynia's side.

"This is my fault," he said, sounding haggard. "I had been trying to organize the week's inventory reports and had no idea he left. All of this kind of thing is not easy for me, and I have to concentrate, and I guess I lost sight of everyone around me."

"Clearly."

His head lowered. "I'm sorry."

Pushing away her frustration, she said, "I should never have placed him in the office. Rowan is not suited to a desk job. He simply waited you out, knowing that he'd eventually find an opportunity."

"I guess I'm not that good at a desk job, either."

"You were never supposed to be. Splitting your time between welding jobs and office work doesn't help, either. You need to be building the Ring, not breaking down reports. Our new factory is going to make it happen. Soon, you'll be doing what you love."

Thick forest towered around the campsite. Lynia often

thought she saw shadows moving in there. She figured that four out of every five times, she was probably right. This forest provided everything a wild animal could want. Tens of thousands, maybe hundreds of thousands, of new species flourished in there. Some had to be curious about their new invaders.

And they were invaders. They had landed uninvited, unannounced, and began clearing land for their campsite. Lasersaws brought down trees fast, and by the end of the first day, they had plenty of lumber to start constructing whatever they needed. The constant sizzle followed by the cracking of a falling tree had since become as ever-present as the scent of seared wood.

Lynia led the way into the Square. Brown and green canvas tents lined the outside forming a wonderful open-air market at odds with the high-tech structures used from the initial landing. Colorful pendants fluttered above each tent to draw attention. While Monclova Industries provided plenty of the basics — food, shelter, clothing — this market filled in the gaps. People were encouraged to grow food to sell or harvest it from the forest. Some used their free time to hunt, eating what they could and selling the rest. Others whittled chess sets or figurines. Some crafted jewelry, and some knitted blankets. Whatever people liked to do on their own, they often found a way to sell it in the Square.

While there was no need for money here, the mini-economy incentivized people into productive activities. Lynia made sure the company supported and encouraged it. Anything that kept idle hands busy and kept the drinking to a minimum meant less people in the small jail, less trouble for the small police force.

Yet she heard plenty of complaints that these side jobs had become a necessary part of their survival, that an economy built on the company providing everything had created competing values on the same product — one for an item sold through the company; one for the same item sold in the market. Twice in recent months, Lynia had to have the police break apart scams where people overbought from the company so they could turn around and sell in the market at a jacked-up price.

In the center of the Square, Rowan stood on the bottom steps leading to the tower platform — an enormous metal pylon that provided limited capabilities for their visi-links. It wasn't much, but it had helped morale for a short time.

"We have all been given a new birth from the Lord and gods." Waving his hands to emphasize the rhythms in his speech, Rowan drew in a small gathering of people. None of the family would recognize him — especially their father. Long hair down to his shoulders, a beard and mustache to match, and sallow skin from lack of eating. He frequently chose starvation as a method for seeing the Divine. Lynia figured it was better than drugs provided he didn't starve to death.

"Just as the Lord and gods flooded the Earth but provided Noah the tools to rebuild, you have been chosen to start anew here, on Miguel. The Lord and gods brought us the Pathway Ring and the Pathway Ring brought us to this new land."

"The Lord didn't bring me nothing," one voice said.

"I'm here because I'm getting paid," another said.

"Fuck off," someone further back said.

Though plenty continued to mock him, Rowan smiled as if sharing the joke. Lynia, however, saw nothing funny in the few people who listened intently, the few who nodded as he spoke.

Rowan went on, "I understand your skepticism. I shared it, too. It's easier to think that nothing exists beyond what we see. It's comforting to know that when we die it's all over and no final judgement awaits us. But I have done something few ever do. I've studied religion. Not simply learned about them, but I have *studied* them. I have come to see how they all are speaking of the same gods, the same ideas, the same values, only in different contexts. The Lord and his lesser gods wanted you to come here, wanted you to hear their message, and they sent me to be their messenger. I was not picked by Miguel Monclova to travel through the Ring. My brother, Varo, was meant to go. But I ended up here instead. The Lord and gods sent me here so that you may hear their words."

Graham tilted his head closer to Lynia. "Do you want me to

end this?"

She shook her head slightly. Sending anybody to stop Rowan's soapboxing would only strengthen his position. Those that mocked him wouldn't care, but those that listened closely, those considering his words, would see any such act as equivalent to a government clamping down on free speech. But ignoring the problem wouldn't solve anything, either.

She walked forward, garnering hesitant looks and a few startled hushes. She joined her brother on the steps, happy to see a flash of shock on his face. He quickly recovered.

"Ah," Rowan said, flapping his arms at her. "I knew it wouldn't take long for those in charge to try to silence me."

"Nobody's silencing you," she said. "In fact, I think everybody here has a right to listen to you or speak out for themselves. But not on company time. We pay you to accomplish an incredible and demanding goal. It's already been hard, and it'll be harder still. But that is the reason we came. All of us. Not to preach. Not to find religion. We are here to build the Pathway Ring."

"The Lord and gods have given us a new world and a new life. We can forge a new society however we choose."

"Not if you want your families to honor and value what you came here to do. Not if you want them to receive the full benefit of your sacrifice. We are here for the Ring. Nothing more. We are not trying to rebuild Society because Society hasn't been destroyed. It's waiting for you back home. Once the Ring is built, once you have completed your contract, then Monclova Industries has no claim to your time. If you want to ignore your families, frolic off with my brother, start a new society in the forest, and deal with the flood of immigrants from Earth and Mars, that's your choice. But until then, Monclova provides you with food, clothing, shelter, medicine, protection, and more, and part of that deal is that we will not engage in religion or anything else that divides us."

The red uniforms of four police officers appeared on the outer edges of the Square. Damn. Graham wouldn't have called them. He knew better. Somebody in the crowd or perhaps one of the vendors in the Square didn't like the gathering. Police were necessary, of course, but Lynia had regular trouble with Chief Lig ever since landfall. He went beyond simply helping maintain peace. He wanted Law to prevail, and he wasn't afraid to break a few laws to do it. She needed to finish this before those eager head-pounders decided to intervene.

"I do not wish to divide." Rowan shifted his posture to appear smaller, weaker than Lynia. He could have been an abused beggar on the steps that the big, mean boss had come to throw into the trash. The moment the effect had been achieved, he rose straight and strong. "It is the goal of all religions to unite people. We need to be united if we are to survive out here. Work is not enough. We need to nourish our souls. What does Monclova Industries know about that? Nothing."

"This is a company job, and this is company land." She noted a few police inching forward, including a fifth officer — Chief Lig. She pushed on. "You've had your chance to speak, but there is work to be done. I've just returned from seeing our first factory. It's a great achievement that we can see, touch, and use. With that in operation, we begin the next phase of this amazing future we are building. That is what unites us. Not some fairy tale that none can prove true. We have the solid work ahead of us and the end result is the Pathway Ring."

From the crowd, Graham cheered. "That's right. Let's build the Pathway Ring."

A few others joined him. "Let's build the Pathway Ring."

Before Rowan could respond, Lynia added, "Go. Work together. Work for our future."

The crowd broke away in unsatisfied clumps. Despite the positive end, Lynia recognized how few had gone along with Graham's cheer. Anger simmered. Frustration. And she couldn't blame them. Too many had risked coming out here with the expectation of working on the Ring — not waiting around eight, maybe ten years before getting started.

As the police officers strutted forward, breaking up those lingering around, Chief Lig led the way. He eyed the people leaving last, perhaps making mental notes, his pale skin reddening under his scowl. In one gloved hand, he held a stun-prod with a firm grip.

Graham joined Lynia and Rowan on the steps. As the last of the crowd dispersed, Lynia clasped her brother's shoulder and dug her thumb in deep. "Unless you want to be arrested, you'll follow Graham. He's going to take you to my home. If you're not there when I'm finished with the police, I'll see that you meet your Lord and gods a lot sooner than you expect."

Rowan did not argue. For all his boasting of supernatural deities, he still understood when reality descended the hammer upon his head.

As Chief Lig reached Lynia, his four officers behind him, he plastered on a generous smile that cut through his thick mustache. "Right hard and ready, there seems to be a bit of trouble here?" he said. Though Lynia knew for certain that he could speak in a fine, eloquent Martian manner, whenever in public, he adopted the evolving vernacular of the workers. If he thought doing so made him more appealing, she would happily ruin that belief. But not today.

"No trouble," she said, remaining on the steps so that she looked down at him.

"I beg different. I saw your brother attempting a religious gathering. I've told you before, we can't have that. It goes against the feking rules that you laid out. Rules we use to keep peace."

"I did lay out those rules, and I can change them."

"Oh? Is that what you're doing?"

"Only reminding you that I'm the one in charge."

"I have no doubts about that. But you need to understand that you're not a monarchy." He poked the stun-prod into the stone step making it sizzle. "I can admit that your dictatorial approach was both necessary and worked well while we were aboard a floating can through space. But now, well, it's like your brother. People start to get ideas as the walls around them spread out. The further we get on in this Pathway Ring project, the farther spread out all the people here are going to be. They'll get ideas."

"Am I to take it that you want to start a government? Can I

guess who you think should be in charge?"

Chief Lig chuckled. "Fek no. I do not want that job. No, ma'am. I'm not even sure we need a government. They don't seem too useful. But we do need some form of justice system. It can't simply be me locking people up because I think they broke the law."

"You surprise me."

"Oh, I would be a good judge, jury, and executioner, but that's not the way things work best. Give it some thought before we have real problems." With a sharp gesture, he sent his police force back to patrol the camp. "One last thing — if I see Rowan on the steps again, he will be arrested. The law cannot be only for the workers. You cannot be above the law nor your brother. You do that, and this whole thing will fall apart faster than you can die in space."

With a wink, he pivoted on one foot and sauntered away. Lynia's mind crowded with plenty of choice words, but she still had Rowan to deal with. Turning in the direction opposite Chief Lig, she headed home.

# CHAPTER 31

THE GROUND SLOPED TO A SMALL HILL that overlooked the camp. Enormous trees formed a spiked wall behind, and Lynia noticed the flicker of some creature high up scurrying around the trunk. The dirt road turned to gravel — more large stones than crushed rock — as she climbed the gentle incline that reached her front door.

Her home consisted of three prefab containers linked together at the long ends. The middle one, she used as her main living area. The one on the right was her private study. The one on the left was her public office used for large meetings and any other official business. It was more space than allotted to any other, but she required every inch. Besides, this wasn't the luxury life of Mars. There were few perks that came with being in charge. Might as well enjoy one.

Well, two — the extra distance and the forest wall behind her dimmed the constant noise produced by the camp. Lasersaws never seemed to stop taking apart trees. Metal clanged on metal in rhythm. Machinery brought from Mars whined and whirred. And the workers talked, shouted, and laughed.

Before entering the house, she gazed over her camp once more, inhaling the rich forest air. Seeing the busy activity, the small world they had carved out, the bright future they all would enjoy — she could admit that it filled her with pride.

It also calmed her. The stresses of timelines, resource reports, worker gripes, Chief Lig, and of course, her brother, all drifted away for those few seconds. She saw the peace and potential of this little town. Yes. Not a camp, but the start of a town.

She shook off the idea. She could not let herself think like that. This was a camp. A temporary worksite. One day, it would all be gone. No sense in believing they could set down roots here.

She clumped through the front door, slung her jacket on the back of a nearby chair, and crossed to the sink on the opposite wall. She ignored Rowan stretched across the corner cot as well as Graham sitting stiffly at the tiny table with the remains of her breakfast rotting from that morning.

Bending over the sink, she washed her face. Plumbing had been installed only recently — another complaint from the people — but soon the entire camp would be connected. At the moment, the pipes dumped in the same area they used for their waste. Once complete, they wanted a treatment station that would clean things significantly. Unfortunately, nobody had that specific knowledge. A few decided to learn it, setting a great example — everyone would have to step up or they'd never succeed.

Once she dried her face, she leaned against the counter. "Mr. Torson, cancel my last few appointments for the day. Reschedule them as you see fit."

Graham bounded to his feet. "Yes, ma'am. Anything else?"

A vague idea hovered in her mind, and she weighed whether she should pursue defining it further. Might as well try. "Set up a meeting with Pel Garner."

"Yes, ma'am, already done."

"You knew?"

Confusion crinkled his mouth. "Knew what?" Perhaps sensing he may have stepped into something he shouldn't, he said, "Pel Garner requested the meeting yesterday."

She remained still, stoic, unable to decide what that could possibly mean. But that would be tomorrow's problem. She did not move until Graham had left.

A sharp look at Rowan, then she crossed her arms and put her chin to her chest. She wondered if Sydney, as the eldest, felt this way — responsible for all the siblings. Of course, Lynia only had responsibility for Rowan, but she often found herself wishing Varo had been the one to go through the Ring with her. A drunken playboy would have been a nuisance and an embarrassment. Nothing more. Rowan, on the other hand, attempted to undermine her authority every chance available, and his actions threatened to ruin the reason for being here.

"I know you feel strongly about all this religion stuff —"

"*Religion stuff?*"

"Don't start playing nitpicking word games and semantics with me. That is the defense of somebody who has no defense. Whether I agree with you or not, you are part of the Monclova family. You should act like it."

"Then don't bother asking me to stop. Because I'm not going to."

Kicking her heel against the lower cabinets, she said, "You stubborn ass. If you would listen, you would hear the truth of what I'm saying instead of making assumption. I am not stopping you from your preaching. I'm only asking you to wait. Our employees need to focus on the Pathway Ring. That's their purpose for being here, and as long as they don't deviate, we'll go home within a decade. But every time you open your mouth, you draw more people away to some other purpose. That means we don't go home."

"I'm sorry, Sis. The Lord and gods have given me a greater purpose than the one from father."

The angrier she became, the calmer he acted. He did it on purpose — digging under her skin as only an older brother could do. He wanted her to challenge him, his ideas, because it would open the door for another fruitless debate. They had been engaging in these discussions for almost seven years and had yet to reach a satisfactory conclusion.

It all had started in space.

After traveling through the wormhole, once they had located a viable planet and set course, once everyone settled into their various duties, Rowan found himself stuck in an unusual limbo. He was not part of the Monclova Industries crew — not a contracted volunteer, not a contracted employee, not a contracted anything. Nothing but the son of the owner. That last part, however, had people treating him special, as if his name alone granted him power. His position as brother to the woman in charge also caused people to want to befriend him, to use him.

Lynia knew she had made one big mistake with him during those years. She should have forced him to take a job, something that required daily duties, something that made him feel like he contributed to the ship. But despite her outward confidence, she was still learning to stand on her own feet and accept her leadership role at that same time. Ordering her brother around felt weird and unnatural. That was back then. She had no problem doing it now. And had she the foresight to have done so when it was necessary, she probably could have avoided this mess.

As it happened, she had ignored her brother, and Rowan found his own way to pass the endless hours and days and months and years. He delved deeper into his religious studies. With every new trinket of information he uncovered, he would attempt to debate her over meals. Usually, he waited until the mess hall had nearly emptied — not confident to argue like now. Lynia thought he might be trying to convert her — a useless exercise — but he never seemed deterred as she thwarted every attempt at his divine propositions.

"None of what you're saying proves whether or not the Lord and gods are true."

He probably had grown sick of hearing that one, but she couldn't help it. It was the truth. He could argue morality or causality, he could argue where science ends and the gaps in knowledge begin, he could argue about the infinite awesomeness of space itself or the idea that science might stop people from seeing the divine — it didn't matter. None of those things, weather true or not, proved the initial proposition that the Lord and gods existed at all.

After each debate, she hoped that perhaps this time she would get through to him. Perhaps this time he would question the things he thought he knew. Yet a day or two later, sometimes a week, he returned to the mess hall with a new approach to debate.

One year before they made landfall, he changed. He refused to provide details — said this was part of his personal journey — but he claimed that the Lord and gods had spoken directly to him. He had found a purpose in his life greater than anything he'd ever predicted. It was the start of his confidence and of his causing her real trouble.

"You won't succeed in silencing me." He rested his head on the arm of the couch and stretched his legs out. "History is full of defeated regimes that tried to stop the Lord and gods."

"I don't think you've read your history very well. But it doesn't apply. Here on Miguel, there is no regime. There's an employer and employees. That's it. I will not allow religion to drive a wedge between these people."

"Something always does. At least, this way some good will come of it."

Clawing into her arms to keep from forming fists and throwing a punch or two, she said, "Chief Lig is sick of it. You go out there talking again like that, and he'll arrest you. I won't be able to stop him."

"I'm not sure you want to try."

"I'm not too sure, either. But it won't matter. I'm done coddling you. You're here, living off all that Monclova Industries provides. You can start earning your way."

Rowan bolted straight up. "A job?"

"Absolutely. And since I don't know any skills you have besides mouthing off, don't expect anything that's above menial labor."

"But, Sis —"

"Report to Graham tomorrow morning for your assignment."

"You can't —"

"I just did. Before you think about not showing, remember that would be a dereliction of duty. Chief Lig would be thrilled to have the law on his side with you. Now, I still have actual work to do. Go home."

Before he could object further, she stormed to her office and slammed the door shut. She plopped down on the hover-bench, letting the air cushion relax her tired legs, and she waited. Took about three minutes before Rowan accepted that she would not return. Another minute before he left the house.

She watched him sulk down the hill, and she wondered — *Am I solving a problem or making things worse?*

# CHAPTER 32

THE NEXT MORNING, GRAHAM REPORTED that Rowan had accepted an assignment to one of the farming details. Lynia wanted to feel hopeful, but her brother had played along before. Her attempts at reforming him had all failed up to this point. She refused to give up on him, though. Not only because he was her family, but because she refused to give up on any of them.

These people had put their trust in her, in Monclova. Even if her own father didn't see her value, even if her own brother followed some amalgamation of religions that often pointed to the same misguided doctrines, she would prove through action that the Monclova name meant something. Besides, before she went through the Ring, her father had changed how he saw things. At least, he seemed full of regret. If a devoted man like that could rethink his ways, then Rowan could, too.

With Graham at her side, Lynia set about her daily rounds. She walked through various sections of the growing camp, checking on the progress of camp development and numerous side projects. The printers had long since run out of their specially formulated base materials rendering them useless at constructing necessary objects. Everything since had to be made the old fashion ways. Plumbing and electrical were on the top of the list of *must haves*, and so far, those teams had performed outstandingly — albeit slower than desired. A kiln, a smokehouse, and more had been built — some based on a hobbyists' knowledge; some figured out through trial-and-error off visi-link databases.

She noticed that Graham had scheduled the meeting with Pel Garner for last of the day. She smiled.

Not for the first time, she wished they had a satellite network in place. The visi-links still worked as computational, document, and storage devices, and the comm-tower in the Square's center allowed limited communications, but the inability to instantly chat with people across any distance hampered daily work. On the plus side, the devices could also be used for recreational purposes — the *Pioneer* had downloaded over two million movies, shows, books, and music — yet after seven years stuck in space, most people had already gone through a significant portion of that material.

To Graham, she said, "Make a note — now that the basics of camp are nearly done, we should look into allowing people to create their own entertainments."

"Um, ma'am, they already do that."

"Oh? More than the little poetry gatherings and a few songs?"

"The latest thing is rhythm bands. Groups of four to eight that use various objects to bang upon and create a music of a sort. I know another bunch attempted to put on a theatrical performance, but that required a larger group and more organization. The whole thing fell apart. I'm sure they'll try again, though. There are sports, too."

"We have sporting teams?"

"Not teams, ma'am. Not organized. Just quick contests — races down a street, various games with a ball, that kind of a thing."

She wondered how she could have missed all of that. Well, staying focused on the survival of these people and the success of the project may have made her a tad myopic. The more she thought on it, the more obvious it became. She had seen the contests, had heard the music — simply never gave her brain the time to process it.

*I have to be better.*

After making rounds, they headed back to her office. Plenty of work still to do, plus several boring update reports. Then, her meeting with Pel Garner.

She hadn't thought about a man or woman like this in so long, it was hard to focus. Though she knew nothing would come of it, she couldn't allow such distractions, she considered it good for her mental health to enjoy the anticipation. A little crush didn't hurt. At least, it reminded her of how the rest often felt.

That brought back to mind her conversation about entertainment and sports. It should not have surprised her that people acted like people. Of course, they would find ways to create and entertain themselves. That was a good thing. But the sports.

Rowan had warned that something always managed to separate a group. She worried about religion doing that, but what if it ended up being sports? If any kind of team event became popular throughout the entire camp, if any type of league were then formed, trouble would brew. People would pick a team to support, and the unified group that was Monclova Industries might break apart. Martian history had plenty of stories about big sporting matches devolving into riots over a bad call or even a surprise win.

A ping from Graham drew her focus to the latest reports from both the scouting team and the survey team. The data downloaded and immediately propagated through the map system. Too much of the map remained empty, but each day, a little more appeared. Once they could get a few satellites in orbit, the scouting team would be able to trek much farther out and simply upload all they discovered. Unfortunately, their satellite experts died from illness during the initial acclimation period. She had several others trying to learn what had been lost, but it would take time.

Her office door banged open. Graham stood in the doorway, face wide with panic. "There's been an accident."

Bounding from her hoverbench, Lynia raced after Graham. They were down the hill and toward the northern edge in minutes. A circle had formed around an injured man, but when they saw her coming, they parted.

The man lay flat on his back, his shirt torn apart, a ragged V-shaped cut starting wide at the shoulder and ending with the point at his chest. Blood pooled out. A little closer and Lynia saw the man was Mar Weltty — a muscular miner who had been helping cut trees and clear land for the growing camp. Another miner, Tawn Pibald knelt at his side, applying pressure with a wad of cloths but pulling them off to check the wound.

Tawn snapped her fingers and pointed at one gawker. "Get the medics." Then seeing Lynia, she stood.

"No, no," Lynia said. "Pay attention to Mar. And stop looking at the blood. Keep the pressure on."

Tawn nodded and returned to her knees.

"What happened?" Lynia asked.

Somebody in the crowd called out, "An animal got him. Big thing. Almost as big as Weltty. That — that's its bite."

Mar Weltty's eyes shot open. He screamed, arching back, knocking Tawn aside and ripping open the wounds that had begun to clot. She jumped back on him, shoving him to the ground, and resumed pressing the blood-soaked cloth against the wide, jagged damage. The man's uneven gasps bubbled in his chest. His legs spasmed.

By the time the medics arrived, he was dead. Everyone knew it, but they waited for the medics to check over him and say something official. All but Tawn. She knew before anybody. The way she walked off, shoulders slouched forward, head hanging, muscles taut as she twisted that sopping cloth — those paying attention, knew it all, too.

"What do you want me to do?" Graham asked.

Lynia pushed forward. She hated this, but the crowd needed something, some kind of acknowledgment. "Let us all take a knee to honor our fallen. Give him a minute of silence."

In unison, the circle of workers lowered to one knee and bowed their heads. She hadn't asked for that last gesture but accepted it. She dropped down, too, and closed her eyes. Then, she started counting. After sixty seconds, she rose.

"If you need to take the day off, do so. If you need to work, then do so. Anybody working near the camp's edge, be extra careful."

With that, she turned away. Graham hastened to her side. Once they had walked a full block away, he asked, "Is that all?"

"What more should I do?"

"I don't know, but I think they expect more."

She stopped and glanced back. "Make sure the body is examined. We need to learn all we can about that animal, what caused it to attack, what to look out for, everything."

"Yes, ma'am. But that's not exactly what I meant."

"This planet is a new frontier. This solar system, probably this whole galaxy is a new frontier. People are going to die out here. It's why the job required voluntary consent."

"I know, but —"

"Whatever else they want, they don't want it from me. Let them get drunk or fool around with each other, or whatever makes them feel alive, feel happy they were not the one to die today. You can take the rest of the day off, too. I've only got the Garner meeting left. I can handle that alone."

Clearly uncomfortable but unwilling to argue, Graham said, "Yes, ma'am. See you tomorrow."

Lynia didn't bother watching him leave. She marched back home, her mind a battlefield of mundane, practical matters at war with the unnerving sight of a man dying in front of her. Perhaps she needed to take her own advice and have a few drinks.

# CHAPTER 33

TODKA HAD BEEN ONE of the original Miguel-grown creations. Figures that alcohol would come first. Made from an oval-shaped root vegetable that grew near the base of the daggerbark tree, the tater earned its name for its similar appearance to a potato. Fermenting it produced a clear, intoxicating liquid much like vodka. Thus, todka.

Lynia downed a shot, poured another, and downed that, too. The bitter drink burned her throat but heated her belly. After a few minutes, her muscles relaxed — as much as she could ever relax — and she sat at her small kitchenette table, letting the day wash away in the fiery liquid burning through her system. Maybe she should have been more lenient about alcohol on the ship. At least, everyone could drink now. Not that turning these hard-working folks into alcoholics was a good idea, but as a short-term solution, it was preferable to brawling — then again, the one often led to the other.

Twenty minutes later, when Garner arrived, she had cleaned up her drink and made sure to be working at her office desk. Her ruminations came to no clear answer. Centuries of battles for and against alcohol with no success proved a simple truth – humans needed relief from the stresses they created.

Garner knocked. She lifted her head as if pulled from some engrossing reports. Hopefully, he did not notice the open game of *Mighty Bits* in the bottom corner as she closed her desklink.

He looked clean, shaven, and smelled wonderful — a natural, woodsman aroma. Perhaps she should have indulged with only one shot of todka. She shoved away her observations along with the risqué images popping in her mind.

"Please, Mr. Garner, take a seat."

"Thank you." Even his voice resonated deep and luscious. He tapped his visi-link against her desk. After a beep, the data and reports he had prepared floated between them. "I've been thinking about our situation and have put together a proposal."

"Our situation?"

"Sorry, I'm jumping in my head." An off-center smile followed a shaking breath.

She held back from touching his hand. "There's no reason to be nervous. I'm just a person."

"Yes, but I'm making sure I don't screw this up." He chuckled. "I've been working on this for a few months now. It's important, and I don't want to ruin it. When I saw you at the factory yesterday, the way you looked at me, I worried you already had made a decision."

Maybe she had but certainly not about any plan by Pel Garner. "I haven't a clue what we're discussing yet, so how could I make a decision?"

"Of course."

Easing back, she hoped her amusement did not look like pity. "Start over. What's this about?"

He cracked his knuckles as he gathered his thoughts. With a demeanor mixing boyish excitement and a dangerous gravitas, he said, "As I understand it, our goal has always been to complete the Pathway Ring in as little time as possible so that we may return to our loved ones."

"That's a fair assessment."

"Unless I'm mistaken, the current plan is to do all our mining, then manufacturing the materials we'll need, then shooting it all into space for a seven-year journey to where we emerged from the wormhole. The construction team will have to be out there to receive these materials, and then they can begin their work — which will require many years as well. Of course, if anything goes wrong in that journey, an even greater amount of material will have to be mined and manufactured. Plus, any accidents that may occur on the Ring will be final. Even minor ones cannot be treated unless we put a medical facility up there as well. Many injuries would still require the employee to return here for further treatment. That doesn't even touch on the issues of maintaining a proper orbit. Not so difficult when we were going from Mars for only a couple months, but it's a whole other thing on a seven-year journey."

"Smart and handsome."

"Excuse me?"

"Nothing." Alarm bells rang within her. She had not meant to make her comments out loud. Perhaps it was the alcohol. "Please, continue."

Garner slashed his hand through the air until he reached the section with his full proposal. "I've outlined here how we can solve these problems and many more listed on the previous pages. It'll take one major change. We build the Ring here."

"Here? On Miguel?"

"If we build the Ring at a northern latitude like a halo on this planet, we won't need to haul all the raw and manufactured materials through seven years of space. We can easily build supply lines that will transport everything where it needs to go. Injuries, accidents, breakage, anything that goes wrong can be handled because it's happening here, on a planet with gravity, and one in which we can breathe the air. All the troubles of working in a vacuum vanish. Now, of course, there are some obvious questions you would have."

"Like the fact that the planet Miguel is here and not next to the wormhole."

"That would be the big one." He swiped to the next page. "I propose an alteration to the Pathway Ring design that adds a simple engine system. It will maneuver the Ring once we launch. We'll have to build two, maybe three, ships that can hook onto the Ring and assist it, tug it all the way, but that's only one seven-year journey, not numerous. Best of all, when we launch the Ring, we can start it up at the same time. The Pathway Ring requires enormous amounts of raw materials to consume as part of the jumpstart process. By building the Ring around a northern latitude that encompasses that amount of raw material, possibly more, we simply start it on the ground. It will eat away the top of the planet, jumpstarting the device, and be fully operating. We won't even need to launch it into space, really. The planet will simply disappear around it. Once we fly it out to the correct location, we can tune the Ring to stabilize our end of the wormhole and, well, it's done."

"So, the trade-off is that now I have to have three new ships built and be okay with destroying this planet."

"Building three ships will require less effort than mining the huge amount of material needed to jumpstart the Pathway Ring in space. Likewise, all of that mining would destroy the planet anyway, just in a different manner."

"Anything else?"

"One of the big benefits to my plan is that it will cut at least three, possibly even four years from our projected schedule. Unfortunately, we'll still lose quite a few lives in the process. While the number of space-related deaths will obviously decrease significantly, there will be a rise in deaths in the wild. Survey teams will be required to hike through more forest and whatever other terrain is out there as the building of the Ring moves around the planet. They'll stumble upon all sorts of deadly situations. Then, as we move into an area, we should expect deaths from interactions with the wild environment much like when we first landed."

Lynia could not suppress her smile — he had no idea how charming, how infectious, his attitude made him. "You really thought this out. I suppose you have an answer to this problem, as well."

"I do." He scooted forward, and as he went to swipe through the link once more, he brushed the top of her hand. Did he blush? Or perhaps he was excited about his proposal. Lynia tried again to push these thoughts away.

Pointing to a graph with a descending line, Garner said, "This is our current population trend. Now, I understand why we've refrained from allowing anybody to procreate, but if we don't start urging the birth of children and build an infrastructure to educate and train them for the tasks we'll need, it's very possible we won't have enough skilled and knowledgeable people to complete the Ring."

Lynia thought about Mar Weltty. To dismiss him as simply a miner would be to dismiss all his expertise on how cave systems worked, how the structure of a mine prevented collapse, how to recognize healthy veins of ore from diminished veins, and much more. The loss of that kind of knowledge could not be replaced on the fly. They needed to start training people now. And while they could train each other, the unspoken implication of Garner's plan flashed like a visi-link sign in her face. While his plan promised to cut several years, they were still looking at a longer projection than originally hoped. They would all grow old. Ten years, even twenty years, they could handle that. But with enough setbacks, they might reach thirty years, and suddenly, the current group of one hundred forty-nine souls would start to lose efficiency. Wait too long, and they would die off.

"I see several problems with your proposal, including the retraining of all our people expecting to work in zero-g space, but most we can overcome. However, if we allow children to be born, some form of civilized society will follow. If we do that, we're setting down roots. How can we allow that to happen, if we're going to destroy this planet?"

"I've given that thought, too."

*I'll bet you have.* She gestured for him to continue.

"We have the *Pioneer* in orbit. We could send a crew around the sun, going in the opposite orbit as the planet Miguel. Their job would be to search where we have not been able to see yet. With any luck, we'll find another planet viable for life. But even a dead planet can be lived on — we've done it on Mars. Or, if we choose, we could move our entire operation to the dead planet — provided it has the right composition of metals required — and preserve Miguel. It's hard to know what the best options will be until we have the data of what's out there."

"Unless there's nothing out there."

"If that's the case, we pack the kids on the ships along with the rest of us and once the Ring is in place and operational, we go through. The children will learn firsthand about the Ring, and we can show them the wonders of Mars and Earth."

"It's interesting. I'll need to think about it." She closed the visi-link. "Don't worry. I really will think about it."

"Another benefit is the fact that you could have a child as well. You can ensure the continuation of the Monclova family."

She could not tell if he was appealing to her sense of purpose for the Monclova family, playing on a presumed vanity for the Monclova name, or offering up his services in fathering a child. Perhaps this was clumsy flirting, but she had little experience in such matters. She had dated a few men back on Mars, slept with a few, too — but she never got the hang of flirtation. Often, she fell back on simply being blunt. That did not seem wise at the moment considering the boss-employee nature of their relationship.

"I'll make my decision soon."

"Of course." He stood. "If you have any other questions—"

"I know how to contact you. Please leave."

She hated the rudeness in her voice, but if she allowed him to stay much longer, she might blurt out one of her blunt thoughts.

His plan, however — the Garner plan — held merit. It had the bonus that if implemented, she would work alongside Pel Garner for many years. Her blunt thoughts could be dealt with then.

# CHAPTER 34

FROM HER MEETING WITH GARNER, she made two decisions. First, Lynia needed to table the Garner Plan and Pel Garner until she could put some distance between her business sense and her less than professional thoughts. Second, she lifted the ban on pregnancy. Even if she ultimately rejected the Garner Plan, she couldn't deny reality. The seven-year travel time to the wormhole caused extra problems that threatened to stall the completion of the Ring beyond a single generation. They needed to make babies now.

Lynia expected the news to travel fast, but she could not have imagined how fast. Everybody knew within seconds of her writing the new order — it seemed, at least — and the line at Medical to remove birth control implants stretched around the block. A festive atmosphere enveloped the camp that lasted a full month. The days were filled with humor, comradery, and warmth. The nights belonged to parties, joyful music, and a lot of moaning.

Making a note for Garner that they should plan for a baby boom in eight to nine months, Lynia headed for the farms. Rowan had requested the visit, and while he could have waited until their weekly dinner, she had to admit that they failed to partake in dinner as often as they should. She often had to cancel due to one pressing matter or another.

But she received regular reports from Akiko Towson, the head of agriculture, which suggested that Rowan had really taken to farming. He worked hard, contributed ideas, and had become a welcome friend to the entire team. Even without Rowan's invite, Lynia had planned to call on Akiko — to make sure the reports matched the reality. After all, Rowan Monclova was a

Monclova. The desire to hide the negatives and highlight the positives in a report had to be expected. Should the assessment be honest, then Lynia wanted to share in Rowan's triumph and encourage this more constructive behavior.

Give him a little time to mature and Lynia thought that she might set him up with a good woman. Get that woman pregnant, and he could be the one to continue the Monclova name, relieving her of that duty. While that would mean giving up the family line, she could put assurances into place that would keep her in control. After all, back on Mars, Sydney and Tephen would be creating little Monclovas of their own, and those children would have first claim to running Monclova Industries there. If Lynia wanted to keep her position — which she did — that meant staying on this side of the Pathway Ring.

She figured at some point she would have to produce an heir to her own throne. If Varo ever figured out a way to remain a bachelor yet have a child that wasn't a bastard or Rowan changed his direction, she had no doubt that their father would favor their children over any born by her or Sydney. He may have changed somewhat before she left through the Ring, but she didn't believe he could change that much.

As she reached the edge of the farming area, a loud explosion erupted in the distance. Browit Cot had warned everyone to expect the noise as the first mines were cut open. Just another piece of percussion adding to the rhythms of the camp. A sound of progress.

Graham met her, and together they walked toward the main farmhouse. Akiko stood on the prefab porch to welcome them. She wore loose-fitting garb that allowed ease of movement and kept the body cool — though sweat did draw spots down her back and under her arms.

"Good to see you both," Akiko said, genuine and guarded.

Lynia had never cared for Akiko. Nothing wrong with the woman. They simply did not get along. Though Akiko never said anything outright, Lynia always felt judged as a product of nepotism. Or perhaps the undercurrent of dissatisfaction flowing throughout the camp caused the friction. Even with a month of nightly bedsheet frolicking, most of the people held a dark scowl as they went about their daily grind.

"I've already sent someone to get your brother," Akiko said, gesturing to a wooden bench for them to wait.

"Thank you. I hope he hasn't been too much trouble."

"Rowan? Not at all. He's really taken to the dirt." Leaning closer, she said, "That's our way of saying he's good with growing things."

Lynia forced a pleasant smile. Two wooden stools had been placed opposite a bench against the porch railing, but Akiko did not sit. Lynia wondered if anybody regularly relaxed out here or if it was mostly for show. She hoped the former. They didn't have time to waste on show.

After an awkward moment, Akiko said, "If there's nothing else, I have a farm to tend. If you ever bother to read my reports, you'll see the progress were making is impressive. The soil here is rich with nutrients."

Lynia looked directly at Akiko. "I read everybody's reports." A pause. Then: "Keep up your hard work."

Akiko's smile faltered. She hastened an exit.

Graham snickered. "That wasn't very nice."

"Is being nice part of my job requirements?"

"No, ma'am." Flipping through his visi-link, he said, "A side note — with the expected increase in population, we're going to need to clothe everybody in ever-shifting sizes. Our printers for clothing are only designed to handle the expected wear and tear of the original team. Throwing in baby clothes, baby blankets, toddler clothes, and all the way on up until adults, we're going to need a new source of fabric."

"Make sure our scouting teams know. Hopefully, they'll stumble across an animal that we can domesticate and sheer for the equivalent of wool. We can also search for plants that make cotton-like material or some other fiber." She sighed. "If we must, we can talk with Akiko about other possibilities she might be able to grow."

"Thank you, ma'am."

She wanted to tell Graham that he could be more direct with

his ideas. Clearly, he had thought a conversation with Akiko was required. However, Rowan came around the house, slapping hands against his legs to remove loose dirt. All thought of correcting Graham's behavior vanished.

Rowan looked happier than she could ever recall. More than a smile or the crinkle in the corners of his eyes, she noticed the way he hopped to the porch, the way he inhaled the air, the way his eyes roamed over the landscape, even the way he shook Graham's hand and sat on one of the small stools. He looked bright and pleasant and full of verve. He looked wrong.

"Thank you so much for coming out here." He spoke in a reasonable, adult manner.

"Are you drunk? High?" Lynia checked the porch, half expecting the farmers to jump out, laughing at the prank they had pulled.

Nobody jumped out. Nobody laughed. Except Rowan. "No, Sis, I'm more sober than ever. I must thank you for it, too. Of course, the real thanks go to the Lord and gods who set us on this path." He wagged a finger at her. "Don't dismiss me so quick. I can see it in your eyes."

"It takes a lot of work to run this entire camp, so if you've brought me out here for another sermon —"

"I asked you here so you could see — but I'm getting ahead. Hold on. Have some patience."

To Graham, Lynia said, "How much time do we have?"

Graham coughed. "Ten minutes. Maybe fifteen. We have to meet with the volunteers for the nursery project."

"Oh, yes," Rowan said, clapping his hands. "I must commend you. More people are exactly what we need to accomplish all that we both want to accomplish."

"You've got ten minutes." Lynia straightened her back. "Don't waste it."

Rowan never stop smiling. She crossed her arms over her chest, clutching her elbows tight.

He said, "When you forced me to start working here, I was angry. I apologize for the terrible names I called you in my head. I was wrong. Getting in touch with the land, its soil, you feel what the planet Miguel truly has to offer. You get a sense of how connected things are. We never experienced that on Mars. I have read about earthlings who had similar discoveries when working the rich soil on that planet, but on Mars — we had nothing but dead rock. Our father always talked about the strength of the stone, and he once put my hand against it in the house, tried to make that connection for me, I guess, but I never felt anything. Out here, though — in an instant. The very first day I started working the land."

"Is that it? You want to thank me for bringing you to your senses? You're welcome." She didn't mean to sound so harsh, but Rowan knew how to rile her — even without direct provocation. He knew the tones, the body language, the expressions, that set her ablaze. Some triggers he knew better than she did — which only ticked her off more.

Trying to pull back on her visceral reaction, she said, "I hope you have a wonderful life on this farm."

Rowan laughed, only this time she heard a condescending tone. "It didn't stop there, Sis. Had it stopped, that would've been enough. I would have thanked you again, right now, and lived the rest of my days providing sustenance for our dear people. But something happened. I received a sign."

Her mouth dried up. "A sign?"

"I know, I know. I sound a bit crazy. But it's clear to me. I have a purpose." Jumping to his feet, Rowan thrust his hand out toward the field that stood most prominent before the camp. "Right there, it came to me. I saw it. Shimmering in the morning sun, and I knew what the Lord and gods asked of me."

He stared off into that field, and she could feel how desperately he wanted her to ask. She didn't want to ask, though, and part of her considered staying silent out of spite. But Graham stole the moment. "And that is?" he said.

Moving his hands to his hips, Rowan stood like an actor portraying a conqueror. "A church. Right there. The First Church of the New Truth. You won't have to worry about me standing on the town steps anymore. I'll build a church here, and I will spread my message without getting in your way."

Lynia jolted to her feet. "Absolutely not." The outburst drew a few looks from farmers laboring the nearest fields.

With an even greater smile and even more condescending tone, Rowan said, "Dear sister, there's no need for that. We're both simply looking out for these people."

All pretense of familial warmth drained away. Her fists shook at her sides. "These people are here for one purpose only — to build the Pathway Ring. That's it. All resources are for creation of the Ring first and survival of the town second."

"I think this is the first time I've ever heard you call our humble home a *town*. Not a camp." He raised his voice, drawing more attention. A few farmers stopped working, and a few others meandered closer. "The Lord and gods promised that I would see you change for the better, and here is the proof."

"Stop it." She stepped closer, lowering her seething voice. "I always thought you came out here to escape our father, to escape all responsibility to Monclova, but I never thought you were insane."

"You accuse me of insanity?" Backing away, he thrust his arms open. "Every single time the Lord and gods have spoken through mankind, those messengers have been accused of insanity. If nothing else, you only prove further that I have been chosen."

"Enough already."

"Soon, dearest sister, soon you will see the light of my words. You'll understand that you cannot stand in the way of the Lord and gods. When that glorious day occurs, you will help us build this great church, and you will follow me."

She shoved him hard, and he stumbled into the stool. The crowd gasped. As if on cue, another detonation burst then echoed in the distance. Graham moved in, but Lynia raised her hand to stop him from interfering.

She loomed over her brother. "You think you're going to supplant me? You think you can become a leader now? Our father gave you every chance imaginable to lead. Sydney was blatantly more capable, yet he handed you the keycards to an empire. But you feared it all. He would have happily taught you to be great, but you shunned it all. Why? Because it came from him? That's always been it. You despised him because he wasn't around enough, because our mother cried some nights over his absence, because — I don't know — because you loved her so much that you had to hate him. You're a psychological mess with delusions of being a religious icon. But it will never happen. Not here. You can read all the sacred books and listen to all the famous speeches, you can cobble together this imaginary new religion and try to sell it, but that won't change reality. It won't change the truth."

"What truth could you know?" Though his darker skin hid his blush, she saw she had embarrassed him.

"There is no Lord, no gods, no proof of any of it. Never has been. None of it ever has made logical sense because none of it is real."

Graham cleared his throat. "Perhaps we should go."

Gazing across the crowd, Lynia considered addressing them, but Graham's nudge on her arm promised she had said enough. The farmers all turned away — some hastening back to the fields, others unhappy to see sister and brother at odds, and still others thrilled to gossip about the event that would be the talk of the night. But most held that dark scowl and deepened the creases on their faces. Without another word, Lynia left.

"You're going to regret this day," Rowan shouted from the safety of the porch. "The Lord and gods will show you how real they are. You'll see."

She and Graham continued to walk away, heading for the next item on the endless list of things that needed to be addressed. Keeping the town running, keeping the project on schedule, keeping these people safe — all of that weighed far heavier than her brother's madness. Yet she couldn't stop part of her from straining to hear if his voice still carried behind her.

# CHAPTER 35

THE REST OF THE DAY DID NOT IMPROVE. High demand on the generators from all parts of the camp led to fighting between numerous groups. The miners thought of themselves as indispensable and thus, holding more rights to energy. Lynia had to explain that they couldn't do much mining without food, clean water, and engineers. Then she had to explain to the plumbers and engineers that without electrical and rocketry all the efforts of the miners would be pointless, amassing tons of ore with nowhere to go. Then, naturally, she had to explain to electrical and rocketry that without the pilots and welders and other Ring builders nothing meant anything. By that point, the miners had gotten ruffled again and it all started over.

At least, the nearby river supplying most of the water could be tapped for power. But building a hydroelectric dam would take time. Even the waterwheels and windmills they had planned would take longer than she thought people would accept. Rolling blackouts tended to irritate even the calmest person. Yet if they had to resort to candles to get by, that was what she would make happen.

As the sun lowered toward the horizon, Lynia went home. She climbed a ladder built into the side of her prefab and settled on the flat rooftop. It needed a pitched roof, but that was a low-level project. Unless they discovered a rainy season, but so far, the storms were manageable.

"Everything is manageable," she said, gazing across the camp.

The honeymoon period had ended. The birth initiative's rise in sexual activity had lessened many problems, but clearly those problems had not vanished. If anything, they had festered in the dark, hidden by a layer of false happiness. The entire town needed some release. Once all the pregnancies kicked in hard, there would be a lot of new stresses to deal with. A final party might help.

Lynia had never organized a party, and she did not intend to start. That was why delegating had been invented. She would give the task to Graham, and either he would handle it or he would delegate it to another. Either way, the party would happen, and Lynia wouldn't have to oversee it.

Something squawked. Leaves rustled. But the insects kept singing and the smaller creatures continued making their croaks and chirps and cheeps. Lynia gazed into the dark forest behind her home. She held still, listening, looking, waiting. The black maw of trees watched back. She could feel it, sense it, knew that at least some of the animals in that dense foliage observed her. If for no other reason than to make sure she didn't attack them. But some — some weighed their options, wondered what she might taste like, tried to decide if breaking into the open was worth the risk of exposure, of possibly dying.

She dropped onto the rooftop and rubbed her face. Staring into the dark of the forest could be disturbing, but if she looked away, she would see the town. There awaited her responsibilities and an endless dump of work.

A bitter chuckle rose through her throat. As a girl, she never understood why her father had to always be at the office, always choose his work over his family. She saw it now. She was the point upon which this project balanced. Without her — or somebody like her willing to do the job — the entire town would fall apart. The disagreements of today would become outright wars tomorrow. She wondered how many times on Mars she had thought ill of her father when he missed a family event, but in reality, he negotiated peace between rival groups within Monclova Industries, staunched resource bleeding that could sink the company, or convinced employees their best interests meant following his plans.

"But did it have to be you?" she whispered. Lifting her eyes toward the night sky, she pictured her father. "That's the other thing — and I figured this out faster than you — we're important but no less indispensable than any other person in any other position. It's not that *I* am important as the leader. I can be replaced as easily as Chief Lig or Graham or Browit Cot. Maybe easier. They have specialized knowledge. All I have is the guts to make a decision and the money to make it happen."

Another bitter laugh crept up. "Y'know, growing up I always dreamt of going on a big adventure like the ones I read about. Well, here I am, and the thing they never tell you is how boring a lot of it can be. Seven years on a ship? They skip that part in a few paragraphs. You only get the highlights. Reality has a ton of waiting."

She picked one of the stars and decided that would be the Sun, that Mars circled it along with Earth, and that Miguel Monclova worked alongside Sydney daily. "I hope you'll still be alive when I get back. I think you'll be happy with all we've managed so far, and what we'll be able to do in the years to come. And I promise, I'll do my best for Rowan."

This time, the snicker had a darker undertone. "I shouldn't say that. What I'm trying to do for Rowan is not what you would want, I guess. You pushed Shendo on him — on all of us — so hard that I walked away from it. But Rowan …"

The rest of her words died in her mouth. She rubbed the *M* pendant with her thumb. Thinking back to Mars, to growing up, she wondered if she would have done anything different had she been in her father's place. Of course, she would have. She had the benefit of knowing the damage his choices had on the family. When she had her own family, she would make sure to put them first. She would value time spent with them and never let the demands of work replace the warmth and love of family. Well, it sounded good, but she acknowledged that only moments ago she had given her father a little understanding for his absences. If only humans were not so consistently inconsistent. All her deliberations of how she would do it meant nothing anyway without an actual family to raise.

Propping on the elbows and stretching her legs out, she gazed at the trees once more. The last of the day's light streaked across the bark, creating lines of vertical gold. And she saw it. Against the trunk of one tree, she would never have spotted the creature if not for the sharp angled sunlight. But there it was.

Clinging to the trunk, the creature must have been around six feet tall. It had a hard shell like an insect — an exoskeleton? — and that shell outlined harder muscles. The forearms clasped back like an old Earth praying mantis. From what she could tell — much of the creature blended in with the bark — it had two arms and two legs. Maybe a tail.

"Mind if I join you?" Pel Garner said, coming over the lip of the rooftop.

She waved him over, and when she looked back at the forest, the creature was gone.

"You okay?" He strolled towards her, silhouetted against a sky with streaks of pale yellow.

Lynia's pulse increased. A queasy sensation rushed through her system. Despite the heat, her skin prickled. But she quickly abolished the intimate images in her mind. It was ridiculous. After all, she had been thinking about the Monclova name, the Monclova lineage, and the various implications of growing the town's populace. She probably would have had similar thoughts if Graham had shown up on the roof.

Probably not.

Besides, she most likely read too much into any look Pel Garner had given her in the past. He was interested in his project getting approved. Nothing more. Keep everything professional. "I'm sorry, but I haven't made a decision yet."

"Oh? I thought the answer was *No*. After you allowed the births, I thought I might hear from you, but then time went by and nothing. I'm glad you allowed the births, at the least. We're going to need that. But am I correct now that you're saying my proposal is still under consideration?"

"All plans are under consideration until we reach the point of having to make a final decision. Until then, it would be rash and foolish to jump into any one lane."

"Of course. That makes sense."

Garner sat on the rim of the rooftop, keeping a respectable

distance from Lynia. She wanted him closer. Wanted to be able to smell him.

She banished those thoughts. The day had been long and stressful. She was tired. That was the logical reason for these missteps in her thought process.

To hide any tells her face might betray, she turned her attention back to the forest. Garner must have noticed because he said, "You think there's anything out there? I mean, anything intelligent."

"We orbited Miguel for a long time, scanned it, imaged it, sent drones through here to explore it. We found nothing. Lots of animals and insects. Plenty of life. But nothing to indicate an intelligent species. No permanent structures. No remnants of a migrating camp. No agriculture or animal husbandry. Nothing."

"Yet, sometimes, I get the feeling that something is watching us."

Her head snapped towards him. The idea that he had also experienced that sensation ran too close with the other thoughts she struggled to avoid. Those intimate images of them bubbled up.

No. She had to stay focused. "Hold on. If you assumed my answer about your plan was *No,* then why are you here? Did you think you could change my mind?"

"Not in the least. I've watched you at work for too many years now. Once you make a decision, that's it. I get it. In fact, my peers warned me never to present my plan to you."

"Why not? Do they fear me?"

"Some do. But they would fear anybody in charge."

"And you?"

He looked off into the forest. "I believe in my idea. I believe in it strongly. I would have brought it to your attention no matter what. But — I have to confess that I had another motive."

She considered that this ulterior motive might involve going into the forest, but then his attention shifted toward the town. The way he moved his head, the way his eyes darted over, her instincts told her that he avoided making eye contact. Either he was ashamed or embarrassed by what he might say. With another man, she might have added fearful, but she believed him — he did not fear her.

"You have another plan? One that, perhaps, you don't feel so strongly about?"

One side of his mouth rose in a charming display. "I do have another plan, but I think I feel even more strongly about this one." He took a deep breath. "My original motive in coming to you last time was because I wanted to meet you. I've been an admirer since the start of all this. I would've spoken to you much sooner, but you had a job to do, a very difficult job, and I didn't see how you would have time for somebody like me. Then my own duties, trying to survive on a new planet, helping build this camp — my time was ripped away every bit as much as your own. It's only recently that any of us have had the chance to think beyond tasks and duties and helping wherever help was needed. Once that time became available, my mind turned immediately to you. I realize that a romantic relationship is not something you probably have room for in your life — I'm not sure I have room — but I don't want to go to my grave regretting not having at least presented you with the choice." Bowing his head, he added, "If I've overstepped, I apologize. Say the word, and you won't be bothered by me again."

"This is refreshing. Usually I'm the blunt one."

"I'm not very good at subtle. I think, I plan, and then I act."

She held back her laughter. She didn't know how to react and didn't trust the competing emotions roiling in her chest. Pushing to her feet, she shared his desire to look at the town or in the forest, but she forced herself to gaze directly at him. "I'm not sure what to say."

Rising to meet her, he said, "You could start by telling me how you feel."

"What if I don't know?"

He stepped closer. "Let your heart do the talking."

She touched his arm. Her mouth dried even as she wet her lips. With an embarrassed shy grin, she said, "This is not like me. I'm — I'm —"

"Beautiful."

She lifted her chin and parted her lips. He leaned closer.

Clutching the pendant around her neck, she said, “It’s not so simple. I’m more than a boss out here. More than a leader. I have to be an example.”

“There’s nothing wrong with showing everybody that you’re human. We all need the warmth of another person.”

She looked back at him. But before she could form another protest or another thought, she heard Graham’s urgent voice from below.

“Ma’am? Excuse the interruption, but this is urgent — your brother has been arrested.”

# CHAPTER 36

LYNIA WHISKED THROUGH TOWN, her heart hammering as her mind vaulted between one possible scenario and another. But every thought experiment ended with the same choice — either let her brother rot in jail or use her authority to free him. Both outcomes held serious repercussions with the town.

Keeping pace, Graham said, "I don't know the charges. However, I heard that Chief Lig is quite pleased with himself."

Halfway to the police station, Lynia realized Pel followed along. She halted. Her thoughts had to be focused entirely on Rowan, yet looking at Pel, her heart hammered for a different reason. This was why she couldn't have a relationship. Back on Mars, it would be different, but when every decision could collapse this fragile group of people, she had to give up other indulgences. Pel Garner had to go.

"You don't belong in this. Go. It's a family matter."

He did not take offense nor did he press her. A perfect response. He made it easy by being understanding. Damn.

A crowd had formed at the steps of the station — many farmers, several people from Rowan's speeches at the Square, as well as numerous onlookers, curious as to what event had broken up a calm night. At the doorway, two red-suited guards blocked the entrance with burly bodies and stern glowers. The front row of the crowd — which included Akiko — all knelt, each with their hands tented at the fingertips and pressed against their foreheads. Whatever prayers they offered, they did so in silence. That quiet plucked Lynia's nerves — this large crowd hardly uttered a sound.

She picked her way through, and the guards sidestepped to allow her passage. Inside, she stomped across the small main room with its two desks and out-of-date map of the town. A door on the left led to the three jail cells that rarely held more than a person in need of sobering up. On the right, Chief Lig's door. It stood ajar, and Lynia slammed it wide open with one hand as she blew in.

"I honestly figured that would take longer," Chief Lig said. He sat at his wide desk with a cup of kama in his hand. The drink, named after its creator Kenidal Afli Moha Anwer, packed a caffeine punch like coffee but created a lot of foam which adhered to Chief Lig's bushy mustache. "I didn't think you cared about Rowan this much."

"You better have a good reason to for this. I'm in no mood."

"Your darling brother tore up a huge section of farmland to build a church." Sitting forward, setting his cup on the desk, Lig swiped over his visi-link without even looking. He had prepared for her.

Photos of the damaged land hovered over his desk. From the placement of the town and farmhouse in the background, Lynia estimated that Rowan and his followers had marked out close to an acre. The church looked to be planned for the center of this land, and they had already ripped out the crops in that section.

"I shouldn't have to tell you how serious this is." Lig swiped away the photos and replaced them with stockpile reports. "I pulled these after I stuck your brother behind bars. I'm not a numbers guy, so forgive me if I made a mistake, but from what I can tell, Rowan's act will cost us a significant amount of food down the line. Might be we'll have to ration slightly for a bit. Not a good thing with your recent baby initiative."

"Do you have anybody at the field right now?"

"You think I'm stupid? I'm not letting these bastards have another chance at ruining our food supply." He closed his link. "I'm sure some of those idiots praying out front are also guilty, but by the time we arrived at the farm, Rowan was the only one standing there. He fully admitted what he had done. As for the rest — we have strong suspicions, but I can't arrest people on that alone. That would be one guaranteed way to destroy everything you've built."

Lynia wanted to run across the building, yank open the jail cell, and pummel her brother. Yet at the same time, part of her wanted to protect him. She lowered into the nearest chair and cleared her mind. There was a lot in play here — Chief Lig made that clear enough with his last comment.

"Thank you," she said, "for doing your job so well."

He put out a hand to stop her. "I respect that you're in charge, and I know he's your brother, but I can't release him. I won't, so don't ask. Doing so would undermine my authority, and without the police to maintain order, you got anarchy on your hands."

"If you don't release him, you'll end up with a riot on your hands. Those peaceful prayers could turn violent quite quickly."

"I doubt that. Just a bunch of religious nuts."

"One of them happens to be Akiko. You understand? The head of farming permitted Rowan and others to stop their work so that they could destroy the very thing she has devoted her life to. She gave up Mars to come all the way out here to farm a new world. That's not an idle idea. That's devotion. Yet she let them tear it all up."

"I'm not releasing Rowan." Lig rapped his thick knuckles on his desk. "I don't care if they want to bring back the Greek gods of Earth, we have to follow our laws. Without that, we'll never get the Pathway Ring done." Leaning back and folding his hands, he added, "I fully expect to have a few grandchildren waiting for me when we get back to Mars. There is no way I'm letting your brother or anybody else stop that."

Lynia held Lig's smarmy glare as she thought. He sipped his kama again, leaving behind more foam in his bushy mustache. A sloppy man. Arrogant, too. But not the arrogance that came with true power. Not even the arrogance that came with overconfidence. Rather, she saw his arrogance as a mask.

A man like Lig only sought to gain another step, to feel powerful without being vulnerable. He wanted to win without risk. Probably, the only reason he accepted this position was that he believed in Miguel Monclova, believed Monclova Industries would never send a bunch of people to the unknown wilds of space without a definite plan — a moneymaking plan — to get back. Why not take all that the company offered, go away for a bunch of years, and return a hero? One that would make his grandchildren proud. A man like that always needed an out. While Lynia could not offer a faster way home, she could help him in other areas.

"You put me in a tough position," she said, attempting to look meek.

Chief Lig reacted as expected — puffing up with self-importance. "Well, it's not your fault, really. It's your brother. We all have family members we wish we didn't have to deal with. Myself, I have a nephew — nothing but trouble from day one. Thievery, drugs, lying — it's because my brother and his wife were too protective, too coddling. But I'll tell you what changed him. He got caught stealing and spent a little time in a Martian jail. That made all the difference. Real punishment can straighten out a lot of crooked minds."

Lynia nodded as if receiving sage advice. "Then let's leave Rowan in jail tonight. He's never done anything illegal before, so I'm sure that would be enough time to fix him up. In the morning, you can set him free, and I'll take care of things from there."

"A week would do a lot more towards helping him and making sure you and I maintain our positions of power."

Turning a sudden laugh into a cough, she refrained from explaining to Chief Lig that he had no power. That wouldn't serve her. Instead, she said, "I appreciate that. I even agree with you. Unfortunately, I don't think the crowd outside is going to be as understanding. We need to consider their feelings upon the situation as well."

"I don't care about them."

"I do."

"That's your problem." Chief Lig stood, hitched his belt, and sauntered over to close the door to his office. "You are under some serious misapprehensions concerning how things operate. It's evident with how you want to handle your brother, but quite honestly, it's been clear to me for a lot longer."

"I suppose you're the one who is going to educate me."

"Life will do that plenty. But I'll give you the cheat sheet." Strolling around the office, he let his footfalls thump loud enough to stake claim. It wasn't much, but he clearly considered this office his kingdom, and he wanted it known that he was the king. "From the moment we arrived, you have acted like a dictator. In fact, you were acting like that before we went through the Ring. Right? You came in, slaughtered the other guys, and then sailed us through the Pathway Ring. Now, I've supported you through the whole journey ins space. I still support you. But you want absolute authority over everyone and everything. That can cause problems."

"I have made it clear, time and again, that this is not a society. This is not a place for government. This is an extension of Monclova Industries. We are a company, operating a company job, and whether you like it or not — or anybody else — that is the way it is. Companies run from the top down. They don't vote or hold elections or have committee meetings."

"Companies do all those things."

"Not Monclova Industries. Not out here. Before, Miguel Monclova was the law. Here, Lynia Monclova is the law. A dictatorship? Perhaps. But I will say what I told my brother. You want things to be different, you want to run things in a different way, then leave. There's a whole planet out there for you."

"Yeah, that was great advice you gave your brother. Look where it's gotten him. If you would have listened to me a week ago, two weeks ago, heck, if you would have listened to me since landfall, you'd find yourself in a better, more stable position. I'm a good resource of wisdom and strength, yet you never ask for my opinion. You act like you have all the answers, and it's getting you in deeper and deeper of a mess. I suppose in the long run, I'm going to be the one to clean it up."

Lynia slammed her hands on his desk as she rose to her feet. So much for placating his ego. "My father hired you, but I can fire you. You can be replaced." Her flaming eyes proved strong enough to stumble Lig's steps.

"Easy there." He returned to his seat. "We were having a friendly conversation."

"I am not your friend. And you are not in charge of this town. You are here to enforce the laws that I make. You are here to protect the property of Monclova Industries — which, in case you don't understand, is this entire town, our employees, and eventually, the Ring. Once it works, I will happily send your ass back to Mars. Then, you don't have to be with me, and I don't have to deal with you. Until that time, you will recognize where you belong in this entire plan. If you can't, well — there's a whole planet out there for you to live on."

"I was only trying to suggest —"

"Here's a suggestion. You want to act like the big man? Go ahead. You keep Rowan overnight. You want him longer than that? Okay. Keep him two nights. Keep him three. Whatever you decide up to a week is okay with me."

"It is?"

"You just let Graham know what you decide." She threw open the door and stepped out into the main room. "But you need to go tell everyone outside what your decision is, too. You make it clear that I gave you the power for this decision. It's yours." Marching toward the exit, she added, "Whatever morning he's let loose, he better be at my breakfast table or it'll be your job."

# CHAPTER 37

THE SUN ROSE A FEW HOURS LATER. Lynia had managed only two hours of sleep, yet she felt rested. She guessed her body would crash by the end of the day. Still, she let out an exhausted sigh when Rowan failed to appear for breakfast.

She never expected it but had hoped Chief Lig would be smarter. When she started to clear her dishes, she heard the front door open. That simple sound jolted her upright.

"Rowan?" she said, rushing for the door.

But Graham entered. "Sorry, ma'am. Just me."

Her shoulders slumped though she tried to keep from betraying her disappointment. Then, seeing the odd look on Graham's face, she stiffened. "What's wrong now?"

He slid into a seat at the table opposite her half-eaten breakfast. "I haven't slept all night, so excuse me if I look a bit off."

"I didn't sleep, either. If I can't get Chief Lig to —"

"That's not the problem. It's not even your brother. Well, it is him, but it's more than that."

With apprehensiveness invading her voice, she sat. "What's *more than that?*"

Graham focused on the table, searching for the courage to speak. Right when she was about to bully him into talking, he lifted his head. "You don't have a full understanding of what's happening here. I didn't, either. But you — you've never really understood these people."

"I understand them fine. I've read their files and —"

"Then tell me who my parents are."

An annoyed frown. "I can't recall every little detail."

"You've shown great ability to recall every little detail

concerning the business operations here. You should have no trouble recalling my parents' names, if you knew them. But you only studied the practical information in the files and clearly avoided all the personal. You don't even know the names of everybody in this place."

"You came here to scold me?"

"No. But what I learned … well, you need to understand these things."

Glancing at the office door, then the front door, before squirming in her chair, Lynia said, "Why? I'd think people would be happy I'm not snooping into their private lives."

Graham's brow lowered as he focused on Lynia's breakfast. At length: "My father was a Shendo monk. It was one of the reasons I was picked for this job. In fact, the whole crew were picked not only for their expertise in various fields but also because they shared the Shendo faith. Your father made sure of it."

"My father's obsession with religion clouded a lot of his thinking. So?"

"You need to grasp what you're dealing with." He rubbed his wrists. "Shendo has three core principles that inform the entire religion. First, and most well-known, is that each person must find what role they fit into best and then best fit that role. Second, the Lord is always watching, ever vigilant that his creations are well-cared for. Third, and perhaps most important, loyalty to self, then the group, then beyond. Though monks debate the exact meanings of these three principles, they agree that these three ideas have always kept the faithful together against whatever obstacles are encountered."

Lynia grinned. "They do rather reinforce each other."

"Exactly. We each find our role, we do our best at it to show our loyalty to others, and we always know the Lord sees our deeds."

"Are you trying to say that I've pushed people towards Rowan because I don't believe?"

Graham bolted from his chair and headlong into rapid pacing. "In any religion, when someone like Rowan comes along, people tend to split into two groups — doubters and devotees."

"This isn't new. I saw it last night at the jail."

"But Rowan's supporters are already more fanatical than you're giving them credit for."

"A few farmers forced to listen to Rowan all day while tending crops doesn't make them —"

"I hacked into Rowan's private link files."

Lynia froze. She wanted to be angry. But this new information also reframed the entire conversation. Her slim breakfast soured her gut.

Swiping in the air to open his visi-link, Graham barreled ahead. "I know I shouldn't have done it, but I've seen the way people act around him. My father warned me about diehard believers and how they could be easily swayed. Your father selected a lot of diehard believers for this job." He pulled up a vid-log which he kept paused on Rowan staring at the screen. "I don't want to hurt your family, but you need to see this." He started the recording.

Rowan floated aboard the *Pioneer*. He spoke in a hushed tone so as not to wake anybody around him. Sitting with disheveled hair and wrinkled pajamas, he said, "It happened again tonight. I'm sure now. The Lord and gods have made themselves clear to me. At first, I thought, no I knew, that I wasn't ready. All my studies have shown that being ready is never ready and I certainly have more to learn. But was Moses ready? The Bible says that only those willing to receive can be taught — or maybe that's Shendo — or possibly a Krishna text — it doesn't matter because they all blend because they all are one." He twitched, gazing off at an empty spot. "My father destroyed Mars and destroyed my mother and destroyed me. If not for the Lord and gods then I am out here because of him. I can destroy him from here. I can be free. And the Lord and gods have shown me the path to righteous freedom."

"*Righteous freedom?* What's that?" Lynia could not hold back the clench in her throat.

Graham said, "Shendo says that not all freedom is truly free. Most leads out of one prison and into another. Or, as with an atheist's freedom, leads to moral decay. One must become free through Shendo. That's the righteous way. But some other religions have similar ideas. He could be referencing those."

"Or just something in his own head."

"That's a possibility, too." He flicked to a different video. This one was another personal log, but it looked like Rowan from the early days on Miguel. A little pale from being sick, but still that vibrant, heightened glint in his eyes.

"This is Eden. This is what the Lord and gods have been showing me all along. But am I ready? No. I must prepare. I must strengthen myself. My resolve. Yes, that's a key. Who would follow me if I didn't have conviction? I will pray for these things. Because when the day comes to cleanse this world of corruption, the Lord and gods will not want me to waver. Father would never waver. The bastard. I wish I didn't have to be part of him, but I trust the Lord and gods. I see how they had me birthed with this man as my father so that I would have the power within to do what must be done no matter how ruthless."

Graham swiped once more. "Now, watch this."

Rowan in the living room of Browit Cot — of course. A small gathering surrounded Rowan, maybe ten people, and they watched him with eagerness. He moved with strength. The crazed soul from the previous video had been replaced with a man confident in his knowledge.

He pointed to a woman — looked like Harma Tsi. "That's a good question. Well, the Pathway Ring is neither good nor evil. The Lord and gods created the universe and have given us the ability to travel it. What we do with that ability is what makes us good or evil. But here's the real question — do we have to do anything with it at all? We have been brought to a new Eden, have we not? We could choose to not built the Ring, to not let unclean thinkers into our world. Or we could build it and only let through those who the Lord and gods would deem worthy. We could have the freedom to create a better existence than we ever had before. One where our children and our children's children can be raised with proper values, good morals, and truly divine guidance."

Lynia snorted. "It's all good when you *raise* your own children to believe whatever crazy crap you believe, but if others do it, it's indoctrination."

Pausing the video, Graham said, "Don't dismiss him. This video was dated fifteen months ago."

All humor and derision left her. "Fifteen?"

"Things are much further along than we realized."

She looked at her brother's frozen face. His conviction worried her almost as much as the adoration of those around him. To Graham, she said, "Go check on Chief Lig. Find out when Rowan will be released — I want a firm answer."

"Yes, ma'am."

Once Graham left, Lynia restarted the vid-log. Her stomach tightened as if punched. *Damnit, Rowan, you should have stayed behind.*

# CHAPTER 38

TWENTY MINUTES PASSED. She remained motionless until the problem became clear. Quiet. She heard nothing. No distant booms of digging mines. No sizzle and crack of trees felled. Not a sound but the gentle, off-pitch hoot of a nickel bird (named by its discoverer, Nick L. Meijor). In the adventure stories Lynia read, this kind of silence usually led to monsters crawling up from beneath the Martian surface, beasts made of rock that wanted to grind human bones.

Children's horrors aside, something serious had happened. She threw on her rugged work clothes, thinking how badly she wanted just a single day without incident, and hurried downhill toward town. When she spotted Graham rushing up, she knew the day promised to get far worse.

"Well?" she said before he had a chance to catch his breath.

"Your … brother …"

"He's been freed already?"

Graham nodded as he hocked up from his chest and spat on the ground. "That's the trouble."

She didn't need to ask where to go. Only one location made any sense. She headed to the farms.

The crowd that had formed near the front of the farming land already included half the town. All activity outside this group had stopped. Nobody worked. Those that weren't part of the crowd watched from rooftops, apartment windows, or let the gossip train bring them the news. Two large display screens had been erected so those in the distance could see the front with ease.

*When did anybody have the time to set this up?* But even as the question popped in her head, she thought about the silence. Nobody working meant plenty of hands to prepare this.

On the outskirt of the gathering, Chief Lig had stationed his officers. Their dark red uniforms stood out, their presence abundantly clear. Lig's eyes scanned the area, seeking out potential issues, making sure that whatever happened, it did so peacefully. Lynia begrudgingly gave Lig an approving nod as she passed by.

He shrugged. "You wanted him freed."

A gentle mist flowed across the open field as the cool morning air kept the crowd milling about calmly. As Lynia weaved toward the front, she noticed that dealing with her brother had become an exercise in navigating her way through crowds. Her frown deepened.

At the front, she found Rowan's followers on their knees, praying with their tented hands on their foreheads. They went three rows deep. That halted her. Three rows. Had Rowan gained that many followers overnight? She thought of the vid-logs. No, Rowan had been building this for a while. She had to keep that in mind.

Two wide planks had been laid across a couple sawhorses, and with the help of a muscular farmer, Rowan stepped upon this makeshift stage. He patted his hands in the air to quiet the crowd that made no noise. Beaming over their heads, he brought his fingertips together and tented his prayer hands to his forehead. After a silent moment, he motioned to the front row that they should stand.

Only when they all had obeyed, only then did he speak.

Lynia's stomach lurched. Though she had broken up several of his speeches in the Square, those could not account for this level of devotion. His arrest and jailing — she had played right into it. He had orchestrated this moment, she could see it on his face, knew it because he was her brother and a Monclova.

"Thank you for joining me this morning and welcome. It feels good to breathe fresh air again." Grumbles from the followers. "I know a lot of you watch me with a skeptical eye, worried I might try to convert you to our religion." He wiggled his fingers as if sprinkling magic dust, and the crowd chuckled. "I don't do that. I will explain to you what I offer, it's not too different from

Shendo, but that's not the point of being here today. That's not the point we want those in charge to hear. We join together today to make a stand for our freedom."

Of course, the front row clapped their hands. However, Lynia noticed several others applauding in the crowd and even a few cheers from deeper in.

"Those in charge of us, in charge of this entire town, in charge of everything you eat, you wear, you think — they don't want you to have that freedom. They have made it abundantly clear that we are here on the company's wallet. We are here because Monclova Industries needs us to build that Ring. And that's fine. They paid for us to come out here. They have some right to request that we behave certain ways — *when we are on their clock*. When we work for them. But the rest of our time? Come on."

Laughter and nodding heads. More and more than Lynia had ever seen before.

Rowan took a few powerful steps on his tiny stage. "Why can't we have our time? When we're working for Monclova Industries, we are building this wondrous human achievement that will put our mark in the history books, something we all want. Why can't we, on our own time, believe in the religion we want? Or even no religion, if that's your crazy idea of truth. Not too long ago, you couldn't even have children because Monclova Industries and Lynia Monclova said *no.* Then she changed her mind, said *yes,* and now everybody is allowed to have kids. They are deciding when and how we have sex. Does that seem right? Does that seem fair?"

"You're a Monclova." The voice came from far back, and Lynia wondered if it had been a plant — perhaps from Chief Lig, perhaps from Rowan himself. Either way, the crowd up front reacted with boos and hisses.

This gave Rowan the gift of quieting them down and seeming reasonable. "Now, now, that's a fair question. I am Rowan Monclova. That's true. But I was not chosen by my father to lead this historic job. I'm an outcast of my family. Why? Because I don't believe in Shendo. I know many of you do, and you have every right to do so. Monclova Industries shouldn't penalize those of us who don't. And while my father, Miguel Monclova, wanted you to believe Shendo, wanted everybody on this trip to be a Shendo follower — well, that would have been just as wrong as what we have now. Lynia Monclova forcing all to be atheists. Especially when the Lord and gods have revealed themselves to me so that I may bring unity to all. There is wonder and gloriousness to be found in all religions. To unify them, much as Shendo had hoped to do, will make us stronger. We do that, and we'll do more than fulfill the promise of the Ring. We'll fulfill the even greater purpose of building a healthy society, of finding love, and of living for now and not being merely a cog in the Monclova Industries machine."

Cheers erupted. At that moment, Rowan looked directly at Lynia. He had known she stood there the entire time, she could see it in the way he winked at her, the way he smiled. It confirmed what those vid-logs had shown — he had been building his following for years, and most here did not need convincing. This wasn't a speech to educate or convert. This was a rally.

Then his face opened into surprise. "Well, look here. My sister has graced us with her presence. Come up here, Sis. I want to be fair. I want everybody to know that I'm not giving a one-sided view. Let's hear from the head of Monclova Industries out here on planet Miguel."

Stepping forward — because what else could she do? — Lynia stopped at the base of the stage. She waited, expecting a hand to help her up on the sawhorses, but no help was offered.

"Well? Do you have anything to say?" Rowan asked.

From the lower position on the ground, she raised her voice. "Monclova Industries and I have no desire or intention of controlling your lives. My only focus has been and continues to be finishing the Ring so we can all go home. Every decision I have made that has brought us across space, discovered this planet, and is helping us survive in a dangerous situation, every thought I've had is toward that goal."

"Yes, always thinking about the Pathway Ring and never about your own people."

"I'm not the one who destroyed a huge part of our food

supply to lay the groundwork for a church."

"The Lord and gods have provided us with an entire planet. This one tiny swatch will not ruin us. If you're going to preach, at least be honest — it's not the food that bothers you. No. You are bothered that this church will give me, will give this community, a place to stand up and be heard."

Her instincts — both business instincts as well as those of a sibling — urged her to fight. But another voice prevailed. It sounded partly like Chief Lig in her head, partly like her father. It told her that at this moment, she could not win in front of this crowd. She needed to lick her wounds and regroup to win the war her brother had started.

*Maybe so,* she thought. *But nothing wrong with a parting shot.* "None of what my brother has told you regarding me or Monclova Industries is the truth. It is the way he perceives it and the way he wants you to perceive it, but it is not how we feel. However, I have listened, and I have seen that many of you agree with him. That tells me that I have not been doing my job well enough. I have not shown how much I care. With that in mind, I'll work harder for you. I'll address the issues brought up today and any others that concern you. But I guarantee one thing — none of us wants to be here longer than we must. We all have loved ones to return to, and that can't happen unless the Ring is built. So, let's call this meeting over, please get back to work, and I promise that in the next day or two I will release an official statement from Monclova Industries and myself that will address everything we have heard today."

Nobody moved. Nobody said a word. All faces lifted toward Rowan.

Gazing down at her, triumph glittered his eyes. "That's all we ever asked for. We want to be heard. All right, everybody, you heard the boss — back to work."

As he jumped off the stage, his followers immediately broke away. The rest of the crowd took the hint and dispersed.

Walking up to her, he said, "I'm sorry it had to come to this, but —"

She whirled away from him and stormed up the street.

Graham rushed to catch up. As they reached the corner leading toward the center of town, Chief Lig stood with his arms crossed and watched carefully for any disturbances. Still, he had time to raise an eyebrow at Lynia.

She glowered at him but said nothing. Nothing needed to be said. He simply shook his head and chuckled.

# CHAPTER 39

BURNING RAGE FOUGHT TERRIFIED WORRY as she moved through the streets. Maybe Chief Lig had been right. Not that Rowan should have spent a week in jail, but maybe she had given her brother special treatment. If she had been harder on him, this wouldn't have happened. Even that thought buoyed Chief Lig's position. Because had Rowan been anybody else, she wouldn't be questioning herself. She would have put a stop to this long ago and forced him to take on a job that benefitted the project. Instead, she had to deal with crap that served nothing but the disillusion of people upset at the cold, hard truths.

Too late for regret. She needed to focus on the current problems. Take them one at a time and find her way through. To Graham: "Rowan has possession of the farms. We can't allow him to grow beyond that. The mines, the factory, everything else must remain in Monclova control."

"Yes, ma'am."

"Start with the factory. It's closest. Meet with Runi Nire and make sure she's loyal. If you have any doubts, get back to me at once. If you're convinced she's with us, move business by business, street by street. We've got to get a read on how many people Rowan has pulled."

"Right away." Graham broke off at the next corner and jogged on.

She continued toward the Planners Office. Though Pel Garner worked there, that was not the reason for going. The office held all the detailed plans — blueprints, phase schedules, ore requirements, camp designs, everything one needed to know to complete the Pathway Ring. She could not risk letting Rowan get ahold of this building.

From the outside, the Planners Office looked small and unassuming. Inside, the building was a mixture of the highest tech on the planet with basic camp building supplies. The walls were wood and stone plastered with mud. Yet the latest in holo-digital advancements projected out of the walls to provide users with a clean, easy-to-read detail of whatever plans they called upon. Several worktables, also with holo-digital tech built in, dotted the large main room.

Pel glanced up from one table while several other engineers huddled over another. "We hear you had an eventful morning."

"Already?"

Ghee Tsung entered from a door in the back. He sipped a cup of kama. "Gossip always travels fastest."

She surveyed the handful of people in the room. Pel, Ghee, their assistants, and three others. Not one of them appeared angry or uncomfortable in her presence.

Best to be sure, though. "If any of you do not trust me, if any of you agree with my brother, you can leave now. Go listen to him at the farm, if you want — I'm sure he'll be giving another speech soon enough."

Nobody moved.

"Looks like we're with you," Pel said.

The flush of pride within the room lasted only a fraction, but Lynia felt it. Striding to the nearest worktable, letting the morale boost lift the room, she connected her link to the holo-digital display and brought up the latest town map. The others gathered around.

Pointing to various streets, she said, "We have to control all major pressure points, and we'll need a new source of farmed foods until this situation resolves." Using her link to manipulate the holo-display, she zoomed in on the main road that cut down the center of town. "Rowan's people are returning to work now."

"Supposedly," Ghee said.

"Some may not, but most will. They don't think of themselves as a cult, but they're not going to be dissuaded by logic, reason, or debate either. They'll follow whatever their leader tells them."

"How can they believe something with no way to know if it's

true?" one of the assistants said — an inky, bald woman with bright eyes, the name Shonana Querl coming to Lynia after a short struggle.

Pel said, "That's faith. And faith brings comfort. The idea that there's no divine plan, no guiding purpose to existence — that can be terrifying."

Lynia frowned. "I thought you all followed Shendo."

"We all said that to your father so we could be hired onto the project. Others did, too."

Ghee said, "But most are Shendo."

"I still don't get that," Shonana said.

Leaning closer to Lynia, Pel said, "She was born and raised atheist."

Ghee added, "I'm sure a lot of our friends here had a big change of heart after going through the Pathway Ring. They had no idea what they had signed up for."

"None of us really did."

"Yeah, but for them, the unfathomable vastness of the universe suddenly became a fathomable reality. That scared them right into the arms of anybody offering an explanation. And Rowan was waiting."

"Enough," Lynia said. "We can debate how we ended up here later. I need all of you to reach out to everyone you know that will help us. My assistant is already shoring up the factory and mines."

Another assistant — Lynia could only recall his first name, Leck — raised a hand. "Um, I've been seeing Wello Patrice. She's second-in-command at Waste Control and Removal."

"Perfect. Go now. Renny Poe is in charge there. He should be on our side, but talk to your lady and make sure. If Poe is with Rowan, keep everything quiet, keep Wello close to him, and we'll deal with it."

As Leck darted off, another worker pointed to the medical center on the map. "I have a few friends that work there. I don't know how high up they can go, but —"

"Anything is good," Lynia said. "I haven't been focused on Medical in a few months. They may be feeling ignored. Get over there and make sure they know we're paying attention, we care, and that we're going to support them."

"If they've already chosen Rowan?"

"Then threaten that I'll make them pay after I destroy my brother."

Pel reached over to Lynia's link and flicked across to drag the map to an unassuming building one block off the Square — the Armory. "What about that?"

"Most important." She lifted her gaze to the room. "Anybody close to a person in the Armory?"

All eyes bounced amongst each other. Pel said, "I guess not."

"Then it's up to me," Lynia said. "I've met with Zural Kin-Nol regularly."

"He's in charge there, right?"

"Yes, but we're not friends. Sometimes, I think he's irritated by me. I tend to ask a lot of questions and often want him to detail their security protocols."

"Just in case somebody tries to overthrow the leadership?"

Closing out the map, she clicked her tongue. "Call me paranoid." To the rest: "I have to make sure the Armory is with us. If you have any friends in charge of any other departments, or if you have friends who are friends with those in charge, please convince them to stay with Monclova Industries. I know this is unsettling. I can see it on your faces. But this is not a surprise. Long before we left Mars, scenarios like this one were run through simulators. We'll be fine. But you must contribute your energy to helping. Understood?" Hesitant nods, but at least, she got nods. "Good luck."

As she turned to leave, Pel joined her side. Before she could protest, he said, "This isn't the day to put bravery ahead of intelligence. You are not going out there alone."

"Ma'am?" Ghee stood as Pel opened the door. "What if Rowan's people come here?"

"Barricade the door. Fight. Do whatever you have to do."

She didn't wait to see his reaction. Didn't want to know.

The trip to the Armory went quickly — she probably walked double-time without knowing it — but she still noticed the growing tension. A lot of people had not returned to work, even at Rowan's command, opting instead to congregate on the streets in small clumps. They all sensed it, knew it, tasted it — something had changed.

Lynia felt how they watched her hurry along. Every eye followed her. Low conversations ceased when she neared. The eerie silence brought on by the lack of daily work blanketed the town.

When she reached the Armory with Pel, they were too late. The front door had been torn off its hinges, and the inside lobby had been ransacked. Zural held a blood-stained cloth to the side of his shaved head while others hurried to nurse wounds on three fallen friends. When he saw Lynia, he limped forward.

He was a burly man, more wide than tall, with thick arms, legs, neck, and even lips. Every part of the man looked heavy and taut. In a deep voice, he said, "I'm sorry, ma'am. Only these three showed up this morning. Everybody else was at your brother's speech. I didn't know that's what was going on, and I didn't think much about it other than to yell at those idiots when they arrived."

"But they never came?" Lynia said as Pel went to help the injured.

"No. Then about ten people showed up. We tried to hold them off, keep some order, but they overwhelmed us. I can fight, but T.R. over there was only helping in the Armory until his skills with rocket launches would be needed. The others weren't well-suited, either. They fought their best, but you can see what happened."

She didn't want to look further in, didn't want the bad news, but she needed to know. "They got everything?"

"No way. I made every single bastard pay even for the attempt. Broke somebody's arm, got in a lot of punches —"

"But they took all the weapons, right?"

Zural gazed over his shoulder. "Half, at least. Maybe a bit more."

"Your head okay?"

He pulled the cloth away to reveal a long gash on his skull.

Blood seeped down the side of his face. "I'll be fine."

She paused to make sure he meant it. Then: "Gather some people that you trust and guard the rest of what we have."

"Yes, ma'am."

"First, though — I need a handgun."

A few minutes later, she holstered a P37 Garrison — subsidiary of Monclova Industries. She had never shot a weapon before, but she had never been in a battle like this. The closest she had ever come was when they hijacked the transit ship for the Pathway Ring. At that time, she acted like a general not a grunt. She gave orders. Never had to squeeze the trigger herself.

"Pel," she called out. When he joined, she said, "We're going back to the Planners Office to figure out how to cut off any further actions of Rowan." He looked a little pale, and she noticed the blood on his hands. "Keep it together. This won't be the last of the wounded."

"It doesn't have to be like that. Talk to your brother. Stop this before it gets worse."

"He's not going to back down."

"Then negotiate. Treat this like a union forming."

Her face chilled. "I watched what happened when Miguel Monclova negotiated with bad faith actors. There is no way I'll make that mistake."

From outside, a metallic voice shouted, "People, listen to me. Gather round and listen."

Cocking his ear, Zural said, "That's coming from the Square."

A block away, but Lynia recognized the voice instantly. "That's Graham. What's he doing?"

# CHAPTER 40

STANDING ON THE STEPS IN THE SQUARE, Graham used his visi-link as a bullhorn, amplifying his voice across several blocks. Though he did not draw a crowd even half as large as Rowan's, some people closed in with curiosity. The last two days had been disturbing to most, and each time another voice spoke out, it provided another perspective, another idea, more clarity, and more confusion.

As Lynia and Pel reached the Square, she saw the eagerness in the people. They wanted to hear from others. They sought to make sense of what they had witnessed or had heard from those claiming to have witnessed. They wanted the truth and knew it would be difficult to learn. It always was.

Pel tried to push through the growing crowd, but nobody budged. A few glanced back, saw him, saw Lynia, but none parted for her. More than anything, that sent spikes of fear through her. Things were changing faster than she could control.

Circling the back of the crowd, they made their way to the far edge. Not a great vantage point, but at least she could see Graham. He shimmered with sweat and his hand shook, causing his voice to waver. Despite having no training or comfort with public speaking, he had planted his feet firmly and managed to talk with little hesitation.

"I will stay here and say this over and over until everybody understands — Lynia Monclova is not your enemy. She has devoted every breath, every moment to our success. And we have succeeded. I'm sure many on Mars assumed we would be dead within the first week, but we have lasted years. We could have torn each other to pieces locked in space travel, but we didn't. We found Miguel. We built a base to work from, and we have a leader who guided us this far. She will guide us safely home. It's not perfect. Nothing ever is. But don't let somebody voicing your minor discontent ruin all the good we have achieved."

"You hear that? Our problems are nothing but *minor discontent.*" Akiko Towson emerged from the crowd. "That's the problem with Lynia Monclova and her sycophants. They see your desire for freedom to be only *minor discontent.*"

"Any idiot knows that's not what I meant."

Lynia cringed. She knew he intended it as an insult to Akiko only, but his ignorance in discourse led him to drop his guard. Sure enough, Akiko jumped on the opening.

"You heard that? He thinks we're all idiots."

"That's not what I said."

"Now he wants to rewrite history." She climbed the steps. "Well, let me give you a little history lesson. Throughout mankind's existence, we have had to deal with the struggle between the bosses and workers. It's always the same. They want to control us. They want to rule over us. They want to be mini-dictators. Tell me, Lynia's lapdog, why can't she simply allow us to be free on our own time?"

If Graham saw it, he had a chance. After all, Akiko was clearly Rowan's lapdog. But either he missed the opportunity or chose dignity instead.

"All of the decisions Lynia Monclova has made regarding the use of off-hour time has been in the interest of unity and efficiency."

Mocking him with a huge roll of the eyes, Akiko said, "Blah blah blah. That sounds like lawyer-talk. You a lawyer? Makes sense that the company would send lawyers out here, too. They like hiding behind the law to screw us over."

An ominous mixture of laughter and grumbling rolled through the crowd. Coupled with the rally that morning, Lynia saw things getting ugly. She surveyed the gathering — a lot of tight, angry faces. Then she spotted a ray of light. A disgusting light that she hated to need, but he was there — Chief Lig.

She moved toward him with a tilt of the head. "Chief."

He glanced over, his expression hidden beneath that mustache. "Lynia."

"Would you please gather your people and break this up? I think we've had enough rallying today."

He shrugged, and the simple gesture carried the weight of disgust, indifference, and defiance. She wanted to yell, but raising her voice would not help at this point. Certainly not in this crowd.

"You had plenty of chances," he said.

"Regardless of how you feel about me, do you really want to see what happens if we lose control?"

He spat on the ground. "You lost control last night. Fek, you lost it years ago. Just too stupid to know it."

Sounding flustered, Graham said, "No, no. I never said — listen to me, please, we have created a great thing here. A foundation upon which we will make the Ring."

Akiko said, "A foundation of our blood and sweat, of our bones and brawn. We deserve the chance to think on our own, to pray how we want. Am I right?"

A strong cheer from the crowd.

"We deserve to be treated like more than just tools to build the Ring. Am I right?"

A stronger cheer.

"We demand the end to Monclova."

Nobody knew who threw the first rock. At least, nobody ever confessed to it. But a rock sailed through the air and hit Graham in the shin. Mocking laughter rippled through the crowd — ugly and cruel — and Lynia noticed no release or relief with that act. Instead, tensions notched up. A vicious anticipation grew like the audience in a boxing match knowing the fighters entered the final round.

Another rock hurled through the air, but Graham dodged that one. "Stop it. We can disagree and have a civil discourse that will—"

Akiko strutted straight to Graham and slapped his face. "We're tired of your crap." More of that hungry, malicious laughter barked out of the crowd.

With his cheek red and his face locked in a scowl, Graham said, "Go on and laugh. It's always easy to complain and point out the faults of those in charge, but it's a big difference when you're the one running things. Look at her. Look at how she's handling this. Pay close attention because she's going to be in charge. If you choose to follow Rowan, this woman is his number one lieutenant. Is this really who you want?"

She slapped him again. The laughter started mixing with grunts. Lynia and Pel tried to get to the front, but those around actively scrunched together, refusing to budge.

Another cheer. Lynia craned her neck to see between the crammed bodies. She caught a glimpse of Graham hunched into a ball as Akiko pummeled him, kicked him. The crowd spurred her on, and a frightful grin flashed on Akiko's face.

Clasping Lynia's arm, Pel said, "I wish you'd get out of here."

She turned to him — not sure if she wanted to argue or agree — when a voice hollered out, "Tear it all down!"

Raging energy burst through the crowd like a massive storm shattering windows and howling through halls. They surged forward, engulfing the steps, swarming throughout the Square. Several people climbed the comm tower, yanking and pushing, screeching like rabid apes.

Lynia stood petrified at the sheer display of hatred. For years, she had minimalized the depths of their fury and dismissed their outbursts as solitary events. But this … "I got it all wrong," she whispered.

Chief Lig strolled through the mayhem, watching as the crowd looted the various tents around the edge of the Square. "Take it as a compliment," he said. "You're not doing it right if you haven't had to stop a riot or two."

"Get your officers. Control this situation."

"Not yet. You've got to wait until their energy peters out. As long as they keep it in here, in the Square, I'm fine with letting them beat each other senseless."

Lynia squinted at him as if he had become blurry. "You say that like you've handled this kind of thing before."

"Your father knew something like this was inevitable. I've run security during strikes and union issues in the past. I assumed he hired me to keep things smooth."

Glass shattered as people smashed through a window display. "He knew this was going to happen?"

"You didn't really think you could keep an iron thumb on the entire town without some backlash?"

As the crowd spread in different directions around the Square, Lynia saw that Akiko still stood over Graham. Rushing forward, Lynia pointed back at Chief Lig. "No more of this. No more waiting. Go get your officers."

As she turned back towards Graham, two seasoned miners marched to either side of him. At Akiko's command, they lifted Graham up — each man taking an arm — and hauled him away. Lynia tried to move closer, but Akiko caught her eye.

"Don't worry about him. Your brother's got plans."

Lynia tried to parse out what that could mean when Akiko pulled out a wide-barreled gun. Lynia's hand dropped to her holster, but then Akiko pointed the gun into the air and squeezed the trigger. A green flare shot into the sky. From other points in the town, green flares responded.

Every single time she thought she understood how organized Rowan's group had become, they proved her wrong. This was not simply a moment that got out of hand — this was a planned assault. Akiko was only part of it. Elsewhere throughout the town, Rowan's people had created the conditions for a riot.

Lynia spun back, looking for Pel but couldn't find him. The chaos made it difficult to single out anybody. Whatever happened to Pel, wherever he had gone, she couldn't do anything to help by standing still.

As she took her first step, however, the air washed from her lungs. Her gut took a hefty blow. Lifted from her feet, she watched the walls of an alley form around her. Slammed into the ground, the last of her air whooshing out, Lynia looked up and understood. Geoff Butcher — a man she knew by name only through reading reports of his repeated visits to Chief Lig's jail. He stood over her having just tackled her to the ground. Thin but strong, black stubble forcing beads of sweat on jagged routes down his cheeks, bald head, and mean, mean eyes — not the kind of man ever to be stuck in an alley with.

"Well, now, isn't this something?" His voice creaked like an old rocking chair, and he cracked his knuckles like crushing rock.

Whatever he had in mind — and Lynia had a good guess — he checked over his shoulder to make sure nobody had followed them into the alley. Lynia allowed herself one breath to regain her self-control, presence of mind, clear thinking, and fast action. One breath. That's all she needed.

Her leg rose swiftly, the point of her boot digging straight into Butcher's groin. He yelped like a wounded dog. She shifted her hips to dig the toe deeper. Forcing him to the side, he fell over, cupping his groin, and spewing out a flood of curses. Rolling in the opposite direction, she popped to her feet.

Running out of that alley required jumping over his body. She knew her kick had been hard, but he acted as if she had done greater damage. Her hesitation had been enough. His howling turned into laughter as he rose to his feet.

"Feisty. Couple inches over and I wouldn't be able to contribute to the baby initiative."

His voice had thinned a little. Perhaps she had struck closer to the mark than he would admit. Reaching behind, he pulled out a work knife — nothing too big but plenty sharp. Plenty dangerous.

"I know things have gotten a bit crazy out there," she said, forcing a calm tone. "When this blows over, people are going to have to face what they've done. You really want to get yourself caught up in all this trouble?"

"You stupid ass. I don't care if it's you or your brother or Lig or anybody in charge. I never wanted to be out here in the first place. I didn't sign up to come across the galaxy. I was told there was a mining job worth a lot of money, it'd take a couple years, and that's it. Your daddy lied to me."

She frowned. That could be true. But if he had lied to everybody, a riot like this would've happened a long time ago.

Butcher went on, "Oh, yeah. Was having a good old bender, three days straight, women and booze and plenty of chems in my blood, and dear daddy signed me up and sent me away."

"It's been more than eight years, and you're just mentioning it now? You're full of crap."

"Maybe. But I should have some excuse to cut you up, and this one sounds pretty good." He swiped at her with the knife. She jumped back, sucking in her gut as the blade cut the air in front of her. She had hoped to talk through this, but the yelling, the shattering glass, the pounding metal, and cracking wood reminded her that there were far more important issues going on throughout the town. She needed to solve this one fast.

Taking a firm stance, she whipped her handgun out, used a diamond hold, and aimed. Geoff Butcher froze.

The splash of fear in his face slipped off fast. He laughed. "You ain't got the guts to —"

She fired. Hit him in the shoulder. He stared at the hole in his arm unable to comprehend this sudden pain followed by blood. When he looked back at her, Lynia fired again. She aimed for his foot. Down he went, the high-pitched screams authentic this time.

As she walked out of the alley, she said, "Save your strength. I don't know how long it'll be until Medical can find you."

Once in the Square again, she looked for Graham or Pel. Unsurprisingly, they were gone. Much of the activity in the Square had died down as the fight moved elsewhere. Small fires littered the ground along with the debris of explosive emotion. Shards of glass, stone and brick rubble, splinters of wood — spread across the Square, a memorial of a tantrum.

With her weapon in hand and her awareness heightened to the fullest, Lynia worked up the streets toward the Planners Office. The speed with which this mob had destroyed their own home astonished her. She thought she had understood her people. After all, they had shared the same experience traveling out here and starting their important work together. Yet in a few quick moments, the bandage had been ripped from her eyes. So many had been behaving one way in front of her and an entirely different way elsewhere. Each one of them was two people — two extremely different people.

The air stank of burning. In the distance, Lynia heard the mob chanting as they smashed through block after block. Turning the corner toward the Planners Office, she found Pel Garner standing outside scanning the street with desperate concern. When he locked eyes with her, relief crossed his brow. He ran towards her.

"We got separated. I didn't mean to leave you alone." He wrapped his arms around her. On another day, it would have been a wonderful moment — it was — but she pushed him back. She needed to get control of the situation.

"I'm fine," she said. "You were smart to come back here."

"I figured this was the logical place to meet up."

"Is everyone in the office okay?"

As if sharing a secret, he said, "There's nobody in there."

Not what she wanted to hear. "What about the Armory? Did you check there?"

"I've been waiting for you. But you can't go to the Armory — it's too obvious a spot for your enemies."

"Enemies? These are my people. My employees."

"If you want it ever be that way again, then we need to get you to safety. You can't help anybody if you're killed."

Arguments and debates rifled through her mind. When she settled on outright denial, reality rebutted before she could say a word.

"Lynia Monclova, don't move." From the far end of the block, Browit Cot led a contingent of four men towards her. They were thick muscled, dirt caked, and sweating as if they had recently emerged from a deep mine. Looking over her shoulder, she saw another three similar men approaching. She considered her handgun, but Browit and one other were armed as well. The rest held various pieces of equipment meant for cutting trees, cutting rock, and other forms of demolition that did not have a favorable outcome when used against a human body.

"Put your weapon down," Browit Cot said.

With hasty, rough treatment, Lynia and Pel were frisked, weapons were secured, and their hands fastened behind their backs.

As they were marched off, Lynia said, "I never thought you were the religious type. But you're devoted."

Browit Cot snorted hard and spit to the side. "I have a strong feeling that your brother's going to reward me well for grabbing you and bringing you to him. That's what I believe."

Snapping out a command, he led the group through the ruined town streets. Around his neck, he wore a necklace with a cross that had a curved bottom. Lynia held back further comment. Up ahead, she saw a familiar hill — the one ending with her house.

# CHAPTER 41

WHILE THE SOUNDS OF DESTRUCTION THUNDERED behind them, Lynia approached her home as if entering an enemy encampment. Her eyes darted everywhere, counting guards, noting weapons, feeling the weight of their presence on her land. Browit Cot strutted to the front door as if he had strapped a leash around her neck. His hand mimed sharp tugs at the air, pulling her to his heel.

Before he knocked, he snarled at her and Pel. "You act respectful in there. You talk back and I'll see that you won't be able to talk back to nobody ever again. Maybe you won't even walk so good."

She could feel Pel tensing behind her, wanting to throw a punch or seven, and she wanted the same. But they lacked the leverage. Moving her head slightly, she hoped Pel picked up her signal. Thankfully, he huffed a breath and said nothing.

Browit gave them one final look over and knocked on the door. The guard that answered — one of the farmers — frisked them again. Then he motioned for them to enter, putting a hand out to stop Browit Cot from proceeding.

"Hey, I brought them here," he said.

The guard, an equally large man, pushed Browit back. "Father Rowan knows and appreciates it. You won't be forgotten." Leaving no time for a response, the guard closed the door.

As Lynia tried to adjust to hearing *Father Rowan*, she also struggled to recognize her own home. Rowan and his people had been quick to clear out everything that made it hers. Her office desk had been brought into the main room and a digital map of the town glowed flat on the surface. All her chairs had been lined against one wall while all other furnishings were gone — either shoved in the other rooms or discarded outside. This was not going to be Rowan's house, then, but rather an operational headquarters.

The office door opened, and Rowan entered. He wore his farming clothes, including the wide sunhat, yet the garb now took on a holy image. There was a reverence to the way people moved around him as he approached.

"My dear sister," he said, pity flowing from his pores. "I am truly sorry that things had to happen this way. I'm sorry for every person that has been hurt by this unfortunate yet necessary day."

"None of this was necessary," she said, her strong tone met with offended stares by his followers.

"I agree. You could have let us build our church. You could have let us have the breathing room to practice our religion. Had you done those things —"

"That's crap, *dear brother*. If we're going to discuss this, let's be honest. Had I allowed any of those things, you would have come up with other demands. If I compromised on those, you'd come back with even more. You were never going to stop until you found something I could not accept."

"Nonsense."

"I'm not an idiot. You've been planning this for years." She turned her attention to his attendants. "You all understand what's going on? He's using you. He doesn't care about a church or a religion or your freedom. He wants the power of being in charge."

"If I had wanted that, then I could have simply accepted our father's decision to make me the leader."

"Maybe you changed your mind. Or maybe you want the power but not the requirement to complete the project. I don't know. But I certainly don't believe your goals are pure and holy."

Clasping his arms behind his back, Rowan said, "I wish you felt different. You are my sister, and I do love you. But the fact is that half of this town already belongs to the New Church, and by morning, the whole town will belong to us. There are a lot of frightened people, unsure of what will happen to them. They're right to be afraid. I don't want anybody else to get hurt, but those who oppose me, oppose the Lord and gods. That cannot stand. The Lord and gods are swift and vicious to unbelievers. We shall be, too. So, work with me. Let's discuss how to transfer control peacefully."

Lynia looked to Pel. "Is he joking?" To Rowan: "You are joking, right? That's not peace out there. It's a coup."

"It's only a coup if you're a government. Are you finally going to admit that you've been a dictator?" A loud thump in the distance, and the ground vibrated. "Sounds like somebody is playing with the mining explosives."

Lynia stepped closer to the window over the kitchenette sink. The town fell apart before her, flames slapping the smoke-filled air, sounds of violence muted by the window yet no less horrid, chaos reigning. She looked down into the sink, not wanting to witness the end of everything she had hoped to accomplish, lost before it even began.

But those garbled voices reminded her that she still had to lead. Even if most chose not to follow.

"You say you don't want anybody hurt. Stop all of that down there. Send the word right now to cease, and I'll step down peacefully."

Rowan appraised her for a moment. "It's a good thing we're siblings. I'm not sure I would trust you, otherwise." He nodded to one woman who rushed out the door. "There. Our first steps towards peace."

"The people who don't want to follow you, those loyal to the company, allow them to risk the wilds. Give them that option. After all, your whole pitch is about freedom."

"Freedom from you, from Monclova, freedom from the shackles of the mortal realm. I offer true freedom that only the Lord and gods can provide. Those who would rather stay by your side will remain here and be retaught, shown the beauty of the New Church."

"And those that refuse to join you?"

He pressed in as he repeated, "Swift and vicious."

Pel stepped closer to Lynia. "I'm not leaving her."

"Oh," Rowan said, giving a playful wink. "I didn't realize you two were together."

"We're not," Lynia said. "I don't know."

"I don't really care. If you want to take him with you, go right ahead."

"Where am I going?"

"Wherever. Just not here. Usually, when there is an unplanned change in leadership, the old guard is executed. But I could never do that to my little sister. Yet I can't have you walking around here. No matter how much I trust you, we both know that you'd start working against me right away."

He wasn't wrong. "So, you're exiling me?"

"And your man can go with you."

Pel slid his fingers between hers.

Lynia said, "What about Graham?"

"Your assistant? No. He will stay."

"He's only valuable because he worked for me. Let him go and —"

"Still thinking you're the center, the most important. Not very nice to ol' Graham. He's going to be on public display to keep doubters in line. He'll be the symbol of the old dictatorship. One day, we'll execute him, and there will be no doubt that the New Church controls the town. Until then, he'll also be my insurance to keep you from doing anything stupid."

Lynia said, "Our father would be disappointed in you. I'm disappointed in you."

"I've always had to cut my own path in the family. This is no different." He turned away. "You better get moving. As word spreads to cease the violence, there will be some who can't calm down fast enough. If they're not as forgiving as me, you may have some trouble."

Tugging on Pel's hand, Lynia headed for the door. She tried to think of some parting word, some jab that might give her a sense that she had undercut his victory, but no words came. Once outside, all such thoughts vanished. The forest awaited them. Dark, vast, and unknown.

Squeezing Pel's hand, she led them in.

# CHAPTER 42

SWEAT STUNG HER EYES. The cuts on her arms itched. Her leg muscles burned.

Two hours hiking through the woods — practically a jungle — and her body wanted to quit. At least the pain and discomfort kept her mind from wandering too far. Any slight deviation often sent her spiraling through the betrayal of her brother, her mistakes as a leader, the ruin of the project, the end of her father's dreams, her dreams, and the dreams of countless people far away on Mars and Earth. Better to focus on pushing her legs another step as she followed Pel.

Thick vines hung from huge trees, and the night turned them into the treacherous arms of humongous monsters. Rustling, snorting, buzzing — the night sounded more alive than the day. It would be exciting if she could see anything. But the darkness only turned those noises into unseen threats.

Lynia stopped. Her chest shuddered. When Pel turned back, she shook her head. "It's over."

Choking down the urge to sob, she bent over. With any luck, Pel would mistake her heaves for the need to vomit. She stared at her muddy boots on the trampled ground. The universe shrank into those boots. She stood there breathing, staring, and all she could see was the drying dirt on the toe. A pinpoint, perhaps the only one, that made any sense.

A warm hand pressed onto her back and rubbed gentle circles. "This always helped me when I was little," he said. Then: "Sorry, that's a lie. It's something I learned later. An old girlfriend taught me that. I don't know why I lied."

Straightening, Lynia said, "It's okay. We've lost everything today. A little lie won't harm us."

"Still, you need to know you can trust me. No more lies. I promise."

She tossed a warm nod that altered into a shake of disbelief. "Why are you even here? I must look pathetic, yet you've thrown away what little you had left to bother with me?"

"How about we keep moving?"

"No. I can't walk anymore."

"Sure you can." He turned back to the path he had been cutting through. "Come on. Follow me, and I'll tell you exactly why I'm here with you."

Despite the exhaustion consuming her legs, she stumbled toward him. Curiosity pushed her some, but mostly, she didn't want to be alone. "Okay. I'm listening. Talk."

Even with his back to her, she could hear his amused smirk as they plunged deeper into the jungle-forest. It lifted her away from the downward spiral in her head, floated her above the ruins of the town she had led, and settled her upon a soft cloud of acceptance. He accepted her. She had failed, yet he was still with her.

That wonderous relief last only seconds. Pel blew out a long sigh, and his shoulders tightened. With a serious edge to his voice, he said, "I was an orphan on Earth. I don't know why my parents gave me away. I like to think it was the most painful thing they ever did, that it wasn't by choice but maybe they ran out of money or somebody threatened them or something beyond their control. Doesn't really matter, though. I popped out of my mother and went straight to the orphanage."

He slashed at the thick leaves blocking their way with a pocketknife that had a button to fire a laserblade function. It had a tiny battery, but with judicious use, Pel said he could make it last longer than expected. After that, they would have to be satisfied with a standard sharp piece of metal. As he spoke, he pressed that button harder.

"The orphanage was run by a Hindu lady, and she raised us all in that religion. Tried to, anyway. I've read old books that tell stories about nuns that ran orphanages and how awful they were. Ms. Chakrabarty must have read those books, too. I think she took them to be instruction manuals. You don't need to hear about it other than to know it was awful. But no matter how much she hurt me, I couldn't believe in Vishnu or Krishna or any of it. I suppose if my parents had kept me, I would have fought against the idea of Jesus or whatever they believed in. None of it made any sense to me."

"Is that why you're with me? Because I refused my brother and his New Church?"

"No. And please, keep walking."

Lynia didn't realize she had stopped. With concentrated effort, she forced her sore legs to trudge onward.

"When I turned eight, I was shipped off to Mars. That's how a lot of orphanages work on Earth. If nobody has adopted you by eight, they get rid of you. Some end up on the Moon, but most go to Mars. The trip over — well, I don't want to talk about that."

"That bad?"

He grunted and offered nothing more. "I didn't understand at the time, but a significant portion of the education I received had been an attempt to make me Hindu. Once on Mars, those efforts went away. Now, those in charge simply wanted to turn me into a piece of machinery. School consisted of opportunities to run machines, to learn how to fix robotics, how to maintain a computer system. Low-level work."

Continuing to weave a path through the woods, he led a wistful pace that seemed at odds with his words. But shortly later, he returned to the rugged state that cleaved at vegetation with his small knife.

"My first week, I saw an advertisement for Monclova Industries. On it was a picture of you with your whole family smiling on a sunny Mars day, and the ad implied that if we worked for your family, then we could become like your family."

"I remember those photos. We had a wonderful day together. I was still young enough to think it was true."

"I'm not that much older than you, and I certainly thought it was true. I stood in front of that ad, looking at that photo, and I wanted to be like the Monclova family. I wanted out of my crappy situation and to have what you had — or, at least, what I thought you had. So, I pulled up Monclova Industries on my link and applied for a job. Lied about my age, but I figured I could get away with that. Growing up, I was always big, and my voice was low enough that I didn't think anybody would bother. Nobody did. That night, I left a bar, looked up an alleyway, and I saw this girl. She walked along as if nobody could bother her. Except two men tried to jump her. I ran up and yelled at them. The girl kicked one guy and ran."

"That was you? Did they beat you up?"

"A little. But every punch was worth it." He hacked at the foliage for a moment. "A few days later, I got the job, and by my second week, I was working the mines for Monclova Industries."

"The mines? I'm surprised you stuck around long enough to get out of there. That's hard work."

"I'm not afraid of hard work."

"Nobody out here is, but that's the kind of work that can physically ruin you."

"That's true. For a lot of miners that's the end of their journey. That's all they want. To work in the mine so that they can be paid well and live their lives until they retire or die or whatever. Not me. This was merely step one toward achieving something much bigger. When the Pathway Ring project started, I saw my chance. Monclova Industries began a program to train people into becoming engineers. I applied, got in, and they covered all my schooling plus a stipend. They paid me to study in exchange for going on a trip through the Ring — possibly. There was no guarantee you would go, but I suppose one of the reasons my application was approved was that I didn't have any family. Nothing tying me to Mars."

"Perfect if you don't ever return." Lynia halted, wondering how many people in town had been chosen for similar reasons. Probably a large number. She had always assumed they had family to go back to, had used that to motivate, but she may have helped drive them away. With that many having no strong ties to return them to Mars, it became easier to see how Rowan manipulated them.

"Keep walking," Pel said. "Anyway, that's how I ended up in the program, but I don't think I really considered what might happen if I went on this trip. I thought about bailing out a month before I would've graduated — I would have learned all my engineering training, could've probably worked my way into a university to finish out with a degree, and get a job either on Mars or back on Earth."

"But you didn't like the idea of screwing over Monclova Industries, did you?"

"The company has been good to me. I'm not dumb enough to think that a company is going to be loyal back, but I still felt I owed something. There was one other thing — a far more important reason I stayed. Once, your father came to speak to my class. He spoke in a lofty way that was both intimidating yet oddly endearing."

Ducking a low branch, she pressed on with an inward snicker. "Oh yes, I know that well."

"After his speech was done, he had to leave for lunch with his daughters. As somebody ushered him away, a side door opened, and you and your sister entered to greet him. I recognized you as the girl from the alley, and I know how this sounds, how weird and strange it might make things feel, but this is the truth — you stole my heart. Right there. Something inside me clicked that I never knew existed. That's why I came here. To be with you."

"Not to be rude, but that's a stupid way to handle big life decisions. You should never throw away all your opportunities over a girl. What if I didn't like you?"

"Then I would be happy from afar."

"What if you didn't like me?"

"Then I would work even harder to get the Ring finished so I could return to Mars." He turned back when Lynia stopped once more. "You need to keep walking."

But her legs cried out at the thought, and the words belched out of her. "Why? There's nowhere to go. We don't even have supplies. We were sent out here to die. You understand that? That's what's going to happen. We're going to die out here."

As if talking with a student who kept making one blunder after another, Pel said, "Do you think we've been wandering aimlessly?"

Pointing in one direction, then another, she said, "It all looks the same to me. We could be going in circles."

"I've been leading us on an exact course. We're following the original scouting paths. Unless the data we've been plotting on our maps is incorrect, there is a scouts' cache just ahead."

Sure enough, after another seventeen minutes of hiking, they came upon a hastily constructed shack. Inside, they found a wealth of food, three canteens with freshwater, tools for making a fire, one torn blanket, and enough room that they could sleep under the shack's limited protection in inclement weather. It wouldn't be a comfortable sleep, but they could manage.

Lynia's fingers danced along the shelves from one item to another. "I don't think I've ever been happier in my life."

"It's a good feeling to know we're not done yet."

"But?"

"But we're not going to do very well if we stand here gawking. We need to set up a fire for tonight. I'm assuming we're going to do it right here near the cache. If that's okay with you."

Holding a can of black beans, she halted. "Me? You still want me to give the orders?"

"Who else is going to? Don't look at me. I learned when I was a kid never to be in charge. Not if you wanted to survive."

Lynia chuckled. "Thanks. That's the perfect thing to hear."

Though cold and tired, finding the supply shack reinvigorated them. At least, for a short time. Enough to clear a small area around the shack, start a fire, heat up some beans, eat, and relax their weary muscles. Feeling the warmth of the flames flickering against her skin, Lynia thought about her adventure below the Martian surface once again. The more she recalled those events, the more she could feel it again, see it again.

She remembered her fright and fury when those men approached her. The way they looked upon her chilled her skin. But then a stranger — Pel — gave her the chance to escape.

When she returned home that night, sneaking into the house

hungry and afraid of getting caught, when she settled into the joy of knowing she could have a good meal and a safe place to sleep, she found it difficult to shake off the adrenaline of that alley. Maybe it was the naïve wishes of a child, but she promised that if she ever ran a city, she wouldn't allow those things to happen.

Naïve, indeed. But there was a confidence within that girl's view, too. Maybe that came from the security of her home and her food and her bed and all their money. She had none of that now. Yet across the fire, Pel rested with his hands behind his head and his eyes gazing into the night. He looked relaxed and confident. But not confident in himself. No, after all he had confessed, she understood his confidence was in her.

If he felt that way about her — not simply some schoolboy crush, but a true confidence in her ability to lead — then others in the town might feel it, too.

Flicking on her visi-link, she pulled up her map. She guessed it would work since the scouts had been able to update Pel's maps from here, but she found the connection tenuous. The riot had probably destroyed some of the infrastructure boost points for the limited visi-link network. Not much of a network, but better than nothing.

"We're going to need to sleep in shifts," she said. "Too many unknown things in the wild out here."

"Absolutely."

"I'll take the first watch. You get some sleep." She started plotting the path they had hiked to the supply shack.

"You're more tired than me. You should rest first."

"No. I want to work on this."

"Why?"

With an incredulous stare, she said, "Because I need to be prepared for when I get my company back."

# CHAPTER 43

WHEN GIVEN THE CHANCE, Lynia still couldn't sleep. Even if her mind had not been buzzing, the night music of a thousand hidden creatures would have kept her awake. Back in town, the constant noise from the forest diminished amongst the buildings, the closed windows, and the softer sounds of humanity asleep. But here, hours deep within the forest, she would have to train her ears to accept the cacophony as soothing signals that the time had come to rest.

As the first rays of dawn reached pink hues across the sky — a sight Lynia could only snatch glimpses of through the thick canopy — positivity gushed in her system. She had developed a short-term plan. Simple, really, but she had learned the lesson well from her father — highly complicated systems all began with simple ones. To build anything on a massive scale, like a planetary company capable of constructing an unfathomably enormous contraption in space, one must start with a basic foundation, meet the simplest needs, and go from there. Build the next simple step and the next and the next. The complexity would grow on its own.

Easy enough to think. Easy enough to say. But to have the patience, to take all the right steps — that was always the tricky part.

When Pel arose, Lynia had already gone over her plan seven more times. "We're not going further away from town. This is where we stay. We use the supply shack as a central point. According to the map I have, and I admit it's not the most recent version, there's a stream running near to the south. That's probably where the canteens of water came from, but we should test it before using it as our main water source. Next, we focus on the immediate area for whatever food is available. After that, we can get familiar with the surrounding area. We've done this before when we first came to Miguel. We can do it again."

Pel stretched his firm arms overhead. "Good morning to you, too." He slapped his hands together and rubbed them. "What do we tackle first?"

They spent the morning clearing brush and stones. Neither spoke unless necessary. More often, a gesture or a nod served them fine.

Lynia found comfort in the quiet. After all the debating, the shouting, the chaos that her brother had instigated, this simple morning work in peaceful silence covered her with protective arms like a hug. The quiet became a warm fire on a frozen night, to the point that when she picked up the empty canteens, when they clanged against each other, the sound startled.

With the spell of silence broken, Lynia made more noise situating the canteens over her shoulder. "I'm going to find that stream. There's a half-full canteen in the shack."

"Next on your plan is food. If it's okay, I'll head north and see what's there."

"Don't go too far. Be back before sundown."

They parted ways, and taking only a few steps towards the south, the forest engulfed her. Their little camp created the illusion of control, but the trees wanted to make matters clear — this belonged to them. The thick canopy cast intersecting shadows on the sloping ground while large fronds blocked the view ahead. Lynia slowed her pace, making sure to cut a blaze in tree trunks every few feet. The trees were right. They owned this forest, and she would be lost easily without marking a trail.

Not long into her hike, she heard the trickling of water. The fresh, woodsy air added a scent of vegetation that loved the wet. On rocks, she noticed a fuzzy growth formed in wavy lines of red. The scouts had already named it *red moss.* A rather boring name. If she had the chance to name something — and it hit her that she would get to name a lot of things out here — she would put more thought into it. Yet as she closed in on the stream, as other possible names filtered through her mind — *blood moss, red fuzzy, crimson water moss* — she discovered it wasn't easy. Every possibility sounded wrong. Add in that the scouts spent a lot of their time naming things, and she could see why they would choose to keep it basic. Red moss. Not bad, after all.

A few minutes later, she reached the stream. Only three feet wide and ankle deep, its waters flowed lazily along. Sunlight beamed through the canopy break in bright, clean shafts, spreading warmth upon the rocks in and around the stream. Leaves drifted like aimless boats, and a few startled splashes promised some kind of life under the surface.

Lynia singled out a wide, flat boulder that poked into the water from the shore. She lowered to its warm surface. Removing a lead from her visi-link, she placed the sensors on the water. After ten seconds, the full report showed no known pathogens. Not surprising since they drank the water supply last night with no ill effects. Still, better to do things right instead of desperate.

She submerged the canteens one-by-one until all were filled. After sealing the last one, she rolled onto her back and let the sun press against her skin. Gazing up, her eyes fell upon another of those large creatures that blended in with the trees. Her skin prickled. This one stretched out over the water, holding on with one hand and its feet, dangling its free hand, perhaps enjoying the sun as well. She could see it clearer than the ones she had observed near tow and found it even more impressive.

The mantis-like arms ended with a four-digit hand, and its shell shaped sturdy muscles throughout its body. More than anything, however, she noticed that this creature had markings on its shell. They formed a red V off the shoulder — not a natural stripe but perhaps painted on.

Lynia didn't dare move. Not out of fear for herself, but fearing she might scare it away. If it could paint a declaration or signifier on its shell, that suggested a level of intelligence, self-awareness, or perhaps tribal society — a level which had not been thought to exist on Miguel.

A fluttering in the distance caught the creature's attention, and it shot off into the woods. Lynia remained on that rock for another ten minutes, hoping V might return. When it became clear that she would not see the creature again, she gathered her canteens and began the uphill haul toward camp.

The entire hike, she thought about V. Sweat dripped off her brow and salted her tongue, but she ignored any discomfort. She had witnessed another intelligence on this planet. All this time, and nobody had ever thought the creatures were more than animals.

At length, she reached camp, set the canteens inside the supply shack, and plopped down near the fire — nothing but glowing embers now. Her angry muscles tried to relax even as her mind whirled from one thought to another. When she could, she cleared away the chaos in her head and simply wallowed in the memory of V leaning out from that tree.

Snorting grew louder behind her, and Lynia's attention snapped to the present. She held her breath and listened. More snorting. Something definitely there.

Careful not to startle anything, she eased around to find a stubby animal on fours, its head smooth and shallow with no neck. With every snort, two proboscises fluttered in front of its short snout. Nudging its head along the edge of the shack, it sniffed and grumbled and inhaled every scent.

About the size of a chubby toddler, the creature looked well fed. More importantly, Lynia thought it looked like good feeding. Its belly dragged the ground, and its meaty flank jiggled as it continued sniffing. Her stomach gurgled. A woman could only eat so many taters.

Moving slow and cautious, trying not to make a sound, she gently rested a hand on her holster. No gun. Crap. She could picture it on the shelf inside the shack next to the canteens.

The creature stiffened. Two flat flaps along the back of its head perked up as its fluttering feelers twitched rapidly. Maybe it caught her scent or maybe she had made a sound without realizing. Uttering a raspy cry, it charged towards Lynia. She crouched, hoping to tackle the thing to the ground, but it barreled straight for her, smashing its weight into her side and knocking her over.

She rubbed her right flank as she pushed up and saw the tree root she had fallen upon. Stupid thing could have killed her. The animal had fled, but as she gazed in the direction it had taken, she heard a deep throated growl. Crap, again.

The animal had not run because of her. Of course not. She should have known better. There was another who would be equally interested in eating the pudgy meal. Turning slowly once more — this time no longer the predator — she scanned the edges of camp. Her heart hammered. She lifted her eyes upward, searching the trees for that bloody V on the shell of the six-foot killer.

Movement to her left. She snapped her head down — towards the ground. Emerging from the trees, rising from where it had hidden flat in the dirt, a lean hunter rose. Not V. This thing moved into camp on six legs, every step showing off muscle that rippled under a thin coat of fur. Lynia counted four eyes — one on each side and two staring straight ahead. But of all its features, the mouth stood out. A long snout that ended in a sharp point. Jagged teeth lined the inside, growing from a hard beak-like exterior.

She had no trouble imagining this thing leaping onto the back of its victim and chomping down. The bite mark would be distinct — exactly like the one she had seen on Mar Weltty, the miner who had suffered an attack while helping cut trees and clear land.

"Got a taste of humans and want some more?"

The sound of her voice caused the hunter pause. She backed away as it sauntered forward, its front eyes never leaving her, never giving her a chance to attack clean. She considered yelling for Pel, but the sudden noise might launch the creature into action.

With controlled breaths, she kept side-stepping. If she could get the thing to circle her as if they were boxers in a ring, she might reach the shack. From there, she would have to dash inside, grab her gun, and shoot the creature before it could stomp her into the ground and bite her neck into pieces.

She didn't like her odds.

It opened its mouth further, and a gray, puffy tongue lolled around its teeth. A strange clicking reverberated in her head — her teeth. Her chattering teeth. She peeked at her hand still on the holster. It shivered. Bile burned up from her stomach, singeing the back of her throat.

One final idea popped in her mind. She could lunge toward this thing. When she got close to the campfire, she could kick the dying embers at it. With any luck, one or two might land into its mouth, burn its tongue, or even destroy its throat.

She didn't think she would be that lucky.

It must have sensed her fear. Or smelled it. Like soured fruit. Or perhaps some other pheromone gave her away. Promised the hungry beast that she had not prepared, that she could not defend, that she had become easy prey.

Launching off its hind legs, the creature bellowed loud enough to force Lynia's instincts into retreat. She stumbled back, her brain trying to catch up with where her feet wanted to go. Smacking hard into the ground, she looked over her shoulder as the beast raced towards her, its slobbering teeth closing in.

A dark blur blasted by from the side, hammering the animal away. Lynia popped up to find V standing over the bleeding creature. A metal weapon with four prongs like an overeager Trident skewered the creature's neck into the ground. It thrashed for a moment, tried to raise its head, let out a long wheeze, and dropped back with a wet smack. Dead.

In a shocked whisper, a shiver in her throat, Lynia said, "Th-Thank you."

V looked down at her before uttering several strange tones coupled with deep rumbles and odd clicks.

Breathing hard and still shaking, trying to catch up with events, she managed to stand. She pointed to herself. "I'm Lynia."

It click-rumbled again, and two other equally large creatures dropped from the trees. Neither of them had markings on their shells. V motioned to its friends — or maybe subordinates? — and they picked up the dead beast to haul it away. V stood motionless the entire time, watching Lynia carefully.

She put out her hands. “I’m no threat.” Stupid thing to say. Once these fellow creatures left into the woods, V gave a final curious cock of the head before following.

Lynia did not move. Not for the next half hour. Not until Pel returned with a handful of taters he had dug up as well as some spicy yellowjacket fruit.

Setting the food down, he looked at her with a frown. “Something happen?”

She collapsed to the ground.

# CHAPTER 44

WEEKS WENT BY AS LYNIA AND PEL focused their efforts on survival. They followed the stream to a mid-sized lake filled with creatures they dubbed *fish*. Pel figured most of the names they gave things would change when biologists investigated, but until then, *fish* would do fine. After catching a few, testing their composition on the visi-link leads, and testing them further by eating only a bite of each, they learned that most could be digested. Only the blue-backed discfish caused stomach cramps.

Pel spent half-a-day designing and constructing a smoker. Lynia dug a cold cellar, and with Pel's help, they walled it off and covered it. Over several days, they marked out and expanded the supply shack, adding on a small room that could be used for sleeping or shelter during storms.

Each day, they drove sweaty and hard. Each night, they slept exhausted. Throughout it all, Lynia looked for a return of V and his friends. She could not recall at what point she began to think of V as male, but it felt right. Part of her acknowledged these thoughts as humancentric. After all, V's species might have a hundred sexes and perhaps as many genders. Yet the human mind liked to categorize, to find patterns. She would have to be cautious. She did not want to start on bad terms with V by calling him male if he was something else.

Collecting firewood one afternoon, she checked the trees like usual, and like usual, she saw no sign of V. She would hate never having another interaction. He had been an impressive, terrifying, exciting creature. She had so many questions. V's weapon had been forged metal. How could another species be advanced enough to make tools and weapons yet remain unseen?

Why hadn't the ship located V's people when first scanning Miguel? Did the forest canopy block all signs of camps or towns? Or perhaps they had been found but nobody recognized the structures as the result of a possible intelligence.

But these thoughts always drifted Lynia toward the one thing that never left her mind — her town. *No,* she remembered. *Not* my *town. It belongs to all of us.*

Except it belonged to none but Rowan now.

"I need to check on the people," she said one night over the campfire.

Pel tossed the last cooked tater into his mouth. "I wondered how long it would take for you to say that."

"Simple steps. We got the camp together, basic needs are in better shape — it's time for recon."

"Sounds great. Let's supply up and head out in the morning."

"Just me. I know you want to go, but I need you to keep foraging a good stockpile of food. Shifts in weather might mean a lack of food later. Plus, we need you to protect the camp."

She could tell Pel didn't like the idea of her alone in the forest. She didn't care for it much, either. But with only two of them handling the work of ten or more, they often had to split the load in unpleasant ways. This was no different.

At least, that was the excuse she gave the following morning when she shouldered her pack and tramped off into the woods. Pel looked unconvinced, but he would obey her orders. For now. No matter how eagerly he wanted to please her, to follow her lead, she figured there would be a point where he tired of her running things.

*Stop that,* she chided herself. Self-sabotage could not enter her mind. Not if she wanted to survive this.

By midday, she ate a meager lunch of taters — of course, taters — spread with a sweet goo on top similar to a mixed berry compote. She checked her map throughout the long hike. The only other time she had taken this route had been the night of her exile. Darkness, anxiety, exhaustion, and disillusionment had overcome her senses during that hike, leaving her memory of the path cloudy, at best.

But Pel had marked her map clearly, and her visi-link wouldn't need a recharge for several more months. Inhaling a mint scent on the air, she plodded on through the thick foliage. She kept expecting her legs to complain, but her muscles had grown stronger. She didn't strain for air, either.

At length, she reached the forest edge and found a vantage point to look out across the camp. Lynia's heart jumped. Everything appeared good. Evidence of the riot such as broken glass, burned market stalls, blood, and ruined buildings, had been mostly cleaned up. Rebuilding of the worst damage had already begun. Rowan's church, not surprisingly, had also broken ground. She could hear the metallic hammering surrounding the mines and even noticed activity around the factory.

Daily life had returned. No, she had to admit the truth. What she saw was a town. A devilish grin crossed her face. All towns needed a name, so she would name it — Sydney.

With a satisfied chuckle, she settled in for a few hours of careful observation. But storm clouds formed in the distance. With them, Lynia picked out the darker side of Sydney.

The police force had increased in size. Small patrols of red uniforms marched along the streets like tiny curses in blood. When they neared regular citizens, fear electrified the air. Even from the tree line, Lynia could sense the unease, the concern, the troubling brows of even the strongest miners. The police moved with arrogant steps, and Lynia pictured Chief Lig sitting in his office like a feudal lord wallowing in his small, muddy piece of power.

A scream that scratched the inside of bone rattled in the distance. Until that moment, Lynia had not realized how devoid of voices the town had become. The noise of work existed, but not the noise of life.

She couldn't locate what had caused the horrible screech, but none of the police appeared bothered. Either they already knew the answer or such sounds of horror had become commonplace. Regardless, Lynia's thumping heart no longer held hope that Rowan had ruled well for her people.

She needed to go. The storm rumbled across the sky, but she

stayed still. She could do nothing for these people. Not yet. But she needed to witness what terrible things had come to Sydney. As testimony, perhaps. Or even self-flagellation.

*Another hour.* Watch for another hour, and she promised herself that she would get moving.

Twenty-seven minutes later, the rain fell. Water glistened on the buildings and muddied the dirt streets. She stared as large puddles formed and wondered if the blood of those murdered in Rowan's coup would pool up from the ground. Perhaps all the death and destruction had not been cleaned. Perhaps it had become a ghost seeping into the bones of every building.

*Perhaps I'm to blame.* Thick raindrops broke through the canopy to splash against her face. With her jaw set and her mind racing, she stomped back into the woods, heading towards camp. She would fix this. She had to.

Water pattering on leaves as it fell toward the forest floor sounded like static. The strong aroma of wet wood and fresh mud plugged her nose, as Lynia trudged along the path back — *home?* No. She could not allow the supply shack camp to be called *home*. It was a staging ground. A place to prepare for the inevitable.

She tried to find protection under the wide leaves of a colorfully-striped bush or beneath a rock shelf, but the wind pushed the storm in all directions. Every time she thought she had evaded the rain, the wind laughed, changing its path and forcing water into her face.

Pushing onward, she climbed a steep incline when a rock beneath her foot sucked out of the mud. Her stomach lifted into her chest. She went down hard on her knee. Hissing as something sharp dug into her skin, she planted one foot to stand again. She grunted. The ground disappeared beneath her.

She tumbled and rolled and flipped through the wet mud. Rocks poked at her back and her arm snagged against a tree, wrenching her around with a vicious bite.

The fall did not last long. It ceased with a thump in her back that thrust the last breath from her lungs. Feeling mugged by the forest, she knew to be thankful the drop had not been further.

That would have been her death.

Panting, she grabbed the nearest tree for a crutch and pulled onto her feet. No broken bones — another miracle. The taste of blood mixed with mud in her mouth.

She didn't have much in the way of first-aid, but even a simple rag to clean her wounds would be welcome. She reached into her bag and —

*Her bag!* Spinning in a circle like a confused dog, she searched all around her. Nothing. The pack with her supplies and food was gone.

# CHAPTER 45

THE COLD RAIN TAPERED OFF, and the resulting drizzle fought the humid forest creating an eerie fog. If she had simply waited out the storm, she would have been fine. That fact boiled a sharp accusatory howl from deep within. Losing the town, the Ring, Monclova Industries was bad enough, but now this planet stole the few supplies she had to get back to the pathetic little camp. She wailed and kicked the nearest tree.

With that release, her mind turned toward the current problems — the ones she could solve. Hiking all the way back to camp would be foolish. Too late in the day. By the time she could climb to where she had fallen from or worked a way around to rejoin the path, night would take over, and she didn't even have a flashlight.

But making an overnight camp would be foolish, too. She had no supplies, no tools, nothing to build with. Searching for her lost pack might be smart, if she found it. Otherwise, she would waste time and energy.

At least, food wasn't an issue. She had snacked while investigating Sydney, and though she expected to feel hunger pangs tomorrow, she could handle that. Food awaited her back at camp. Might only be taters and a fruit spread, but it would fill her stomach.

She needed a place to sleep safe from the elements — if the rain returned — and from predators. A quick survey of the area did not reveal any caves or overhangs. However, there were plenty of trees. Not perfect, but at least hiding in a tree provided some protection.

Picking the nearest one that had branches low and sturdy enough, she climbed. But the mossy bark had turned slick from the rain. Her feet slipped, her hands could not get a firm grip, and she dropped. Only a few feet, yet the forest floor pounded the air from her and jostled her head with vigor.

She let loose a string of curses. Her mother would have been appalled. That thought made Lynia laugh. That laughter contained a few tears.

Gazing up at the tree that had rejected her, she noticed movement two trees over. Peeking through the fog, one of V's kind maneuvered toward the ground. Had it been following her? Or perhaps it had been watching the town, too. After all, these creatures had been observing Sydney since the beginning. She had seen them without knowing it, and now she spied this one—

Except she was no spy. The creature dropped down and approached her, picking her out of the dissipating fog with ease. The moisture on her arms chilled her goosebumps.

It stood over her, a blue square painted on its chest, and it rattled off a series of clicks and grunts. This one seemed more curious than threatening — although, it did carry a bladed weapon, the shaft of metal about as long as her head. She recalled how V had killed that charging beast with one strike. These creatures had great strength. She made sure to move without any threat — at least, what she hoped would not be perceived as threat.

A second creature came up to the Blue Square's side. They seemed to exchange looks, yet their faces didn't move. Lynia tried to understand, but she found nothing familiar to latch upon.

Five excruciatingly long minutes passed. No attack came — that much was good — but the creatures did not back away, either. They stood over her as if waiting for her to attempt an escape. She imagined that knife slamming into the back of her skull and coming out the front with several more inches to go.

Then V arrived. He spoke harsh noises at Blue Square who clicked rapidly back. Body language suggest a disagreement that threatened to boil into a fight. Or perhaps Lynia misconstrued the entire exchange. At length, Blue Square leapt onto a nearby branch and disappeared into the trees.

A long stare from V, and the other creature stepped aside to give him room. He watched the trees for a moment. Apparently satisfied that Blue Square would not return, V crouched toward Lynia's feet. He placed a large, folded blanket before her.

She hurried over, and her sudden movement riled the other one. But not V. He remained like stone.

Smiling, hoping to convey friendship, or at least a lack of hostility, she reached out to touch the blanket. Thin fur lined the top, and that one touch made it clear — the blanket had been created from the hide of the beast that had nearly killed her. A beautiful gift, indeed.

But it was more. The edges looked exact — machine-made perfection — as was the soft, waterproof cloth underneath. In each corner, she unfolded a triangular metal hole. A grommet. This could be used for more than a blanket. It could be tied into a tarp, a cover, even a tent. An incredibly versatile, useful object. So simple yet so valuable.

"Thank you," she whispered.

Offering no more than a slight head movement, the creatures backed away.

"Wait," she said, causing V to grip his weapon tight as he scanned the trees.

Lynia stepped closer. She knew what she wanted to do, yet part of her hesitated — resisted. She hoped her father would understand.

Taking off her necklace with the M pendant, she presented it. It was the only thing of value she had left.

V glanced back at his friends before accepting the gift. He held it up to see the dangling M closer. Lynia had no idea if V's species created jewelry or even understood it, but as the others faded into the forest, V wrapped the thin chain around his wrist.

In a low rumble, he said, "Thank you."

As he disappeared like his friends, Lynia watched, unable to move, heart beating in her ears, sweat breaking across her body, icy rainwater trickling down her spine. It seemed impossible. A mind trick. An illusion. But she knew what she heard.

The creature had spoken.

# CHAPTER 46

THE REST OF THE NIGHT BLURRED under patches of rain. Laying her new blanket between the branches of two trees, she created a covering that sloped behind. This kept her dry and drained the rainwater away. But nothing kept her mind from reliving those final moments with V. She thought of nothing else.

An hour before the sun rose to a clear sky, Lynia had already folded her blanket and hiked a quarter of the way to camp. Most of her remained stunned by V. Finding life on Miguel had not been surprising. With the unfathomably large size of the universe and all its galaxies and each galaxy chock full of planets, some were bound to hold life of a sort — bacteria, micro-organisms, plants, fungi, even small animals. Finding a planet that had a larger ecosystem, such as Miguel, had been an exciting bit of fortune. But to have intelligent life — life that could not only decorate its body and forge metal weapons but also speak — that astounded her.

Lynia considered that perhaps similar worlds attracted the wormhole. Perhaps having the Pathway Ring lock one end of the wormhole near Mars and Earth required the other end to seek out a similar area — a part of space also near a world with intelligent life. She had no idea if physics could work that way, and she suspected that one day a lot of smart people would figure out such things. They might even become famous for it. If she earned any fame for the Monclova name, however, she at least had claim to making first contact.

Not long before midday, she arrived at camp. Pel had been positioned to see her enter, and he bounded to his feet.

"Welcome home," he said. Warm. Filled with relief.

She eased onto a log bench near the campfire. "Thank you."

The words caught in her throat. Two simple words that people said to each other all the time, yet now she only heard V's deep rumbling voice utter those same words.

"What happened to you? Where's your bag?" Pel looked over the blanket with a frown. "Did you make this?" His roving concern shifted to her. "You're hurt. I'll get the shack's first aid kit."

She tried to stop him but could barely lift an arm now that she had halted. After such a long day and night, she only wanted sleep. Pel returned with a small box as he pulled up first aid information on his visi-link.

He tended to her scrapes and bruises with gentle care, cupping her elbow to inspect her upper-arm, lifting each leg as if carrying porcelain. She felt like a cloud handled her. With each pat of antiseptic and each bandage applied to a cut, she could see his brow easing. When he finished, he turned to the fire.

"You hungry?" he asked. "I caught some giraffe fish from the lake."

Long-necked swimmers like a cross between an eel and a trout — at least, Pel described it that way. She had never seen underwater life except in nature shows. But she knew the fish tasted great, and as he set two filets on a flat cooking rock near the fire, the smell instantly caused her to salivate.

After the meal, sleep finally caught her. When she awoke, night had arrived. She sat up in the bedroom attached to the supply shack. No recollection of moving there, but she felt so much better having several hours of rest.

"You're up," Pel said, entering the room. He lowered to her side. "Let me change the bandages on your arm. The rest of your injuries look okay, but that one really bled."

As he unrolled the arm wrap, careful not to pull the skin in the process, he watched her. The intensity of his gaze stirred her deep inside. She imagined what his chest would feel like pressed against her skin.

Shaking her head, she pushed those thoughts away. It was the rooftop again, and while she had no objection to exploring those possibilities someday, she wanted to tell him about what she saw at Sydney and all about V.

"You won't believe what happened out there," she said.

"Don't worry. I won't doubt you."

"Oh … I didn't mean …"

"I know. I just want you to know that I trust you."

He shifted to get more light on her arm, moving his body closer. She could smell him — sweaty from a day's work. How could that be so appetizing? Her tongue licked her lips, imagining the saltiness his skin would taste like.

He finished wrapping the new bandage before letting go. Her skin tremored as if clamoring for his touch to return. When he lifted his head, they stared at each other, faces close enough to feel their tentative breaths.

Hearing her own voice as if from afar, she said, "I thought I should tell you about what I found."

"If that's what you want. Is it? What you want?"

Before she could talk herself out of it, she leaned closer, pressing her lips against his. They were hungry yet unhurried. She lavished in his embrace and flushed with his warmth. As he pressed her softly down, she let her fingers trace his chest.

When they finished, she slept again. Only this time, she cradled her back against him. Nobody guarded the camp, yet she felt safe anyway.

# CHAPTER 47

THE DAYS THAT FOLLOWED MELDED into a long series of lustful encounters, brief moments of restoration, and further physical exploration. Lynia had taken lovers in the past, but nothing had prepared her for the sensations Pel created. Though part of her knew that survival instincts and the threat of losing all contributed to her heightened sexual experiences, she refused to believe that explained everything. A bond had formed, and its physical expression surpassed any she had known before.

Reality could only be ignored for so long, however, and the needs of camp broke apart their frequent unions. In the weeks that came and went, they caught fish, foraged edible plants, prepared food for storage, improved the campsite, and worked at surviving. Early on, Pel had listened to a detailed telling of the town's condition as well as Lynia's exchange with V, and this proved to be the only coarse friction between them.

One afternoon, while cleaning up their lunch, she mentioned V again. Pel frowned, dismissing her enthusiasm.

"But don't you see how incredible this is?" she said. "The creature actually spoke."

"It mimicked you, but yeah, it's great."

"Then why do you sound upset?"

"Because animal behavior studies aren't important when Sydney is still under Rowan's thumb. What's the plan for getting the town back? I'm enjoying our time together, I'm glad you've found these creatures interesting, but I came out here to regroup, to strike back, not to hang our head defeated."

"I know."

"Then how do we get control of Sydney?"

She shrugged. "I haven't figured it out. Not yet."

"Maybe our relationship is diverting your attention."

Trying not to lose the loving bubble surrounding their camp, she rubbed his shoulders and kissed his cheek. "What we have is the one thing keeping me sane. I'll figure this out. Have some patience."

He stomped away from her. "We've been living out here for months. Half-a-year, maybe. I've lost track. That's fine for us, but what about the rest of them. They're more than just employees. Many of them are my friends, and they're stuck. From what you said, they've got to worry about the police, Rowan, and who knows what else — and I'm sure they all cling to the hope that you and I are working on some way to fix this."

"We are working on it."

"Doesn't feel like it. Feels more like we're indulging ourselves." Gazing back at her, his head dropped. "I'm sorry. You know I'm happy with us, but I feel guilty. We can't do nothing."

"I promise you — I am thinking about it. I'm trying to find an answer."

He started to speak, stopped, then shook his head. "I'm going to the lake."

She watched him leave. They had debated this before, but this time felt closer to the bone. Pel felt guilty. He had never expressed it so plainly, never let it be heard out loud. She had guessed as much, but to see the pain on his face — she wished she had an answer. While she had been working through different scenarios on how to win back Sydney, she admitted that Pel's body offered a delightful escape from dealing with these problems. But using him to avoid their problems only delayed matters. It didn't solve them.

When she finished cleaning up, she walked the path to the lake. She couldn't say what possessed her, but as she neared the shore, she squatted low behind a purple bruise bush and spied on him. He swam to the opposite side, pulled up onto a rock, and stretched before the sun.

Seeing his wet, naked body reminded her that there was a clear reason she had been losing herself in all this pleasure. He had a wonderful physique. Trim and fit. She looked between his legs, remembering how it filled her, igniting her senses.

He dove back into the water, staying under long enough for the waves to settle. She quickly removed her clothes, set them aside, and scurried to the shoreline. The water felt cool on her feet as she eased in. With a smile rising on her lips, she swam.

By the time she reached the middle, he had resurfaced. She continued over, placed her arms around his neck, and pulled him close, pressing her flesh against his. She kissed him, refusing to release his lips until he stopped resisting and returned her kiss.

"Apology sex doesn't work on me," he said, though he sounded as if it might.

"The sex isn't my apology. This is — since all of this started, since Rowan ousted me, I've been caught up in my own head. You've been here for me, and I have used you but never really paid you the attention you deserve. I act like I'm in this alone. I hope you know that I couldn't have come this far without you."

"It's tough being the leader."

"That doesn't excuse how I've been. Sydney is your town, too. I won't forget it."

Pel's hand reached down her back as he lowered his head to kiss again. But he stopped. His eyes shifted beyond her, toward the shore. Turning, she saw V standing by the purple bruise bush. Ten more of his kind emerged from the forest, five to each side of him, stretching along the edge of the water like shadowed sentinels.

Lynia's heart flipped. She could not hide the thrill at seeing V again. She wanted to speak more with the creature, learn about him and his people, discover what secrets he knew about this world. More than that, she wanted to share it all with Pel.

But why would the creature arrive with an armed squad? Her pulse hammered. Each one carried one of those big, multi-pronged weapons. Perhaps she had been wrong. Perhaps V had never intended friendship or even peaceful curiosity. This could have been a series of cautious steps with a new organism he had discovered, and now that V had concluded his study, he would conquer his enemy.

Except none of their time together suggested any of that. V wasn't Rowan. She had no reason to distrust the creature. Not yet.

Regardless of his motivations, one fact rang clear. V's presence — along with ten others — marked the end of her little paradise with Pel.

As if confirming her thoughts, V reached out a hand, and in a booming voice that shivered across the water, he said, "Come."

# CHAPTER 48

OVER THE NEXT SEVERAL HOURS, Lynia swirled between excitement and frustration and concern. Every step through the jungle-forest meant a step closer to something new. After leaving the lake and getting dressed, V led his people in a long line. Lynia and Pel marched in the middle of the group. They moved with coordination — not quite military precision, but rather with the orchestration of a well-honed team that had spent a lot of time together.

Even more of a thrill — Lynia noticed her necklace had been tied into a bracelet around V's wrist. It stood out against his dark shell, catching glints of light like a promise of their newly born friendship. Or perhaps she imagined that.

Because all attempts at communication failed to get any response. Even from V. She wanted to show Pel what these creatures could do, yet not one of them spoke. Of course, Pel had heard V's single request — or command — but that had sounded different, less honest. That had been the words of somebody performing a required duty — not the voice of a native creature trying to express an emotion to an alien creature. Or, as Pel had suggested, it could be mimicry.

Using a wide, curved blade, V hacked at the red arch fronds blocking their way. They came upon a steep, rocky rise. Without pause V and his squad started up.

Lynia looked to Pel. "How are you at climbing?"

"We're not tree hoppers like these things, but I think we'll manage."

Scrabbling their way up the incline — only requiring assistance twice — they reached the top without embarrassing all of humanity. Lynia noticed she hardly sweat, didn't gasp for air, and felt invigorated rather than exhausted. Another forty minutes brought them to a sweeping view of the jungle-forest. Far in the distance, lines of smoke rose — Sydney.

V did not give them time to stop. Later, when they crossed a stream, Lynia bent down to get a drink, and V shouted in his clicking language, waving his hands at her. She froze, water dribbling out of her cupped hand. He slapped the hand open, splashing the water against the rocks. Her stomach tightened. She braced for an assault, for a shift in behavior that made no human sense, but probably made perfect logic to an alien mind. But then, V pointed to the rocks protruding from the stream. A crimson fungus grew along their edges, staining the stones and releasing an oily substance into the water.

"Poisonous?" she asked, but V did not answer.

Pel, however, did. "I think it best to assume that's what he means."

Straightening, she gestured for them to continue onward, her chest tapping rapidly as she took a few shaky steps. V brought them downhill for a while. At length, the ground evened and the trees cut away into a clearing. Several large coverings, each similar to the blanket Lynia now owned, had been fastened high above between the trees surrounding the clearing. From further up, it must have looked like a gray pool of water or another shadowy section of thick overgrowth.

The ten creatures that had accompanied V spread around the clearing's perimeter while V walked straight toward the middle. A mud hut had been constructed in the center — tall enough for V but only wide enough for one inside. In front, another of the creatures sat, its shell dusty, less-vibrant, perhaps an elderly one.

V stopped several feet short of the older creature. With a swift motion of its mantis arm, the older one permitted V closer. V stepped forward and lowered to his knees. He set his weapons at his side and bowed his head to the grass.

From the edge, Lynia could hear the deep tones of a conversation. Her mind whirled in an effort to take in all she witnessed, let alone understand it, but at the very least, she comprehended that these creatures had a social structure, a language, could craft with metal, could construct buildings, and possibly a lot more.

She noticed Pel moving his hand over his wrist. A soft, muffled beep. Smart. He had turned on his visi-link. It would record this meeting's audio, and if he could manage it, they might even grab some video or a few pictures.

"Come," V said, gesturing toward Lynia and Pel.

Her throat constricted. Hoping she looked serious but friendly, she approached the two creatures and stopped at V's side. Pel followed a few strides behind. Smart again. By this simple act, he established her leadership without a word. She made a mental note to give him the ride of his life when they returned to camp.

V motioned for them to sit on their knees. Not wanting to be rude or start off wrong, Lynia complied and Pel followed.

The old creature bowed its chin to chest which Lynia took as a sign of respect. But then it reached behind its neck, she heard several sharp snaps, and it pulled off its head. No, a covering. The hardshell was a covering. Headgear. Or a battle helmet.

*Like armor,* she thought.

The shell had given the creatures an insect-like appearance, but now Lynia saw its real face — a pale thing resembling a hairless hound. The skin itself looked thick and tough. Leathery.

"I name Osto. You, Lynia. You, Pel."

Lynia's eyes could grow no wider. "You know our names? How can you speak our language?"

"Speak not well. Not yet. We watch when you came. We watch."

"You really were observing us. Listening. Learning."

Osto's hound lips pulled back into a grin. "More talking good. Help us learn faster."

Lynia allowed a genuine smile to rise. "Well, on behalf of humanity, I say hello." She put out her hand, but Osto stared in confusion. She made a circle in the area encompassing herself and Pel. "We are called humans."

"Humans. You are Lynia, a human. He is Pel, a human."

"Yes. And you?"

Osto uttered three clicks and a grunt followed by, "Dahtien."

She tried to make the same sounds, but her throat and tongue could not get the right pitches. But she did manage the verbal part. "Dah … tee … en. Dahtien. You are named Osto, a Dahtien."

The old Dahtien nodded. "Humans live above. Dangerous animals."

This one took Lynia a moment. It sounded as if Osto had decided humans were dangerous — not a wrong conclusion — but then she pieced it together. "The Dahtien live underground?"

"Yes."

She thought of all the beasts that had killed her people and nearly killed her. "There are a lot of dangerous animals here. Is it safer underground?"

Osto paused. At first, Lynia thought the Dahtien had not understood. But the way its lips moved, a soft whisper escaping to sound out the new words, she gathered that Osto digested a newfound understanding of some aspect of human standard. When it spoke next, she heard a clearer, better usage of her language. Amazing.

"Dangerous animals are everywhere. But, yes, it is safer underground. Humans dig into our home. Why?"

Osto surprised her again. Without any further preamble, this creature had shifted Lynia into a negotiation. Already, it claimed the land for the Dahtien — their home. Humans had a long history of screwing up first contacts with each other, and now she had to represent all humankind in a first contact with another intelligent species. She wanted to make the right impression but also gain acceptance of their presence and their purpose. Otherwise, things would eventually turn ugly.

She decided to start with tentative honesty. "We are builders. We have constructed a tunnel far in the sky. It starts at our homeworld and stretches all the way out here. Our job is to finish the tunnel so that we may return home. To do that means we need metals found deep in the ground."

Osto tapped a finger in V's direction. "Building tunnels." This seemed to be part of a larger discussion or argument between the two, and Osto appeared to have scored a point in its favor. To Lynia: "When the tunnel finish, you return home. Other humans come?"

"Yes. To explore, to live, to meet you."

"And to give things?"

"What things? Gifts?"

Osto frowned, shaking his head. "Tregacy give the hide to you. You give the gold chain."

"I see," Lynia said, trying to rebrand V as Tregacy in her mind. "That's called a *trade*."

"Trade. Trade." Osto savored the word a moment. "Yes. Humans come through the tunnel to trade."

"Many will, I'm sure. It's also possible for you to go through the tunnel — we call it the Pathway Ring — you could go through it and visit our worlds. Trade there."

This appeared to astonish Osto, though Lynia had to keep her assumptions in check. Clearly, the Dahtien had reacted, but she could not be sure what its various facial expressions meant. Yet the same curving of the lips she had seen before — that she thought of as a smile — returned to Osto's face.

"Trade is good. Building is good."

"I agree. It helps to create strong friendship." She realized the word *friendship* would not have come up much in observing a mining town's daily functions. Friends did not often throw around self-referential words like that. "Um … *friendship* … um …" She pointed to Tregacy. "Like him and me." She clasped her hands together and smiled. "Friends." She made fists, punched them at each other, and frowned. "Enemies." Then returned to smiling and clasping. "Friends."

Osto picked it up fast. "Yes, yes."

Taking a breath, Lynia reached her hand out toward the old creature. "Humans want to be friends of the Dahtien."

Reaching back, Osto wrapped its large hand around hers. "Friends."

But Tregacy leapt to his feet. Blue Square rushed in from the edges. The rapid click-grunt talk raced between them. Like Lynia,

Osto stood still, listening and watching. Unlike Osto, Lynia had no idea what anybody said. She only understood from the tones and the urgency.

Tregacy spoke to Osto next, but the old leader made a calming gesture until the younger Dahtien sat, head bowed. With a shift of the body, Osto put all its attention on Blue Square. That Dahtien quickly returned to the perimeter.

Lynia kept silent, doing her best to observe. She waited for Osto to return its focus upon their meeting, the one that had been going so well until this point, and she wondered if they could bring matters back to where they were.

Osto said, "The Dahtien are friends of Lynia."

"Yes. And we humans are your friends. Let's continue from there."

"I, Osto, speak for Dahtien. But Lynia does not speak for humans."

"I do. I lead this project to build the Pathway Ring."

Osto's thick skin wrinkled across its brow. "Then why are you away from your people?"

"The town? Well … that's a long story."

"You, Lynia, the leader?"

"Yes, but —"

"Why allow so many deaths?"

The question reached into her chest and tangled around her lungs. "Deaths? What deaths?"

Osto slipped his headpiece back on and clicked it shut. "Tregacy will show. I prepare for you and I next meeting."

As Tregacy stood, Lynia followed. Pel got to his feet, too, brushing off the dirt, and fell in behind her. She nodded her head toward Osto — no matter what else happened, at least she heard the words *next meeting*. She hadn't totally botched things.

Tregacy pointed to three others, and they hurried close. After issuing orders, he said to Lynia, "Hike. Long."

With his first steps, she knew where they headed. A long hike, indeed. But knowing there were deaths in Sydney — enough to draw concern from an outside species — that twisted her stomach even as it hardened her steps.

# CHAPTER 49

IT WOULD TAKE HALF-A-DAY OR MORE to reach the supply shack, then another to reach Sydney. And that was without a contingent of four Dahtien plus Pel or the stop at the shack to eat and rest — something Lynia had not done in almost a full day. None of it could happen fast enough, and the longer the day dragged, the worse her imagination dove into horrible ideas of what Rowan had become and what he might be doing to her people.

Rain poured for hours. The driving sheets of water pushed against every trudging step. Despite Lynia's fears of moving too slow, Tregacy kept their pace strong. Even through the storm. Even after it dissipated without warning, leaving thick mud behind.

When they finally reached the tree line, Lynia no longer wanted to see Sydney. If she could preserve the town in her memory, she wouldn't have to know. But those intruding thoughts belonged to a child. She shoved them away. No matter what had happened down there, she still considered herself the town's leader. That meant facing the ugly side of things — even when the ugly side was her own brother.

"Fuck me," Pel whispered, gaining an odd glance from Tregacy. "It's a curse word." Tregacy shook his head. Pel said, "I'll explain later."

Lynia wanted to swear, too, but that required her throat to open enough for sound. Instead, she shuddered, never taking her eyes off the horrors below.

At the southern end of town, along the dirt road that reached the first buildings, two rows of bodies had been lined up. White and brown tarps wrapped each one, though some had dark spots where blood seeped through. Further south, two men operated a tracked hauler used for carting heavy tubs of fuel and ore over uneven ground — only this one carried several corpses. Their path led Lynia's eyes to a burning pit. The smoke of death rose dark gray in the air.

Looking back up the road, the buildings lining the southern entrance had been set up as offices for all the various departments that needed access to both the town and the land — mining being chief among them. But red-suited officers now traipsed in and out of those buildings. In a few cases, they shoved downtrodden folks through the doorways. She recognized one. Zural Kin-Nol, the head of the Armory. Lynia surmised that these were prisoners either being brought in for interrogations — attempts to weed out any of her supporters — or being locked up in makeshift jails.

"Is this like you saw last time?" Pel asked.

"This is worse. This is organized."

"I can't believe your brother would go this far. Or that people would follow him."

"You didn't see his vid-logs. He's been grooming his followers for years. They see him as nearly-divine, and he believes in destroying the enemies of the Lord and gods."

Pel sneered. "It isn't murder when your gods tell you to do it."

"Exactly."

Tregacy nudged Lynia. "Go. Better see."

She followed along the tree line as they worked toward the northwest of town. She wished she had stayed in the south. From this new vantage, she had clear view of the Square. Long metal bars had been fastened at right angles to the ruined comm-tower. Off each one, a body had been hung. Four bars. Four bodies. Bags covered the heads, and from the way nobody paid attention, Lynia guessed they had been hanging there for a long time.

That same terrible silence from her earlier visit pervaded the town. Nobody spoke. The only sounds came from physical labor. Surveying the area in a broader scope, she noticed that only a few buildings looked to be in use — mostly by the police.

Except one, of course.

The most activity surrounded the church. Its base structure had been completed, and the framework of a tower rose from the far end. A wide porch ran along the front. On the corners, two workers chipped away at large boulders, slowly carving out a statue each. She had strong guess who the statues would depict.

One of the front doors opened, and Rowan stepped out with Akiko by his side. He wore a long, white robe and had a wreath of red and green swirling leaves crowning his head. Akiko held a slightly bent posture as if always bowing toward him. Several others followed a few steps behind, recording what he said or running off to fulfill an order he had given.

A gust of wind blew across the town, swiping Lynia's breath as she noticed her brother's hand. He had a rope wrapped around it. The rope dragged along the ground behind him, sloped upward, and connected to a collar locking the neck of the last person out of the church — Graham Torson.

Lynia whipped out her small knife as she jumped to her feet. "That son of a —"

While the Dahtien watched her, perhaps unsure of what her behavior signified in the larger context of their new relationship, Pel grabbed hold of her from behind. His strong arms clamped tight. She thrashed and kicked.

"No, no," he said. "You can't run in there."

"I'm going to kill him."

"You'd never get anywhere near him, and having you dead won't help Graham."

She strained, thrusting her knife in Rowan's direction. At length, though, she went limp. Pel lowered her to the ground. "I'm okay," she said.

"You're not. But I don't think you'll do anything rash now."

Taking his hand, she brought it to her lips.

Tregacy angled his head toward the forest, as did the other Dahtien. Then he turned to Lynia. "We go back. Osto ready. Talk more."

She had noticed this behavior before, but in the past, she had discounted her thoughts because when he was V, she thought him an animal. However, now that she had experienced a sliver of Dahtien intelligence, she wondered if they had developed a type of communication system similar to the link. Perhaps those shells were more than simply armor.

For the moment, she had to be content with following Tregacy away from the town. She hated leaving Graham behind, leaving any of them behind. She hated leaving. Rowan should be the one banished from this land. None of her people should be suffering, imprisoned, murdered.

Silently, she made a promise — the next time she came back to Sydney, she would not leave again.

# CHAPTER 50

THE JOURNEY BACK GREW into the longest hike of Lynia's life. Moving further away from Sydney required impossible effort. The dead reached for her back, chilling her spine, plaguing her with the simple thought — the more time she spent away from town, the more bodies would hang, the more dead to haunt her.

Despite her perceptions, the slog through the forest ended at the supply shack sooner than expected. Pel even remarked that they had traveled the path enough to limit the need for cutting too much vegetation. After a short rest and resupply, Tregacy insisted they continue.

"But the sun is almost down," Pel said.

"Need no sun."

Though Lynia and Pel did not agree, tried to explain that human eyes could not work as well in the dark, Tregacy left no room to argue. He did make sure to keep his squad on the forest floor with only one scouting ahead in the trees. This worked well enough. Even when the sun vanished, Lynia could see the Dahtien in front of her. She stumbled a few times but managed to stay upright.

"Are you okay?" Pel asked at one point. "Tired?"

She should have been. While being in exile had done wonders for her physical stamina and overall athletic health, she had not been ready for two day-long hikes with minimal break. Yet pushing her body onward required little effort. Adrenaline could only account for some of it — she couldn't run on that alone for an entire day. Euphoria? Over what? She had seen her town ruined.

When she finally guessed the answer, her trudging steps

became stronger. Even without a firm plan in mind, she knew she would succeed. Pel had been waiting for her to come up with a strategy, to act in that direction, and she had done nothing. Thought about possibilities but never moved them closer to that target.

Yet now — now she had new friends. She didn't feel alone. In fact, the answer came with clarity. It peeked out of her subconscious, waving like an overenthusiastic child. All she had to do was convince her new friends to help.

Her father had once taught her that negotiations never amounted to one discussion. Even when it appeared everything had been worked out, negotiations continued throughout the life of any relationship. As Tregacy returned them to the clearing, as she realized this was a different clearing set up like the first one but much larger with three huts in the center, she saw that Miguel Monclova was right. She wanted another negotiation, and it appeared the Dahtien wanted the same.

Like before, Dahtien lined the perimeter of the clearing, but this time, they encompassed the entire thing with numerous Dahtien shoulder-to-shoulder. In front of the center hut, Osto sat, its shell removed from the head. On either side, two other elder Dahtien sat — also with their headgear removed — and behind them all, Lynia guessed around fifty more Dahtien crowded the clearing.

The one to Osto's left had a slight bluish tint to its shell. The one on the right, a darker green. The Dahtien behind the huts and standing on the perimeter also bore these subtle differences. Lynia wondered if these were different governments, different states, or no difference at all — simply alternate colorations.

With a single gesture, Osto summoned Lynia and Tregacy forward. As she had done the first time, she approached and knelt alongside Tregacy.

Osto indicated the Dahtien on his right. "This is Warthem." Then to the left: "This is Vinip." Then with both hands out: "We are the three strongest families of the Dahtien. They want to hear about trade."

Lynia thought about all the negotiations her father had gone through. Whenever he managed to be home for a meal or a visit, she could always get him talking if she asked about his business. He loved to explain the intricacies of a good negotiation like a chess game. Or a war.

Understand the opponent. Think several moves ahead. Hide strategies in plain sight. There were so many nuggets, but she needed to pick the right ones now. Much of her father's approach could not be counted on. He dealt in adversarial negotiations, bad faith negotiations. But here, she needed to trust the Dahtien as she hoped they would be — friends and allies.

From her previous meeting with Osto, she knew two definite things — the Dahtien spoke direct, no preambles, no false pleasantries; and the Dahtien wanted trade.

She launched into a straightforward explanation of the Pathway Ring, their intent to build the connection to her world, and the great possibilities for trade between humans and Dahtien. Osto translated, and the other leaders clicked and nodded. The large groupings of Dahtien in the back also reacted as if they could hear the softer conversations between the leaders.

When she ended her initial talk, Vinip spoke. Osto then said, "Vinip's family asks if all families will trade or just the Osto family. I told him all. He needs to hear you say that, too."

"Yes. The Vinip family, the Osto family, the Warthem family are all welcome. Any other families you wish to be involved, too. We value trade with everyone."

After more translation and conversation, Osto said, "The concern now is over the killing."

She expected this and had prepared an answer. It helped that her answer was also the truth. "I lead the Monclova family. Rowan Monclova, my brother, has broken away to start his own family."

"The same has happened with some of ours."

"Then you understand. He causes these killings. If he continues to lead, more killings will occur. Worst of all for you, he has no intention of finishing the Pathway Ring."

Vinip spouted a rapid grunting. Osto said, "If you do not

build the Pathway Ring, then there is no trade. No reason to talk."

Not the conclusion Lynia had sought, but she would work with it. Another key lesson from her father — turn every failure into an opportunity. If she could win today, it required one of these Dahtien to broach her plan first. Make it look like they instigated the entire thing; otherwise, they would never agree.

"I guess Vinip is right," she said, letting her shoulders sag like a deflating balloon. "With only Pel and myself, there is no hope to take back the town and get construction moving again. I'm sorry to have wasted your time."

She waited. No response. Making a greater show of feeling dejected — in case human emotions didn't translate as clearly — she shuffled toward the edge of the clearing.

"Stop."

She halted, striving to hold back a victorious grin. When she turned, she found Tregacy standing with a hand reaching toward her.

Tregacy? This surprised her.

He rushed closer to the leaders, dropped to the ground again, and rattled off a short speech. Osto listened with care, as did the other two. Behind them, the various Dahtien rumbled about, acting agitated — or, at least, Lynia interpreted their movements as agitation. She had to remember that even a simple wave of the hand could mean anything, including *hello.*

Debate continued amongst the three leaders, and as Vinip became more forceful in his phrasing, those behind the huts sharing Vinip's bluish tinting also became forceful. Osto appeared defensive, as did its black-shelled counterparts. Lynia would have found the entire gathering an astonishing scientific wonder, if she didn't need to focus on anything beyond the purpose of the meeting. Negotiations could be fast when both parties knew exactly what they wanted and worked together to achieve it. When talks dragged on, two things usually governed the situation. Either the parties did not trust each other or one party did not trust itself. Lynia feared the latter described the Dahtien.

*Just another opportunity,* she thought.

At length, Osto motioned for Lynia to return. A good sign. She took care not to rush, not to look too eager.

When she settled on her knees, Osto said, "Tregacy wants to help you, and we agree it is good. But also danger." Vinip tried to speak, but Osto warned off the interruption with a glower. Back to Lynia: "Dahtien kill to eat. Long ago, Dahtien kill each other, but no more."

Tregacy's arms dug into the ground. Lynia wondered if he didn't agree with Osto's representation of Dahtien history. Maybe their internal warring wasn't so long ago.

Osto had stopped talking. Lynia counted to five, but when no further words came, she knew she had to take her gamble now. Her father would have said that the door had been cracked open. Time to kick it down.

"If you fear the danger, I will not say it would be entirely safe. But I promise that my approach will give us the best chance to take back the town peacefully." Scanning their faces, she guessed they had expected her to say as much. She went on, "If you want strong trade, you'll need to do more than stand behind me when I take that town. I can do all in my power to mitigate the damage to the Dahtien as well as to my people, but damage will be done. It has been done already. I have seen the dead. Tregacy has seen them, too. Not all the humans will remain when I return. Some will have to go. To have trade, the Pathway Ring must be completed. Without all the humans to work, so many dead, others sent away, it will take most of our lives to complete — the strong, healthy years anyway."

*Be direct.* She had to keep in mind that the Dahtien did not think like humans. She was being too wordy. Even without the language barrier, she would have lost them.

Mimicking Tregacy's earlier gesture, she put up a hand. "Let me speak again."

Osto nodded. "We understand. We speak different."

"Yes. I will be clear." She took a breath. She narrowed her eyes onto Osto. "Help me take back the town. Stay and help me build the Pathway Ring. Do all that, and years from now, when the Ring is complete, you will have endless trade."

The three Dahtien leaders entered another round of discussions that caused another round of reactions behind them. Lynia stayed silent. She wanted to peek at Tregacy, get a read on what the others might be saying, but she kept her eyes forward — not that she could read anything from his headgear.

At length, when the three faced ahead, Osto placed his hands on his knees and stood. The others followed, and since Tregacy also rose to his feet, Lynia did, too.

Osto said, "We will help."

# CHAPTER 51

FOR THE THREE DAYS REQUIRED to organize the Dahtien families and march through the jungle-forest, Lynia's adrenaline continued to ramp up. Sleep came in short spurts, often leaving her more tired than before closing her eyes. Pel appeared to suffer the same, and their anticipation only strengthened as they closed in on Sydney.

Most of Vinip's people stayed in the trees, their blue-black tint blending with the silhouetted canopy and sky beyond. Warthem's people preferred to remain on the ground, their green-black tint acting as excellent camouflage. Lynia thought a little red dashed in would have been perfect. She wondered if that was Tregacy's motivation for the red V on his shell. Except then, why would Blue Square choose a blue square?

Yet even allowing her mind to wander around Dahtien peculiarities could not free her from the mounting tension. The second night, she had sex with Pel — mostly to relieve her stress — but it barely helped. In fact, she found only one positive to the long hike — she had plenty of time to prepare.

However, despite all the hours to think and plan, Sydney appeared between the trees before she felt ready. The sun burned high in the sky, and no clouds threatened an incoming storm. Perfect weather.

They had arrived.

Meeting with Tregacy and Pel at the tree line, Lynia said, "We'll enter through the south side where the corpses are deposited. Not a lot of people will want to be around the dead which should make our approach easier. We keep advancing until we reach resistance. Then, we fight our way to the Square. Once we control the Square, the town is ours. I know it's not the most strategic position — stuck in the center of the entire town — but it's a symbolic one that will hold great weight. There will be pockets of resistance from Rowan's deepest followers, but that should be a minor nuisance for a few days."

Tregacy asked questions regarding words he did not know, and after clarification, he said, "Too much killing."

With a more diplomatic tone, Pel said, "The plan is a good start, but it needs refinement."

"I suppose you both have ideas." Lynia disliked the combative tone in her voice and tried to soften it. "I'll do my best to listen."

"Wait for night," Tregacy said. "Small people."

"Because fewer people outside means less killing. The only problem is that if we wait until dark, our appearance will feel more like an attack than a liberation — that word means freeing, freedom, being set loose."

"Understand."

Pel said, "We should wait some. Especially when you hear my point."

"Which is?" Lynia asked.

"Well, um, I noticed you didn't mention your brother. He must be dealt with, and it can't be in some quiet way. It has to be public. People have to see his failure, or you'll be dealing with more than a few small pockets of his diehard followers."

Lynia mulled over these contributions, but her mind locked onto Rowan. Walking deeper into the woods, she said, "I know."

Facing Rowan had been part of her plan. She knew it had to be done. But she clung to the hope that the problem might solve itself in the chaos of their appearance in town. He could run away, or he could change and give up. A darker side of her thoughts guessed that he might be killed. She didn't want that, but she acknowledged that his death would solve a lot — provided he did not perish in some dramatic martyrdom.

"You okay?" Pel said as he approached.

"Just because we're having sex doesn't mean I need you to be my confidant."

He took a step back. "No, but I figured being the only other human being on your side at the moment gave me that right. You can't do all this alone."

Clenching her jaw, she waved him closer, and pulled him into a hug. "I know. I know all of it. Doesn't make it any easier to swallow." After a few moments of quiet, she added, "He's my brother."

In any battle throughout history, hot or cold, massive in scale or simple in structure, between armies or between two combatants, luck always played a factor. After waiting until early evening, when the sun seemed to hover before its final descent to the horizon, luck arrived. A loud bell clanged — swiped from a data library of prerecorded sounds from Earth and Mars — and all the townspeople migrated toward the church. Many looked disgruntled, yet others appeared elated. Even the red uniformed officers left the buildings converted into jail cells. Clearly, Rowan demanded everybody's attention for this mandatory call.

"How's that for no killing?" Lynia asked Tregacy. To the rest, she said, "Get ready. It's time."

It had taken so many days to reach this point, so many hours to reach the edge of the forest followed by more hours of waiting, yet as Lynia approached the southern road, as she saw the white and brown wrappings of the dead, all that time vanished. Her pulse quickened, her senses heightened. Her life, the lives of the town, of Monclova Industries, of possibly all Earth and Mars and Miguel, awaited ahead.

Pel, Tregacy, Blue Square, and four of Blue's squad followed behind her. The remaining Dahtien held back under the cover of the jungle-forest.

With corpses outlining the road long before it formally began, Lynia thought of how skulls and heads on pikes had been used ages ago to strike fear in approaching outsiders. She wanted only to look forward. If she could manage that, she would not have to count the bodies or think about the faces underneath the wrappings. Even after nine years, she did not know all her people well, but she knew their faces. Every single one.

Avoiding faces proved simple compared to avoiding the stench that permeated the area. All rotting flesh carried a familiar foulness, a warning not to eat the poisonous meal. But when that flesh was also human, the body's natural reaction invoked horror, disgust, and a desire to escape that bordered on blind panic.

Lynia's brow tightened. With each new body they slogged by, she turned those faces into tight fists. With each breath of rancid air, she turned that instinctual panic into a clenched jaw.

"Madness," Tregacy muttered.

Lynia didn't want to know where he had learned that word. Instead, she snarled. The flattened grass beneath her feet disappeared, packed into dirt, and the first buildings marked the edge of Sydney.

She headed straight for the building on the left, a small office used for maintenance services. The structure combined one of the original modular units with a wooden addition. When she entered, she found an abandoned desk with an old monitor displaying supply records. Behind the desk, where a door should have been, metal bars had been hastily welded in place. Some of the bars had been hinged to act as a doorway, and inside this makeshift jail, Lynia found Runi Nire, head of Sydney's first factory, curled in the back corner like an abused animal.

"Runi, what've they done to you?"

"Ms. Monclova?" Runi said, lifting her head. Her eyes lacked any spark — a sad sight for such a brilliant mind.

"Let's get you out of there."

"Sure. That'd be nice." She rested her head back. Her wasted body suggested she had not eaten much in the last months, and she must have thought Lynia was a hallucination.

However, once Lynia rooted around the desk, found the keys, and clanked the door open, Runi's head popped up. A glint sprang into her eyes.

"I'm real," Lynia said. "Come on. Time to leave."

As the older woman hobbled out, she rested a hand on Lynia.

"I knew you'd come back."

Once outside, Lynia quietly guided Runi to the south. "Don't be scared," she said, as they approached Tregacy and the others. "These are the Dahtien. They're going to make sure you get some food and water."

Tregacy offered a slight dip of the head. "Please. Come. We help."

Further on Blue Square repeated, "Medicine. Medicine."

Runi froze, her mouth agape. "This can't be real."

"It is," Lynia said. "Now go with the kind alien so I can free the rest of you."

Though confusion fought with disbelief across her face, Runi allowed the Dahtien to escort her toward the forest where several of Warthem's people had set up an aid station. Pel stepped from the building across the street with two young ladies leaning on him as they stumbled toward freedom. Not wanting to waste a moment, Lynia hurried to the next office-jail. And the next. And the next.

In minutes, they had freed a dozen prisoners — each one behind bars for supporting Lynia; each one made to suffer. She guessed these individuals had been kept alive for their expertise, but Rowan must have had trouble breaking them. She made sure to thank each one before handing them off to the Dahtien. Astonished gasps followed.

With Pel at her side, Lynia pressed on. Tregacy kept close. They strode up the road and would have reached the Square easily, if not for the lone police officer who fumbled out of a building on the right. From her harried appearance and rushed actions, Lynia guessed the officer had overslept and now feared the consequences of her tardiness to Rowan's gathering. When she spotted Lynia and Pel, however, her attitude shifted. No longer worried about being late, she adopted a firm stance and pulled a handgun from her shoulder holster.

"Don't move," the officer barked, her weapon shaking as she strode closer.

# CHAPTER 52

LYNIA AND PEL HALTED, raising their hands shoulder high. To her side, Tregacy became stone still. He looked like a weird sculpture brought along for some unclear purpose. The officer gave Tregacy a curious glimpse, dismissed the statue, and poured her rising fears into the real and known threat in front her.

"His Grace always said you would return, but I never thought it would be so soon." Her red hair had been tied back in a ponytail, but strands flew out in different directions, some dangling in front of her face. She kept blowing at them.

That hair clicked something in Lynia's head. She couldn't recall the woman's name but knew that before being a frightened police officer, she had worked in Electronics. As Lynia's thoughts galloped through approaches to appeal to this woman, Pel walked forward, keeping his hands up.

"Kasidonna, right? Like the city on Mars?"

The officer reared back and wrinkled her face. "I don't know you."

"We met a few times but always in passing. You might remember before we went through the Ring — you were nervous, and I handed you a bag of salt crisps."

Kasidonna's eyes narrowed. "Be quiet. Leave. Or I'll arrest you all."

"My name is Pel, and —"

She firmed her stance, though her weapon shook. "You move towards me, and I'll shoot."

Lynia had enough. She gestured toward Tregacy. "Please introduce yourself."

When Tregacy moved, Kasidonna hopped back with a yip

escaping her lips. Her unsteady aim darted from one target to another. "What is that thing?" She returned her focus to Tregacy. "Trained some animal to attack us?"

Lynia said, "Not an animal."

Tregacy extended his hand. "Please. No killing."

Holding a breath in shock, Kasidonna watched the Dahtien. And watched. And watched. And forgot to start breathing again.

She passed out.

Lynia snapped her fingers at the nearest office-jail. "Put her in a cell. Tie her hands and gag her." To Kasidonna: "We'll free you when this is over. For now, I can't have you warning anybody that we're here."

If the woman understood — or even heard — Lynia couldn't tell. That red hair had fallen over her face, yet Kasidonna's shocked wide-eyes peeked through. She put up no resistance as Pel followed his orders. With the last of the prisoners freed, and with their newest prisoner locked up, Lynia led her team forward.

Sydney had become a ghost town. The Square had been cleaned up from the riots, market stalls replaced, even trash had been swept away, yet the comm tower remained in shambles. The most important piece of equipment for the town to communicate with each other, and nobody had bothered with it. Proof that Rowan either didn't know how to run a complicated organization like a company town or, and more insidiously, that Rowan wanted to limit communication between his people.

Lynia shuddered as echoes of Rowan's speech reached the Square. She gazed off in the direction of the farms and the church. She knew this moment would come — it was inevitable and, thus, planned for — but the idea of standing in front of Rowan once again, of seeing him after all he had done, sickened her. That they could be of the same blood made her doubt the strength of DNA.

Walking toward the farms, she said, "Pel, Tregacy, please get everything ready."

Pel said, "Where are you going?"

"I need to have a chat with my brother."

With every block closer, Lynia worked to calm the rage inside. No good would come from yelling in front of the town. As much as she wanted to march right up to Rowan and punch him in the nose, the townspeople were intelligent and would not be swayed by violence. At least, she once thought so. But she had to admit that among all those engineers, scientists, agricultural specialists, mining experts — many had been duped by a false prophet.

"When the Lord and gods came to me, they did not ask that I break my back, that I risk my life for the enrichment of another."

Loudspeakers had been mounted on the wooden corners of the church. As they blasted his message, Rowan stormed across the boards of the church's porch. His white robe flowed around him like a magic cape and his red-green crown caught sunlight that made his head seem to sparkle color. His closest followers, including Akiko and Browit Cot, stood with their backs against the church wall, glaring at the audience, acting as if at military attention. The audience — the townspeople — all those still alive, filled the dead field in front of the church. Some looked despondent. Some shamed. But too many wore shirts with the words *New Church* across the top and the symbol of a cross with the curved bottom like a scimitar. Another shirt had a smiling face on the back and the words: *he set us free.*

"I know for some this has been a difficult time. Change, even good change, is disruptive. We become comfortable in our shackles and wary of those who try to bring us to freedom." Rowan stopped and lowered his head. "It has been unfortunate that a few have chosen to reject what the Lord and gods have offered. It has led to difficult and, at times, ugly choices. But to make a garden flourish, you have to do some weeding."

Lynia's stomach flipped at the cheers that arose.

"But don't worry. Walk with your heads high and have no fears. I am resolute in the task assigned to me. I will not fail you. The desires of the Lord and gods will be followed. I will see that we have freed every willing member into the welcoming arms of the New Church. The rest will not corrupt us. They'll be no more."

Applause and hooting. Even those who Lynia expected to oppose Rowan clapped albeit unconvincingly.

"And so I —" Rowan stared out over the heads of the town — stared straight at Lynia. "I'd started to think you had given up."

The townspeople turned towards her. A few smiles lifted to greet her. A few sneered. Most gazed upon her with cautious confusion — unsure of what they hoped for but knowing that they hoped for something.

From the porch, Akiko shot forward. "Arrest her."

Clad in New Church shirts and hats, two large men and a burly woman pushed towards Lynia. But Rowan called out: "No, no. Make a path for her. If we are ever going to rid ourselves of this disease, we must bring it to the light." Rowan's followers reluctantly stepped aside. Little by little, others backed away, leaving a ragged aisle that unrolled straight to the church steps.

Lynia moved forward, keeping her chin high and her stride moderate. Too slow would have been obnoxious and rude. Too fast would have looked frightened or threatening.

When she reached the porch, Rowan chuckled. "Right here, not too long ago, at this spot, we sparred words that led to the end of your reign."

Aiming for a tone both full of strength yet not belligerent, she said, "Fitting that it will now be the end of yours."

# CHAPTER 53

WITH FALSE MAGNANIMITY, Rowan performed a slight bow. "This is it, my dear sister. You have the entire town listening. You want to convince us that we should deny the Lord and gods, that we should obey your company rules, that we should handcuff ourselves to your Ring project, that you should acquire more money than anybody could spend in lifetimes. We all want to hear this. The floor is yours."

Feeling like a bug trapped in a glass jar, she said, "No."

"Did you hear that? She's giving up already. How disappointing."

"I didn't say that."

A weird reaction rippled through the audience. Some had started to laugh before she denied giving up. Then they became still, paying closer attention. Rowan heard that change, too.

"Stubbornness won't win this for you."

Crossing her arms, Lynia said, "Neither will lying."

"I haven't lied."

"The way you presented me was manipulative at best. All these people are smart. They recognize it." She hoped the latter was true. "You've tried to make it so that I had to prove the position, but I'm not the one making the claim. I have been clear from the start — this entire project is about returning home, about building the tunnel that will connect this world with ours. That's it. I've made no claim otherwise."

"You claim that there is no Lord and gods."

"I do not. But you know that. It's why you're lying. You misrepresent my position on purpose. All I've ever said is that there is no evidence for any kind of god. I don't deny the possibility that one could exist. We don't know. That should be the default position of any rational human being. I don't believe in books that tell me gods exist anymore that I believe in books that tell me dragons exist. Show me evidence that they do, that they roam around or rule the universe or whatever you want to believe, show me irrefutable evidence and I'll believe. But it has never been done. The nonsense that is brought forth as evidence is easily debunked. So, dear brother, you are the one with the burden of proof."

Rowan clapped his hands slow and mocking. "You actually brought life to the same old, tiring arguments all atheists make. It's a shame, really. I had prepared myself for a much stronger adversary."

Lynia scanned the crowd. Nobody acted as if they might join her side and overthrow Rowan. Even those she suspected felt that way wouldn't dare reveal their thoughts. Not with rows of corpses lining the southern road.

She had wanted to ease the townspeople into this, but Rowan gave her no choice. "Okay. You want me prove that your Lord and gods don't exist? I'll give it a try."

Laughter erupted. "Well, well," Rowan said, prancing about his makeshift stage, winking at members of his audience. "I guess she has some fight in her after all. If you think you can do it, we're ready to listen."

More laughter.

"Obviously, I can't prove a negative."

Folding his arms, he said, "Changing the rules now? Typical."

She bit back a snide retort. When she started to speak again, she paused. His robe — his divine robe that made him appear holy, special — the bottom was frayed and muddy. "The truth. That's what we all really seek. We want to find the truth."

"That's what I provide."

"Your religion, the New Church, would it be fair to say that you follow the ideas of the Old, New, and Shendo Testaments? Perhaps also the Quran and the Bhagavad-Gita?"

"The Lord and gods have used many paths to speak to different peoples."

"And in all of those the Lord, and in some cases the gods, are all-powerful, all-knowing, all seeing. They are beyond the concept of Time. They know the past and future — they even know about this debate we're having and whether or not I will succeed."

"I doubt success is in your future, but yes, that's all correct."

Lynia checked the back of the crowd. "Now, I don't claim to be as well read in those books as you — after all, you've been studying them since you were a boy. I suspect that's true of a lot of so-called prophets. But though I don't know those books like you, I am familiar with them. I'm certain that in the majority of these religions, there is a belief that the gods created the universe, particularly the Earth, for mankind."

"Most religions share many common ideas."

"All of this, the universe, the planets — it's all for us."

"Every atom, every molecule, every breath of air has been provided to us by the Lord and gods."

"The plants and animals? Them too?"

"Absolutely. The Lord and gods provided plants and animals to feed us, to work for us, to clean our air — it's a remarkable system that could only have been designed by a brilliant, flawless creator."

"And it's all for us."

"It is."

Addressing the audience, Lynia said, "Then this would explain why we've never found any other intelligent life in the universe. Because the Lord and gods created it for us exclusively. Correct?"

"Yes." Rowan drew the word out, uncertainty creeping into his voice.

"It's an interesting thought. In our pets, in the animals of Earth, we have found creatures that can think, but never have they reached the level of sentience, of understanding, like a human. Why should they? The universe doesn't exist for them. Yet if we did find intelligent life, alien life, that would be hard evidence that all those books were wrong. Not just wrong about some small detail, but wrong about the creation of life, the purpose of the universe, the entire reason for those books existing — namely, to explain it all to us. They would be wrong because their explanations, which came from the Lord and gods, would be wrong, and thus, the Lord and gods would be wrong as well." Gesturing to the back of the crowd, she said, "Well, there stands your hard evidence. His name is Tregacy."

As had been done for her only moments before, the crowd turned toward the back and parted down the middle. At the far end, Tregacy stood.

"Welcome to my planet," he said.

# CHAPTER 54

A SHOCKWAVE RIPPLED THROUGH THE CROWD. Some gasped in awe. Some in fright. A group crowded tight around the Dahtien while others broke off into small packs murmuring in shock, pointing at him, and in a few cases, glaring at Rowan. But plenty moved closer to Rowan, begging with their eyes and their tented prayer hands for an explanation.

Fumbling at the railing, Rowan said, "This does not mean the universe was not created for us. If anything, it only strengthens the idea of the wonder of the Lord and gods." He stomped across the porch as if his booming footfalls could drum back those that turned away. "Their majestic touch is all over this. Who but the Lord and gods could create another intelligent species, one put down here for us to communicate with so that we are not alone in the universe?"

His followers nodded in relief. A few sneered at the crowd around Tregacy. Lynia had expected this. Those most devoted to Rowan, those that truly believed in him would never admit they were wrong. To do so, to let go of Rowan and see him as a charlatan, meant accepting their actions. If the Lord and gods were not real, then all those righteous deaths were murders. All those violent acts were evil.

With the steady rumble in the crowd strengthening, Lynia could not hear what Tregacy or Pel said. However, somebody yelled out, "They want to trade with us."

Lynia smiled inwardly. She did not want her expression misconstrued as arrogance or any measure of superiority. Though Rowan still charged about the porch, Lynia stepped forward to block his path. In a quiet voice, one too soft for the microphones to pick up, she said, "Let's not repeat the bloodshed from when you took over. Let's make this peaceful."

Truly lost by this comment, Rowan said, "Why would I ever turn the souls entrusted to me over to you? A blasphemer. You are no better than a demon brought forth to steal the souls of the deserving." Pushing her hard, he raised his voice to pull the crowd's attention back. "A demon! Don't be fooled. This deceiver has brought evil and cloaks it in scientific wonder. Don't be manipulated by her clever words and her well-trained pet. They are nothing but demons and must be cast out."

"Shut up."

Lynia could not tell who had spoken, but the reaction emboldened her. Laughter, once again, but not at her. She put a gentle hand toward Rowan, but he slapped it away.

"Brother, you've lost. These creatures, the Dahtien, they truly want to trade, and that has reminded our people why they came out here. This is no longer a project that will only benefit Monclova Industries. Trade means jobs for centuries, and they know that."

"Is that true?" he addressed the crowd. "Are you all so fickle that the mere presence of a well-trained animal will make you doubt your beliefs? Is your faith so weak that you want to return to my sister's dictatorship so —"

Lynia shouldered her brother aside. "I will not run things the same. I learn from my mistakes. I pay attention to the truth and do my best to grow. I was wrong in how I handled this coup, all of you, and the project. The Ring is a company job, but we are more than company people. We will do better, different, together."

A shattering scream. But not from Rowan. Further along the porch, Akiko pushed off the wall and charged. She formed a fist and smashed it into Lynia's jaw.

When Rowan had instigated his coup, he had done so strategically. He riled his people until they lashed out against a perceived unfairness. He wanted a mass of followers to lose all sense of themselves, to explode upon a fevered wave, until they exhausted all resistance from the leadership and the town. He wanted the chaos.

But as Lynia dropped to the floor, her jaw radiating fire, she saw that this would not be a riot.

The brawl outside the church had components of anger and release, even of a battle against injustice, but it fast became organized on both sides. Akiko commanded the loyalists on the porch, sending out Browit Cot to wrangle smaller units of followers into squads. Pel and Tregacy joined with Shanana Querl, one of Pel's workmates from the Planners Office, to do the same on their side.

Within minutes, both groups had broken away from the muddled violence, forming a crooked dividing line down the center of the field. Insults flew across this narrow no man's land, as did clods of dirt and the occasional spit, but nobody launched a second attack. Not yet.

Lynia knew it would be coming, though. They all did.

"No fight," Tregacy said.

Lynia cringed. The Dahtien's words would only enflame his opponents. Sure enough, a voice yelled back, "This ain't your business."

Rolling on her side, she had to trust that her team could handle the situation. Her jaw hurt too much to yell out orders. Besides, she had other tasks to accomplish for their plan to work. That began with standing up.

Easier to think than to do.

Struggling, she leaned on the porch railing. The arguing and yelling and scuffling roared behind her, but she turned her attention to Rowan. He looked blurry as her head strained to clear, and he sounded fuzzy, yet for an instant, she saw her true brother. Her blood. A Monclova that cared about her.

"Are you okay?" he said. "Akiko shouldn't have done that."

"No fighting," Tregacy repeated, but nobody responded in the growing commotion.

A steady *thrump* grew in the distance. With the precision of a metronome, it approached. As it became louder — *thrump thrump* — the bickering crowd became quiet. Pulling Rowan's attention back, he gripped the railing to peer at the streets, the farmland, and the woods in the distance. Lynia did the same.

Pounding his weapon on the ground, in time with the *thrump thrump*, Tregacy bellowed, "No fighting."

From all sides, Dahtien appeared. They emerged from the tree line, from across the farms, from all directions. Standing shoulder-to-shoulder, the tall creatures trooped forward, grim and determined. The closer they came, the tighter their form until a smaller group had to break out and move ahead. *Thrump thrump* they marched. They stopped only when they encircled the church and surrounding area three-rows deep.

A breath.

Another.

A third.

The longer the stillness lasted, the more hopeful Lynia felt. If this show of force could be enough, if this woke the New Church followers to the truth …

But Akiko raised a fist and roared. "Liar!"

She blitzed across the small gap and leapt upon the nearest person. The others on both sides launched into a brawl. All fists and kicks. No weapons discharged.

Oddly, that also gave Lynia hope. It struck her like siblings fighting. They wanted to release their anger, they wanted to dominate, they even wanted to hurt the other, but no one had the desire for blood, for death.

Tregacy must have noticed the same, for he held back a command for the Dahtien to engage. They stood guard, preventing anybody from leaving the tight circle, and simply let the strange aliens fight each other. Lynia tried to get his attention, to nod her appreciation, but he was too far away.

Rowan stepped from the railing and drifted into his church. He shuffled with a slow gait, far removed from the man Lynia had seen riling up the crowd. His robe dragged on the floorboards. She worried he might be considering something drastic, and that worry increased when she gazed through the church door. She caught a glimpse of a bare leg and bone-thin arm. A body chained to the back wall.

Graham.

# CHAPTER 55

THE VIOLENCE IN THE CROWD DIMMED as Lynia entered the church. A warm light met her. Dozens of candles lit the large room, filling the air with the smell of a birthday. Lynia half-expected Rowan to appear with a cake while singing an ancient tune.

But the illusion broke at the full view of her assistant, Graham. Bruises covered his body. His hair looked greasy; he smelled even worse. He had lost a dozen or so pounds. A stained mattress had been placed beneath him, and each small motion he made rattled the thick chain shackled to his ankle. Fixed into a metal plate in the wall, the chain limited his range severely — far enough to enter the bathroom a few feet away. Nothing more. This was a church, after all. Nobody wanted him defiling it with his own filth.

She hurried towards him, but he did not gaze up with joy or relief or hope. Instead, he fixed his attention on a spot behind her. Midway to him, she stopped.

Knocking on the new wood proscenium that framed a podium on a small riser, Rowan said, "The old churches and temples were made of stone. More permanent that way. Once I've settled things, I'll start using the mining operation to push in that direction. Maybe throw in some gold or silver, depending on how much we find. Might take a generation, but we'll build a cathedral to rival the old ones on Earth."

Lynia shifted towards him. She wanted to show compassion, but her lips lifted into a sneer. "Father would be disgusted with you."

"He wouldn't be too thrilled with you, either."

"The difference is that I never had a chance. From the

moment I was born, the moment he saw that I was a girl, he decided I could never be good enough for the Monclova name."

"That didn't stop you from trying. The Lord and gods may have —"

"Can you quit the religious routine? Please. Nobody's in here but us and Graham, and somehow, I get the feeling you don't care what he thinks."

"You still believe I'm faking this."

"I know it started out that way. But you wouldn't be the first to fall for his own lies. Maybe that's what Father spotted was wrong with you. Maybe that's why he focused on Varo, instead — even if he was a useless drunkard."

"That's our brother you're defaming."

"Doesn't make it any less true."

"Ah, that's still your whole thing," Rowan said, as if he had uncovered a great secret. "Ever since you were little, you cared so much about what was true. Never really focused on how people felt, how they perceived things. With you, it's always hard true or hard false. That's the real reason you never got Father's approval. He required more than a loyal soldier."

Lynia moved toward the podium, but for every step closer, Rowan countered back another. "And you tried to be the religious believer he never got out of the rest of us. But you screwed it up. You let our mother poison your mind against him."

"Mom was not a poison."

"She wasn't any better than our father. I used to think she was innocent, a person who got trampled by the stampede of Father's ambitions —"

"So poetic."

"— but when I saw how she used you, used all of us, it sickened me. And you fell into being her weapon. You took one of the things dearest to Father — his religion — and you attacked him with it."

Arching forward like he did when they were children and Varo picked on him, Rowan said, "You're just as bad. You think he wanted you to go through the Ring? To be the leader of

Monclova Industries out here?"

"I think he came around to it."

"He had no choice. And look at the mess you've made of the whole thing."

Lynia knew she should be angry, but she pitied her brother, instead. He projected his own disappointments, attacked through his own failures.

"You're right," she said.

He frowned, moving closer to the podium as if it could protect him. "You admit it?"

"We both failed Father. But then, we never could give him what he wanted. He had this dreamchild conjured up in his head, some amalgam of Sydney and Varo, you and me — none of us could live up to that."

"I don't know if that's exactly right."

"It doesn't matter anymore." She reached out, resting her hand atop his on the podium. "Father isn't here. He doesn't know about the Dahtien. He probably never imagined such a thing could exist. But we are here. We do know about them."

He shook his head, gripping the podium tighter but not removing his hand. "It doesn't matter. These creatures — maybe they're intelligent —"

"They are."

"Maybe not. But if the Lord and gods —"

"Look outside. The Dahtien are a truth you cannot deny. The people out there know it, too. If I had brought out a dog-like creature and said that it was an alien species equivalent to us, not one of those people would fall for it. They all can tell what is real, what is true. If they couldn't, they wouldn't bother fighting. Not like that. That's an outpouring of loss. Your followers — most of them — are realizing they've been wrong. It makes them angry. So, they punch and scream. But they won't kill. People don't murder when they don't believe."

"You think this somehow disproves the New Church? Plenty out there still believe in me."

"That's because you have leadership within you. That's because you have charisma. They don't believe in what you say as much as they believe that through you, things will be better. But things weren't bad before. I'm not saying I was perfect, but nobody suffered. You made them believe they were in trouble, in bad shape, and only you could solve everything."

Rowan glanced out the window, a sharp look before he lowered his head toward the podium. Sweat dappled his brow. Gasping, he said, "I'm not a fraud."

"I know that. You believe what you say. But belief in a thing doesn't make it true."

He hissed and shoved away from the podium. "The Holy Books are truth."

"No." She pointed to Graham. "Your books say that treating a man like property is okay, and never do they correct that mistake. But you know that's wrong. Your books say that murdering those who disagree with you is okay, and then they say it's wrong to kill, leaving the reader confused. Those old books, those old ways, they served a purpose long ago, but we have evolved beyond them. We are better. We can create a better world than the one they strived for. If you truly believe in the Lord and gods, then do you think they would want you to keep following the books that lead to self-destruction? Shouldn't we do better with the universe they have created for us?"

Rowan gazed at Graham. Like a fish, he opened and closed his mouth, making no sound. Thrusting his arms out wide, he knocked over several candles but didn't seem to notice. "You win." A little bitter, but mostly, he snickered. "I think you'll have a hard time with my loyal followers. You think they fight because of loss, but it's more than that. When someone is wrapped up in a belief, they can't let it go. Not without unravelling."

He turned his back on her and shuffled toward the stairs leading to the unfinished bell tower. As he climbed out of view, flames licked up the wooden walls.

# CHAPTER 56

THE HEAT INTENSIFIED FASTER than Lynia thought possible. The church became a flickering, orange madness. Sweat dropped out of her, and she had to squint through the thickening smoke.

Rushing to Graham's side, she reached for the chains. They weren't too hot, but that would not last. She checked over the lock on the ankle shackle. It looked sturdy. Well-made. Of course it was. Nothing but the best craftsmen had been brought on this trip.

Graham tried to speak. Only a scratching gurgle came out.

"Don't," Lynia said. She handed the chain to him and gripped it closer to the wall. "Help me."

Together they leaned back, pulled on the chain, groaning with the effort while the snapping of wood behind them sounded like dozens of breaking bones. Gasping for air led to a bout of coughing. They tried again. And again. The metal plate connecting the chain to the wall would not budge.

"Key," Graham managed.

Lynia rushed to the podium, but the blaze had consumed it in a pillar of orange. Despite the danger, the church smelled as welcoming as a friendly campfire. She noticed a small desk near the entranceway. As she darted towards it, sparks blasted up from an unseen source, forcing her to shift to the side. A plume of flames caused her to double back and find yet another way forward. Finally, reaching the desk, she yanked open the single drawer, spilling its contents across the floor.

The entranceway door kicked open. Pel peered in, covering his mouth and nose with one arm. In two large strides, he reached Lynia, grabbed her arm, and headed outside. But she pulled back, freeing from his grip.

"You've got to get out now," Pel yelled over the crackling flames.

Despite the brightness of the fire, the dark smoke billowing across the ceiling made seeing more and more challenging. Lynia dropped to her knees to sift through the desk's contents. No key. Nothing even close to a key.

"Leave," Graham said.

"Shut up."

"It's … okay."

Bolting to her feet, she said, "No, it's not. You hold on."

Stumbling and coughing as she emerged from the church, Pel followed out, sticking closer to her side. People tried to talk to her, but she waved them off. The wall of Dahtien ringing the farm watched the fire, ready to quash it much like they had been ready to stop the human violence from spreading.

That caught Lynia — the violence had stopped. Akiko, Browit Cot, and the rest of Rowan's diehard followers had been lined up in rows, on their knees, hands clasped behind their heads. Others sat nearby, their wounds being treated by a contingent of human and Dahtien medical teams.

"I see you all!" Rowan's voice rang clear from the platform atop the tower. "The Lord and gods see you, too. They are one. They rule us all."

Akiko gazed up, bright and hopeful. "The Lord and gods are one!"

The other loyalists took up a low chant — *The Lord and gods are one. The Lord and gods are one.*

Lynia hastened by them. She stopped when she found Tregacy. "Please," she said. "There's one more inside."

Earning her endless respect, Tregacy never hesitated. He charged toward the church, forcing Lynia to hustle behind. He uttered several clicks and noises and a few other Dahtien stepped forward, creating a tighter circle around the prisoners.

Once inside the furnace, Lynia pointed toward Graham who lay sprawled unconscious. Tregacy leapt over a glowing red pile of wood, gingerly placing his feet while moving fast toward his target. When he reached Graham, he grabbed the chain near the metal wall plate. His pincer arms clamped tight. They must have burned, but Lynia saw no reaction — perhaps the Dahtien shell protected him from severe pain.

Two strong pulls. The plate ripped out of the wood in a shower of sparks. Flames shot towards the hole in the wall, seeking the fresh oxygen outside, while the glowing embers inside ignited anew.

Tregacy lifted Graham's limp body and turned toward Lynia. She reached out to take the man, but Pel appeared beside her. "I've got him," he said. "Go outside. Our people need you."

As Pel accepted Graham into his arms, Lynia headed for the exit. But Tregacy did not follow. She looked at him. "Come on."

"One more," Tregacy said, gazing toward the burning base of the church tower.

As if in response, Rowan's voice seared over the flames. "The Lord and gods are one!"

"You can't save him," Lynia said.

But Tregacy moved toward the tower, and Pel nudged her to the doorway. They stumbled out into open air, and as two people rushed to aid Graham, Lynia fell to the ground. She hacked black goo from her lungs.

"The Lord and gods are one," Rowan chanted. His most loyal repeated the phrase back.

Gazing toward the top of the platform, Lynia spotted her brother. He stood tall, waving his hands in triumph, reaching out towards his followers. Sparks danced behind him. She searched for Tregacy but did not see him. Everything below, the entire church, had become a ball of raging reds and orange — even a few spots boasted white-hot flames.

A crack and boom shot a stream of fire up the tower. It engulfed the structure, swirling around the wooden framework and blinding the crowd with sudden brightness. The tower pulsed heat across the town as one of its beams split in two. It tilted, whining as it went, and for a moment, it sounded as if Rowan screamed in burning ecstasy. Then the entire thing crashed down through what remained of the church ceiling. A shockwave reverberated through the foundation that barely held its form at this point. No more. The building crumbled, the walls collapsing upon themselves, sending fire and smoke high into the darkening sky.

It happened in seconds.

But for the next few hours, nobody moved. Akiko and the New Church followers watched their dreams burn, and they wept for Rowan. The Dahtien watched in confusion. If they wept for Tregacy, no human could recognize it. And Lynia — she wept for them all.

Nobody survived this unscathed.

# CHAPTER 57

LYNIA SAT AT HER DESK IN HER HILLTOP OFFICE once again. And once again, her visi-link inbox overflowed with reports, data, and decisions that needed attention. But it no longer rested on her alone.

In the months that followed the demise of her brother, she made sweeping changes. One of her first steps was to form the Monclova Council consisting of herself and elected representatives from all the major branches within the company. Everyone in the town got to vote, including Akiko and the rest of the New Church.

That last bit helped sway a few more away from Rowan's fold. Lynia figured within the next year or two, the New Church would only have a dozen or so followers remaining. Those like Akiko who would go to the grave believing.

Lynia made other changes, too. She worked to foster a healthy relationship with the Dahtien, and they, in turn, joined with the humans to rebuild the town. Many Dahtien became passable in speaking standard while several humans tried to speak Dahtien with miserable results. Apparently, the human throat could not create the sounds and intonations required. They did, however, learn to understand the language even if they could not speak it.

The most controversial decision she made involved the police force. Despite several on the Council who disagreed, Lynia permitted Chief Lig to remain in charge. "He goes with the wind," she said at the meeting. "Wherever the power blows, he'll side with it. That's a known quantity we can work with."

"But he's allowed people to be murdered," Browit Cot, representative of the miners, said. Like many of Rowan's former followers, Browit Cot managed to say things that ignored what he had done. Pointing this out only caused belligerence.

Pel called it cognitive dissonance. Lynia called it a sick nuisance she had to endure. There simply weren't enough people to allow one to slip away. Soon though, the population would grow, and years from now, when these babies were young adults, she would have enough people that she could ignore the Browit Cots of the town.

"Lig doesn't care what the laws are, as long as he's the one to enforce them. If we put together a clearly defined set of laws, we won't have trouble from him or his officers."

Once the rest of the Council picked up on the fact that they would all help make those laws, they agreed. It took several weeks of long debates, but they finally established that clear set of laws and punishments. The justice system would take some more work, but Lynia found that all the members of the council, even Browit Cot, approached these decisions in good faith. She had full confidence that they would make a fair system.

"Excuse me, ma'am," Graham said, knocking on her door.

Lynia shut down her visi-link and rubbed her eyes. "Come on in."

She liked seeing Graham walking around — he had spent more than a week in serious condition, died and resurrected once, and gave Lynia more than a few jolts of adrenaline along the way. Though he had a permanent limp and had yet to regain all the weight loss, the doctors promised he would be fine. Physically, anyway. The therapist wouldn't divulge anything — mental health confidentiality prevailed even in Monclova Industries — but Graham assured her that he was working through his trauma. She had nothing to worry about.

Still, she worried.

Especially with his current nervous look. "If this is about the Council pushing for more time before we resume the Ring project, I'm not going to bend on that. We've a job to do. It's going to take a long time to complete the Ring, and we've lost too much already."

"No, ma'am, I'm not here about that."

"Good." She waited. Then: "Out with it."

Approaching her desk, he reached into his pocket. "Now that the funerals are over and the church wreckage is cleared, I thought maybe we should put some kind of memorial on that space. Maybe even a special note about the Dahtien that saved my life — since we couldn't be at his funeral."

When the fires had cooled enough to be sifted through, Blue Square led a small team into the ashes to remove Tregacy and take him back into the jungle-forest. Lynia asked to go along so she could pay her respects at his burial. The Dahtien refused. She wasn't sure if something was confused in the translation or if she truly wasn't welcome, but in the end, she decided to let them handle a death of their own however they saw fit.

"I think it's a wonderful idea," she said. "It would be nice to have a place to visit both my brother and my Dahtien friend."

"Um … well … one more thing."

"Oh?"

From his pocket, Graham pulled out a charred necklace with a Mars rock pendant. The letter *M*. He placed it on the desk. "I found this in the rubble near where … where they had me. I thought you should have it back."

Lynia's flesh prickled. She sat frozen, staring at the necklace. She barely took a breath. Graham had to have sifted through tons of debris to find this. He certainly did not come across it by accident.

"Thank you," she whispered. Then, clearing her throat, she added, "Anything you need, you let me know."

With a pleased bow, Graham exited the office. As he left, Pel entered. They shared a look, and Lynia instantly knew that they had been searching for the necklace together.

"I thought he should be the one to give it to you," Pel said. "He's been through a lot."

"You have, too."

"Yeah, but I got to spend my exile with you. He was chained to a church wall surrounded by zealots. He deserves whatever small happiness we can give him. Besides," Pel bent over and kissed her gently, "I have something else for you."

"I don't have time for that."

"No, not that."

From his pocket, Pel set a new pendant on the desk. "I had some of the welders make it from genuine planet Miguel ore." It was shaped into a V. "I couldn't decide between this and a *T* for his name, but I thought this was better."

Tears dribbled down Lynia's cheeks. She nodded. "It's perfect." The words catching as she uttered them.

She picked up the V and added it to her necklace, then she clasped the whole thing around her neck. Pressing her palm against it, she closed her eyes and vowed never to remove it again.

"You okay?" Pel asked.

Lynia chuckled. "Better than you know."

"What's that mean?"

She had intended to wait longer before telling him, but with her emotions swelling through her, she decided the time had arrived. She rubbed her belly and grinned.

"What?" he said. Then his eyes widened. "Really?" He wrapped his arms around her tight, kissed her hard, and laughed. "I know religion isn't a thing with you, but would you object to a marriage? I'd really like for our child to have a mother and father that were married."

"You aren't the only one on this planet who wants some of the old traditions. The Council has already put in place a marriage procedure. So, yes, I'll marry you. But one condition."

"Anything."

"We keep the Monclova name."

He laughed again. Harder. "I can be Pel Monclova. No problem."

"Good. Now get out of here. I've got to finish my work."

Actually skipping as he left, Pel shouted, "I'm going to be a daddy!"

Lynia stretched her arms and walked out of the office. She motioned Graham back to his desk as she stepped outside. Pel was already near the bottom of the hill — still announcing his impending fatherhood to everybody he passed.

She climbed the side ladder to the rooftop. Breathing in the clean air, she gazed across the town of Sydney. Though she could see plenty of problems on the horizon — particularly with what the Ring would do to the planet, the Dahtien homeworld — Lynia still felt hopeful. She would not abandon her people nor would she abandon the Dahtien. They could overcome every obstacle together if they faced it in a truthful, honest manner.

Clasping the two pendants on her necklace, she said, “I hope you’re both proud of your people. I promise to lead them well.”

# ZILL GRACE

BRACKEN TURNED THE CAR onto a series of sideroads that lacked the welcoming appearance of Professor Kovaric's neighborhood. Economic policies and political attitudes kept the citizens at a basic level of subsistence, but some areas thrived with achievers while others rotted on that bare minimum. Watching the lack of upkeep in these blocks left Zill no doubt which area they had entered.

Chovar rolled his lips. "I never heard so many horrible things about Rowan. In the family histories I've read, he was always portrayed as an unruly man who pushed Lynia into being more of a leader. But the idea that he was the one who went against her, that he was a religious madman, that he went against the family … if you weren't connected to Professor Kovaric's research, I wouldn't believe any of it."

"Sadly, plenty never stopped following him. I read once that most major change in any society only occurs when the previous attitudes die with those who hold them."

"I know that one — *a previous generation must die out to quash a previous and unwelcome idea.*"

"Akiko Towson, Browit Cot, and others reassimilated in order to live, but they died still believing."

The final stretch of driving left Zill and Chovar to think in silence. At length, Bracken parked in front of an ugly apartment building — a square concrete block with thin windows and no life.

"7291 Orstead," he said.

Together, all three exited the car and approached the front door. 7291 was on the bottom floor. Chovar knocked. When no answer came, and after he tried two more times, he moved his head at Bracken. Before Zill could ask what to do now, Bracken pressed against the door and fiddled with the lock.

"Is he —"

Chovar said, "We were just at a crime scene tampering with a dead body, and now you're getting worried about lockpicking?"

Scanning the area to see if anybody watched, Zill avoided Chovar's eyes. "I guess not."

A click and the door opened. Inside, Zill found a dismal single-room apartment — the only privacy afforded to the bathroom via a hanging curtain. Wall rugs covered every bit of wall and floor, including the slim windows. A single desk sat in the middle with an old computer on top and a hanging light overhead.

"This is his," Zill said.

Chovar poked at the wall rugs. "You sure? Lots of people still own these things."

"Not like the Professor. No other furniture, too — that's another thing he liked in a workspace. What he absolutely needed. Nothing else to distract."

"His home had plenty of furnishings."

She ran a finger along the desk. "Maybe that's why he had a secret office. To get away from everyone and everything. But I can't believe he never told me about this place."

"You are part of everyone and everything."

Except Professor Kovaric never made her feel that way. Once he had accepted her, included her in the research, he opened his bubbled world to her. She knew all about … except she didn't. She saw that now. She thought she had full access to his life and his work, but this office proved he had facets she never encountered. Chovar's connection to him proved it more.

Sitting at the desk, she pushed the computer's power button. An old-fashioned whine ramped up as the ancient machine came to life. While waiting for the boot sequence to complete, Zill opened the desk's single drawer. A few coins, a pen, and a packet of ten datacards.

Chovar reached over and plucked the top card off. "I haven't seen one of these since I was a kid. You ever use one?"

"Not with the Professor, if that's what you mean."

"I meant at all, ever."

"Not really. By the time I was old enough, holos had taken the place of all that. I've seen datacards, the University has lots of old equipment gathering dust, but I never had to use one."

Chovar slipped the datacard into a side slot on the computer. "Might as well see what's on it."

Zill wasn't sure she agreed, but an icon appeared on the screen that suggested the datacard was being read. A second later, the screen lit up with the single statement: ENTER PASSWORD. Zill did not hesitate. All the Professor's devices used the same initial password — *Dahtien.* In a flash, a directory of the datacard appeared. She recognized the Professor's haphazard organization instantly.

Pointing to a file marked *ZG1,* she said, "That's my research. Based on the dates listed, he created this file right after I started working for him and kept it current."

"What about those?" Chovar pointed toward a series named *foundationMMLM.*"

"That would be everything I've already told you. *MM* is Miguel Monclova."

"And *LM* is Lynia."

"Those files would include background on both of them. Hospital records of their births and any visits to the emergency rooms over the years. School records. Everything we could find. I've read through just about every file on this card. It's a big part of what he had me doing."

Chovar slanted his head towards her. "Your focus was limited to the first generations of my family? I thought you knew everything about us."

"Professor Kovaric knew it all. My initial research was this foundational work. Then he had me focusing on some of the final years on Miguel — during the presidency of Coyote Monclova and all that happened with her brother, Rio. I only did the surface work on that period, though. The bulk of my latest work focused on the years after, the journey through space and all that led to our arrival here on planet Newarl."

"But back on Miguel, the years in between Lynia and Coyote?"

Zill removed the datacard, reached into the drawer, and sifted through the others. Little lines were written in the corners of each datacard label. That was the Professor's way. A simple but quiet ordering system. She had always thought his desire for secrecy came from the sensitive nature of researching the Monclova family. Also, she pegged him as a little paranoid. Clearly, she was wrong.

Selecting the datacard with two hash marks, she inserted it into the computer. "This should be the next generation or two of your family. Probably includes all the events with Pel Monclova, too."

"And her son?"

"Behr Monclova? Of course."

When the file directory appeared, it held hundreds of folders, each with hundreds of files. As she set her fingers toward the screen, Chovar grabbed her hands and lowered them to the table.

"These files — and those on the other datacards — they could end up contradicting everything you've told me. You could be wrong."

Zill kicked out her chair as she shot to her feet. "I've been very clear about the veracity of what I told you. All the major events happened, and while some of the details are unclear to us at the moment, I've done my best to fill in those gaps with the most accurate approximations we have available. If you doubt my ability, then you must doubt Professor Kovaric's as well. We worked like one unit, and I have no problem boasting that I was the best damn researcher he ever had."

Chovar's eye bore down on her, but she refused to let the Monclova gaze shake her nerves. He turned toward the computer, read from the screen, then walked to one wall and pressed his back against the hanging rug.

"I want to thank you for helping me to this point. I promise you that, provided you keep our conversations private, you have nothing to fear from Monclova Industries or the Monclova family. You can leave now."

Zill's mouth dropped. "What?"

"You're no longer required. Bracken can drive you home."

"No," she said, moving away from Chovar's imposing assistant.

"Please don't do this."

"You need me." She flapped her hands at the computer. "You might be able to read all of that — or pay somebody to do it — but you won't understand how it fits together any more than you would have understood how Lynia and Rowan's relationship shaped the outcome on Miguel. You're looking for an answer about the Pathway Ring. I have to know why Professor Kovaric died. These files might have both. Besides, without me, you'll have a much harder time breaking the passwords."

Chovar did not move as he thought it over. Then: "I'll give you a week."

"This will take longer. At least a month."

He exchanged a look with Bracken, and Zill couldn't stop from shuddering. With his brow pulling down, Chovar said, "I am truly sorry that I've brought you into this. I shouldn't have, but it seemed, well, that is to say that I don't often consider —"

"How other human beings feel?"

"I suppose. But look at this room. Look at those datacards. He put password protections on the data, put it on an ancient tech making it difficult for modern parties to work with, stashed it in this secret location — he didn't do all that because it was harmless."

"I've been working for years on this research."

"And he never let you know the full truth. He tried to shield you from it. Now he's dead." He glanced at the desk and computer as if the Professor's body lay in front of him. "Kovaric was a good man. Even a friend, at times. I don't think he would want you going any deeper."

"I need to know what happened. I need to know why."

With a pained expression, he sighed. "You've given me enough to get started. The rest will come when my tech people work at it. They'll break his passwords eventually."

"You're not listening." She stomped to the computer and sat.

"I'm your best chance of getting any worthwhile information from this machine. More importantly, I owe it to the Professor to see his work completed."

"Please, don't. I acted rashly when I had Bracken take you to my home. I panicked."

"None of that matters now. It happened, and I'm here."

A pause. A sigh. "If you pursue this further, there's no changing course. I'm offering you an exit right now. You should take it. Go and live a better life. Forget all this horrible stuff."

She rested her hands on the datacards. "I was raised to believe in the truth. Knowing what is real holds all value. The truth allows us to make good decisions, moral decisions, because we know the reality we deal with. Fairy tales are comforting, but they are a poor way to decide the fate of people. And lies — even little, white lies — are evil and destructive. You want to know whether to use the Pathway Ring you built. That requires the truth. If you merely guess or take it on faith, then you might destroy the entire planet like what happened on Miguel. So, with all respect, Mr. Monclova, I'm going to finish this."

Chovar patted her shoulder. "You've got a month. Then I want a report on what happened after Lynia gave birth."

Zill never heard Chovar and Bracken leave the office. She had already jumped into the deep waters of the Monclova past.

# Acknowledgements

This book has a long history. In fact, this book took longer to get into your hands than any other I've written so far. Over a decade. It began with an idea about siblings trying to build a massive project on a planet far from our solar system. I didn't have the skills to pull off the story way back then, but it sat in the back of my mind. Then about seven years ago, I wrote *The Pathway Ring,* a standalone novel that tried to do way too much in a short space. After my wife and son made it clear that this book was nowhere near ready for publication, I set it aside to write a Max Porter novel and figured I'd come back to it later in the year. When I finally got back to it, five years had gone by, but I thought I might have learned enough to be able to tackle the project. First thing I realized right away: this book is actually a series of maybe four to five books. And I went from there. The result is this first book of a series you are reading.

So many to thank that got us here, but above all, my wife and son deserve a huge amount of credit. Not only did they suffer through the first version years ago, but they went through this book and helped me work out all the broken parts.

Also, big thanks to Luis Peres who managed to do the wonderful artwork for the cover in a slim amount of time. He's been awesome to work with, and I can't wait to see what he comes up for the rest of the series.

Many of the usual suspects deserve thanks, and many of them don't know the part they played. So, my thanks go to Darin Kennedy, Joelle Reizes, John Hartness, Matt Dillahunty, Forrest Valkai, Matthew Saunders, James and Cheryl Maxey, Kenny Seay, and of course, book Santa himself, Dino Hicks.

Last, but always first, is you, my wonderful reader. Without you, none of this matters.

Thank you.

www.ingramcontent.com/pod-product-compliance
Lightning Source LLC
Chambersburg PA
CBHW030517310726
48979CB00010B/1704/J
*9781963517187*